GIRLS' NIGHT OUT

"Did you look for a ring?" JoAnne asked me, pointing a stalk of celery at me like an accusatory finger. "I mean, before you flirted?"

"I didn't even think to look," I admitted. "I was just . . . so . . ."

Abby nodded. "Smitten."

"Well, that's not exactly the word I would have chosen," I said, "but yeah. I was smitten."

"Not all married men wear rings," Maggie pointed out reasonably. "So even if Erin did look and didn't see a ring, she'd have been none the wiser."

"So, when did you finally spot the ring?" JoAnne pressed.

"When he shifted his coat from one arm to the other," I said.

"Smooth."

I gasped. "You don't think he was hiding the ring on purpose, do you? That's ridiculous!"

Maggie grimaced. "It's been known to happen, Erin. Men are manipulative. They'll use any weapon they can when they're on the hunt."

JoAnne just shrugged and took another sip of her Bloody Mary.

"You don't understand," I said. "You're making it sound all sordid and cheap. It was just . . . just that he didn't seem married!"

"What the hell does that mean?" JoAnne, Abby and Maggie exclaimed. At the same time. They grinned at one another, proud.

I kept my mouth shut. How could I expect anyone to understand something I could barely articulate? Something I was still figuring out myself?

Books by Holly Chamberlin

LIVING SINGLE

THE SUMMER OF US

Published by Kensington Publishing Corporation

Living Single

HOLLY CHAMBERLIN

KENSINGTON BOOKS
Kensington Publishing Corp.
http://www.kensingtonbooks.com

KENSINGTON BOOKS are published by

Kensington Publishing Corp.
850 Third Avenue
New York, NY 10022

All Kensington Titles, Imprints, and Distributed Lines are available at special quantity discounts for bulk purchases for sales promotions, premiums, fund-raising, and educational or institutional use. Special book excerpts or customized printings can also be created to fit specific needs. For details, write or phone the office of the Kensington special sales manager: Kensington Publishing Corp., 850 Third Avenue, New York, NY 10022, attn: Special Sales Department, Phone: 1-800-221-2647.

Kensington and the K logo Reg. U.S. Pat. & TM Off.

First Kensington trade paperback printing: September 2002
First Kensington mass market printing: March 2004

10 9 8 7 6 5 4 3 2

Printed in the United States of America

As always, for Stephen.
And this time also for Donna.

ACKNOWLEDGMENTS

The author would like to thank the Women's Lunch Place for its wonderful work with the homeless and poor women of Boston. She would like to honor the memory of her beloved friend, Fifi. Finally, she would like to thank her editor, John Scognamiglio, for giving her this opportunity and his endless support.

Prologue

This is the story of a year in the life of a thirty-two-year-old single woman. It's my story and I'm telling it because I need to tell it. Also, because I want to.

Consider it a cautionary tale. Consider it a good laugh. Consider it a little of both.

My name is Erin Weston. I recently celebrated—a slightly optimistic way of putting it—my thirty-third birthday.

Jesus Christ was crucified at the age of thirty-three. Not being a rabble-rouser, I'm hoping for a far less spectacularly troublesome year. After last year, I could use the rest.

Anyway, I made it out alive and yes, even well. Imagine that.

Overall, life's been good to me, though on occasion its macabre sense of humor is distressing.

But enough summarizing. My story begins last January, exactly a year ago to this day.

I hope you like it.

Chapter One

January in Boston is probably like January everywhere in America. At least in the sense of its being a month of grand resolutions and well-meant gestures—as well as a month of postholiday disappointment and incipient depression as the resolutions and gestures begin to break down.

Nice time of the year to be born.

I'd just turned thirty-two. And I was a workaholic.

Not really. Though sometimes, especially on those days when I was the only one left in my downtown Boston office after six-thirty, I'd get all panicky and think that if I wasn't very careful I could very easily slip over the line and go from being your typical hardworking single woman to being a painfully skinny spinster, scarily devoted to her filing system and not so secretly in love with her abusive, Scotch-swilling boss.

Or, maybe I would go the other way. Maybe I would wind up a coldhearted, hard-assed, too-tanned, slave-driver type female executive with helmet hair, no husband, and surprisingly few girlfriends.

But I was determined not to allow that slippage to occur, either way. Absolutely not. Because I'd decided I wanted something significantly different for my life.

I wanted legitimacy. The kind that, for a woman, doesn't come even with a solid career.

And my career was solid. In fact, my annual review was scheduled for the following day. If it went well, there was a chance—slim, but I was hoping—that I would be named a senior account executive at EastWind Communications. That's the marketing/PR firm where I'd worked for the past five years. It's a smallish firm, owned by a guy named Terry Bolinger, and its work focuses on nonprofits and organizations that barely make a profit.

I liked being at EastWind.

More information. I lived—and still live—in the South End, officially an historic district of Boston. I own a condo in what was once, way back in the nineteenth century, a single-family brick house. Think New York brownstones but brick. Thanks to the building department's controls, the structure is still charming, as is the entire block, with its brick sidewalks, huge old trees, and lovely, well-tended front gardens.

I had—and still have—a cat named Fuzzer. And yes, on occasion I was definitely frightened of becoming a looney cat lady. Especially if the single situation persisted for much longer.

Which, I vowed upon turning thirty-two, it wouldn't. It couldn't. Because things were going to change. Five, ten, twenty years ahead when I looked back on my life, I was going to refer to this as The Year. The year I met my husband, the man of my dreams.

Tall or medium height, it didn't matter. Neither did hair or eye color. He'd have a fine intelligence and a large sense of humor, i.e., he would appreciate the Three Stooges as well as Jerry Seinfeld, and Margaret Cho as well as Monty Python's Flying Circus. He would be kind and loving and he'd be a hardworking man, as laziness is, for me, the ultimate turnoff. Above all he would have a huge capacity for love and devotion and treat me like a great gift and be respectful of my parents and tolerate with grace—if not really like—my more difficult friends and family members.

The man of my dreams.

Well. That was the hope, anyway. That I'd meet my husband in the very near future. I didn't have much of a plan. I didn't even make an official resolution. I'd never gotten very far with resolutions. In fact, the last official resolution I'd made—at least, the last resolution I'd remembered making—was during my sophomore year in college when for some unaccountable reason I was dating a born-again Christian and inspired by lust I resolved to spend my life as a missionary in some "godless savage land." Those were his words.

Okay, I knew why I was dating the guy. He was gorgeous. Extremely disturbed, but very, very nice to look at. Which is pretty much all I got to do because, you know, those born-again Christian types aren't into premarital sex. Catholics aren't either, but we all cheat. We're all going to Hell, but it just might be worth it.

Anyway, though my common sense and my experience in the dating trenches and my recently acquired cynicism about everything romantic told me I was nuts to be thinking in terms of finally meeting Mr. Right, my heart, that disturbingly powerful organ, told me otherwise. It told me that if I just approached it with openness, I would, indeed, meet my very own hero.

Okay, sure, delude yourself. Knock yourself out. It's your funeral, Erin.

That was Reason. It spoke to me several times a day. Often, it interrupted my sleep. It just had to share its opinions; it just had to pass judgment.

It was one of those workaholic days.

The phone rang just as I was about to pack up for the fifteen-minute walk home. I debated whether to answer it. I checked my watch. Six-forty-five. Not an unheard-of time for a disgruntled client to call and lodge a lengthy complaint. Then again, maybe it was bad karma not to take the call, being on the verge—possibly—of becoming a senior account executive. I was—am—nothing if not responsible.

I picked up on the fourth ring.

"Erin Weston."

"Hi. It's me, Abby."

Relief.

"Hi. I wasn't going to pick up the phone. After-hours cranky clients."

Abby laughed. "Tell me about it."

Abby worked—and still works—as a fund raiser for the Boston Symphony Orchestra. A career in development or, if you like, advancement, sounds all sophisticated and civilized until you start to hear stories about the people Abby has to deal with on a daily basis. Mainly, the outrageously childish women of the Brahman set. My take on the situation is that these women have far too much money and far too much free time on their hands. My Grandmother Morelli had a favorite saying, one she usually delivered with an ominous look at my habitually out-of-work cousin Buster: "The devil finds work for idle hands."

Anyway, how Abby hadn't already put one of those vicious, gossipy, nastily meddlesome ladies—potential donors, all—out of her misery, I just didn't know.

Well, I did know. Abby was genuinely nice. The genuinely nice person is a rarity. I am nice but perhaps not genuinely. I mean, I'd never laugh openly at someone with a silly walk but you can be sure I'm guffawing inside.

"What's up?" I said.

"I thought you might want to have dinner. I know it's last minute, but . . ."

"I'd love to," I said and I meant it. Spending time with Abby would be a great way to ignore my mounting nervousness about the next day's review. It also would be a chance to talk about my mother and her latest escapades. Selfish reasons, mostly, for wanting to get together with a friend, but understandable.

"Great," she said. "I was thinking Biba. Is that okay?"

It was. I agreed to meet Abby in half an hour—she was cabbing over to Boylston Street from Huntington and Massachusetts Avenue—and hung up.

From my office on Boylston Street, Biba was only a three-minute walk. I decided that instead of hanging around the deserted office, I'd take a brisk walk through the Common. Not that my office was in any way unpleasant. The entire EastWind Communications floor had been redesigned about a year earlier. The space was well-lit and nicely decorated in calming beige and taupe with artful splashes of warm colors, deep reds and yellows. My own office boasted a hypermodern beechwood and black leather couch and two matching chairs for clients. And I had a large, south-facing window with a ficus jungle in colorful Aztec-influenced pots.

Still, I was a big fan of walking, not as much for the exercise as for the stimulation of urban sights and sounds. Plus, the Common is such a beautiful place to walk, rich with history. Back in colonial seventeenth century, the land was the common grazing ground for local farmers. As Boston grew and became less rural, more urban, somebody had the wisdom to preserve the land as a public park. Now, it's laced with tree-lined paths, scattered with monuments to the heroes of liberty, and largely safe at night.

I bundled into my brown mouton coat, a piece I'd bought ten years before in The Antique Boutique in New York. The coat, which I call the Bear, is the warmest coat on the face of this Earth. Over the years I'd managed to find an almost perfectly matching hat. A cream-colored wool scarf, brown leather gloves, and I was ready.

The air was cold and clear, and even though the holiday lights had been removed from the trees, and the annual ice sculptures had melted or been chipped away by bored kids, there lingered the scent of celebration. And the enticing, ro-

mantic scent of smoke from the fireplaces in the homes along
Beacon Street. It's one of the few joys of winter in Boston: A
lungful of cold, crisp air laced with a hint of cozy hearth.

I was not alone in enjoying the evening. It seemed lots of
people had chosen to cut through the Common on their way
home or to meet friends. In spite of the freezing weather, a
couple embraced on the little bridge. In the spring and summer, tourists ride the stately swan boats back and forth under
that bridge. I imagined for a moment that the scene was
frozen on canvas. I even gave the painting a title: "The Dream."

Sentimental? Sure.

Then—I heard excited shouts and laughter coming from
the Frog Pond, frozen over for late fall and winter. It's the
city's most popular and picturesque skating venue, a brain-
child of our mayor.

I decided to watch the skaters for a few minutes. It had
been a long time since I'd worn skates—white, with rabbit
fur pom-poms—and it would probably be a long time before
I ever wore them again. When it comes to most sports, I am
strictly a spectator. I do après ski quite skillfully.

The Frog Pond was jammed with skaters. Lots of couples.
Mostly young, one probably in their seventies, looking spry
and healthy, typical hardy New Englanders. A boy about
twelve, wearing a striped Dr. Seuss *Cat-in-the-Hat* hat, shot
around the slower skaters, zipping backward, then forward
again, making loop-the-loops. A girl about ten in a fancy red
velvet skating costume, trimmed in white fur, did careful pirou-
ettes at the exact center of the rink. A group of teenagers, baggy
pants wet from trailing on the ice, hauled each other around
the rink by the hand. Fell on each other. Screamed and hooted
with hormonal glee.

It made me smile. Fun is catching. Two golden retrievers
bounded around and around the frozen pond, barking excitedly, agreeing with me.

Then, I spotted a family of four. Father, mother, two little
kids, maybe five and seven. All members of the same team,
all bundled to the teeth in shiny ski jackets and mile-long

scarfs and fuzzy woolen mittens and goofy, brightly colored knit hats. Laughing. Hanging on to each other, grabbing arms and legs. The father catching the mother as she slipped, kissing her on the nose.

And suddenly, I didn't feel like smiling anymore. This happy family had so much. I didn't begrudge them their riches. I just . . .

So simple. It should have been so simple to fall in love, marry, build a family. But sometimes it seemed so impossible, such a far-away dream. How did you start the process? Was there a magic word or ritual? Did you just have to want it badly enough?

Would it be too insane, I wondered, to go up to the wife/mother of that happy family and ask her for some pointers?

Reason told me, Sure. Go ahead. Make a jerk of yourself.

Here's the bitch of it. At twenty-one, the dream—husband, family, a lovely house with a dog in the yard, a cat on the hearth, an antique mirror over the beautifully upholstered couch—seemed too mundane and dead-end to consider.

I was different.

It wasn't something I could explain very easily. I just wanted something—else.

That dream of husband and house seemed so easy to acquire, so unquestioned. Everybody did it. Why would I want what everybody else had? Wasn't I glad to be different, to go my own way, make my own life, all independent?

Okay. I was young. I thought I'd chart a new course. I thought I'd be some kind of new woman. I thought too many women fell for the dream that started with the white gown, princess for a day, and ended bitterly in divorce court. Didn't almost all women fall into marriage and family, only to learn that the dream's daily trappings were stifling to the self and the soul?

Yes, maybe my mother taught that to me, often, though obliquely, hinting that this was the case with her. She'd married at twenty-one and I'd never seen her happy, only put upon, and used up. Or, it occurred to me, much, much later, acting that way.

Okay. So I had made my own way, built a career, traveled, dated a fair share of exciting, interesting men. In retrospect: self-centered artists; self-absorbed Internet gurus; self-aggrandizing brokers—none with an ounce of energy for anyone but themselves.

And then I'd turned twenty-eight. And the pangs began. Mild yearnings at first, for what, exactly, I couldn't even name.

Just something—else.

Suddenly, going to a friend's wedding dateless didn't seem like striking a blow for the happy, independent woman.

It just seemed—lonely.

Lacy white gowns and sparkling headpieces are fun!

That was Romance speaking up. It was new in town. Reason had tried to shut it down. But the yearning was big and clear and specific and Romance would not be silenced. It had appeared to remind me that I wanted to be married to that intelligent, funny, kind, and hardworking man. Okay, with brown eyes. It had appeared to remind me that I wanted to have children. Two, maybe three, healthy and happy and bright-cheeked. It had appeared to remind me I wanted a big, Victorian-style house on a tree-lined street, with a backyard big enough for a picnic table and a swing set and, of course, a barbecue. It had appeared to remind me I wanted there to be a little white church in the center of town—not Catholic—where my beautiful husband and children and I would attend Christmas Eve services. It had appeared to remind me I even wanted to be a soccer mom—as long as I didn't actually have to play.

But Reason mocked me. There's just one little problem, Erin, it would say. Time's running out. Your biological clock is ticking away. Did you know that a woman who gives birth at the age of thirty-five and older is considered to be of Advanced Maternal Age? AMA. And therefore she and her baby are at much greater risk for all sorts of calamities than, say, a twenty-five-year-old and her baby. So get a grip. Accept the reality. The door's just about to close.

I looked at the mother/wife and her brood. It was hard to tell at that distance, with her face mostly covered by her scarf, but when she laughed her voice sounded young and clear. I guessed she was about my age. Give or take a year. Which meant that she'd had her children in her twenties.

Let's face it, Erin. Reason again. If a man can date a twenty-five-year-old, he will. Even if the twenty-five-year-old makes less money and has less experience than the thirty-two-year-old he thought he might want to ask out. Until the twenty-five-year-old came along. Oh, sure, in the man's mind, the thirty-two-year-old woman definitely has something the twenty-five-year-old doesn't. Wear and tear.

I didn't want to feel bitter, really.

And I couldn't even blame anyone for my being in that place. I'd made the decisions all along the way. The decisions that got me where I was—thirty-two, single, and with no good prospect on the horizon.

I loved my job and I was proud of my career and my condo and my travels. But at the same time, I wanted what I suspected it might have been too late for me to have.

I wanted to fall in love. I wanted it to be real. And I wanted it to last forever.

I watched as the skating family tumbled off the ice. For a moment, I listened to the laughter and shouts of the other skaters, to the excited barking of the dogs.

Then I pulled my coat closer around me and walked on.

Chapter Two

"I don't know what to order."

"Abby, you never know what to order," I pointed out. "But you always wind up liking what you choose."

"That's true. So why do I spend so much time agonizing over the menu? When the waiter comes I should just close my eyes and point."

"Wait. What if you point to mussels? You're allergic."

"Oh, right." Abby sighed. "Maybe I'd better just . . ."

"Ladies? Can I take your order?"

I shot a look of minor panic at Abby.

"Uh, just a few more minutes," I said apologetically.

"Thank you," Abby added. "I promise we'll be ready."

The waiter smiled, said, "No problem," and walked away.

"He's nice," I said, returning to the menu.

My friend JoAnne hates when I do that. "You're paying him," she says. "He's working for you. Why are you apologizing? Why is he 'nice' because he's doing his job? That's what people are supposed to do. Their jobs."

On general principle, JoAnne takes no prisoners.

"Okay, I think I'm going to have the . . . No, wait. Yes, definitely the chicken."

"I have my annual review tomorrow," I said.

Abby looked up from her menu and smiled. "I'm sure it'll go wonderfully."

"How can you be sure? I can't even be sure," I said. Wanting Abby to be right. Wanting her to reassure me.

"Easy. History has proven that every single time you're sure you're going to be fired, you're not. Instead, you're given a bigger expense account or new company car or whatever else people who work for profit-making companies are rewarded with. Extra vacation days. A nicer office."

"Still, anything could happen," I argued. But I felt better already.

Abby nodded. "You're absolutely right. Anything could happen, at any time, with no warning. Which means something good as well as something bad. For example, maybe tonight's the night you'll meet Mr. Right."

I laughed. "Now that would be something!"

Wouldn't it? I don't know, maybe it was watching that skating family earlier, the thoughts and feelings they stirred up, but when I'd walked into the busy restaurant, for a fleeting moment a thrill had run through me. A physical thrill, a big flutter or tingle, like something important was about to happen, something amazing.

Like meeting that special someone?

Not impossible, I thought, given the fact that Biba was a Boston hot-spot and that the room was filled with a fair number of twenty-to-forty-something, well-dressed, good-looking, financially successful men. Okay, there were also a fair number of twenty-to-thirty-something, well-dressed, good-looking, financially successful women, including Abby and me, so the competition was a bit stiff. But I wasn't totally without confidence. Cupid had been known to strike in much stranger places.

Reason snorted derisively. Get a life, Erin, it said.

Romance countered. Abby is right. Anything can happen—if you just want it badly enough. If you just believe!

It was a Thursday, a seriously busy restaurant night in Boston, as it is in most cities these days. Maybe the busiest, with the possible exception of Saturday. But Thursdays were more about singles and people who lived and worked in town than Saturdays, when married couples and people from the suburbs took over.

I preferred eating out on Thursdays. Far more opportunity to meet the intelligent, funny, kind, and hardworking man of my dreams and get going on the mortgage for that Victorian house.

The waiter returned.

Abby ordered the pasta special, not the chicken, something with butternut squash, which seems to be the hot vegetable right now. I ordered the steak frite, rare.

The waiter went off to place our orders. Abby and I sat back to sip our wine, talk, and take in the restaurant's ambiance. With slightly spoolly hand-crafted modern light fixtures, a bar made out of concrete, and floors striped in alternate panels of oak and chocolate-colored walnut, it was a unique and funky salute to Crafts-movement chic, with a distinctly new millenium twist.

"I love your suit, Erin," Abby said.

I laughed. "Thanks, so do I." I'd bought the suit on a trip to Ireland the year before. This was the first time I'd worn it. A long, slim-fitting, single-breasted jacket with a high closure. Slim-fitting pants, cuffed. All wool, in a beautiful shade of deep rose, almost red, that complemented my pale skin, blue eyes, and ash blond hair.

I'm not vain, but I know I'm not exactly hideous.

"Don't you know that man?" Abby said, nodding toward the front of the restaurant. "The tall one, dark hair, in the three-button suit?"

"Where?"

"He just came in. At the end of the bar. He's with another man. A guy with a camel coat. Oh, he just took it off. And a woman in a red coat and an odd fuzzy hat."

I glanced over my shoulder. The bar area was crowded with people stopping by for an after-work drink with a friend or conversation with a colleague, with people waiting for tables with their dates. At first I couldn't pick out the man in the three-button suit. How could Abby even see such a detail from this far away, through a dark and busy restaurant? And there had to be more than one man with a three-button suit . . .

Then the crowd at the end of the bar parted as the hostess led two women to a table and I spotted a red coat.

Behind Red Coat woman, Three-Button. Yes. I knew him. Jack Nugent. He worked for a big marketing/PR agency named Trident. I'd met him at various times during my career at EastWind. I liked him. Jack was nice, a family man, decent, and very good at his job. I admired him even.

But it wasn't Jack Nugent that riveted my attention. It was the man with Jack and the woman in the red coat and odd fuzzy hat. The man with the camel coat over his left arm. The man with the air about him of nonchalance and confidence. Not arrogance, something subtler and sexier. A man at ease with himself.

I'd never seen Camel Coat before. I would have remembered. Even at this distance of about thirty feet I knew I was seeing this man for the first time. Somehow, I knew it would not be the last.

The thrill ran through me again, familiar now but more powerful, and nestled deep inside me.

"Erin?"

"Huh?" Reluctantly, I turned back to Abby.

"What's wrong? You do know that man, right? The tall one?"

But there wasn't a need to answer because Abby's raised eyes and perfect social smile told me Jack had spotted me staring—how could he have not?—and was coming over to say hello.

"Erin?"

"Jack, hi! How are you?" I said brightly. Ignoring Camel Coat at his side. Red Coat woman had disappeared.

"Fine, great. Glad the holidays are over, though. Too many parties and too many relatives."

Jack smiled to show he didn't really mean any of it. Jack

was a guy who actually arranged annual family picnics and barbecues. A patriarch-in-training.

Camel Coat looked at me. For a moment I was sure he was going to say, "I know you." Like he recognized me, like he'd known me at some distant point in his life. It was a look that seemed to want to place me, identify me, remember me. Take me home.

And I looked at him, betraying all those questions and feelings and desires.

He smiled a smile—amused, triumphant, predatory—that acknowledged he'd seen the need and desire and urgency in my eyes.

I wanted to die with shame. I wanted to press my body against his.

Just then Reason chimed in. Don't make an ass of yourself, Erin. Get a grip!

Smile brighter, Erin, Romance countered. He's very attractive!

Ignoring both, I smoothly carried out my social duty.

I smiled back blandly, told my eyes to go blank. Then I turned to Jack.

"Jack, this is Abigail Walker. She works in development at the BSO."

Jack greeted Abby with an open, socially acceptable smile and a brief handshake.

"And this is Doug Spears," he said. "Doug, Abigail Walker and Erin Weston. Erin is at EastWind Communications. Erin, Doug just joined Trident from IdeaONE."

Doug Spears shook Abby's hand first. He leaned in closer to do so. My eyes focused on him like laser-guided heat-seeking missiles. His face was Harrison Ford-like, uneven, manly, with both smile and frown lines, unbearably sexy. His face told me that he was not a young man. But he wasn't old, either. Maybe somewhere between forty and fifty.

His hands looked strong, like he was used to physical labor or some skilled craft, maybe performed out in the sun, wind, and rain. He wore a gold link watch, not as fancy as a

Rolex but well designed, not inexpensive, maybe a Tagheuer. His hair was thick and brown but might once have been honey-blond. The short cut didn't conceal a slight natural wave. He was not very tall, shorter than Jack, maybe five-foot-eleven. Perfect for my five-six. His shoulders were broad. He wasn't skinny but was in no way fat. He gave the impression of compactness, of bottled energy, nothing wasted. He gave the impression of focus and strength.

Doug Spears turned to me. Almost unaware, I put out my hand to be shaken.

"Nice to meet you, Doug," I said. Trying to sound bland and blank, no more than a passing business acquaintance. "I'm sorry, I'm not familiar with IdeaONE."

Doug Spears took my hand and held it just a second longer than necessary. His eyes were an odd and compelling shade of golden brown. Like a lion's or . . .

"It was my own firm," he said, releasing me. "I sold the business to Trident and came on board as Senior VP of branding."

"We'd been trying to get Doug in-house for years," Jack explained.

"What made you sell?" I blurted, and immediately regretted asking such a personal question.

Reason sputtered wildly.

But Doug Spears didn't seem to mind.

"Money comes in handy," he said. Looking only at me. "But mostly, it was probably boredom. I needed a change."

"And are you happy now?"

Another inappropriate question for one stranger to ask another. Except that Doug Spears somehow was not a stranger. He couldn't be. I'd recognized him somehow . . . hadn't I?

Reason found its voice. Have you gone insane! it demanded. Do you realize you're behaving like a lovesick teenager?

Doug Spears looked more deeply into my eyes. Everything—even Reason—fell away at the sound of Doug Spears's voice.

"Oh, I think I might be," he said. Provocatively. Teasingly.

I would make you happy, I thought. I . . .

"Sir? Your table is ready?"

I started. The universe expanded back to its normal size. I stumbled back into consciousness of a world inhabited by more than just me and Doug Spears.

The hostess. A loud burst of laughter from the bar. The sound system playing Diana Krall. Abby. Jack.

Jack smiled again. Had he seen? Had he sensed what was happening between Doug Spears and me?

"Good running into you, Erin," he said easily. No. He'd noticed nothing, I was sure of it. "And good meeting you, Abigail. Enjoy your dinner."

"Thanks, Jack," I said. "You, too."

At least, I think I said that. I know I was thinking, This can't end yet. Please, let him say something. Don't let him walk away. Maybe I should . . .

Reason growled. Keep your mouth shut, Erin.

Romance said, Give him your card, at least!

Doug Spears nodded at Abby. To me he said, "Until next time."

I looked up into his fabulous eyes and promised that yes, there would be a next time. With a smile, I promised other things, too. And begged him to promise me back.

Doug Spears began to walk away. As he did he shifted his coat from his left arm to his right.

And I saw the wedding band.

"Erin?" Abby said quietly, as Doug Spears faded into the boisterous crowd.

"Yeah?" I said, avoiding her eyes. Knowing she'd seen it, too. Hoping we'd both mistaken a school ring for something more important.

"Don't even think about it."

Chapter Three

The very last thing I needed on the morning of my review was a postcard from my mother. The very last thing I needed the morning after meeting the love of my life and two minutes later finding out he was married was a postcard from my mother.

All right, maybe not the very last thing. The very last thing I needed would have been something like a lousy case of the flu.

But it certainly wasn't a good thing, a postcard from my prodigal mother. Because with a mere twenty words or so, spoken or scrawled on a piece of paper, my mother could knock me flat. Just knock me down, deflate me, make me want to crawl back into bed and pull the covers over my head. For about a week.

She was a powerful person, my mother. Though her motives have always been somewhat unclear to me, puzzling, from the beginning I've admitted her power to crush and strangle. And then to graciously offer to help her victim stand. It's a strange and vicious cycle. And I fell for it every time because in spite of it all, I loved her, which meant I always opened up to her—just before she zinged me again.

So I did not need a postcard from her, that day of all days. The day that I was sure I would be fired. Which event would lead rapidly and assuredly to my losing my apartment and being thrown out onto the street. Where, no doubt, I would be killed by a pack of rabid squirrels within a week. My rotting body not found for months.

Review day was not a favorite day of mine.

Despite the fact that, yes, thus far in my career review day had always resulted in a raise and quite often a promotion. (Or a bonus. Sometimes all three.) Despite the fact that by the time I'd gone to bed the night before I'd managed to work up a pretty good supply of confidence. But I think that might have been due to the wine. Wine and lust and an unbelievably ridiculous determination to win Doug Spears away from his no-doubt nasty wife.

And then morning had come. The glaring light of day. And with the return of consciousness, Reason awoke and reminded me just how dangerous it was to be thinking romantic thoughts about a married man. And, it added, it's ridiculous and a major waste of time to judge someone—his wife—without even knowing her.

And then Reason's nasty cousin Negativity slipped into the room and took over. Negativity tends to sound like a sonorous, Old Testament prophet of doom. Or a ranting, decrepit oracle.

Pride goeth before a fall, Negativity cried. Things can change at any time. You never know what will happen. You can count on nothing. And never, ever rest on your laurels!

You're only as good as your last win, Reason added, unnecessarily.

Everyone is replaceable, Negativity roared.

Even a wife? I asked.

Neither responded.

I found the postcard when I opened the door to leave for my office. It sat on the cheery WELCOME! mat I had put down the first day I'd moved into this apartment, a first-time homeowner. A sanitary, hospitable measure I'd picked up from my mother. Back in the days when she cared about things like sanitation and hospitality. And home. And family.

The mailman must have put the postcard in my neighbor's box again. This was common enough. Ike, the mailman, was a nice guy. He always had a chatty comment to make about the weather or an opinion to express regarding the failed marriages and impending tragic breakups of Hollywood couples. According to Ike, Brad and Jennifer had four years, tops. I tended to agree. Ike had called the Meg Ryan-Dennis Quaid breakup, an event I had not at all seen coming.

But in spite of his likeable personality, Ike was no rocket scientist. In fact, I wasn't a hundred percent certain Ike could read. Which could be a tricky sort of handicap for a mailman to work around.

Anyway, there it was. A postcard from my mother. Marie Weston. Fifty-six years old. Divorced after thirty-five years of marriage to my father, John. Currently living in an Un-identified South American Country. See, since she'd gotten on a plane and headed south, it had been difficult to keep track of her whereabouts. She moved from here to there, only occasionally sending a scribbled line or two. Once, I'd tried to contact her at the address on the back of a card, some small, slapdash resort. The snakey proprietor told me she'd left weeks before. With some guy from the town. And asked me when I'd be coming to enjoy the pleasures of Villa Loco.

The brightly colored photo of a brightly colored bird on the front of the postcard was somehow offensive. Clearly, the photo had been taken on a hot and sunny day. This fact annoyed me. Along with the fact that my mother currently lived in a year-round warm climate.

I did not. January in Boston, Massachusetts, is not a whole lot of fun. It was cold, twelve degrees with a wind-chill factor of minus two at 7:30 A.M., according to the telephone service weatherman. Not unusual weather for the Northeast Coast.

There was ice on the ground, too, the extremely tricky, all but invisible black ice which forced me to walk like the very frail and nervous ninety-year-old woman I will be in exactly fifty-eight years. Shuffle, really. And look constantly for something to hang on to. A signpost. A mailbox. A stranger's arm.

On icy days I was not in the habit of actually lifting my feet off the sidewalk. No one has ever accused me of being physically reckless.

I was dressed for the bitter winter weather in a smart, wool-blend, gray pin-striped pantsuit; an ankle-length, black wool coat I'd bought at Banana Republic the year before; a black beret and black, slim-fitting leather gloves; and a gorgeous gray cashmere scarf, a present from my father two Christmases ago. And I was beginning to sweat, standing in an overheated hallway, staring down at a picture of some stupid tropical bird. I didn't even like birds. They frightened me.

My mother used to know that.

Okay. Several options faced me. I could pick up the card, I thought. Verify it was indeed from my mother. Though who else did I know in South America? Who else would be sending me a photo of an undoubtedly smelly, beady-eyed, flea-infested, claw-footed creature?

Option number two. With my booted foot, I could slide the postcard under the WELCOME! mat. Pretend I never got it. "Oh, my God, Mom! Really? Wow, I never got that one! Gee, I'm sorry. That's too bad."

The guilt would haunt, then kill me.

Back to option number one. I could pick up the postcard and walk directly to the trash can under the kitchen sink. Alternately, I could pick up the postcard, tear it into many little pieces, and walk directly to the trash can under the kitchen sink.

Another thought occurred to me. I could go off to work, leaving the postcard where it was on the WELCOME! mat. See if it was still there when I got home. Might be. Might not be.

Still another idea. My imagination is fecund. I could pick up the postcard and put it, unread, on the kitchen table for that evening's reading adventure. Which last two plans, I immediately realized, meant that all day long I would be dreading the moment when I had to face the thing again. Dreading and dwelling, going crazy with curiosity and driving myself insane with worry.

Reason and Negativity have a stepcousin named Panic.

Because what if the postcard is a cry for help? Panic asked. Good question. What if my mother was withering in a horrid, dank, rat-ridden jail cell in the Unidentified South American Country? What if she needed my help, now?

I could make it to the USAC's embassy in half an hour. Provided the USAC had an embassy in Boston. I would call a lawyer. Yes, my father was a lawyer, perfect! Maybe Mom had sent him a postcard, too. He could rescue her and she'd be so grateful she'd declare him her hero and beg him to take her back. . . .

Wait! Reason shouted. Just back it up, Erin.

I took a deep breath. Okay, how likely was it for South American jailors to allow their North American female prisoners to purchase colorful postcards with the word *"Hola!"* printed in yellow on the front? How likely was it for them to allow their prisoners to send such cards to their families and friends back home, scribbled with words like "starving" and "putrifying" and phrases like "lice-infested" and "water torture" ? And when had my mother ever been in serious danger before?

I sighed. Felt a drop of sweat trickle down my back. I was screwed. No matter what I decided to do I'd feel regret. Possibly shame. Inevitably, I'd feel like a very bad daughter.

There was no winning with her. There never had been.

I picked up the postcard. I read it.

> *E—Having a fabulous time with Roberto. Latino men are simply the most wonderful lovers! Our work with the villagers was unexpectedly halted when one of the young girls accused Roberto of . . . Well, anyway, we're on our way—somewhere!—*

so won't be in touch for a while. Oh, hope the holidays were fun! M.

P.S. I chose this card because I know how much you love *birds!*

Chapter Four

By eleven o'clock that morning I was senior account executive.

I figured it was probably all luck, though Terry, my boss and EastWind's owner and founder, said otherwise.

And since waking that morning I'd only thought of Doug Spears once. Every hour.

That night, Friday, while most of Boston's single people were out celebrating the start of their forty-eight hours of freedom, I brought in some Thai food and settled on the couch with Fuzzer to watch *Providence*—which only sometimes annoys me with its goody-goody heroine—and then to pop in a tape of a movie I'd rented on the way home. *Butterfield 8*, with Elizabeth Taylor and Lawrence Harvey. It was one of my all-time favorites. John O'Hara wrote the book and for some reason I'd never gotten around to reading it.

But the movie is brilliant enough—Taylor's performance won her her first Oscar as Best Actress. That night, I was particularly compelled and haunted by Taylor's character, Gloria, a self-employed, high-class call girl who falls in love with one of her married escorts. Tragically, of course.

My interest in the movie that particular weekend had nothing at all to do with my brief encounter with Doug Spears. In spite of what Reason made sure to point out to me.

Saturday morning I cleaned the bathroom and kitchen, did two loads of laundry, waited for the grocery delivery. The usual. At one o'clock I met my father for lunch at Joe's American Bar and Grill on Newbury Street, one of his favorite lunch places. We had hamburgers and beer and I tried to cheer him up by being funny and light-hearted but the sadness in his eyes just didn't budge.

We talked about our jobs. Dad told me about an interesting new case the firm had just taken on. I told him about my promotion. After that, there was a lull in the conversation.

"Have you heard from your mother?" Dad asked abruptly.

"Actually, I just got a postcard from her," I said neutrally.

Dad nodded. I knew he didn't want to ask if she was okay and happy. I also knew he really did want to know.

"She seems fine," I said. "She didn't say much; you know Mom. She said she hoped we enjoyed the holidays."

Dad was not so far gone into misery that he couldn't spare a wry grin. "How considerate of her," he said.

I returned the wry grin. And into my head came rushing a scenario, played out instantaneously, of Doug Spears sitting in his living room, alone, at night, lonely and miserable and not wanting to join his wife in their bed, but thinking of me. Yearning. Of his getting up, packing a bag, driving into the city, and appearing at my door.

"Well, Dad," I said, reaching for my bag, suddenly uncomfortable, "I guess we should get going."

We parted with a promise to get together for dinner later that week.

At seven o'clock I met my friend Damion and his new boyfriend, Carl, at the Loews Cineplex to see the new Russell Crowe movie. There was a lot of noise and flesh and blood. Afterward, the three of us went for cocktails at Vox Populi. At eleven-thirty I was in bed with Fuzzer, reading the new Barbara Kingsolver novel.

And the entire night I'd been obsessed by thoughts of

Doug Spears. Even Russell Crowe shirtless—even hotter, in my opinion, after his role in *A Beautiful Mind*—couldn't block out the unbidden fantasy of Doug Spears taking my hand in his on a warm and starry night, of his drawing me close, of his kissing me.

Doug Spears even haunted my dreams that night. In those dreams my hair was dark, not ash blond, and I wore a tight-fitting dress much like the ones Elizabeth Taylor wore in *Butterfield 8*. Otherwise, I was me and Doug Spears was himself, utterly gorgeous in that manly, imperfect way, and wearing a dark suit and the camel coat.

In the dreams the same thing happened, over and over, with only slight variations. I stood in the middle of an office hallway. To get past me, someone would have to slide to the right or left. At the far end of the hallway, Doug Spears suddenly appeared and began to walk rapidly, purposefully toward me, straight at me. He's coming to kiss me, I'd think. And then, as he trod on, I'd realize he didn't even see me. And as he got closer, his eyes focused far beyond me, on some distant goal, I'd panic and try to move out of his way. But I was never able to move even a finger. And as Doug Spears crashed right into me, not really seeing me, I woke up.

Sunday, I met Abby, JoAnne, and our friend Maggie for brunch at Aquitaine, on Tremont Street, only a few blocks from my home. Brunch is a major social event in the South End so I'd made a reservation for us on Wednesday. We had a booth close to the front of the restaurant and were blinded by the white winter sun streaming through the large glass windows. There we were. Four thirty-something women, eating brunch, wearing sunglasses. Very cool.

We ordered. Eggs Florentine for me; ditto for JoAnne; banana pancakes for Abby; a mushroom and cheese omelette for Maggie. Coffee all around and a Bloody Mary for JoAnne.

And then somehow, inexplicably, the conversation got around to my wayward mother. And to the uncomfortable fact that I still had not found the strength or maturity to forgive her. I mean, I wanted to forgive her—for ruining the family and upsetting our lives and all—but I just didn't seem to be able to do it.

"Why don't you buy that book," Abby suggested innocently. "You know, *Mothers and Their Adult Daughters: The Dance Continues.* I've heard it's very helpful."

JoAnne barked a laugh. "Where, on *Oprah?* Please. Self-help books are useless. Only pathetic losers read them. Or buy those self-affirmation cards. Yes, I am such a loser I can't even afford therapy."

Maggie shrugged. "Hey, my attitude is: Whatever works."

"Here's an idea," I said. Suddenly, changing the topic from my mother to anything else—even nuclear physics, about which I knew virtually nothing—seemed an important idea. "Let's come up with a series of self-defamation cards. I bet there's a market."

JoAnne's eyes twinkled. "I've got one. 'I'm fatter today than I was yesterday and I'll be even fatter tomorrow.' "

My turn. " 'I suck and am going to Hell.' "

"Too general. Let's keep it specific," Maggie suggested. " 'No matter what my mother told me, I am not at all special.' "

" 'I am just like everybody else,' " Abby said.

JoAnne shook her head. "Could be taken as a positive. The point here is to demean. Here's another one: 'I am my parents' least favorite child.' "

" 'I was an accident and will live to regret being born.' "

" 'The mirror does not lie. My butt looks like a sack of cottage cheese.' "

" 'No matter what my friends tell me, I am not attractive to men.' "

" 'I am so pathetic I can't even come up with a self-defamatory statement brutal enough to approach the sad and sorry truth of how big a loser I am.' "

I raised my coffee cup. "To JoAnne. The winner, as usual."

"Next topic?" Maggie asked after the waiter had delivered our food.

"Men?" JoAnne suggested. "Anyone have anything new and interesting to tell?"

"Erin does," Abby said.

"No, I don't," I said. Panic reared its ugly head but Reason quickly beat it down. What was I afraid of?

Too many feelings to acknowledge.

"Yes, you do," Abby insisted, turning to JoAnne and Maggie. "Erin met someone the other night."

"It's nothing," I insisted. What was Abby thinking! "I didn't even really meet him. I mean, there was a man and I was introduced to him . . ."

"So, you did actually meet him?"

"Yes, but it wasn't a special introduction, like someone wanted us to meet, it was . . ." I poked at my eggs and spinach and Hollandaise sauce.

"He's married," Abby blurted.

"Erin?" JoAnne singsonged. "Is this true?"

"And they were flirting."

I turned to Abby. I felt the blood rise in my cheeks. "You know, I can speak for myself. And while I have the floor, are you for me or against me? I'm having trouble telling."

"I'm sorry," she said, patting my arm. "I'm for you, Erin, of course. And I know you can speak for yourself. But I was afraid you wouldn't and I think you should talk about this and get him out of your system. You know, before something . . . happens. I saw the way you looked at each other," she added. "It was . . . intense."

"Abby," I protested lightly, "I talked to him for less than two minutes. He's hardly in my system."

At which point everyone lowered their sunglasses and gave me the look. The look that said, "Cut the crap."

Okay. There was no way out of this conversation but to be honest and up front. Right? At least about the bare facts.

"Look, I met this guy Thursday night at Biba. His name is Doug something. He works for a big competitor. And . . . yes, I was attracted to him. I am attracted to him. A lot."

"But he's married."

"Yes, that fact has been established."

"Did you look for a ring?" JoAnne asked, pointing a stalk

of celery at me like an accusatory finger. "I mean, before you flirted?"

"I didn't even think to look," I admitted. "I was just . . . so . . ."

Abby nodded. "Smitten."

"Well, that's not exactly the word I would have chosen," I said, "but yeah. I was smitten."

"Not all married men wear rings," Maggie pointed out reasonably. "So even if Erin did look and didn't see a ring, she'd have been none the wiser."

"So, when did you finally spot the ring?" JoAnne pressed.

"When he shifted his coat from one arm to the other," I said.

"Smooth."

I gasped. "You don't think he was hiding the ring on purpose, do you? That's ridiculous!"

Maggie grimaced. "It's been known to happen, Erin. Men are manipulative. They'll use any weapon they can when they're on the hunt."

JoAnne just shrugged and took another sip of her Bloody Mary.

Mood dip. Instinct told me to go on defense.

"You don't understand," I said. "You're making it sound all sordid and cheap. It was just . . ."

Just what, Erin? Reason prodded. Just that you went all stupid and slobbery? Tell them the truth!

"It was just that he didn't seem married," I blurted.

"What the hell does that mean!" JoAnne, Abby, Maggie. At the same time. They grinned at one another, proud.

I kept my mouth shut. How could I expect anyone to understand something I could barely articulate? Something I was still figuring out myself?

"It means he was pitching as well as catching," Maggie ventured finally. "Right? He was playing the game back? Feeding you lines."

"It wasn't that," I repeated. It seemed I was going to try

again to explain the unexplainable. My feelings. "It . . . it just seemed like he was supposed to be mine."

Reason choked on its words. Good, I didn't want to hear them anyway.

My friends fell silent again. Admittedly, I had uttered another interesting statement. Another statement that made sense only to me.

But what business was it of anyone's what happened between me and Doug Spears?

It's his wife's business, Reason snapped. Mostly, it's your business and you're on the verge of conducting it very, very badly.

"Well," I said testily, angry at all the voices around and inside me, pissed off at all the intruders. "Since Abby so thoughtfully brought up the topic, and if I say I don't want to talk about it anymore you'll just ignore me, why don't you all tell me your opinions. You know, about everything."

"I'm off men, totally," Maggie reminded us. "Married, single, fat, skinny, whatever."

"Yeah, but don't you have an opinion?" JoAnne pressed.

"Of course. But my opinion should make no difference to Erin. Besides, I learned a long time ago that most times it's better to keep your opinions to yourself."

At least someone didn't feel the need to lecture me.

Maggie Branley. Red hair, blue eyes, and pale skin. Maggie's got a Ph.D. in Urban Design from MIT. She's smart and funny and yet private in a way that makes you think she's suffered some pain that just won't go away. Which, I'm guessing, was caused by her disastrous grad school marriage to an Italian Lothario, about which JoAnne and Abby knew nothing. And she respects other people's privacy in a way that's very comforting.

"Anyway, this is not really about men and women," Abby said. "It's about morality. Right and wrong."

"Duh! If it's about morality, it's of necessity about men and women," JoAnne snapped. "This Doug person is a man.

Erin is a woman. The two big questions here are: Will a married man cheat on his wife? And will Erin let herself be used?"

"Thanks," I muttered.

"You wanted our take on the situation," JoAnne reminded me.

Not really, I thought.

"Sexual ethics. Sex as power. Sex as acquisition," Maggie recited, mopping up the last of her omelette with a piece of buttered toast. "Doesn't it ever seem boring? It does to me."

"Here's my favorite argument for male infidelity," JoAnne said. "One of them, anyway. 'Men need variety and change.' "

"Oh, God, we're back to the biological imperative," I said, not enjoying the conversation at all. Wishing we could just drop it. Doug Spears wasn't like the average man. I just knew. Through the clashing in my head and the fire in my heart, that one truth shone clear. I just knew.

"Yes, sir!" JoAnne pounded her fist on the table. A fork jumped to the floor. A very handsome, very gay waiter raised his eyebrows. "Men must sow their seed over the face of the land."

"Yeah, and how many men stick around to reap what they sow?" Maggie said. "How many stick around to cultivate the love? And the kids?"

"It's not about sticking around," JoAnne said with a grin. "For men it's all about sticking it in. The consequences are the woman's problem."

"Which is why women should stick together," Maggie affirmed. "Okay. There's my opinion."

JoAnne turned to me. "Here's a question for you, Erin. Does this Mr. Married Man of yours have kids?"

"He's not mine," I answered hotly. "And I don't know."

"I suppose he could be separated," Abby said in an oddly hopeful voice. "Or maybe he's a widower."

"Now that's a happy thought," JoAnne said. "Anyway, I don't really care one way or the other about the morality or ethics of an affair. Till death do us part is a ridiculous sentiment. One true love—please. Why pretend anyone can attain a goal that's clearly unattainable? Cheating is an unpleasant fact of life. End of story. Just watch yourself, kiddo. If you decide to play footsie with this guy, set some rules up front. And don't expect him to leave the Mrs. for you. Most men don't have the balls. And try to get some jewelry out of it. Something you can sell later. When the bastard goes slinking back home."

JoAnne Chiofalo takes no crap from anyone. Ever.

JoAnne is wiry and olive-complected with long, very dark, very naturally curly hair. She's also a well-known and highly respected pediatrician. And in a city famous for its top-notch medical community, that's no small feat. Kids love her and she loves kids. Which is kind of interesting when you consider that among the four of us she's the least interested in getting married and having a family. If you said that JoAnne's a romantic it would be like saying Louis Farrahkan is white. Severe misunderstanding of the situation.

"You're not going to do it, are you, Erin?" Abby said. "Go out with him?"

What could I say? What should I say?

What did my friends want to hear?

"Abby, I don't even know if I'll ever see this guy again. And I'm certainly not going to call him," I lied. Because the thought certainly had occurred to me.

I could admit to curiosity, pure and simple. How could that be wrong? The desire to know what, if anything, Doug Spears had in mind. A one-time flirtation? An ongoing, teasing dance, a platonic friendship with a kick? A one-night stand? An affair?

Marriage?

"Because it would be wrong, Erin," Abby went on. "Besides being a total waste of your time, it would be wrong. Just think of his poor wife, sitting home alone every night, wondering why her husband has to work late again."

"I won't allow myself to be a cliché, Abby," I lied again. Because Friday night, still heady from the too-brief encounter, my head filled with images of Gloria the call girl and her married lover, I had stood in front of the bathroom mirror and tried out the title of "mistress." Just to see how it fit. Just in case.

Mistress. It felt odd and exciting, a little dirty, and I had to look away from my reflection.

Then I tried "the other woman," but it just sounded too 1940s Hollywood. I couldn't take it seriously. I felt I should be wearing a hat with a black veil over my face, long black gloves, a cigarette in a holder between my fingers.

Finally, I tried "girlfriend on the side," but the only image that came to mind was a plate of cold peas. It made me laugh and I turned off the lights and went to bed.

Abby reached for my hand. "Just promise me you'll try to do the right thing, Erin. You always have, I know, but, well . . . things are different now. I know you're upset about your parents and sometimes when we feel someone has hurt us we're so—upset—we hurt someone else back. And that's bad for everyone."

JoAnne removed her sunglasses and eyed Abby critically. "Are you sure you're not moonlighting as a talk-show hostess?"

Abby released my hand and blushed.

Abigail Walker. She's the prettiest among us, in a classic kind of very feminine way. Long, sleek brown hair; peaches-and-cream complexion; big hazel eyes; slim but not skinny. Abby's almost totally unconscious about her looks, has no clue that beauty equals power. Which is partly what makes her bearable as a girlfriend.

That and the fact that she's smart and kind and surprisingly true to her ideals. Which sometimes I admire and sometimes makes her a big pain in the butt. Abby might look like a pushover, with her propensity for hair bows and sweaters embroidered with scotties, but just try to get her to bend on the issue of, say, gentrification. Or extramarital affairs. Good luck. Abby is New England's version of a steel magnolia.

What would that be? A hard-shelled lobster?

"Look, everyone," I said, feeling suddenly like I had to

protect my friends from an uncomfortable reality. Me. "He probably won't even call. And if he does . . ." I hesitated. My heart actually beat faster at the thought. "And if he does, and it's for any reason other than strictly business, I'll tell him right off that I don't date married men."

Reason spoke. Good girl, it said. Stick to your guns. Don't do anything stupid. I'll be watching.

"That's my Erin," Abby said.

"Betraying another woman is betraying yourself," Maggie added. "His wife thanks you. We all thank you."

JoAnne smiled enigmatically.

There. I'd given my friends what they were asking for, hadn't I? At least what Maggie and Abby were asking for. An assurance that I would turn my back on Doug Spears, starting now.

But it wasn't that simple. Because I knew it was not a promise I could easily keep. Wasn't at all sure it was a promise I wanted to keep.

Why had I opened my mouth if all I was going to do was lie? Answer: To regain some privacy, someplace within which Doug Spears and I could come together without being harrassed.

To cherish what happened the other night, Romance reminded me in a soothing, persuasive voice. Because you've never felt this way about a man before. This compelled, this in need. You have to pursue the feelings! It would be fatal to your soul to ignore them. This man could be your destiny. You cannot let arbitrary social mores stand in the way of your one great love!

I would say one final thing. For effect. To keep up the role of reasonable, self-respecting woman, someone a friend could be proud of.

"If Mr. What's-His-Name suggests any hanky-panky, I'll just tell him to go jump in the Charles."

JoAnne tossed her napkin on her plate and slid out of the booth. "I'm out of here."

"Have fun," Maggie said.

"Oh, so you're meeting someone else?" I asked. "More exciting company?"

"Martin. The lawyer I told you about."

"Do you like him?" Abby.

"He keeps me out of worse trouble." JoAnne turned to me and grinned. "Like dating married men."

Chapter Five

My father and I had made plans to meet for dinner. If it were anyone but my father I would have canceled, rather than subject myself to being outside any longer than strictly necessary. It was a particularly bitter January day with more than a hint of snow in the air. The damp New England cold has a way of seeping through just about any gear you might don and chilling you head to toe.

This kind of weather sucks. Not only does it suck, it blows. And bites.

I do not like it. I know people who claim that Boston is no colder in winter than New York but I beg to differ. I've been to New York. I know what I know.

By the time I got to the Legal Sea Foods at Park Square I was beyond miserable but determined to snap into a good mood. The last thing my father needed was to be dragged down further than he already had been by the last several months of divorce hell and postdivorce blues.

He was waiting for me at a table for two. He'd ordered a bottle of wine and poured me a glass as I struggled out of the requisite layers of winter gear.

"Cold enough for you?" he joked.

I rolled my eyes. It was something my Grandfather Morelli used to say and it had always driven me crazy.

"Ha ha." I bent down and kissed his cheek, then sat down. "How are you?"

"Can't complain." He made a face. "Well, actually, I could complain, but I won't."

"I'd listen if you wanted to complain, Dad."

"No thanks. Hey, I ordered some bluefish pâté to start, okay?"

Well, if my father didn't want to bitch and moan, I wasn't going to force him to bitch and moan.

For a while we ate and drank and talked about mutual acquaintances and stuff going on at his office. Then, boldly I said:

"Dad, do you want to get married again?"

His answer came quickly and definitively. "Yes."

That was a surprise.

"I . . . why? I mean, after such a bad experience with Mom . . ."

"Erin, it wasn't a bad experience with your mother. Well, the last part was, but not the entire marriage. Honey, there were lots of good things about our relationship. At least, I thought there were. I guess your mother didn't share my opinion."

"Oh. So . . . you wouldn't have left her?"

Dad sighed. "No, I wouldn't have. Maybe I should have, maybe we both would have been happier in the long run if we'd parted earlier. But I'm not a boat-rocker, Erin. I liked the comfort of our family life. I liked the status quo. I felt—lucky."

"Oh." Then, I said, "Do you think Mom was happy being married? I don't mean to you, necessarily, just—being married."

"I tried to make her happy."

"I know you did."

"Thanks, Erin. But, honestly? No. I don't think she was all that happy."

"Even in the beginning?"

"Even then. Your mother loved me the best she knew how, I believe that. But I don't think marriage was for her. Remember, Erin, there wasn't a whole lot of choice for a woman like your mother. Given her family, especially her father, the church, her own lack of ambition. Your mother did what she thought she had to do."

"You're awfully forgiving, Dad."

Dad laughed. "I'm not saying I'm not angry. Or hurt. But I can't see the point in punishing your mother or in lying about her."

I wondered if Doug's wife would be so generous with him if . . .

"Yeah, okay."

"Each of us in a marriage makes a deal—with ourselves and with the other."

I smiled. "How did you get so smart? Have you been in therapy and not told me?"

Dad laughed. "Old age, Erin. With age comes wisdom. If you let it."

"You're not old, Dad!"

"I'm old enough. And I've had enough experience to realize that nobody knows what goes on in a marriage but the two people wearing the rings. That's why it's usually not a good idea to interfere in someone's marriage based on what you see at a dinner party."

"Aside from bruises."

"Of course."

We ate in companionable silence for a while. Then I began to think.

"So, Dad," I said, "if you're so smart and fine with things and all, does that mean you're ready to start dating?"

Dad laughed. "Oh, no. Not yet. Maybe not for a long time."

"Well, someday you'll be open to meeting someone, right?" I prodded.

"I suppose. Why don't we just wait and see what happens, okay?"

"Okay," I agreed. Truth be told, I was in no great hurry to see my father out there on the singles' market. For a variety of reasons.

"Dessert?" Dad suggested with a mischievous grin. "I remember how much you loved German chocolate cake when you were a little girl."

Who could resist him?

"Oh, yeah."

In spite of—or maybe because of—our busy work schedules, JoAnne, Maggie, Abby, and I tried hard to get together once a week. We were each other's touchstones and, to a great extent, each other's family—without the emotional garbage that comes with one's biological family. I admit that sometimes I didn't want to meet for dinner or brunch, that I would have preferred to hunker down alone with a book or in front of the TV, but the few times I succumbed to that desire I found myself regretting my decision. Being alone is fine—it is even healthy—but one can easily overdo it. Isolation is not an admirable goal.

The four of us met for dinner at Ambrosia on Huntington Avenue. Inevitably, the conversation turned to men—dating them, loving them, avoiding them.

"Who's left to date in this town?" I wondered aloud as three twenty-something idiots whooping it up at a corner table were asked to keep the noise level down to a low bellow.

"I want someone—innocent," Abby said, frowning at the idiots. "Do you know what I mean?"

"Yeah," JoAnne said, replenishing her glass of wine. "Oddly enough, I do. But face facts. We're in our early to midthirties. We can't possibly avoid dating a guy who's either been married, at least once, or who has kids. I mean, unless you're into dating twenty-five-year-olds like the idiots in the corner—and good luck there."

"Or you're into dating eternal bachelors and playboys, and then you're just a masochist," Maggie said.

"If a guy hasn't settled down by the time he's thirty-five,"

JoAnne said, "look out. Steer clear is what I say. He's either obsessed with his mother or a serial killer. A serial killer obsessed with his mother."

"Isn't that part of the job description?" I said to no one.

"So, what's the alternative? We just have to deal with ex-wives and stepchildren?" Abby asked mournfully.

"It doesn't have to be an entirely bad situation," JoAnne said. "It depends on a lot of factors."

"Right. Like, was the divorce amicable," I said, thinking of my parents and their divorce. "Their" divorce. Their marriage, their child, their divorce. Yet another thing they shared. Who would get the divorce when they died?

"No divorce is amicable," JoAnne said dismissively. "The question is: Is the woman a furious psycho?"

"And, why did he get divorced in the first place?" Abby added. "Did he cheat on his wife? Did she cheat on him?"

"And what's their settlement like? Does he have to give almost all his money to her and the kids? If so, for how long? And how much money does he make? How much can he spend on you?" Maggie paused thoughtfully. "If you get married, can he afford to let you quit working to have kids?"

"Isn't that jumping ahead just a little?" Abby asked with a frown.

"I'm trying to help you here. You're the one who wants to get married."

"And what about the kids?" I said, thinking now of when I was a kid myself, about five or six, and we lived next door to a girl named Jeannie Connor. Jeannie's parents were divorced. Five days a week Jeannie lived with her mother and went to my school. On Friday night Jeannie's father would drive up to her house in a green Dodge Dart and park at the curb. From the living room window I'd watch him walk up the path to the front door, ring the bell, and wait for Jeannie and her little blue suitcase to appear. I'd watch as Jeannie's father took her hand and led her to the car. As he carefully put her suitcase in the backseat and then opened the passenger side door for her to climb in. I'd watch them drive away.

On Sunday nights at about seven-thirty, I'd push the living room drapes aside again—just a crack—and wait for Jeannie to reappear. She always did, with her suitcase and a large stuffed animal or doll clutched in her arm.

Where did she go on those weekends, I'd wonder. What did she do? What adventures did she have? Somehow Jeannie's life seemed glamorous to me. Two homes. A suitcase. A new toy every week. Jeannie seemed like a minor celebrity, living an exotic life of travel and surprise, while I sat trapped in my stable and happy home, peering at her through a wall of double-hung glass. I didn't have a suitcase. And I got a new toy only on my birthday or Christmas. I was just like everybody else I knew. Except Jeannie.

I always wanted to ask Jeannie what it was like to be divorced. "To be the child of divorced parents," my mother corrected. "To be the product of a broken home." But I never did. "It would be rude," my mother said. "Just don't say anything. Pretend nothing is wrong."

It seemed to me in those days that Jeannie was happy. I wanted her to be happy. But I never knew what she felt. Jeannie and her mother moved to Los Angeles at the end of the school year to be closer to Jeannie's maternal grandparents. I never saw her after that.

"Do the kids spend every weekend with the father?" I said, thinking of that little blue suitcase. Thinking of Doug Spears. Did he have children? "Are you ever going to get away to the Cape or the Vineyard alone together?"

"And then there are the holidays." JoAnne raised an eyebrow and sipped her wine.

Communal groan.

"Does he have the kids for Thanksgiving?" Maggie counted off the questions on her fingers. "Does his wife? What about Christmas? Summer vacation? Spring break? When do the kids see the grandparents?"

"Some people take the kids from their first marriage along on their honeymoon," Abby said. "With the second spouse, I mean. That's kind of sweet."

"That's kind of sick."

"And then there's the depression," Maggie noted seriously. "Even the laziest, most incidental father gets all weepy and blue on a holiday when he can't see his kids. There's a guy who teaches in my department who's absolutely unbearable from mid-November through mid-January. 'Tis the season to make everybody around him as miserable as he is."

"Too true," JoAnne said. "I once dated a guy who, by his own admission, never gave a shit about his kids' school plays and stuff. Then when his wife left him, he couldn't get enough of the kids. Went to every piddling little first-grade nonevent and ninth grade basketball game. Basically drove his family crazy, showing up all over the place, suddenly Mr. Dad."

"Guilt," I pronounced.

"Or transference," Maggie wondered. "Like being with the kids might get the wife back."

"He couldn't have been a very nice man if he didn't care about his own children," Abby said, as if the thought had just that second occurred to her.

JoAnne smiled falsely. "I figured that out. Eventually. Point is, girls, dating a parent is a bad deal."

"You know, joining a convent is looking better and better," I mumbled. "How bad could it be? Except for the shoes. The shoes are horrendous."

"Maybe becoming a lesbian," JoAnne said. "Which, from what I hear, might turn out to be pretty much the same thing as joining a convent."

"Or just swearing off relationships altogether," I said now, inspired. Depressed. "Just having sex every once in a while. Every time you get in the mood. You know, keep the juices flowing."

JoAnne rolled her eyes.

"Well, sex is good for you," I said. "It's healthy."

"That's not why I like it," JoAnne said.

"Or just holding out for your soul mate," Abby said. "Even if he takes forever to show up," she added gloomily.

"Well, ladies," Maggie said, over the idiots' fresh bout of

whooping, "another fun Saturday night has just come to a crashing end."

Okay. Sometimes staying home alone on a Saturday night is the best thing to do after all.

Chapter Six

It was late January when it happened. I met Doug Spears again, again in the presence of colleagues.

Hank McQueen, an account manager at EastWind, and I had signed up for an all-day presentation/seminar called "Going for the Jugular: Guerilla Marketing for the New Millenium," given by The Saturn Group. Lunch—a meal sure to include rubber chicken—in one of the hotel's dining rooms would break up the day. Generally speaking, I'm not a big fan of such seminars, but in this case, the topic interested me greatly. Hank, I think, just wanted some time out of the office.

Before the seminar got under way, the participants gathered in a smallish, carpeted room for coffee and muffins. I skipped the rather anemic-looking muffins and went for the rather weak-looking coffee. Hank was shoving a blueberry muffin into his mouth when . . .

I coughed, recovered, patted my mouth with a napkin. Doug Spears was standing not three feet from Hank, his back to me. But not for long.

Doug Spears turned, saw me, and smiled a slow smile.

Suddenly, I felt extremely self-conscious, glad I'd worn a

skirt that day, stupidly angry that I'd not taken more time with my hair that morning.

A guy with Doug spotted Hank, then he and Doug moved closer through the crowd.

"Hank, how's it going?"

Hank introduced me to the guy. A second later, I'd forgotten his name. Doug and Hank nodded, murmuring the greeting of men who'd met briefly before.

The guy then turned to Doug.

"Doug, do you know Erin Weston of EastWind Communications?"

"Yes, we've met," he said and that particular smile was back, the one that said, "I know what you're thinking and I'm thinking it, too." He extended his hand—the one without the wedding ring—and I took it for the requisite handshake. It was brief and unusual except for the last second when we released our grip and Doug let a finger trail across my palm in a way that was most definitely unbusinesslike.

Unless I'd imagined it. Doug didn't meet my eye, immediately turned away, and in a perfectly neutral voice spoke to his colleague.

I felt unaccountably embarrassed and extremely turned on.

I don't remember what topic was discussed and at the time was only half aware of what was being said. I know I nodded wisely once or twice and am pretty sure I said, "Exactly" at least once. All that was happening for me then was Doug. He was the content and the context of that ten-minute chance meeting of colleagues. His face was the visual; the tone of his voice the audio.

Doug Spears, I thought later, is a huge and hugely powerful magnet and I am a pile of tiny, silvery iron filings, completely helpless against his command. A tired simile, maybe, but an accurate one.

At lunch, Doug sat with his colleagues from Trident and some other guys—all men—from another big firm. Hank and I sat with a few people we knew from our work with nonprofits, as well as with several junior-level creative staff from a company so small it made EastWind look awesome. Doug was at the cool kids' table. We were the dorks. Because cool kids don't mess with dorks, there was no chance for another interaction. Though I glanced his way a few times, I never saw Doug glance in mine.

Which doesn't mean he hasn't been glancing at you, Romance tittered.

Oh, get a life, Erin, Reason snapped.

At the end of the seminar, long after Doug and his group had left the hotel, I worked up the nerve to mention him to Hank. Curiosity was eating me up inside. Maybe Hank knew something heartening about his personal life. Like, maybe Doug Spears was getting a divorce.

"So, who is that Doug Spears guy, anyway?" I said, gathering my things busily. "He's new, isn't he? At Trident, I mean."

Hank shook his head. "I don't know much about him. I mean I read an article about him and his former company, but that was a few years ago. Word is he's a hot shot, but beyond that . . . Couldn't tell you. He's way out of my league."

"Huh," I said. Wrong person to ask, obviously. I'd have to ask another woman. Women are far better at gathering personal information than men. But now the problem was this: The last thing I needed was for my hoped-for informant to question my motives for questioning her. The word that I had a major attraction to Doug Spears must not get out.

This would require finesse. Or a great deal of luck.

Which is what I got when I asked Hank to wait for me while I visted the ladies' room on the way out of the hotel.

The stalls were all empty. Two women stood at the sinks, reapplying their makeup. They stopped talking, glanced at me, then back at the mirrors. I entered the far stall. The women resumed their conversation.

"Kathy says he's a tough boss, but fair. I wish my boss were fair. Jeez."

A laugh. "I wouldn't care if he were tough and totally unfair. Doug Spears is hot."

Hello.

"And married. And has two kids. Taylor and Courtney. Can you imagine how cute they must be?"

"Yes. Their father is totally hot."

"You have a one-track mind."

"So?"

"So, what would you do, come on to your boss? Anyway, who says he cheats? Kathy says he's very devoted to his family."

"That doesn't mean he's very devoted to his wife, does it?"

"Ugh. Come on, let's get out of here."

A moment later I heard the door to the ladies' room shut. I sat there longer than necessary, afraid to let anyone catch a glimpse of my burning face.

Chapter Seven

February, Boston

February in Boston is without a doubt the ugliest and therefore most depressing month of the year. It makes even usually optimistic, even-tempered types despair of ever again feeling the warmth of the sun against their skin.

February breeds discontent.

> *Erin—Roberto went back to his wife. For the best as Julio was becoming v. jealous. Did you take my Hermes scarf? Can't find it, plse send. M.*

We four met for dinner at Franklin Café. No one was wearing a party dress. I was, however, wearing my mother's Hermes scarf. The one she had given to me before she left the country. The one she was not getting back.

Two women about our age sat two tables away. Franklin Café is small and wasn't crowded that night, so we could easily hear their conversation, such as it was. One had just gotten engaged and was waxing poetic about the enormous rock on her finger. The other was alternately squealing and sighing.

Thankfully, they'd gone by the time our appetizers arrived.

"I don't know why so many women in their thirties are so hung up on getting married," JoAnne said irritably. "I, for one, am having a fine time dating a variety of men. My social life is full and totally under my command."

"Well, bully for you," I said gloomily. "No, really."

"Leave me out of this discussion," Maggie said. "I'm fine on my own. At least for now."

"What about you, Abigail?" JoAnne asked. "A special man in your life?"

Abby groaned. "I so wish not! Has anyone ever had a much younger guy have a crush on them?"

"What's much younger?" Maggie asked.

"Um, sixteen."

"What are you doing with your free time that you're meeting sixteen-year-old boys?" I said. "Or maybe I don't want to know."

"Please, Erin! He's an intern at the BSO. His mom's on the board so I assume she got him the job. He comes by after school two days a week and sort of files and staples and things."

"And he's fallen in love with you?"

"It's just so embarrassing! He looks at me with those . . . those . . ."

"Big puppy dog eyes?" JoAnne suggested.

"No. With that pimply face and I just want to scream, 'Ew! Don't look at me!' "

"You could leave a tube of Clearasil on his desk." JoAnne, again.

"Don't be mean," Abby said. "I really don't know what to do. He's so sweet and so young and I really don't want to hurt his feelings but . . ."

"But he's making you feel uncomfortable in your workplace?" Maggie asked. "Are you afraid of him?"

"Oh, no, nothing like that. I mean, Mrs. Rogers is on the

board of directors and she's one tough cookie. I can't imagine Pierce having the nerve to step out of line with a woman." Abby seemed to hesitate. "Okay, I'm going to show you something but promise me you won't laugh, okay?"

"I can't do that," JoAnne said, already grinning. "Show at your own risk."

Abby sighed and took a folded piece of pink paper from her slim leather purse. "He gave this to me today, just before I left to meet you guys."

"What did he say!" I cried.

"Nothing. Well, I think he mumbled something, or maybe it was more like a mutter. Anyway, I couldn't make out any words. He just shoved this at me, kept his head down, made some noises, and ran off to the men's room. It was heartbreaking."

"I wonder if he threw up." JoAnne.

"Let me see, Abby." I put out my hand and Abby gave me the pink paper. "Should I read it out loud?"

Abby sighed again. "Oh, okay, you might as well."

"Okay." I sat up straighter, cleared my throat. "Here we go."

> *Abigail*
> *You are like an angel*
> *with bright, shiny wings.*
> *You are like so many,*
> *many things.*
> *Like my favorite cereal, Fruit Loops*
> *And a bright sunny day.*
> *I will tell all who want the scoop*
> *To them I will say,*
> *Abigail is like the moon*
> *All bright and shiny.*
> *To her my heart I give*
> *Utherwise, I canot live.*

"Can puberty be terminal?" I said to JoAnne, wiping my eyes. "I mean, could this poor kid die of it?"

"In my considered opinion, yes."

Maggie reached for the paper. "Hmm. Needs some help with spelling, too."

Abby looked miserable.

"You could talk to his mother about his crush," I said to Abby. "Maybe she could, I don't know, talk to him about his behavior being inappropriate in the office."

"How humiliating for poor Pierce! He'd know I said something to her. He'd quit immediately."

"Maybe his mother won't let him quit," Maggie said. "Maybe she'll think it would be a good lesson for him to have to face Abby every day . . ."

"A good punishment, you mean. That would be so cruel." Abby considered. "But knowing Mrs. Rogers, not unlikely."

"I say the way to get little Pierce to lose interest is have a date pick you up early one day. Confront him with a real man." JoAnne nodded sagely.

"No." I had a better idea. "What Abby needs to do is introduce Pierce to a nice sixteen-year-old girl. She needs to show him she's too old for him."

"Hey!"

"Well, you are, you know."

"Maybe Pierce should just grow out of his crush all by himself without anyone interfering," Maggie suggested. "These things don't last long. Usually."

"Well," Abby said suddenly, "something had better change because I'm tired of people in the office laughing at me. Everyone thinks it's a big fat joke. I need to be taken seriously!"

"At least you have a date for Valentine's Day," JoAnne said slyly.

Abby put her head in her hands and sighed.

I'd long thought that Valentine's Day should be banned from the face of the Earth. At the very least, it should be ignored by the unmarried. Unless, of course, you have a boyfriend with whom you are madly in love and who is truly, madly and deeply in love with you. And prepared to offer you a big-ass diamond ring.

Or, unless you were JoAnne Chiofalo and claimed not to give a crap about Valentine's Day in the first place.

Not that I was bitter or anything. It's just that I was facing yet another Valentine's Day without that special someone. Without even a jerk-off temporary boyfriend. And, of course, without Doug Spears.

The morning passed quietly. Just before noon, the receptionist buzzed my line.

The receptionist's voice was singsongy. "Eriiiiiiiin . . ."

I rolled my eyes. What now?

"Yes, Heather?"

"There's something out here for youuuuuuu."

Probably a summons, I thought, sighing and getting up from my chair. What could I have done to deserve having to appear in court? Or maybe—oh, no, please don't let it be my mother!

Now the question was to go running toward the reception area, arms wide, or dash back into my office and lock the door behind me.

No good. The door didn't lock from the inside.

Shit.

I walked on past private offices, then the kitchen and listened closely but heard no voice from the reception area but Heather's. Well, she had said "something" not "someone," I reminded myself. A person's not a thing. . . .

Three or four more steps and I'd be around the bend and face-to-face with . . .

A reception area empty but for the top of Heather's head peeking out from behind a massive bouquet of red roses arranged with ferns and baby's breath in a cut crystal vase.

"These are for youuuuuu!" Heather came dashing out from behind her desk and grabbed my arm. "Aren't they gorgeous!"

Yes, they certainly were. But who . . . ?

"Who brought them?" I asked.

Heather shrugged. "Some guy from a florist. He said they were for Erin Weston. Go ahead and read the card! Aren't you curious?"

I looked at Heather. Did everyone at EastWind Communications know I wasn't involved in a serious relationship? That my receiving flowers on Valentine's Day was an unexpected event?

I glanced at the hall down which I'd come. Heather had been beating the drums. Heads were peering out of offices, faces were expectant.

Jeez. Casually, I pulled the small white envelope from a plastic stalk tucked into the arrangement.

"This is so exciting!"

Yes, it was. And private. I turned away from Heather and slipped the card partway from the envelope. And felt as if I were going to be sick. And faint. Maybe both.

"Well?" Heather prompted.

I tried so hard to keep the grin from my face I felt it morph into a grimace. "Oh, they're from my dad," I said brightly. Amazing how easily the lie came to my lips. "Sorry to disappoint you."

All along the hall, heads withdrew into offices. Heather looked deeply confused.

"Oh. Well, that's sooooooo nice," she said, in a voice that smacked undeniably of pity. "He must be a real sweetheart."

Carefully, I lifted the vase of Doug's dozen red roses. "Oh, he is," I promised. "A real sweetheart."

Let the game begin.

For a day or two I did nothing, made no response to Doug's extraordinary gesture. I felt confused and elated and thrilled and frightened. I was not in a state of mind conducive to clear thinking.

I told no one the truth about the flowers, especially not JoAnne. Actually, I didn't tell my friends about the flowers at all. What they didn't know wouldn't come back to bite me on the butt.

Finally, I began to wrestle with the notion of making a response. It was only polite to thank someone for a gift, right? Especially when the gift was unexpected. I mean, my mother might be wacky but she'd brought me up to know the social graces.

Reason snorted derisively. Any excuse to make contact, eh, Erin? The guy is married. What he did was a huge breach of etiquette—not to mention a betrayal of his marriage vows. The smart thing to do would be to do nothing. Make no response. Let it go.

Romance cried: Don't listen to Reason! Do what your heart tells you is right!

My heart and good manners.

I could, of course, send Doug a thank you note. But somehow that seemed wrong, responding to such a personal gift with such a formal gesture.

E-mailing was out. I was sure nobody at Trident knew their senior VP of branding had sent flowers on Valentine's Day to a woman not his wife. And I certainly wasn't going to be the one to tell.

So, that left a phone call, to the office. A discreet phone call, made behind closed doors. The thought scared the wits out of me but no matter what Reason advised, I knew I was going to attempt contact with Doug Spears in some way or another so . . . It might as well be the most direct way, short of appearing at his office in a silk teddy.

Okay. I'd do it. I flipped through my Rolodex, got Trident's general number, and dialed.

"Uh, hi, yes. This is Erin Weston, from EastWind Communications. Is . . . is Mr. Spears in?"

"Doug?"

Okay. So Trident wasn't as corporate as I thought it might be.

"Yes, Doug Spears. Douglas. Spears."

"No, he's not in at the moment. Would you like his . . ."

"Yes. Please."

". . . voice mail?"

"Yes."

Well, that had gone smoothly.

After three rings I was connected. Doug's message was brief, to the point, professional. Nothing extraordinary at all. Frankly, I didn't even recognize his voice, having spoken to him only twice, and in person.

The voice stopped. My turn. Panic stirred but I shoved it down.

"Hi. It's Erin. Weston. Of EastWind?"

I blanked. What now?

"Um, I . . . uh, someone sent me some flowers the other day and, well, the card was signed with your name. Printed, actually, with your name. So . . . well, I was wondering . . . If the flowers were from you, um, thanks. Okay, I . . ."

I was cut off. Nice blab job, Erin, I scolded. But I doubted it would have gone any more smoothly if Doug had been in the office and I'd had to speak with him directly.

I counted my blessings and told myself to put Doug's gift out of my mind until I heard from him again. Which was somewhat difficult, what with twelve pungent red roses a mere twelve inches from my nose.

Someone knocked on the door. I jumped.

"Come in!"

The door opened and Maureen, Terry's executive assistant, peered in. "Erin? Meeting with Terry about the Johnson account in five. You okay? You don't usually close your door."

I stood, grabbed some loose papers on my desk, felt and knew I looked utterly the guilty fool. "Fine, fine. Just, you know, busy. Let me just grab the file . . ."

Maureen shrugged and left, closing the door again behind her.

I collapsed into my chair. My cheeks were hot. I panicked and wondered what was running through Maureen's mind right now. Did she think I was planning to leave EastWind, that I'd been talking to a prospective employer? Doing something to oneself that should only be done in the privacy of one's own home? Did she think I had been leaving a message for the married man who seemed to be courting me?

The time of deception had begun.

Chapter Eight

Two weeks had passed since Valentine's Day, since Doug had sent me the roses and I'd left a thank you message on his voice mail. Two weeks of thundering silence. I began to feel angry. I began to feel hurt. I began to wonder if I'd imagined the entire thing.

Reason had a thing or two to say. Forget him Erin. If it really was Doug Spears who sent the flowers and not some prankster, he's obviously had time to regret such a stupid move. So you should, too. Move on. Go on a date. Forget the bum.

Romance, of course, did not agree. Oh, Erin, it said, be patient! Let true love take its course. Just trust to the future with your soul mate.

But for the moment Reason won out—or I let it think it had. I'd met a guy named Alan Grey at a small business get-together back in January and he'd called me at the office afterward, suggesting we have dinner. I'd yet to call him back. Now, I would—and I'd apologize for not getting back to him sooner, say I'd been really busy, which wasn't a lie.

I looked at the remains of the roses in the vase on my desk. A bit sorry-looking, aren't they, Reason said. Time for the garbage. True. But before I brought them to the kitchen sink to dump the fuzzy water, I pulled one wilted blossom from the dozen, broke off most of the stem and put the wilted bloom in the top drawer of my desk.

Hope isn't dead yet, Romance whispered. I just knew it.

> *E.—Have run into a bit of difficulty. Please wire some money to the address below? Promise to pay it back. Don't tell your father. Five hundred dollars would be good. M.*

Date number one of the year. I met Alan Grey for dinner at Capitol Grille on a Thursday night. It was my choice; he'd suggested I pick the restaurant.

I wore a camel-colored wool suit with a brown silk blouse and slender camel-colored pumps with brown piping. I was a class act. Alan wore a navy, two-button suit, conservative but nicely made, and a pale blue shirt. I noticed as we sat that he was thinner than I'd recalled. His wrist was not much wider than mine. Huh. It certainly wasn't as wide and strong as Doug's wrist.

Stop it, Erin, Reason warned.

She can't help but make a comparison, Romance argued.

Okay, okay, I thought. I'll behave. I'd made a vow to myself to focus on the date and not to let my mind wander to fantasies of Doug Spears. And I was going to keep that vow. At least, I was going to try to keep that vow.

The waiter took our drink order and handed us two menus. I began to peruse.

What I really wanted to order was the prime rib. But I hesitated. The last time I ordered the prime rib it was bigger than my head. And my head is not a small one. I ate the prime rib, all of it. It was delicious. But I was with my girlfriends and though Abby kind of stared in wonder, no one really cared that I could easily consume a piece of beef the size of—well, my head.

Tonight, however, tonight I was with Alan Grey. And on a first date. There were serious implications to every gesture and every word. I would be judged and rated and evaluated on every syllable to come from my mouth, every smile to dawn on my face, every turn of my well-manicured hand. Was I a slut or a potential wife? Mrs. Right or Ms. Right Now?

And there was also this question: What impression did I want to give to Alan Grey? Who was I, at least for tonight? Did I even like this man enough to really care? Well, I didn't know. It was a first date, after all. How could I know anything more about Alan than that he seemed to like navy suits and parting his hair on the right? Could I extrapolate his entire personality and moral character from these and similar stylistic traits? Of course not.

I wanted that prime rib. And the garlic mashies that came with it.

"Erin? Are you okay?"

"Hmm?" I looked up from the menu. "What? Oh, yes, I'm fine."

Alan Grey smiled. "It's just that you were . . . Well. It looked like maybe you were in pain. I mean, your forehead was all . . . Uh, do you have a headache?"

Was Alan Grey hoping I had a headache so he could end the evening early?

Don't be ridiculous, Erin, Reason scolded.

I smiled brightly at him. "Oh, no, I'm fine. I just couldn't decide what to order. But I've made up my mind."

He smiled brightly at me. "Good. I'm starved."

He signaled the waiter. The waiter came to the table and turned to me. The lady was privileged to order first.

"I'll have the Oysters Rockefeller to start," I said. "And then the prime rib."

"How would you like that done?"

"Rare."

"Mashed potatoes or french fries?"

"Mashed potatoes."

"Blue cheese, vinaigrette, or ranch on your salad?"

"Blue cheese, please. And when you have a chance, another glass of wine."

"Of course. And you, sir?"

The waiter and I turned our attentions to Alan Grey. His expression was—odd.

"I'll skip the appetizer," he said. "And have the steamed halibut for an entrée."

"Mashed potatoes or french fries?"

"Can I get steamed rice with that instead?"

The waiter hesitated. "I'll check. And on your salad? Blue cheese, vinaigrette, or ranch."

"Vinaigrette, on the side."

"And how are you doing with that drink, sir?"

The waiter and I looked at the man's almost full glass of heart-healthy red wine.

"I'm fine, thank you."

"Very good," said the waiter. He walked off to place our orders.

I wondered. Would it be rude to say to this man, "I thought you said you were starved!" Yes, I decided, it would be, so I didn't.

"You know," Alan said, "the prime rib here is very large."

Was this man afraid I'd waste his money? Did he think I was one of those women who just play with the food on their plate?

"Oh, I know," I said, with only a trace of annoyance in my otherwise perfectly modulated voice. "I've had it before."

"I see. Do you eat this way, I mean, do you eat red meat often?" he said.

Hold the phone. Back up the train. This man was a virtual stranger. Was it any of his business what I ate and how often? No, it was not. Wait, maybe I was taking offense where none had been intended. That had been known to happen on occasion.

"I guess," I said, noncommittally.

Alan Grey's face grew stern. "I take my health very seriously," he said. "And to be honest, I can't see myself being with a woman who abuses her body . . ."

"Whoa." I held up my hand. Offense had indeed been intended and now had indeed been taken. "Are you accusing me of abusing my body because on this particular night, the only night, I should point out, you have ever seen me eat, I ordered red meat?"

"Oysters Rockefeller has a lot of cheese. Your meal is loaded with fat. And the blue cheese dressing? You know, once you hit your midthirties, that all settles right around the middle."

This was not happening. It was my worst nightmare. A man—a virtual stranger!—was trying to control my food intake! It was my mother all over again but with a new and horrid twist. How did this man know I hadn't eaten a salad for dinner the night before! The fact that in reality I'd eaten three slices of pepperoni pizza was irrelevant. Alan Grey was not speaking out of love and commitment and genuine concern. This man was speaking way, way out of turn.

Ladylike, I folded my hands on the table. I smiled nicely. And I said, "Here's the deal. You're going to leave now. I'm going to sit here and eat my dinner. And I'm going to enjoy it immensely. You're going to cancel your order or pay for your dinner. I'll pay for mine. I can, you know. And you're not ever going to call me again. How's that for a plan?"

Alan Grey shook his head and got up from the table. "It's your funeral, Erin. I tried to help."

"No you didn't," I said. "No, you're not about help. You're about hurt." I smiled very brightly. "And that's just not fun."

"Oysters Rockefeller." The waiter placed the plate on the table. He did a very good job of pretending not to notice Alan standing with his coat over his arm.

"Thank you. The gentleman will be leaving," I said. "But the lady is staying."

Over the waiter's bent shoulder I saw Alan Grey walk toward the maître d'.

"It was the steamed fish, wasn't it?" the waiter whispered.

Yes, it was the steamed fish. And it was the five hundred hard-earned dollars I'd wired off to my mother that morning.

And it was Doug.

* * *

Date number two, a few days later.

My first impression upon meeting Alex Barry was—okay, this is nice. My final impression differed vastly.

I suppose my first clue should have been the state of his clothes. Neat is far too tame a word for Alex Barry's appearance. Alex Barry was impeccable. Every hair was in place; there was not one stray hair on the back of his neck. I wondered if he trimmed his hair every day.

His shirt was starched—obviously so. His trousers boasted a perfect, blade-sharp crease. His shoes shone. He smelled—fresh. His nails were professionally manicured, no doubt about it. Alex Barry was squeaky. It was a pleasure after some of the slobs I'd known, guys who couldn't keep their fingernails clean for five minutes, guys whose shirttails were stained with pee.

We met on neutral turf, in the Oak Room of the Fairmont Copley Plaza Hotel. A nice choice on Alex's part, a civilized, quiet room. It was too early for the jazz trio's first set so we chatted about nothing in particular over a drink. We'd made no plans for dinner but thus far the conversation had been so pleasant—if not exactly stimulating—that Alex suggested we get something to eat.

We could have stayed at the Oak Room. We should have stayed at the Oak Room.

Ordinarily, I don't bring a man to my apartment until the third or fourth date. But Alex Barry was someone my colleague Hank at EastWind had vouched for and the weather was so lousy, and Thursday nights are notoriously busy nights for South End and Back Bay restaurants, so I figured there wasn't great harm in suggesting we go back to my place and order in.

Alex seemed slightly taken aback but okay with the plan.

The trouble began when I put the silverware on the table. Alex eyed it warily.

"What's wrong?" I said.

Alex gathered the silverware carefully. There was an odd look on his face.

"I'm just going to give these a quick wash."

"Why? They're clean."

Alex said, "Oh, that's okay, I don't mind," and took the silverware to the sink where he proceeded to vigorously scrub away the nonexistent dirt.

I don't claim to be the world's greatest housekeeper but neither do I admit to being a slob. The silverware was plenty clean when I'd placed it on the table. I didn't know whether to be insulted or excited by the dim possibility of a husband who enjoyed housework.

When Alex had finished his task, we went into the living room with our glasses of wine—glasses also freshly re-washed—to wait for the delivery guy from Appetito.

"Sit anywhere," I said, settling into my favorite chair, the one in which I liked to spend rare precious hours reading.

Alex hesitated. He peered suspiciously at the cushions of the couch.

"What?" I said.

Alex murmured, "Nothing," removed a very white hand-kerchief from his back pocket, and proceeded to dust—yes, dust, with a flicking of the wrist—the couch.

Now I was insulted. Mr. Clean was very close to riding my last nerve.

Dinner arrived. We'd ordered two pizzas and a salad. Alex cut his slices of pizza with a fork and knife. Okay, nothing wrong with that, Italians in Italy do this. But do they blow on each and every bite, long after any possibility of the food being too hot to eat? And do they wipe their mouths after each and every bite, from left to right, from right to left, end-ing with a pat in the middle?

I thought of offering Alex a steel wool pad but resisted the temptation.

My appetite was not its usual healthy size that night. Eating in front of Alex seemed somehow offensive. I stopped after one slice and promised myself I'd chow down when he left. Which I wanted him to do in a very short time.

While I wrapped the leftovers, Alex excused himself to

use the bathroom. He was in there for some time. I refused to consider what he might be doing.

I waited for him in the living room. Finally, he came out of the bathroom and gave me a look.

Here we go again, I thought.

"What?"

He looked a little pained. Maybe slightly sick.

"Uh, your bathroom floor is . . . crunchy."

"What? Oh." I shrugged. "It's only cat litter. I have a cat, you know. He's sleeping."

"You could, you know, uh, sweep up the litter."

I pretended to consider this. "Yes. Yes, I suppose I could."

"Well, I did it for you. This time."

I smiled brightly. "Gee, thanks! You know, Fuzzer just tracks litter all over the place." I watched Alex's face closely. "Even in the bed. Because you know, Fuzzer sleeps with me. On my pillow. Every night. He has a slight snoring problem, but you get used to it."

Yes, Alex definitely looked sick now.

"So, you should leave now," I said.

Alex nodded, grabbed his coat, and bolted.

"Fuzzer!"

The beast came stalking out from the bedroom, yawning widely. I scooped him up.

"You missed all the fun, guy."

I hugged Fuzzer and wondered how Doug Spears felt about cats.

I decided he liked them.

Chapter Nine

After Mr. Fastidious and Mr. Anorexia, there was Mr. Toot. Yes, once more I forged into the breach, gave it the old college try. I don't know why I did. Looking back, I suppose that even Mr. Wonderful would have come up short in my estimation. My heart just wasn't into finding anyone but Doug Spears worthy of my attention.

Nevertheless, when Jim Keeley asked me to see a movie with him, I accepted the invitation. Jim was a guy I'd known for a few years. He was a dedicated member of the Harvard Writers Circle—a group not associated with the university, I might add—and though I was a far less dedicated member, making an appearance about once every three or four months, he didn't seem to hold it against me. A few times a group had gone out after a meeting for drinks at Casablanca and Jim had proved to be quite the funny man.

In yet another effort to take my mind off Doug Spears, one Monday night I took the Orange Line to the Red Line out to Harvard Square in Cambridge, paid my five dollars, and settled in for a rousing though largely imbecilic discussion about a member's largely imbecilic script. Not having read the script beforehand didn't seem to matter as the discussion was impossible to follow. The room was warm and after a half hour I found my eyes beginning to close. Then: "Ow!"

Jim grinned. "Sorry," he whispered as the others glared at me. "Didn't mean to hurt you."

"You didn't," I whispered back. "It's just something I say when someone pokes me in the ear."

"You were falling asleep."

"I know. It's more bearable that way."

"Next time I'll leave you alone."

The discussion droned on around me for another half hour. At the end, I declined Jim's blanket invitation for the group to head for Casablanca. Something told me I wasn't wanted. Maybe the continued glares of the self-important others. My attempt at distraction had been a disaster.

"I'm glad you came tonight, Erin," Jim said as we clunked down the stairs to the lobby.

"I'm not so sure I am," I said, then added quickly, "I mean, it was good to see you, though."

Jim laughed. "Nice save. Hey, would you like to see a movie with me sometime?"

The question caught me off-guard. I'd never thought of Jim in any romantic sense. He was smart and funny and kind of good-looking in that bland, boy-next-door way, but he'd never made my blood race. Still, I was on a quest for a Doug-free life so I accepted. Jim said he'd call me the next day to make plans and true to his word, he did.

I had no great hopes for our date but knowing what I did of Jim—admittedly, not much—I felt fairly confident it wouldn't be a horrible experience.

Note to Self: "Don't ever, ever assume anything. Ever."

I met Jim at the nineteen-theater Loews cineplex on Tremont. He gave me a peck on the cheek. I didn't protest. He paid for my ticket. I didn't protest. He asked if I wanted popcorn and I said yes. He bought that, too, and got himself a soda and a box of candy.

Jim looked nice. He wore a pair of nicely faded jeans, a

simple navy pull-over sweater, and an L.L. Bean jacket. Not a fashion plate, but acceptable.

We headed for theater twelve and settled in. The previews provoked some amusing comments from Jim. The popcorn was yummy. Things were going just fine. The lights went down. It was time for the main attraction.

And then it began. No, Jim Keeley didn't grope me. He didn't take out his dick and ask me to touch it. No. Jim Keeley did something far, far more offensive.

He farted. Not once, not twice. Many, many times. He did not apologize. He did not acknowledge the farts. And they were smelly farts, too.

What does one do in such a situation? In my wildest nightmares I'd never imagined a scene like this. After the initial shock and disbelief, I thought, Oh God, the poor guy has a serious irritable bowel problem. Then I thought, So, why the hell doesn't he take something for it! Then I thought, Does he think this is funny?

I glanced at Jim. He was looking straight ahead, absorbed in the action on the screen. Around us whispers were rising. Some expressed disgust. Others, amusement. Those latter voices belonged, of course, to the teenage boys in the audience.

After the tenth or eleventh explosion of noise and smell, I was beyond angry. I was scared. Jim Keeley was a lunatic.

Carefully, I took my bag from the seat on my left and mumbled something about getting a soda. Jim grunted, still absorbed in the movie. Loath to give the people behind us yet another reason to rebel, I hunched over and practically crawled to the end of the aisle. God, I thought, I hope no one thinks I'm the farter!

I dashed out of the darkened theater and into the corridor. Fresh air was in order.

"Young lady!"

Somehow, I knew the words were for my benefit.

I turned back. A very dignified older woman had followed me from the theater. She did not look happy.

"It wasn't me!" I cried.

"Your husband's behavior is despicable," she said. "I am lodging a complaint with the management."

"He's not my husband! I hardly know him!"

Great. Someone finally assumes I'm married and it's to a public farter.

The older woman glared. "Then I advise you to choose your gentlemen friends more wisely in the future."

"Okay," I squeaked. And then I ran.

I decided it was far, far safer to hang out with my girlfriends than to risk another date right then. Clearly, my stars were not aligned with the moon, or Mercury was in retrograde or God was pissed at me for entertaining lascivious thoughts about a married man.

It was a stroke of seriously good luck that Maureen's husband had four tickets to the Celtics vs. Bulls game at the Fleet Center for Tuesday night. Not just tickets, either. Supremely fine tickets, on the floor, just behind the team bench. Tickets Mark couldn't use. Maureen didn't tell me why he couldn't use them, but I guessed it had something to do with the fact that she'd bought tickets for the theater the same night. Mark and his buddies hadn't stood a chance. The pregnant wife rules, as she should.

As often happened, the pregame talk turned to relationships, a topic I considered toxic after Anorexia, Fastidious, and Toot. Still, I couldn't help tuning in.

"What is it you're looking for, anyway?" JoAnne was asking Abby. "No, really. I want to know."

"A soul mate." Abby's answer was unhesitant and definitive.

JoAnne snorted. "Please. How old are you? Twelve?"

Who's twelve? I thought. JoAnne really should watch the snorting.

"I don't see why I can't hold out for my soul mate," Abby said.

"You don't? Okay, I'll show you why. Turn around. See those women up about ten rows, in the center." We all turned around to look.

There were four young women, twenty-somethings. They looked like maybe they were Hispanic. They looked like Jennifer Lopez. They had gorgeous long hair, gorgeously done. They had flawless skin and fabulous makeup. They had tight, curvy bodies poured into expensive, very hip clothing. They had enormous diamond rings and long, French manicured nails. And they all looked supremely bored.

They were the players' wives.

"There's the reason," JoAnne said as we all turned back to face the court. "You think those women held out for their soul mates? No. Those women knew a good thing when they saw it. A freakishly tall, very rich basketball player."

"Those women are like prostitutes," Maggie said quietly. "They prostituted themselves for a husband. I'll give you sex, you give me money. Here's my heart in exchange for a fistful of cash."

"Yeah, and that's such a bad thing," JoAnne said, laughing. "Gosh, I wonder how they live with themselves."

"Don't judge them, Maggie," I said. "You don't know anything about them, really." I sneaked another peek. Damn. I would kill to look that good. Even one day in my life.

And if I did, would Doug Spears suddenly love me?

"They can't be happy. Can they?" Abby mused.

"Oh, yes they can. And they probably are. I would be."

"That's the difference between us, JoAnne," Abby said heatedly. "You don't have a romantic bone in your body. You're so pragmatic about everything."

"Look," JoAnne went on, "I'm not saying I want to marry for money alone. I'm saying that if I did, I'd make the deal and be happy with it. It's all about what you want. You decide that first, then go for it. Women have been making deals since the start of time. You think marriage was always so loaded with the frou-frou of romance? Please. That's a relatively modern concept. Marriage was—and is—a deal. A business arrangement. If you want it to be romantic, too, fine. But that's your choice. Not everybody has that choice, you know. Not every woman can be Elizabeth Bennet and land Mr. Darcy. Some women are Charlotte Lucas and take a Mr. Collins when he comes along because they know they're not going to do better. Unfair? Sure. Life's tough, get a helmet."

"JoAnne," I mumbled, "I think we get the point here." Maybe I can drown out the sound of her voice by slurping the last of this soda, I thought. Maybe the game will start soon. Maybe someone will blow a really loud whistle.

JoAnne thought we needed more convincing. "You and me and Maggie and Erin, we're lucky. We're white women in the richest, most powerful, and probably most liberated country on the face of the earth. We get to choose what we do with our lives and who we marry. Do you realize how great that is? Do you realize how much more we have than the average Afghani woman?"

"Yes," Abby said firmly. "It is wonderful to have a choice. And I choose to wait for my soul mate."

Now it was me who sighed.

"Look, Abby," I said, "here's a wild and crazy concept for you. Did you ever think that maybe a soul mate isn't found, he's created? Or grown or built, whatever. Meaning it's the relationship you make with someone that creates the best friend, perfect lover, soul mate thing? I mean, do you really think there's someone out there exactly perfect for you, just as he is, without knowing anything at all about you? And that you're absolutely perfect for him without even knowing if he likes opera or country or whatever? I don't. I think that's naive thinking."

"I think it's romantic thinking. I'm a Romantic."

"You also haven't had sex in six months," JoAnne said through a mouthful of popcorn. "This is all I'm saying."

And then the lights went down for the overly dramatic laser show that would introduce the stars. And everybody finally, finally shut up.

Chapter Ten

March, Boston

March in New England is a big fat tease. Forsythia suggests that yes, there is life to come. Icy rain states flatly that there is no point in going on. It's contradictory and perverse and frustrating.

Some people prefer to cut a New England March short by escaping to a tropical island for a time. JoAnne is one of those people. Early in the month she took off to Cancun for a week—during which time she celebrated her birthday—with a guy she'd been seeing on and off for about six months. His name was Martin Something-or-Other and he was a hotshot corporate lawyer—or so JoAnne told us.

We almost never got to meet JoAnne's dates as she never invited us to. Once, about two years ago, I ran into JoAnne and a podiatrist she was seeing (for the free foot rubs, she said). JoAnne looked distinctly uncomfortable, almost guilty, though for what exactly I couldn't imagine. She overbrightly introduced me to Dr. Whatever-His-Name-Was and hurried him off for a supposed dinner reservation at Bob the Chef's—a reservation I highly doubted she had. JoAnne was not a big fan of soul food. Anyway, after that one chance encounter—which neither of us mentioned when we next met—I hadn't seen hide nor hair of JoAnne's men.

JoAnne's trip to Cancun made me think. Going away for an entire week with a guy—even one you'd been sleeping with on and off for half a year—seemed like a big step to me—and a risky one. So much could go miserably wrong spending seven days together, twenty-four/seven. You could find out you hated each other. Worse, you could find out you bored each other. You could also find out you were in love.

Maybe that's what JoAnne was hoping for—a resolution one way or the other to the relationship. Did she and Martin want to spend their lives together? Or did they make each other sick?

I scratched that notion almost immediately. JoAnne still claimed—in very strong language—that she wasn't at all interested in having a steady, building relationship with any man. And I believed her. JoAnne knew what she was doing, going away with Martin.

Right, Reason said. Just because you can't figure out what she's doing doesn't mean that she's not perfectly in control.

It was mid-March before I heard from Doug Spears again. Several weeks and several disastrous—and yes, amusingly so—dates after the dozen red roses and my awkward voice mail message.

He called me at the office one morning around ten. He was no-nonsense and to the point. He made no reference to the flowers or to my response. He asked if we could meet for lunch so he could pick my brain about one of Trident's accounts. I said, yes, though his request seemed slightly unusual as I was a newbie in the business compared to Doug Spears. We made a date to meet two days from then at twelve-thirty at Radius. When I hung up the phone I felt sick.

The good sick, not the bad sick. The pit-of-the-stomach

whirring kind of excitement that you first feel when you're about twelve and Billy Jenkins, the most popular boy in eighth grade, swaggers into class.

Two days. I had two days to dwell and to fantasize and to plan an outfit. Time to swing by Radius and get a look at the lunch menu so I'd appear decisive when it came time to order— a good quality for a professional woman to possess, decisiveness.

I told no one at EastWind Communications that I was meeting Trident's senior VP of branding for lunch. Partly because that would make the lunch open territory—colleagues would question me upon my return to the office, hoping for information EastWind could somehow capitalize on. Even if the lunch did turn out to be wholly about business, I wanted, for the moment, to keep it to myself. The other reason I said nothing about my lunch plans was this: I thought—I hoped— that my meeting with Doug Spears would be about something other than business. And if it was, if it really was about me and Doug and not about clients and their accounts, what then could I say to inquiring colleagues?

I admit that along with a sense of anticipation about my meeting with Doug there was a sense of guilt just as strong. Why was I hoping for a married man to cheat on his wife— with me? Was I so depraved and so devoid of moral standards? Hell and damnation were rapidly upon me. . . .

But, the truth, sorry or not, is that I couldn't quench the desire for something romantic to happen with Doug. I was curious and compelled and at the time no amount of leftover Catholic fear of eternal damnation could match the intensity of my desire. A desire I couldn't fully explain—a sort of desire that was new to my experience. A sort of desire I thought I could get used to.

> *E—gave yr address to nice young man and his gfriend—pregnant—going to USA to make better life. Expect them in 2-3 weeks! M.*

Thursday. I wore a crisp, white, fitted blouse with the collar upturned; the cuffs were French. At my neck I wore a triple strand of pearls, very Jackie Kennedy. My suit was black, with a pencil skirt to the knee, and a short, waist-skimming jacket. The outfit was sophisticated yet alluring.

Not an outfit for a woman dreading the possibility of two broke kids from somewhere in South America landing on her doorstep. Definitely an outfit for a woman hoping for something more than a meaningless business lunch.

Our reservation was for one o'clock. I left my office far too early and wandered around the not particularly scenic South Station area. At precisely twelve-fifty I went into the restaurant and asked for our table. If Doug was late he'd never know how early I'd been. If he was on time, I could honestly say I'd just gotten to the restaurant a few minutes earlier. The point was not to appear overeager and yet, in case this meeting was all about business, to appear professional.

Doug was five minutes late. Things were going swimmingly.

He came striding into the restaurant with that air some men have of owning the space through which they move. I saw him spot me; his face registered the slightest, controlled flicker of pleasure.

"Erin, good to see you," he said and sat down. No handshake.

His suit was olive; his shirt, peach; the tie a pattern that combined both colors along with taupe. An interesting choice. Very nice.

As for his face . . . Doug looked as though he'd been in the sun recently, though it was only March and March in New England isn't known for its sunny warmth. Maybe he and his wife had slipped away to a tropical island for a weekend. . . .

"I hope you don't mind if we get right to business," he said, at the same time gesturing for our waiter. "I've got a busy schedule."

Okay. For a split second I was annoyed. He'd asked me to lunch, after all, not the other way around.

"Of course," I said. "What exactly did you want to talk about?"

He told me. He wanted to talk about a client's account. Keeping within the bounds of confidentiality, of course.

And all through the meal—I had the Warm Maine Crab Tartlet and Doug ordered the Golden & Red Beet Cannelloni— we talked about his client. I offered a perspective. Doug countered with a different perspective. I acknowledged its wisdom. But I never could quite figure out why Doug had needed to talk to me about Trident's most reliable and oldest client. There was no current crisis and none imminent. Doug admitted so.

Strange. More strange at least to me: There was no mention of the Valentine's Day flowers. Or of my dorky thank you message. There was no hint of flirtation, no hint of anything in the least personal. It occurred to me then, as the waiter took away our plates, that maybe Doug had asked me to lunch to put an end to any idea I might have gotten that he was interested in me. By talking only business maybe he was saying, There's nothing between us, Erin. There never was and there never will be.

Romance began to snuffle.

Reason said, It's better this way, Erin, and you know it.

"Are you interested in art?" Doug asked abruptly.

"Yes, sure. I'm not an expert but I took some art history classes in college and I belong to the MFA . . ."

Doug was looking at me in a way that made me cease my babbling.

"What do you think of the paintings here?" he said.

I glanced around. "I don't know. I mean, I hadn't really looked at them."

"Something else more interesting to look at?" Doug said and grinned that knowing grin.

I blushed and blurted, "I think they're for sale. It's like a . . . like a show."

"So, let's look now. What about that large canvas, over there?"

Doug nodded toward the back of the room. And then he put his hand on my arm, just above my elbow and said, "Do you like it?"

The painting was okay. Doug's touch was electric.

"Yes," I said, a bit breathlessly.

"What do you like about it?"

Oh, Lord.

I kept my eyes straight ahead and on the painting.

"It's . . . it's powerful."

Do you see what's going on here, Romance whispered excitedly.

I wish I didn't, Reason answered darkly.

"Yes. Powerful." Doug's breath tickled my ear and I shivered.

He took his hand off my arm and moved away.

"We should get the check," he said. "It's on Trident."

I could hardly find my voice. Doug was looking at me amusedly but steadily.

"Thanks," I finally said. "For lunch."

Doug smiled. "We should do it again."

I smiled though the smile might have been goofy.

"Okay," I said. "I mean, yes, we should. Meet for lunch. Again. Sometime."

I hastened off to the ladies' room, taking coat and bag with me, while Doug took care of the bill. My face was flaming and I was pretty sure it wasn't the result of the one glass of wine I'd had with my meal.

God. I'd been so wrong, thinking Doug had brought me to Radius to end what had never really begun. The truth was that Doug Spears and I had just been on a date. I knew a date when I saw one. Even more so when I was on one.

Suddenly, powdering my nose, I was sure I couldn't go back out there and face Doug Spears. I was utterly convinced I'd made a jackass of myself, getting all gooey when all he'd intended was . . . What?

A date, Erin, Romance sang. A romantic rendezvous. The beginning of a beautiful friendship!

The beginning of trouble, Reason said darkly.

"I can't go out there," I said to the mirror. How was I going to handle this? What if Doug asked me if—if he could kiss me? Oh, God, did I want that to happen?

Yes. And no.

My panicked thoughts were interrupted by the ladies' room door swinging open and a woman in a navy suit entering. She gave me the requisite ladies' room half smile and I gave her the same. Suddenly, it occurred to me that if I stayed where I was any longer Doug would be compelled to ask a waitress to check on me.

I hurried from the ladies' room and walked briskly toward our table, vowing to handle whatever happened next with aplomb and grace. Except . . .

It was no longer our table. Two hefty Irish-American types were settling in and Doug was nowhere to be seen.

The table's waiter saw my puzzlement.

"The gentleman is waiting outside," he said. I did not miss the smirk.

My hopes were dashed. And I was enormously relieved. And disappointed. And . . .

No decent man left his date in the restaurant alone. He waited for her, either at the table or by the bar.

I found Doug, as promised, on the sidewalk.

He stuck out his hand and mine shot forward in automatic response.

"Thanks for joining me, Erin," he said in a perfectly neutral tone.

"Thanks for asking me," I said, now utterly confused. Would he again mention our getting together in the future?

No. He would not.

"I've got some errands to run, so I'm off."

"Okay," I said and tried desperately to hide my disappointment.

Doug smiled a perfectly neutral smile and walked off down High Street.

I stood staring after him, feeling like the proverbial village idiot.

Not far away, I heard Reason clear its throat.

Chapter Eleven

Erin—Hola! Man and gfriend not leaving coun-
try; her family demanding immediate marriage.
Sorry; you wld have liked them! Have never been
so tan—you wouldn't recognize your own mother.
Stay out of the sun. Mama.

Abby had found herself a man closer to her own age than poor sixteen-year-old Pierce. The guy was a teacher at a private high school for kids with emotional problems. Delinquents. Druggies. Kids who stole Daddy's car and wrecked it on an average of once a month.

Bob Cleary was either a saint or emotionally perturbed himself to choose such a career.

Anyway, that afternoon he and Abby had gone to a movie. Later, Bob told her he'd like to accompany her to her date with us at Flash's. He wanted to meet her dearest girlfriends. That was nice.

But we were not impressed.

JoAnne watched Bob Cleary leave the restaurant. When he was out of sight, she leaned in.

"Is he hung?" she asked Abby in a stage-whisper. "He's so skinny! It looks like there's nothing there. He looks like a Ken doll, no bulge." JoAnne considered. "Or like Gumby."

"Maybe he tucks," Maggie said.

"I thought only transvestites and cross-dressers tucked," I said. Mostly for effect.

"I don't know if he's, er . . . I don't know what's down there," Abby admitted. She leaned forward, eyes wide, voice low. "He's a virgin. He's very religious. He's saving himself for his wife."

Okay, emotionally perturbed.

JoAnne hooted. "Holy crap! That proves it! He's a pencil dick. Hung like a raisin. He has a subpenis. He's going to lure some poor unsuspecting girl, some Born-Again-Virgin, into marriage and she's going to be all, ooh, I found such a perfect gentleman and I don't have to deal with ex-girlfriends or STDs, blah, blah, blah. And then, on the wedding night, big anticipation, she's been burning up with lust, can't wait to get into his pants. He comes out of the bathroom, she's sitting on the bed trying to look shy, not too eager. He drops trou . . . It's all over. Right then and there, the marriage is over. Unmitigated disaster."

"What if the girl was a real virgin?" Abby mused. "What if she doesn't know any better?"

"She will," JoAnne said darkly.

"Oh, come on. It's not the size of the ship, it's the motion of the ocean." This from Maggie, who, as far as I knew, hadn't had a date in at least three years. At least.

JoAnne laughed. "Oh, my God. Are you high? Are you on drugs?"

"JoAnne's right," I said. "That's the biggest pity-lie ever. Of course size matters. Come on, have you ever been having sex with a guy and suddenly you realize, oh, crap, is it in? I mean, you can't even tell! But you don't want to hurt the guy's feelings, you're a nice person and all, so you decide you'd better make some noise just in case it is in.

Thinking, when the guy hears the noise he'll up the activity, so maybe you'll feel something after all. Instead of intense boredom."

"Wait. Back up just a minute." JoAnne turned to Abby. "You're not saying you're a virgin, are you?"

"No! But, well, I just thought that if, you know, things work out with Bob, I could wait. I mean, it's not like I can't live without sex."

"Got that right," Maggie confirmed with a nod. "I'd rather live without sex than be involved with a guy who is lousy in bed. Or a guy who cheats on you."

"Sure. Who wouldn't," JoAnne agreed. "But what happens if you wait until your wedding night and discover that, A, not only is he a pencil dick, but B, he hasn't got a clue in the sack. Huh? And how would he have a clue if he's a virgin. What's his experience level, jerking off to X-rated videos? Are adult virgins even allowed to do that?"

"I'll teach him."

"Better you than me." Maggie.

"What if he can't learn?" I wondered. "I mean, what if he has no natural ability. Or what if he thinks you're a whore because you like sex and know more about it than he does. What if he equates you with the girls in his X-rated videos? What about that?"

"It's a bad deal all around," JoAnne confirmed. "Divorced men, fathers, virgins. Cross them all off the list. At least for a serious relationship. Virgins, no use whatsoever."

"Add postal workers—no, wait, all federal employees. And professional athletes," Maggie suggested. "They all cheat on their wives."

Abby looked suddenly indignant. "That's not true! Look at Lance Armstrong. No way he would cheat on his wife. He's got three little children and oh, I love their names! Luke, Isabelle, and Grace. And he's so hot! He's always so intense and focused and he looks so . . . so, ferocious when he rides!"

JoAnne grinned amusedly. "And I bet he stinks to high heaven when the race is over."

I nodded. "Outdoor Man Smell. OMS. The worst."

"Well, I'm sure Lance takes a shower before he has sex with Kirsten," Abby said, somehow hurt. "Lance Armstrong is a gentleman. I can just tell."

"I'll say this much for him. He's cancer's hottest poster boy. If I were single . . ."

There was a moment of stunned silence. I wanted to slink under the table.

Then: "You are single, Erin," JoAnne said forcefully. "Get a grip. Your fantasizing about a married man doesn't translate into your being in a relationship."

Why had I told JoAnne about having lunch with Doug?

"It was only lunch," I said inanely.

Abby and Maggie each gave me a strange look. The looks said: Erin is strange.

"You're hiding from the truth, Erin," JoAnne went on. "You're hiding from having to build your own future. Is it really better to be someone's sidecar than to be behind the wheel yourself?"

"Why do you have to do this to me?" I said angrily. "Why can't you just let me live my life."

"Because unlike someone whose name I will not mention, I love you. Now, let's order. I'm starved."

I asked Maggie if I could walk her to Back Bay station after dinner. I wanted to talk with her, alone.

"You don't hate me for being interested in Doug, do you?" I said after we'd walked about a block in silence.

"No. Of course not. You're my friend."

"But you don't respect me for it, do you?"

"Erin, I respect you," Maggie answered patiently. "That doesn't mean I have to respect or approve of every decision you make. Besides, it's your life, not mine. Only you know what's really in your head and heart. Only you know why you need to make a certain decision."

"Thanks."

There was something I'd been wanting to ask Maggie about her own life, but had hesitated to do so. It had been a long time since we'd discussed her romantic past; as far as I knew, there still was no romantic present. What I wanted to know about was Maggie's hope for a romantic future.

"Maggie? We're always going on about meeting someone special, getting married and all. Do you . . . I mean, I know you went through some bad stuff, but it's been a while. Do you ever think about meeting someone special? Or do you just humor us when we babble on?"

Maggie laughed softly. "Well, that was awkwardly put."

"Sorry."

"It's okay. I enjoy babbling as much as the next woman. I love being with you guys. And, yeah, sure. I think about meeting someone special. Who doesn't?"

"Okay."

We walked on in silence for a bit. Then, Maggie said, "I guess I just want someone to, you know, catch my drift. Like in the Alanis Morissette song."

"You even have a drift?" I teased.

"Everyone has a drift."

"So, what's yours?" I asked.

Maggie shrugged. "I don't know how to describe it. I don't think you're supposed to talk about your drift."

"You're just supposed to—have it?"

"Yes. You have it and you hope that someday, somewhere, someone else catches it. And, I guess, that you catch theirs back."

"You're really talking about Abby's soul mate thing. Right?"

Maggie shrugged again. "Maybe. But I prefer to think in terms of drift."

As long as we were talking openly . . .

"Did you think you'd found someone who caught your drift when you married Vittorio?"

"God, I can't imagine what I thought at the time! I mean it. That Maggie is a different person. Grad school Maggie. I was so young! I suppose I must have thought he was—okay—

my soul mate. I don't think I would have married him otherwise. But I was so shy, so stunned he was interested in me, this sexy Italian guy, I was so charmed by his stories of Italy and his accent . . ."

"Ugh."

"I know, I know." Maggie sighed. "You live, you learn. That's also from an Alanis song."

"That's also a big cliché."

"It's true, though, isn't it?"

"Yeah. It's true."

We walked along in silence again for a few mniutes. Then, I said, "So, what if the person who catches your drift is married to someone else. What do you do then?"

"I don't know," Maggie said. "Maybe he hasn't really caught your drift. Maybe you only think he has."

Okay. Fair enough.

"What if your soul mate turns out to be not at all what you expected?" I said then. "How would you even recognize him? Say, you're expecting a musician and he turns out to be a dentist."

Maggie laughed.

"You worry too much, Erin," she said.

Again: Fair enough.

We'd reached the Clarendon Street entrance of the station.

"Well, good night, Maggie," I said. "Be careful."

"You, too, Erin. Good night."

Chapter Twelve

April, Boston

A Boston April can be a fine thing. Or not. Happily, that April was sweet and warm. The four of us met at Sonsi on Newbury Street and took a table facing the sidewalk, close to the wall of open glass doors.

Abby was the last to arrive. With a thud, she dropped a stack of magazines onto the table. The stack began to slide, allowing a quick glance at each cover. *Vogue. W. Bazaar. Allure. Elle. French Vogue.* Together, the magazines had to weigh ten, fifteen pounds.

Abby scrambled them together into two shorter piles and sat.

"Welcome," JoAnne said.

"Do you actually read all those magazines every month?" Maggie asked in disbelief.

"Of course," Abby said. "Though not every article in every issue. For example, I wear only clear nail polish so I skip articles about the newest nail polish shades though I look at the pictures so that I know what's going on out there. I like to be informed."

"And I thought I was being informed by watching CNN," Maggie quipped.

"And what am I thinking reading all those medical periodicals cover to cover?" JoAnne added, wide-eyed.

"Hey, information is information," I said. Secretly, I devoured *Allure* and *InStyle* each and every month. I knew where Abby was coming from. Except that I didn't make it a habit to carry my magazines with me.

Abby shot a glance at a middle-aged woman who'd just passed our table.

"See that woman?" she whispered. "Her hair is far too long for her age. A woman of a certain age shouldn't have long hair. Definitely not below where her neck meets her shoulder line. And it should be worn very neat, not all wild and flyaway."

"You're ready to impose that rule?" I wondered.

"It's just my opinion. When I'm of a certain age I'll cut my hair."

"What's 'a certain age'?" Maggie demanded. "Who determines that?"

"Well, I think it's a little different for every woman. You know, depending on her looks—her face and figure, and her style. But I'd say the cutoff is fifty. Absolutely no long hair after fifty. That's just too horrible."

"You never cease to fascinate me," Maggie said. "Where do you get this stuff? From those magazines?"

"Yes. And I just learned it, growing up. From my mother and aunts, you know. You learn the rules and the exceptions to the rules. Erin knows what I'm talking about."

Leave me out of this, I protested silently.

"Well, knock yourself out," Maggie said. "I can't be bothered with the 'rules.' I just hope this doesn't mean that when I'm sixty and have a gray braid hanging down my back you're going to snub me in public. Does it?"

"Oh, of course not. But I think your hair might be too thin by then for a really nice braid."

JoAnne groaned. "Can we please change this stupid topic?"

"It's not stupid," Abby protested.

"Are you from another century or something?" JoAnne asked. "Next you'll be saying you believe a woman should hand over her rights as a citizen and all her property to the man she marries."

"No! Of course not." Abby considered. "But, I do believe that a husband and wife—or life partners, whoever—should share their finances."

"I believe in keeping finances separate," Maggie countered. "I think a woman should always be prepared to get out while she can—and have something to live on. Do you know how many women are totally screwed in divorces, even if the law 'provides' for them?"

"Men get screwed, too," I said. Not because I felt great sympathy for those men—like Doug?—but I did feel they should have some representation.

"Not as often as women," JoAnne said darkly. "Especially if there are kids."

"Well . . ." Me, again. Lame devil's advocate.

"Why don't you buy a place, Abby?" JoAnne challenged. "Renting is such a colossal waste of money. You build no equity, renters' laws only go so far to protect you, there's no point in wasting money on great furniture that might not fit into the next place. Half the time if you paint the walls with some special technique you have to pay for them to be repainted white when you leave."

"I don't care," Abby insisted. "I'm not buying a house until I get married. Then my husband and I will buy together."

"That's ridiculous!" I said. "What if you never get married?"

"I will get married."

How could I argue with that logic?

"Why not own property now?" Maggie urged. "Make an investment in your own future. You can always sell the apartment when you get married or have kids and need a bigger place."

"No. I don't want to." Abby flipped open the copy of *W* and pretended to ignore us.

"You're avoiding maturity," Maggie pointed out.

"Maggie's right," JoAnne said. "A woman should take care of herself and plan for her future. Abby, put the magazine down and look at me. What kind of retirement plans do you have? Insurance? Investments? Who's your broker? Financial advisor? Or do you handle the research and paperwork on your own?"

"I . . ."

The poor thing needed some help.

"Abby, I know it's scary but we can all help," I said. "Look, my father helped me through the paperwork when I applied for the mortgage on my apartment. I was petrified. I just didn't know terms, I didn't know anything. I mean, when we did the closing I think I paid for about six different kinds of insurance. Who knew you needed title insurance, fire insurance . . . it never seemed to end."

"Well, you can trust your father," said Abby.

"Right. And he's a lawyer and he's bought houses before, so he knows the ropes. Buying your own home is a very scary thing."

"I don't know . . ."

"Look, Abby," I went on. "I'll admit that on some level I saw buying my own place as sort of giving up the hope of ever getting married and buying a house with a husband."

JoAnne snorted. I gave her the evil eye.

"I know that sounds ridiculous, but it's true," I said. "Part of me felt elated and powerful and finally totally independent. Part of me felt like I'd finally grown up—which was both good and bad. And part of me felt—alone. Like I'd finally acknowledged just how alone I really was. No husband. No children. No immediate possibility of either. It was just me and Fuzzer. Not that Fuzzer isn't the best."

"Well, if I were a man," JoAnne said, "I'd find a woman who owned her own home attractive. I'd think maybe she wasn't looking for me to sweep in and take care of her. I wouldn't feel so much pressure."

Abby looked worried by this. "Do you really think a man cares so much about whether a woman rents or owns?"

"I don't know about that," I said, "but I'll admit I find a man who owns his own place a lot more attractive than a man who rents. Unless he's in transition or something. Like looking for the perfect place, or he's just been transferred and he's living in corporate housing, or his architect and contractor are taking longer than expected perfecting his two-thousand-square-foot loft."

"A home is security," Maggie said.

"It's power."

"Your own home is where you can be Martha Stewart."

"If your husband isn't sickened by wreaths made out of colored pipe cleaners and smelly potpourri."

"Isn't potpourri smelly by definition?"

"Would you own a house with someone you weren't married to?" JoAnne asked. "If you were living with the guy, would you pool your finances, share a checking account, save for the future together?"

"Never." Abby.

"Depends," I said, thinking, what if Doug's wife holds up a divorce and Doug and I live together before we can marry?

"On what?" Maggie demanded. "How many generations of destitute women does it take to teach the rest of us a lesson about protecting our assets?"

Now, I was depressed.

"Abby?" I said. "Can I borrow your *Vogue?* The French one."

Erin—hi. please get diamond brooch from s. deposit bx., sell, send money. it's mine from great-grandma. send to address below. know i promised it to you. take coral beads instead. Mom

Sometimes I think I'm a frustrated party planner. Or maybe my desire to be a hostess has something to do with growing up an only and often lonely child. Either way, it occurred to me that with the early April weather being so unexpectedly fine, we city folk should take advantage. I suggested to about twenty people, mostly from EastWind, that we meet at the Barking Crab for an informal get-together. I'd thought about asking Doug but didn't have the nerve. Besides, I thought, what if he brought his wife along? What if he met my invitation with coldness?

JoAnne arrived wearing a clingy, wraparound dress in cobalt blue and black, and black strappy sandals. Of course, she looked unbearably sexy. Thank God she didn't have a thing for older men, I thought later.

I'd opted for low-on-the-hip pants in taupe, a fitted blouse in khaki, and canary yellow strappy sandals. I've never been afraid to wear bright and colorful shoes, provided they are beautifully designed and well crafted. And somewhat within my budget. And worn as the splash needed with an outfit in neutrals.

Good thing the occasion didn't call for the diamond brooch, the last remaining Morelli heirloom. I'd sold it just like my mother had wanted me to do. I was a good daughter. An angry daughter, but a good one.

An impulse I couldn't understand had made me ask my father to join the party. Much to my surprise, he said yes. Until the last moment I hadn't expected him to show. I'd expected him to beg off, citing too much work or a crushed spirit still not ready to socialize.

I was wrong.

John Weston appeared at the Barking Crab in a smart navy blazer, crisp white shirt open at the neck, and neat, sand-colored chinos, got himself a drink, and began to socialize.

I watched with some surprise.

"Your father is looking quite handsome these days," JoAnne said. "Your mother's—absence—seems to be doing him good."

"Yeah, who would have thought? I mean, I know he's sad and I think he's still in a bit of shock, but . . ."

"So, has he started to date yet?"

"What?" I laughed. "No. I mean, I don't think so. At least, he hasn't said anything to me."

"Honey, you might be the last person he'd tell."

"Why? We're close."

"And you're his daughter. He might have to get comfortable with the idea of dating before he introduces you to his new girlfriend. It's a classic recipe for trouble—the two women most likely to hate each other, the daughter and the new woman."

"Oh, come on, JoAnne! I'm an adult. I want my father to be happy. I'd be very glad if he was dating someone nice.'

"And old and frumpy. No challenge to you."

"What? You're insane."

Is she? Reason murmured.

"You mean to tell me you wouldn't be—upset—if your father showed up at your door one night with a bombshell on his arm?"

"Well . . . I might. If the bombshell was using him or just after his money or something. I mean, what kind of daughter would I be if I didn't want to protect my father?"

"Protect him from what, evil women? Or protect your place in his heart? Face it, Erin, John's a big boy now. He's a successful lawyer and he's not about to be bamboozled by some floozy."

"You know, you piss me off, sometimes, JoAnne."

"I try, honey, I try. Someone's got to be the realistic one in this friendship."

"I'm walking away now," I said, haughtily. "I feel the need for a glass of champagne. Maybe a two-pound lobster on the side. With lots of butter."

JoAnne raised her eyebrows.

"Overindulgence won't change the truth of my words," she said.

No, I admitted to myself. But it might help me to forget.

* * *

If JoAnne wasn't going to be all warm and fuzzy—or at least, nice—I'd talk to Maggie for a while. After a snack.

We chatted a bit about doings at the Women's Lunch Place, the shelter at which Maggie volunteered, and about EastWind's involvement with a new client, a local public radio station. We admitted to not yet having seen the latest installment of *The Lord of the Rings*. And then I turned the conversation to a more serious topic, one I had not indeed forgotten, in spite of the champagne and lobster.

"Do you think it's odd that Abby's been talking to my father for"—I checked my watch—"over half an hour?"

Maggie glanced over her shoulder then looked back to me.

"Odd, how?" she said. "They've met before, right? You know how Abby is. Once she gets going you can't shut her up. Poor John."

Poor John? He'd been laughing for most of ten minutes now and I hadn't seen that twinkle in his eyes since . . . Actually, I'd never seen that twinkle in his eye. It was quite—attractive.

And since when did he drink champagne?

"She's probably just trying to make him feel better," I said firmly, turning away, hoping to convince myself of Abby's purely disinterested motives. "You know, after my mother's leaving him and all. Abby's so sweet."

"That she is. Look, Erin, this has been great, but I've got to run."

"So soon? It's so early."

"I know, but I have a deadline for an article I'm writing for *Urban Dialogues* and if I don't spend at least an hour a night working on it for the next two weeks, I'm royally screwed."

"Your self-discipline is amazing," I told her. "I mean it."

Maggie shrugged. "Not really. I'm getting five hundred bucks for the article. I'll do just about anything for five hundred bucks."

"Send me a copy when it's written?"

"Like you'd understand a word of it," Maggie drawled.

I smacked her arm, then kissed her cheek. "You're mean. Be careful getting home."

When Maggie had gone, I got a glass of wine and resumed Abby-and John-watching. It was not a sport I'd ever imagined myself a spectator of.

Abby looked adorable—fresh and clean and pretty like Grace Kelly in *High Society* somehow—in a pale pink linen skirt suit, bone-colored, kitten-heeled mules, and her hair lightly curled. She looked like an expensive confection. An expensive flirtatious confection. I wanted to bundle her away, out of sight of the newly single John Weston.

Why was I even thinking such a thing, imagining such a . . . such a . . . such a mind-blowing atrocity as my best friend flirting with my father? Had I gone completely insane? It was not without precedence in my family. My mother's uncle Larry had been "put away" years ago after a rather embarrassing incident involving a chicken and a roll of packing tape, and rumor had it that her "crazy cousin Ellen" had become convinced she was Scarlett O'Hara—or was it Tallulah Bankhead?

Either way, I was doomed. Maybe in my case the lunacy was just kicking in early. Or maybe it was the several glasses of wine and champagne I'd consumed. I looked at the half-empty glass in my hand, grimaced, and put it on the nearest table. Sober was the way to accurately assess this situation.

But I never made it to Abby and my father. Halfway across the floor I was waylaid by Hank and his wife, Erica. By the time I managed to extricate myself from chitchat about the latest Big Dig scandal, Abby and my father were no longer in sight.

I never found out where they disappeared to, but a half hour later I spotted Abby talking animatedly to some thirty-something guy not part of our group. Dad took his leave of the party soon after and I sighed a big ole sigh of relief. Literally.

Chapter Thirteen

A day or two after the informal get-together at the Barking Crab, I began to seriously regret not having asked Doug to be there. If he'd accepted the invitation and shown up with his wife, so be it. I'd have lived. Maybe. At least I'd have known what Carol looked like. I'd overheard someone at EastWind mention having met the Spears at a function, but couldn't glean more information about Carol than her name. Now I had a burning desire to know just who I was up against. And Doug's bringing Carol wouldn't necessarily have meant he wasn't still interested in me. If he was ever interested in me at all.

I couldn't get Doug Spears and our possibly nonexistent relationship out of my mind. I wanted very badly to call him. I was mildly obsessed.

Reason was stern. Mildly obsessed? That's like being sort of pregnant. Face it, Erin, you're obsessed and you've got to cut it out. Now. Do not make the call. Do not.

Romance had its own opinion. Don't deny your heart's desire, Erin, it urged. If you don't act, you'll never know. You'll live the rest of your life wondering what might have been. Take the next step. Take it!

Why can't he take it, I thought petulantly, but I wondered if my petulance was in reality an excuse for my backing away from the idea of placing a call to Doug Spears.

Screwing up one's courage—it's an interesting phrase, and quite an accurate description of how one's stomach feels in the decisive moments before daring action. All screwy and twisty and whirly.

Okay. I'd make the call. Maybe.

But what would I say when he answered the phone? If he didn't answer and voice mail kicked in, would I have the nerve to leave a bright and witty message, or would I just hang up, face burning. Bottom line: I wanted very badly to hear his voice.

Another question: To pretend or not to pretend. To create a false pretense for calling, such as a burning question about a troublesome client—unnamed, of course, because fictional. Or to simply say, "Hi. Want to have lunch sometime this week? No reason. Just thought you might."

It could go several ways with either scenario. If I created a professional reason for meeting, Doug could say he was too busy that week but reschedule. How can a colleague turn down another colleague's request for help? If Doug did indeed say no to a meeting and make no move to reschedule—well, that would be a clear sign that whatever romantic possibilities he'd had in mind were no longer in play. The end.

Second scenario: If I gave no reason for my invitation other than an interest in getting together, Doug's response either way would be clearer. Right? If he said no and didn't suggest a rescheduling, I'd know flat out that he didn't want anything to do with me in a personal way. If he said yes, even if he had to choose a later date, it would mean he was open to—romance?

Okay. If I called I'd be honest. But did I have the nerve to make such a bold move?

Yes. It turns out I did.

* * *

Carpe diem.

At ten o'clock one morning, I dialed Doug's office number. The receptionist put me right through. Doug was in.

"Doug Spears."

"Doug?" I said, and then thought, What a flaming idiot, Erin!

"Yes, it's me," he said, clearly amused. "Is this Erin Weston?"

He recognized my voice!

"Yes. Yes, it's Erin."

"Well, hello."

"Hello." What next?! "Uh, how've you been?"

Doug laughed mildly. "Busy, nothing unusual. How've you been?"

"Oh, fine," I said. "You know. Fine."

There was half a moment of supremely awkward silence—at least for me it was awkward—and then Doug said, again with a note of amusement in his voice, "Erin, is there some particular reason you called?"

Do or die.

I asked him if he would like to have lunch the next day. Or some day that week. Whatever worked for him. If he wasn't too busy. If . . .

Mercifully, Doug cut me off.

"How about instead of lunch we go to a gallery opening I've got an invitation for? It's Wednesday evening, from five to seven."

Oh, Lord. Negativity roared. Had my offer of lunch been too boring? Did I live to eat? Dark self-doubts kept me from responding. I was a glutton, a greedy thing, a hedonist, a sybaritic waste of oxygen. . . .

"Erin? What do you think? I remembered you said you were into art. There'll be appetizers and champagne."

"Sounds great," I said quickly. "The opening, I mean."

Doug laughed. "You don't have to hide your appetites from me. I like a woman who lives large."

"Okay," I said. A brilliant response.

"So," Doug said, "I'll see you at the Biddle Gallery on Newbury at, say, five-thirty, Wednesday?"

"Sure. Great. And, thanks," I added. Thanks for not hanging up on me.

"For what? You called me. I should be the one thanking you."

"Okay," I said, more easily. "You're welcome."

"See you Wednesday, Erin," Doug said and his voice was warm.

"See you Wednesday, Doug," I said.

Another move in the game.

I was a player after all.

Damion Finn and I had met several years ago when he'd joined EastWind Comunications as a graphics designer. I'd been attracted to him from the start. He was handsome and funny and intelligent and very mature. Though he was only about three years my senior, he seemed somehow much older. I liked that about him. However, it wasn't long before I realized that while Damion might become a friend, he would never become my lover. That was okay. Better some Damion than no Damion.

He left EastWind after only a year for a go as a freelance designer. Unlike most office friendships, ours survived the change in venue and actually grew. Though I didn't see Damion as often as I would have liked—his schedule was even fuller than mine and included two pugs who needed to be walked three times a day and who attended regular grooming sessions—when we did get together the time spent was quality. Unfortunately, he'd been out of town the night of the Barking Crab get-together; I would have liked his take on Abby's monopolizing of my father.

On Tuesday, we met for lunch at Elephant and Castle. We each had a Caesar salad, mine with anchovies, Damion's without.

"How's Fuzzer, the Great Beige Beast?" Damion asked.

"Wonderful. Demanding and vocal as usual," I said. "He's the best. How are your babies doing?"

"Lucy and Ricky are wonderful, thriving, just passed their yearly physicals with clean bills of health."

"They have a good daddy."

Damion grinned proudly. "I know."

"How are things with Carl?" I asked.

"Carl is history," Damion said shortly.

"Oh, Damion, I'm sorry. Jeez. What happened? If you feel like talking about it . . ."

Damion shrugged. "Why not? Long story short, I caught him cheating on me. With some twenty-year-old sales clerk from Structure. Can you imagine? Anyway, I sent him packing. Good riddance to bad rubbish, as my dear departed grandmother used to say."

"Wow. I'm sorry. You really liked him, didn't you?"

"Until he cheated on me, sure."

Damion's tone was firm. I didn't really want to suggest he try to work things out with Carl. I'd never been overly fond of him, myself. But, given my own personal situation—potential involvement in an illicit, behind-the-backs romance—I was compelled to seek leniency for all cheaters everywhere.

"Would you give him a second chance?" I asked, tentatively.

"No. I draw the line at infidelity."

"But, you two didn't know each other for long. Maybe . . ."

"Maybe what, Erin? Maybe I should be all forgiving and wake up three years from now sunk in a relationship with a chronic liar? No. My life is too precious. My peace of mind and my happiness are too important."

I wondered how Damion had come by his strong sense of self-respect. I admired him for it, and I was envious. At the same time I still felt that maybe Damion was being a bit harsh with Carl. Lots of relationships were bumpy at the start, right?

Your standards are too low, Erin. That was Reason.

I think she's right. Love is all about forgiveness, Romance offered.

What ever happened to love being "never having to say you're sorry"?

Romance huffed and didn't respond further.

Besides, I thought, just because someone cheated didn't necesarily make him an evil, unredeemable person. Look at Doug. Did he ask to be attracted to me? Not that he was cheating on his wife. Not yet. Not technically, if by technically you meant that he'd had sex with me. He hadn't.

"Enough about me," Damion said suddenly. "What about you, my dear? Any eligible men on the horizon? Anyone special I should know about?"

Someone special, yes. Someone special Damion should know about—no. Not after hearing about the Carl episode.

I frowned. "No," I lied, "unfortunately, no one special."

"Concentrating on work these days?" he asked, with a sympathetic frown. "I know you tend to take on too much at the office."

"Yeah, that's it," I said. "The same old story."

I gulped my lunch and left soon afterward, claiming a deadline, pursued by a nagging sense of shame.

Chapter Fourteen

I didn't tell my friends that I had called Doug. I didn't tell them that we were going to the opening of a show at the Biddle Gallery. I didn't want them to know. I was afraid of their knowing, afraid their disapproval—spoken or implied—would ruin the night for me.

Childish? Maybe.

Face it. When you're in your twenties, your getting involved with a married man meets with almost universal curiosity and interest among your friends. When you're in your thirties, a bit more bruised and jaded, your getting involved with a married man meets with cautionary tales and concern. A twenty-something woman can take care of herself; she has plenty of time ahead of her in which to rebound. At least, that's the general assumption. A thirty-something woman is no longer so lucky. Time is wasting. Forty looms large. Abandonment and perpetual singlehood are no longer distant nightmares, but real possibilities. Thirty-something women start saving money in a serious way and thinking about having a baby on their own if they're not married by thirty-five or forty. They don't pursue a married man for what is sure to be just a fling, not something secure and long-term.

But that's just what I was doing. Only I didn't think too hard about the goals of my relationship with Doug. I was immersed in the thrill of the moment, tossing aside the occasional doubts and fears.

Go ahead, Reason said, disdainfully. Waste a year or more on this bozo. Then what?

It won't be a waste, Romance said, confidently. True love is never a waste of time or energy.

True love? Reason scoffed.

Yes, I thought, maybe. Maybe true love.

> *E—send recent photo; want to see how you look.*
> *hope bad haircut has grown out. too bad you*
> *have your father's hair. M*

I wore a soft brown Ann Taylor pantsuit with a shimmery violet blouse, and matching shoes and purse I'd splurged on just for that pantsuit. My hair looked just fine.

I got to the gallery at ten minutes after five. Doug wasn't there and for a second I thought, He's not coming, and, Maybe I should just sneak off now, and . . .

Then he was walking down the street. He spotted me and nodded and kept coming. There was no way out and I was glad.

Doug was wearing a black suit with a white shirt, open at the neck. He looked very male.

"Hey," he said when he'd reached me.

"Hey, yourself."

He smiled and nodded toward the stairs that led to the upper story gallery. "Want to go in?"

We did. The room in which the opening was being held, in which the paintings were hung, was small but well lit. Two waiters circulated among the twenty or so viewers with trays of finger foods; at the far end of the room was a table set with champagne glasses. A waiter poured Veuve Cliquot; seltzer for those who preferred something nonalcoholic.

"Be right back," Doug said, touching my elbow as he headed

toward the champagne table. I watched him go, noticed the set of his shoulders, the breadth of his back. I watched him return, noted strong thighs through the excellent cut of his suit pants.

Doug handed me a glass of champagne. His fingers brushed mine as he did.

"You strike me as the champagne type," he said.

"I'm also the Yoo-Hoo type."

"A woman of contradictions."

"No. Just a woman of complexity."

Doug grinned. "Let's look at the paintings."

The paintings were—well, they sucked. They were nicely hung, but they sucked. I refrained from sharing that sophisticated, learned judgment. Doug made no comment, either. We circled the room and after only five minutes, we were done with the show.

What next, I wondered.

"Is the artist here?" I asked.

Doug said, "The owner said he might not make it. Car trouble. We don't have to stay, if you'd rather . . ."

"No," I said, far too quickly. "I mean, let's stay for a bit. Unless you . . ."

"More champagne?"

"Yes, please."

While Doug was getting the champagne I grabbed a mini-quiche from the tray of a passing waiter. I hadn't eaten since half a salad gobbled at noon. The last thing I wanted was to get silly.

We drank another glass of champagne and talked and drank yet one more glass and talked some more. Our conversation was light and flirtatious. It was some time before I became aware of the fact that except for two other men, the room had emptied of viewers.

"Uh, I think the opening's over," I said, trying to hide the reluctance in my voice. "I should go."

I thought: Please suggest we have dinner.

"Can I give you a lift home?" Doug asked.

Rats. No dinner.

"Oh, that's okay," I said. "I'm not far. I live in the South End. I can walk."

Doug smiled. "I know you can walk. I've seen you do it. I'm asking if you'd let me drive you home."

Oh, God, yes.

"Yes. Thanks. I'd like that," I said brightly.

Doug's car was parked on Newbury close to Dartmouth Street, a miracle spot. We walked the few blocks in silence. Maybe Doug was comfortable with it; a—pleased?—smile played about his mouth. I could stand it no longer.

"So, what did you think of the work?" I said.

Doug shrugged. "Mediocre. Derivative. Did nothing for me. You?"

I laughed. "What a relief. Frankly, I thought the work was pretty bad. But I wasn't going to say that after . . ."

"After?"

"Well, it was your idea that we go," I said awkwardly.

"Yeah, but I'm not responsible for the art, am I? You can be honest, Erin. I wish you would be."

We'd reached the car. Doug unlocked the passenger side and opened the door for me. When I was safely in, he closed the door.

Score another point.

"Do you know the artist?" I asked when Doug got behind the wheel.

"Yeah. He's my cousin. Nice guy but lousy with a brush. He should have stayed in law school."

"Oh. Should you have stayed to see if he ever showed up?"

"If I'd wanted to stay, I would have."

Doug's own honesty impressed me. No false emotion or dainty words to cover up the truth of what he thought. Imagine.

"Where am I going?" he said and I was startled. Where, indeed, was he going? Where were we going?

"What?" I said. "Oh, make a right on Clarendon and I'll point the way from there."

More silence.

"So," I said, "how long will it take you to get home?"

What a fool, I scolded. Why did you have to mention "home"? Doug's with you now. Enjoy it while it lasts.

"Not long," he said.

A few moments later we turned onto Warren Avenue and stopped in front of my building.

"Nice block," Doug said. "Do you like living here?"

I nodded. "I do. I own my place, so . . ."

So, what?

Doug's hands were on the wheel. Clearly, he was not sticking around.

"Can I call you?" he said suddenly, seriously.

I could hardly breathe. Hardly believe that we were sitting there in the dark, so close together . . .

"Of course," I said. "Okay."

"Good night, Erin."

Please, please kiss me, I begged. Come upstairs and . . .

Doug leaned in and gently kissed my cheek. It was innocent and not. He smelled so good. His lips were so soft. His cheek was slightly stubbly.

He drew away and that little knowing smile was there and his eyes held mine.

"Good night," I whispered, and somehow I got out of that car.

Chapter Fifteen

May, Boston

May in Boston is beautiful. The South End is in bloom and fragrant with lilacs, the sidewalks are slippery with apple blossom petals, and the garden competition is fierce.

On a Thursday night, JoAnne, Maggie, Abby, and I had dinner at Truc on Tremont Street. The South End had become a serious restaurant center in the mid to late 1990s. Most nights, the diners were mostly South Enders and other Boston dwellers. Saturday nights, people from the suburbs, such as Lincoln and Brookline, drove in, had their cars valet-parked, and took tables from the locals.

Truc is small and while not precisely cozy, inviting in feel. We ordered—pan-roasted chicken *"grandmère"* for Abby and me, Long Island duck breast with carmelized rhubarb for JoAnne, and steak frites for Maggie—and began to relax with a bottle of Merlot.

JoAnne suddenly looked up and down the narrow front room. Every seat was occupied.

"Why are we all white?" she said suddenly.

"What?" I was sure I'd heard incorrectly.

"Why are we all white?" JoAnne repeated. "I mean, look at this table. Look around this restaurant. White white white white white. Why are we all white?"

"I don't know. I came out that way. What are you even talking about?" I made a face. Please, let no one else hear this conversation, I prayed.

"Would you date a black man?" JoAnne challenged.

"Where would I even meet a black man?"

"See? This is what I'm saying."

"Is he a professional?" Abby asked suddenly. "You know, did he go to college and grad school? Because if he did, sure, why not, I'd go out with him. If I really liked him. And if he wasn't a jerk."

"I'd probably go out with him even if he was a jerk," Maggie said. "Knowing me. Which is why I don't date anymore."

"See, in New York, this wouldn't happen. Boston is so weirdly segregated. I feel so—apart." JoAnne gave a weird little shudder.

"Oh, and you're telling me that when you lived in New York you were hangin' with the bruthas and sistas?" I laughed. " 'Cause I'm not believing that."

"He'd have to be cute," Abby said. "Is he cute?"

"Is who cute?"

"The black guy. The one who went to law school."

"Abby, there is no black guy," I said slowly. And quietly. Sometimes, it's like talking to a child. "We're having a conversation about a hypothetical situation. It's make-believe."

"Oh. Well, I'd still go out with him. If he was cute. And if he smelled nice. I wonder if he wears Grey Flannel. Oh, I looove Grey Flannel!"

My father wears Grey Flannel, I thought distractedly.

"Check, please," Maggie mumbled.

* * *

Doug called almost every day after the night of the gallery opening. Our conversations were often brief, as we were both at the office, but I lived for them.

We met again for lunch. Talk of business faded quickly and we laughed about the president's latest verbal gaff and bemoaned the Red Sox's ever-growing injured list. Doug had seen the latest super-hyped sci-fi flick and hated it. I'd seen it, too, and hated it for the same reasons. That seemed significant.

Doug walked me partway back to my office before veering off to his. Obviously, on a public street and in broad daylight, he couldn't kiss me, but I knew he wanted to by the look in his eye. At least, I hoped he wanted to. During lunch, which was otherwise wonderful, he hadn't so much as touched my arm. I watched him walk away—and was glad that I did. At the corner, Doug turned, as if he knew I'd be watching, waved and smiled. I waved back and felt my heart soar.

And all during those days and weeks of an almost old-fashioned courting, I asked myself: Erin, do you know what you're doing? And I answered: Yes. No. I have to do it. I can't— I can't say no to him. I don't want to.

It will be all right, I told myself. Everything will be fine.

Abby e-mailed me one morning, asking if I could meet her for lunch. She said she'd come over my way. I E-mailed back saying "sure."

At twelve-thirty we met at Au Bon Pain for a quick soup and salad.

Abby looked terrible. I mean, beautiful as always, but nervous and—scared?

"What's up?" I said, concerned.

"Erin, I have to tell you something."

"Are you okay? Did something bad happen?" Panic cried, She's dying of cancer, her apartment has burned up, she's lost her job.

"No! No, nothing bad."

That was a relief.

"At least—well I hope you won't think it's bad."

I laughed. "What does it matter what I think?"

"It matters a lot, Erin."

"Oh, okay," I said, somewhat chastened. "I just meant you shouldn't do or not do something based on my opinion."

"Your father—I mean John—well, he called last night when I got home from the restaurant, and he . . . he . . ."

"He . . . ?"

"He asked me out. On a date. For dinner."

I laughed. "Oh, Abby. Are you sure it's a date? I mean, he's . . ."

He's what, Reason said. A man?

I tried again. "You're . . ."

A woman. Very good, Erin.

"It's a date, Erin. He made it very clear he was asking me out on a date. He asked me if I was okay with that."

"Well, did you tell him you were absolutely not okay with that!" I said, leaping to my own foregone conclusion.

Silence. Abby looked off to her right, toward the juice bar.

"What . . . what did you tell him?"

"I told him yes," she said, looking back at me. "I told him I would be happy to go out with him."

Huh?

I was thoroughly confused.

"Since when . . . Abby, you've met my father before and nothing . . . Did you always have a crush on him?"

I remembered Abby in her pale pink suit the night at the Barking Crab and wondered if my father had been the one with the crush.

"No, Erin, of course not," Abby said. "When I first met your father he was married and I would never even think about . . ." Abby blushed and changed course. "There was something different about him the night at the Barking Crab. He seemed—like a man. Like a person, not just Erin's father. Do you understand?"

No, not really, I thought. But—yes.

"So . . . are you okay with this?" Abby asked gently. "My going on a date with—John?"

If I weren't, would it make a difference? I didn't want to know the answer to that question, so I lied.

"Yeah, sure, Abby. I mean, I'm surprised, that's all. But . . . you know. Yeah."

Abby smiled as if the sun had suddenly come out after a month of hiding.

"Thank you, Erin," she said. "Thanks."

When I got home that evening after work I checked for a message on the answering machine even before feeding Fuzzer.

"Erin, it's Dad. Give me a call when you get in. I want to talk to you about something important. Nothing bad, I know how you worry. Just something—important."

I didn't return the call.

I wanted Doug.

Chapter Sixteen

Erin—got $, txs. how are you? will be out of touch for a while, going into jungle. ever think your ma wld be an explorer?

I hadn't wanted to know exactly when my father was taking Abby out on their first date. The entire concept was disturbing enough; the last thing I needed was the opportunity to dwell on what might be happening during the specific hours of their rendezvous.

However, not wanting to seem a bad sport, I hadn't asked either my father or Abby to keep the details to themselves. So, they hadn't, at least the detail of day of the week. So, during the evening of the twenty-first, between the hours of seven and eleven—the time I deemed appropriate for a first, Thursday night dinner date—I dwelt and stewed, indulged in self-pity, and was bombarded by unbidden scenarios of debauchery.

I don't know which fantasies were more disturbing: The very creepy ones involving my father and my best friend, or the ones involving me and Doug and the unexpected arrival of his irate wife.

It was not an enjoyable evening.

I called JoAnne, ready to rant and rave about the travesty of Abby's dating my father, but JoAnne didn't seem to think there was anything wrong with their behavior.

"They're adults, Erin," she'd said. "And they're single. What's the big deal?"

"Well, if you don't know, I'm not going to tell you," I snapped childishly.

Then I called Maggie. Her reaction was not much more comforting than JoAnne's.

"Sure," she said, "I can see why you might feel a bit uncomfortable about it. But there's no point in wasting your time over something you can't change. Just wait and see what happens."

Maggie can be infuriatingly reasonable at times.

I finally went to bed at eleven-thirty but could not get to sleep no matter how many relaxation techniques I tried. Morning dawned and I was a mess, eyes puffy from lack of rest, head hurting from tension.

If this was going to be the result of my father dating my best friend, the dating had to stop now. At this rate, I thought, I'd be dead in a year.

Getting ready for work, I knew the worst was yet to come. More than likely, Dad wouldn't call with a report. It was not what men did; it was not what my father would do to his daughter. But Abby was sure to call. She was naturally discreet; I knew she'd never give gory details, especially in this situation. Still, I dreaded the call.

By midmorning, Abby's call had not come and visions of my father and Abby rolling around under the sheets, playing hooky from the office, rampaged in my head. There was only one way to put an end to my morbid curiosity. I picked up the phone and dialed Abby's number at the BSO.

She answered on the first ring. She sounded harried.

"Hi," I said.

"Oh, hi, Erin. God, what a morning."

Gulp.

"The phone's been ringing off the hook and we have a bit

of a crisis brewing, never mind what it's about, but I haven't even gotten to my coffee yet. Ugh. It's cold!"

This boded well. John, my father, was not the uppermost topic on Abby's mind this morning. Maybe the date had been less than spectacular. Maybe they'd agreed it had been a mistake, going out, and that they'd just "see each other around." Maybe . . .

"Oh, but Erin, I had such a wonderful time with John last night!"

Crap. Abby's tone of voice had changed completely. From stress there'd come happiness.

"Really?" I squeaked. "That's, uh, great."

"First we went to dinner at Anago . . ."

First? There was more?

"And then we went to Limbo, that fabulous jazz place downtown, to hear this singer your father likes. She was wonderful. The whole night was wonderful. John is such a gentleman."

"Wonderful," I said lamely.

"We're seeing each other again tomorrow night," Abby said.

I didn't respond.

"Erin? Are you okay?"

No. No, I was not okay.

"Yeah, I'm fine," I said. "Just . . . Maureen's motioning to me. Maybe another call I need to take. Sorry."

"What is it about Fridays?" Abby said with a laugh. "It's supposed to be a slow day but it never is."

"Yeah." I laughed, too. "Look, I'll, uh, I'll talk to you soon. Gotta go."

I hung up. I didn't hear Abby's final good-bye, though I'm sure there was one. I put my head in my hands and felt desolation overtake me.

I had to talk to my father about his behavior. I couldn't have both my parents acting irrationally, now could I? Someone had to be the reasonable, responsible parent. If not, that left me—where? Emotionally orphaned? The thought embarrassed me so I shoved it away.

Shove harder, Reason suggested. In fact, abandon this train of thought entirely. You're a big girl now.

Whatever. I arrived at my father's apartment at about seven that evening.

He'd just gotten home and was, naturally, surprised to see me.

"Erin, hi. Why didn't you return my call the other day? Did you get it?"

There was no hint of nervousness or guilt in his voice or manner. I looked hard for them and found none.

I followed him into the living room and remained standing when he gestured toward a seat.

"Erin, is something wrong?" he asked, clearly concerned. And then, his eyes changed. "Ah, I see what this is about. Abby and me."

"Dad," I blurted, "why are you doing this?"

"Why does any man ask a woman to dinner?" he answered.

"You know what I mean. Why are you betraying me like this?"

Well, that was a little stronger than I'd intended, but the words were out there now.

Dad looked at me with the eyes of a surprised but entirely rational man.

"How is my dating Abby a betrayal of you, Erin? You're my daughter. Abby's my—my girlfriend. Okay," he admitted, "that's a word that makes me feel creepy, but . . ."

"But, Dad, why can't you date someone closer to your own age?"

"I don't mean to be harsh, Erin, but it's really none of your business whom I date."

"Even when it's my best friend?"

"Even then." Dad sighed. "Sit down, Erin."

I did, sullenly.

"Let me amend what I just said. Of course I appreciate

that you're concerned about me. I know you don't want me to get hurt. And to that extent, yes, it is your business whom I date. But in this case, you know Abby, you know she's got a heart of gold. You know we both can trust her."

But I can't trust you, I thought at him. You're a poacher. You stole my best friend. Abby and I will never be quite the same.

Change is inevitable, Reason reminded. Would you rather grow or stagnate?

Don't ask me that right now! I cried. My best friend is a bitch. She stole my father!

"I've got to go," I said.

"Do you want to stay for dinner?"

"No, I have to go. Thanks."

My father didn't try to stop me with word or gesture.

When I got home a half hour later, I sat down with Fuzzer and cried.

My mother was traipsing through the wilds. My father was dating my best friend. Both were truly lost to me.

More than anything else—more than anyone else—I wanted Doug Spears.

Chapter Seventeen

June, Boston

A Boston June opens enticingly with a lovely, long-awaited warmth and goes out with full-blown haziness, heat, and humidity.

At least, that particular June did.

JoAnne asked me to come over to her house in Charlestown late one Saturday afternoon. I hadn't seen her all week, hadn't even had a conversation with her. Her usually busy schedule had seemed extraordinarily so. I welcomed the chance to spend an hour or two just hanging with her. Maybe we'd go to the Warren Tavern for some lunch. And not talk about Abby dating my father.

I took the Orange Line out to the Bunker Hill Community College stop and walked up to Bunker Hill Street and JoAnne's house. The weather was getting sticky. I stopped at a bakery for a half dozen donuts, even though I knew that JoAnne's eating habits were far healthier than my own. Oh, well, I reasoned, more for me.

I knew something was up immediately. JoAnne grabbed the bag of donuts, peered inside, and inhaled deeply.

"For me?" she said.

"For us, greedy. Since when do you crave donuts?"

"Since when do you care?"

Huh?

"I don't care. I mean . . . Okay, whatever. Eat them all if you like."

While JoAnne bit into a jelly donut and chewed consideringly, I noticed that her hair was unwashed. And that her sweatshirt—which ordinarily she would rather be caught dead wearing anywhere but the gym—was stained.

Oh, yeah. Something was up.

I sat down in one of the high-backed chairs in the living room and waited for JoAnne to come up for air.

"How was your week?" I asked finally. "Busy?"

"Mmm." JoAnne poked her finger into the bag again and frowned. "Only one jelly donut?"

"They were out. No new batches until tomorrow. Sorry."

JoAnne tossed the bag onto the coffee table and dropped onto the couch across from me. Where she sat staring at a Miro print on the wall over my head.

"So," I began again.

JoAnne looked down from the print and straight at me.

"So, I might have breast cancer," she said.

"Jesus Christ, JoAnne," I cried, "your presentation sucks. And, damn it. I'm sorry. How . . . what made you suspect something was wrong?"

JoAnne laughed.

"What do you think? I was doing my usual self-examination in the shower and I felt something—odd. So, I scheduled an appointment with my doctor. Typical story."

"Oh." God, I thought. When was the last time I examined my breasts? Had I ever?

"I'd have been so scared," I said uselessly.

JoAnne shrugged and poked now at the stains on her sweatshirt. "It happens. Knowing is better than not knowing. The sooner you find out something's wrong, the sooner you can start to fix it. The sooner you can start to kick its ass."

I laughed weakly. "I think that when it comes to my health I'm more into ignorance being bliss."

Suddenly, JoAnne's face hardened into a mask of anger.

"Don't talk about things you know nothing about."

I was—stunned.

"What? Sorry, I . . ."

"No, no, I'm sorry. I . . . it's just . . ."

"JoAnne, what?"

She rubbed her forehead, sighed, rolled her eyes.

"Look, don't go telling anyone about this yet, okay? The only reason I'm telling you now is . . . I don't even know why I'm telling you. So, promise, all right?"

"I promise to keep my mouth shut until such time as you see fit to lift the injunction."

JoAnne eyed me. "Not funny. Here goes. When I was six I was diagnosed with leukemia. I . . ."

"JoAnne, I . . ."

"Don't interrupt, Erin. Let me just get it out."

I nodded, chastened.

"I was pretty sick for a while. Two years, in fact. You know, the whole bit, drugs, chemo, radiation. Long story short: I got well. My parents didn't. They were financially ruined by the whole thing. I mean, my father was a forklift driver in a warehouse. He didn't exactly have fabulous, comprehensive health insurance. My mother raised me and my brother, so she brought nothing to the table in terms of money. They had no savings, just a huge fifty-year mortgage on the house. Which they lost. The house, not the mortgage. Two years after my remission, they split. It was just too much for them to handle. My almost dying, the lack of money . . . They were good people but they had no real emotional skills, you know? And nothing to fall back on, no rich parents, no trust funds. They tried, they just . . ."

"It must have been horrible," I mumbled. What does one say?

"I guess . . . I guess I've always felt it was my fault, their getting divorced, losing the house. I mean, intellectually I know I didn't do anything wrong, I didn't ask for cancer. But . . . still, it was because of me that my family fell apart."

"And you've been living with that guilt all these years?" I said. My heart was breaking. "Guilt for something you had no responsibility for? Oh, JoAnne. Have you ever talked to anyone about this, a professional, I mean?"

JoAnne laughed and it wasn't happy. "No. Please. I was too busy catching up in school and working part time as soon as I could to help out at home, and then getting scholarships so I could go to med school because there was no way anyone could help me with tuition. I was always just too—busy. Look, if you keep busy you don't have time to dwell on your problems."

"So they fester. Problems don't go away just because you ignore them."

"Thank you, Dr. Laura."

"That's mean. I brought you donuts."

"Whatever. The point is . . . Okay, I know it sounds weird but hell, I'm spilling my guts so . . . I can't help but feel that if I ever got married and had kids I'd ruin that family, too. I wouldn't do it on purpose—I don't think I would—but I'd ruin it all the same. It's better—and safer—for me to stay single and concentrate on your work."

This was amazing. JoAnne revealing true, deep feelings. I ventured. "Like somehow by keeping other kids alive you're . . . I don't know, healing yourself? Repairing the damage you thought you caused?"

"I haven't thought it all through, Erin, but please, feel free to. Just let me do what I do. I'm fine. I always have been and I always will be."

That point could be debated, I thought, but said nothing. After a long silence in which JoAnne grabbed her bag from the floor, removed every card and scrap of paper from her wallet, examined them, tossed a few, and put the rest back into her wallet—all with what seemed like an enormous amount of concentration—I again ventured to speak.

"Why didn't you tell me this before?" I said.

JoAnne snapped her wallet shut. "Yeah, there's an ice breaker. Hi, my name is JoAnne and I had cancer as a kid. How about you?"

"It wouldn't have gone like that."

"No? And what would you have said? Immediately I'd have been setting myself up as an object of pity. No thanks."

"That's not fair. I would have felt sorry but I wouldn't have pitied you."

"What do you feel now?" JoAnne challenged.

I thought for a minute. "Frankly, a bit hurt you didn't trust me enough to talk to me about this before. Sorry, too. Sorry that you were sick and that you felt you couldn't say anything. I mean, jeez, JoAnne, I've told you about . . ."

"About what?" she snapped. "What's more horrible than a sick kid? Your best friend's making out with your boyfriend in college? Your grandmother's heart attack?"

That was low, even for JoAnne.

"Are you saying my life isn't as valid as yours because I didn't almost die when I was six?"

"No, no. No, of course not. It's just that . . ."

"When will the test results be in?"

"Tomorrow. Or the next day. A friend's pushing them through."

I hesitated. "If . . . if something needs to be done . . ."

"Then it needs to be done. I've researched options. I'll talk to my doctor. I'll do what it takes. What else can I do?"

Tears glittered in JoAnne's eyes but I knew they would not fall.

Chapter Eighteen

Erin—Am back from expedition. Tell yr. father hi for me. M. P.S. how's yr job?

JoAnne's bombshell had given me a lot to think about. That night I begged off going to a movie with Damion and hunkered down with Fuzzer and my thoughts.

I'd never given my breasts much thought, except in terms of how a jacket fitted or a blouse hung because of them. I mean, I'd never consciously associated my breasts with my own sexuality or womanhood. Maybe because I'd yet to have a baby. Maybe because my mother bottle-fed me. Maybe because I'd been told by so many men that my legs were my best physical feature, apart from my smile. Maybe because my Catholic upbringing had condemned the consideration of one's body as other than a faulty vessel for the soul. Whatever.

Now, with JoAnne facing the awful possibility of losing a breast to save her life, I became suddenly aware of my breasts as part of me, as integral to my womanhood—if more for their potential than their current function.

As considering my breasts was still not a particularly comfortable exercise, I allowed my thoughts to drift on to related topics. Women and men; perception and projection; image, reality, and fantasy. Flesh and blood versus fairy tale.

I thought about how not long before I'd made an interesting discovery. Well, it was more that I'd had a revelation, really, a putting together of information in a new way that caused an "Of course," a "Eureka!" in my head. Recently, I'd realized that I was All Women to all men.

And that, quite possibly, every woman was All Women to all men.

What did this say about me? About women? What did this say about men?

Here was my own case: In the years since I turned seventeen, I had been said to look like and/or remind a man of Grace Kelly, Uma Thurman, Goldie Hawn, even the ill-fated Carolyn Bessette Kennedy. God, someone even mistook me for Sissy Spacek a long, long time ago while on line for the bathroom during the intermission of a ballet. Could be why I never quite took to ballet. And, now that I think about it, it was a woman who made the Sissy Spacek observation so that example, thankfully, doesn't count in this scenario.

You remind me of my mother, men say, my teacher, my sister, my grandmother, my first girlfriend.

Again: Was every woman All Women to all men? Were we so fundamentally interchangeable? Were we at once both mythic and unimportant in and of ourselves?

Better minds than mine had pondered these questions.

All I knew is that we found this flattering on the whole, the fact that we were known in some way, that we were recognized, though not for who we really were. Strange.

Fuzzer yawned and shifted in my lap. It's easier for kitties, I thought, isn't it? It's all about hormones and instinct and the simple, ruthless life force.

Yes, it was much harder for humans.

Who would JoAnne be without her breasts? To herself, to her friends, to men? I fervently hoped she would never find out.

* * *

Doug managed to call from a pay phone on Sunday. I couldn't imagine how far and wide he'd had to go to find a working pay phone. I didn't ask. I also didn't ask how he'd gotten my home number.

Looked it up in a phone book, Reason said, clearly bored. Called Information.

How bold! Romance crowed. Not to ask for your number, but just to seize it.

I told him about JoAnne. I figured it was safe as he'd never met her and had no reason to tell anyone else her secret. Besides, I had to tell someone. It was too dark and bothersome a secret to keep inside.

Doug responded with sympathy, and with the promise of concrete help. "Look, Erin, I'm on the endowment committee of my kids' school with a guy who's the best at reconstructive surgery. If it comes to that, let me get your friend in to see him. I know she's a doctor, too, but trust me, this guy's got a waiting list a year long. He owes me, he'll see her quickly."

I was touched. Tears sprang to my eyes.

"Thanks," I choked.

"Hey, don't cry. Come on, we'll deal with this thing. Okay?"

I nodded, but he got the message.

We hung up soon after that. I imagined Doug skulking around outside the bathrooms in a mall, looking over his shoulder for anyone he knew, hoping to get away unnoticed.

He was such a good man.

Two nights later I was sitting on the couch watching *King of Queens*—a secret vice—when the phone rang. I adjusted Fuzzer ever so slightly—he glared anyway—and answered.

"Hello?"

"It's me. The biopsy was negative."

Tears sprung to my eyes and I screamed. Fuzzer glared again.

"Oh, JoAnne, I'm so so so happy! You rule!"

JoAnne laughed. I thought I heard genuine emotion in the laugh.

"God, honey, I am so relieved. I feel . . . I feel like . . ."

"Like this is a turning point? Like you got a new lease on life?"

For a moment, JoAnne didn't answer.

"JoAnne? Are you there?" I asked worriedly.

"Yeah. I am." She hesitated. "Erin, you're right. That is what it feels like. Like I got a big ole wake-up call." JoAnne laughed again, this time more loudly. "And, honey, things are going to change! JoAnne Chiofalo is a new woman!"

"I liked the old woman, but okay, you've got my support. So—what are you going to do first?" I asked, Kevin James and Jerry Stiller long forgotten.

"Celebrate, honey. Meet me at the bar at Mistral in an hour."

"On a school night?" I joked.

"Just be there." JoAnne hung up.

"Well, Fuzzer," I said, rubbing his lovely beige head, "looks like our quiet night at home just got canceled."

Chapter Nineteen

I'd suggested that Abby meet me at my apartment before we had to meet Maggie and JoAnne at Hamersley's. Since she'd started to date my father, I'd avoided most of her calls. I missed Abby but I was also still angry at her on some deep, childish level. Angry at her for stealing away my daddy. But I was not so far sunk in self-pity that I didn't also feel ashamed of this childish anger.

So, I decided it was time I got over it. At least, it was time I pretended to get over it. "Act as if" self-help gurus suggest, and reality will follow. Besides, the more time I spent thinking about Doug Spears, the less time I had to think about Abby and Dad—doing it. I was ready to make peace.

Abby arrived at seven, looking spiffy in a powder blue, knee-length dress with a matching, single-breasted jacket.

"John likes me in blue," she said when I complimented her outfit. Immediately, she clapped a hand to her mouth.

"Oh, Erin, I guess I shouldn't have said that. I'm sorry."

I breathed and said, "Abby, it's okay, really. Can I get you anything?"

Abby sat at the kitchen table, a look of relief on her face. "Seltzer? Erin," she blurted, "it's so hard not to be able to talk to you like old times. I'm afraid that anything I say about—about me and John will be wrong and hurtful. I don't want it to be that way."

So, break up with my father, I answered silently, but suddenly, that didn't sound like the right thing to be thinking.

Abby didn't approve of my interest in a married man. I didn't approve of her interest in my father. The last thing I wanted was for Abby to ride my butt about Doug. So, the last thing I'd do is ride her butt about Dad. I mean, John.

But that didn't mean I couldn't ask for some ground rules. I handed Abby a glass of seltzer and sat at the kitchen table with her.

"Can we make a pact about something? Can we agree not to talk about—uh, the personal stuff between you and—John."

"You mean, sex?" Abby said in a whisper.

I put my hands over my ears. "Oh, God, yes. Please, please don't even say that word. I so swear I'll never ask for any information about—that. Promise me!"

"Of course, Erin. I promise."

"Good. Thanks. Is there anything you want me to promise in return?" I asked. "Apart from—the personal stuff question."

Who knew I was such a royal prude?

Abby thought for a moment before answering. "No. I don't think so. But if I do think of something, I'll let you know. Oh, wait. You could promise not to try to break us up."

"Of course," I said, mildly annoyed. "I promise." What did it matter now? I'd already tried and failed.

The phone rang. I welcomed the interruption.

It was Maggie. We spoke for barely a minute.

I hung up.

"Hmm. That's odd."

"What is?" Abby asked.

"Maggie canceled for dinner. It's the third time she's canceled in the past month."

"Maybe she's just busy. She works really hard, you know."

"No, of course, I know." Still . . . "Abby, do you think she's mad at me?"

"At you? Why, what did you do?"

"Nothing! But I can't help wondering . . . Maybe she's bored with us. Maybe she's found new friends."

Abby rolled her eyes.

"Erin, this is not grade school. Adults don't just drop good friends to hang with a cooler crowd."

"Yeah, you're right. I just hope she's okay. Maybe something's bothering her. Maybe she's sick. Maybe I should ask her . . ."

"I think we should leave her alone. Maggie's a private person, Erin. She'll talk to you when she's ready."

I smiled. "You're right. Sometimes I forget how smart you are."

"Thanks," Abby said. "I think."

A package was delivered to my office from Trident. I picked it up at the receptionist's desk and brought it back to my office. It had to be from Doug.

It was. Inside was a book entitled *Erotic Tales of Ancient Japan.* I opened the cover to find a handwritten inscription. It read:

> *To a woman of wonderful complexity—From her avid admirer.*

I stuffed the book into a drawer of my desk and tried— unsuccessfully—to wipe the telltale grin off my face.

Things had just been kicked up a notch.

JoAnne came by my apartment that evening. She was early. I left her to her own devices while I finished doing some hand laundry in the bathroom sink.

When I returned to the kitchen, she was pacing.

"Uh, have a seat?" I said.

JoAnne ignored me, opened the refrigerator, sighed, and shut it again.

"You want something to drink?" I said. "I'll be ready in a minute. As soon as I feed Fuzzer." The beast was slamming his head into my ankle as I popped the top of a can of Fancy Feast.

"No, I'm fine."

I spooned beef chunks in gravy into a bowl and was about to put the bowl down when—

"Oh, here's news," JoAnne blurted. "Martin dumped me."

"What? Nobody dumps you."

Fuzzer yowled. I gave him his dinner.

"You're the dumper," I said. "You can't dump the dumper."

"Apparently you can," JoAnne replied archly. "Because Martin did. For the first time in my life, I'm the dumpee."

"Well, what did he say? Why did he dump you?"

"Seems I made a huge mistake in telling him about the possibility that I was sick. He couldn't get off the phone fast enough. He said he wasn't good with sick people. And that he felt we'd been getting too involved and that he wasn't ready for a commitment."

"The little prick." I flung the empty kitty food can into the sink. Fuzzer didn't even flinch, so absorbed was he in his dinner.

"Well, I'm not ready for a big commitment, either."

"I don't mean about that," I said. "I mean his running away the second he thought you might need him. The second he thought he might have to hold your hand instead of fuck you. What a weenie!"

"Yeah."

Something about that suddenly dispirited response caught my attention. Then—

"You . . . you cared about him, didn't you?" I said. "Oh, my God, I never knew. JoAnne, I'm so sorry."

JoAnne shrugged dramatically. *"Que sera, sera.* Life goes on; tomorrow's a new day."

"You're taking this rather well." Too well, I thought. It was suspicious.

"Actually," she said, rubbing her temples, "I feel like a day-old chicken part."

"What does a day-old chicken part feel like?"

"Like shit. It feels like shit."

Now, that was more like it.

Fuzzer sped out of the kitchen, bowl empty.

"Do you still want to go out?" I asked.

"Hell, yeah." JoAnne grabbed her bag from the back of a chair. "I'm not dead yet."

We saw a mediocre movie, then went for a quick bite at Joe's American. I was home by eleven; JoAnne had lost steam much earlier than she usually did. I wasn't surprised. Before we parted, she told me she was going to tell Abby and Maggie about the cancer scare, if only to reinforce for them the importance of self-examination. I told her I was proud of her. She grimaced.

When I got home I found a message on my answering machine from Doug.

Hey. It's me. I miss you. I hate not being able to talk to you. . . . Call me first thing Monday, okay? Bye.

The sound of Doug's voice in my home made me smile. And it made me think.

What was it about JoAnne that had attracted Martin? Clearly, it was her strength—or his perception of it—not her vulnerability. It had to have been everything she gave, like sex, and not anything she wanted or needed, like friendship. The moment JoAnne needed support, the moment she needed Martin to be a friend as well as a lover, he'd bailed.

Not for the first time I wondered what exactly it was about me that attracted Doug. Surely, he didn't need the grief and pressure of a girlfriend on the side. If he was choosing me and doing it under less than perfect circumstances, something about me in particular, something about Erin Weston, had to be uniquely necessary to his happiness and fulfillment. It was an embarrassing thought in some way; I wasn't used to considering myself as indispensable to someone.

What drew me to Doug? A million things and yet, nothing I could describe. It seemed futile to try to explain the reasons for an emotional, physical, spiritual attraction. You could make a list of traits—I love him because he's funny—a list of examples from true life—I love him because he rescued that stray puppy—but did any of that ever really touch the magic of an attraction that couldn't be denied? No.

So, I thought, what's the point of even trying to analyze an attraction? Sure, therapists made a lot of money helping people analyze why they married the bums or bitches, the clearly "wrong" others they married. But . . .

I was content to let the truth stand unexplained and unadorned. Truth just is, I told myself. Truth is beautiful. And the beautiful truth was that I loved Doug Spears and though he hadn't ever said the precise words, I knew that Doug Spears loved me.

I slept very deeply that night, and dreamlessly.

Chapter Twenty

Erin—never got photo of you; have you gained weight? Am down to 110 and look fab. M

Friendship is about tolerance. It's also about wearing each other down over time so that there are no hard edges keeping people apart. It's about joy. When it isn't about sacrifice.

Each of us had hobbies or interests that not everyone else shared. Like, JoAnne's devotion to exercise. She went to the gym regularly and when she couldn't get there for some reason, worked out on a machine of some sort at home. Abby, Maggie, and I wouldn't be caught dead going to a gym, each for her own reasons. Wisely, JoAnne had never even attempted to recruit us as gym partners.

Occasionally, though, one of us would get interested in something and urge the others to join in, at least to give it a try. Like Maggie and volunteer work for the Women's Lunch Place. She hadn't fully brought any of us on board, but she was working on it. Or the time I got into bonsai and dragged everyone out to a class at Bonsai West in Littleton. Turned out no one shared my enthusiasm for severe pruning under the hot summer sun. Not even me.

Or the time JoAnne convinced us to go skiing in Vermont for a weekend. None of us—including JoAnne—had ever been on skis, unbelievable as that might sound. The result was less than successful. After fumbling for twenty minutes with the stupid boots, I finally got myself clicked into the skis, fell facedown, and spent the rest of the weekend doing après-ski by the fireplace. Abby's fur parka—once her grandmother's—was stolen. Maggie sprained her ankle while stumbling downhill on the baby slope. And JoAnne? JoAnne—the only enthusiast among us—got called back to Boston two hours after we arrived at the lodge. One of her hospitalized patients had "taken a turn for the worse."

Now, it was Abby's turn for a hobby. Somehow she'd gotten interested in scrapbooking and begged us to come to a home class she was hosting for a friend who was a consultant for Life Expressions, a scrapbook company. Maggie, much to my surprise, said yes, immediately.

"You're worse at crafts than I am," I'd said. "Remember how we met? At that awful wreath-making workshop? Our wreaths were hideous. Even that eight-year-old made a prettier wreath than ours."

Maggie had shrugged. "I don't know. I think it might be interesting. Plus, our being there means a lot to Abby, so . . ."

Well, if Maggie could spend the evening being sold scrapbook stuff by a woman sure to be perky, so could I.

"No way," JoAnne had said. "It's going to be like a Tupperware party and I've paid my dues in that department."

"Tupperware is a good product," I said. I didn't really know that from personal experience but my mother had sworn by it when I was a kid.

"Sorry. You and Maggie have fun, though."

In the end, JoAnne had come with us. The argument that had convinced her was the opportunity to buy Christmas and Hanukkah gifts for her staff in one fell swoop. JoAnne hated malls.

At seven o'clock we gathered at Abby's, a total of twelve

women—none of whom I knew except for Abby, JoAnne, and Maggie. Talk was light and focused on the weather and the big sale at Ann Taylor. After some flavored tea and sugar cookies, Candace Recklet, the Life Expressions consultant, did her thing.

After the pitch—which I have to admit was interesting and well-delivered—we were each given a blank white twelve-by-twelve scrapbook page and some materials and told to get busy. I'd brought a handful of photos I'd taken of Fuzzer. JoAnne had neglected to bring any photos so I gave her three of mine to crop and we moved off to the far end of the table to work. And to talk.

"Our friend Abigail is suffering from a serious Cinderella fantasy," JoAnne whispered, pushing aside a plate of cookies.

"What brought that up?" I asked. "Anyway, aren't we all, to some extent?"

"Speak for yourself, honey. I rescue myself."

I wondered. "You know, sometimes I think I see myself as the prince. The rescuer, I mean."

"Nothing good can come of a woman rescuing a man from himself."

"Who said it's from himself? Maybe it's from, I don't know, a corporate dragon. Pass me a cookie?"

She did.

"Your metabolism amazes me," she said. Then: "Honey, the story is all about Cinderella being rescued from her own life. It's about her being relieved of responsibility and the need to earn a living and the need to think on her own. A rescued woman is bad enough. But a rescued man? Disgusting. A pitiable wretch."

"I see you've thought about this before," I said dryly.

"Of course. Abby is a classic little princess just dying to be swept off her feet and taken care of. And if it happens, she'll be suicidal by forty. And maybe an alcoholic. Most ex-princesses are."

"I think you underestimate Abby. She's not as helpless as

she seems. Besides, she is dating my father. That's a—a good thing. A sign of some maturity," I argued.

"Maybe," JoAnne admitted. "Maybe she has the potential to be her own woman. But she hasn't tapped into that potential yet. Abby should rescue herself from her silly fantasies first, then go out there and find a man. No offense, Erin. I mean, a real man, not a fantasy father-man. He won't be a prince—he might actually work for a living and so will she—but then she won't be miserable for the rest of her life, either."

JoAnne had a point.

"It all comes down to self-respect, doesn't it?" I said, shuffling my photographs around the page. "If you don't respect yourself, then how can you expect someone else to respect you?"

"That and independence."

"Interdependence is healthy." Or so I'd heard.

"To be successfully interdependent you need to be truly independent first," JoAnne corrected. "You need to know your boundaries. You need to be able to spot when someone is crossing his own boundaries and getting too close to yours."

It was beginning to sound as if we were talking about invading armies and international warfare rather than two people in a loving relationship.

"My head is swimming." I said. "Let's change the subject."

"Gladly."

"You used to be fun, you know that?"

I reached for something called a corner rounder and began to snip.

"Honey, I was never fun. Witty, yes. A smart ass, yes. Fun, no. Now, we'd better start making these pages or the kindergarten teacher over there is going to scold us."

"Ladies!" the consultant called. "Let's go around the room and share the work we've done so far. Tell us a bit about the pictures you brought with you tonight?"

There was a general murmur of agreement. It did not come from us.

"Nancy, why don't you start?"

Nancy stood and showed us her page in progress. "These are my two little boys," she said. "They're twins, Jason and Jacob. I took these pictures on their first day of nursery school. Aren't they adorable!"

JoAnne raised an eyebrow at me and whispered, "I've seen cuter."

Maria went next. She had brought pictures of her honeymoon in Barbados.

Maggie passed me a note. It said: "I prefer Europe."

Rebecca had brought pictures of her wedding.

Abby made a subtle face at me. I knew the look. It meant, "Horrible dress."

"And what about you, Erin?" Candace Recklet asked. "What did you bring?"

Show-and-Tell should be outlawed after kindergarten.

I remained seated and very quickly said, "Just some pictures of my cat." What was I supposed to have done? Ask Doug for some pictures of him with his kids and try to pass them off as my own?

"Well, stand up and show us," the consultant said brightly. "I'm sure we'd all love to see them. After all, our pets are important members of the family, aren't they? Especially when we have no other special someones at home."

I felt my face begin to burn. There was no way in hell I would be able to stand up and brag about Fuzzer in front of this group of happy wives and mommies. And how the hell had she known I lived alone? Did I look so obviously lonely?

"Well," JoAnne said, standing, her voice loud and brooking no interruption. "I didn't bring any pictures with me. But if I had, they probably would have been of me and one of the fabulously handsome and wealthy men I date. Maybe Martin and me in Cancun. He looked so yummy in that itsy-bitsy bathing suit. Or Wayne and me at the Plaza in Manhattan.

No man wears a tux like Wayne. He owns three of his own. Or . . ."

"Thank you, thank you," the consultant said, laughing nervously.

Show-and-Tell was over after that. JoAnne shrugged and sat down.

"I owe you one," I said, impending tears going back to where they'd come from. Deep inside.

JoAnne grinned. "No problem. It's what I live for."

In the end, Maggie bought a baby album and wouldn't say why. I bought a wedding album because I wanted to torture myself even further. JoAnne bought a travel album, a practical gift for herself, and several small albums and accessories for her staff. Abby bought everything. Candace Recklet gave us each a business card and packed up her many black bags. I tossed the card in my purse and forgot about it for a long, long time.

Chapter Twenty-one

*E—rmbr to send b-day card to mrs. cirillo. she's
yr godmother, after all. rmbr respect yr elders.
M.*

On a beautiful afternoon in late June, Doug and I went to
the movies. Our first movie together. I told Terry that I had a
dentist appointment and left the office at three. Doug met me
in the lobby of the Loews along the Common on Tremont. It
was risky; someone we knew might see us. But to the outside world we were simply two friends spending time together, nothing illicit about it at all. Or so I tried to convince
myself.

We each paid for our own ticket. That seemed right. Doug
asked if I wanted anything to eat or drink. I shook my head
no.

We sat in the back of the theater, Doug's choice. It was
largely empty. The tension between us was enormous. It was
an entity in and of itself. It was a welcome intruder.

We mocked the pre-preview Hollywood quizzes. We commented on the previews: "I'd see that" or "No way."

And then the lights went all the way down.

Doug's knee touched mine and didn't jerk away. I could hardly breathe. I didn't want to ruin the moment, have him think I was sending a signal for him to move his leg away.

His hand took mine. I squeezed his hand gently.

I can't speak for Doug but I was barely conscious of the movie on the screen, some two-bit comedy we'd chosen because both of us knew our going to the movies wasn't about the movie. Doug's touch, the length of his leg against mine, our hands clasped—I felt almost sick with desire.

When the movie was over and the lights came up, Doug finally released my hand.

"Pretty good, wasn't it?" he said softly.

"Yes," I answered. "It was."

Later, alone at home, with the TV tuned to E!—perfect for when you're in the mood for sound but not for serious listening—I thought about that afternoon. Doug and I definitely had taken another step closer to each other—and closer to a full-blown affair.

Was I really okay with that?

The fact was, I'd never considered seeing a married man. I mean, the notion had never even crossed my mind. How many women, I wondered, actually said to themselves, okay, I think I'll date a married man for a while. Who would choose that path?

Well, maybe a woman who wanted the minimum of commitment and the maximum of freedom, while still having somewhat regular sex.

Even that sounded—odd. So I thought more about it.

Fact: After a while, two single people in a relationship either broke up or got married. But a relationship involving one married partner pretty much precluded the second eventuality. How many married men having affairs actually left their wives to marry their girl on the side? Not many.

So, what would motivate a woman who said she wanted to get married to get involved with a married man?

There was only one answer, I thought. Well, maybe one answer with several parts. Passion. Overwhelming desire. Intense need.

Obsession? No, I didn't like that word. Addiction? To what, danger? Was a woman who would sleep with a married man a thrill-seeker? Huh. I'd never thought of myself as a thrill-seeker but . . .

So, what was it about Doug Spears that overrode the fact of his being married to another woman? Besides his incredible sexual allure, of course.

The answer: Doug made me feel smart and competent. He regularly asked for my input or advice on everything from what to buy the secretaries for Secretaries' Day to the wording of an opening paragraph in a proposal. Sometimes it seemed as if he were the only person in my life at all interested in me. Abby had my father; my father had Abby. JoAnne had the pursuit of a new JoAnne. Maggie had withdrawn from all of us with no explanation.

Except for Fuzzer, Doug was the only person I saw or spoke to or got a message from every day. He was beginning to feel like family.

And family is a powerful thing.

Even when they forget that their daughter's godmother has been dead for over a year.

Still, I held out.

Our conversations—if they merited that term—went something like this:

Me: "I can't do this."
Doug: "Why not?"
"It's wrong."
"Not everyone would agree."
"It will hurt Carol."
"It won't affect her life. I won't let it. She'll never know."
"What if she finds out?"
"She won't."

"What will people say?"

"They won't know, either."

"What if people find out?"

"Screw 'em. It's none of their business. Besides, it would only be a rumor. We'll be careful. No one will see us when we're alone."

"Could I tell my friends?"

"The fewer people who know the better. But do what you have to do."

"No one at work should know."

"Of course."

"What if my boss found out?"

"He can't fire you because of your personal life. And remember, it'll only be a rumor. No one can prove anything."

"I'm scared."

"Of what?"

"I don't know. Everything."

There were slight variations on the theme but the content was always the same: I resisted, Doug persisted; I shied away, Doug pursued; I hesitated, Doug urged a seizing of the moment.

As time passed, my protestations grew weaker, even to my own ears. Doug knew and I knew that it was only a matter of time before I capitulated. Because I wanted so badly to be with Doug Spears. I'd never wanted anything so badly in my life.

I talked to Doug about lots of things. I talked about my father dating my best friend. Cautiously, at first, not spilling the jumble of my feelings about the situation, unsure of the level of conversational intimacy that Doug and I shared. It's not wise to share family trauma with someone you haven't yet slept with. Chances are that if you do, the sex part will never come about.

Here's what he said: "Don't think about it, Erin. Don't

waste your time on something you can't control. Think about yourself. Think about me. Think about us. Think about something you can control."

I couldn't let it go quite that easily. "So, you don't think it's—odd—that my father is sleeping with my best friend?"

"I don't think anything about it," Doug said, taking my hand in his. "I think about us."

Doug and I had dinner at Ginza in Chinatown. We went mad on sushi, which I've always found to be a highly sensuous—and visually beautiful—food. Several cups of sake later, Doug walked me to the corner of Kneeland Street and Harrison Avenue, where I could catch a cab home. He put my arm through his as we walked. I couldn't look at him. Because if I did . . .

Just before we reached the end of the small, alleylike street, Doug kissed me. In one swift motion he stopped us, turned me to him, and kissed me. I kissed him back. It was so simple.

"Why the hell haven't we done that before?" he breathed finally, his mouth at my ear.

There's no turning back, I thought. I felt his erection against me.

"I don't know," I breathed back.

Doug pulled back a bit and looked at me.

"Your lipstick's gone," he said.

"I don't care."

"I like your lips naked."

"Good," I said. "Sake is a good thing."

Doug laughed. "You think that's what gave me the courage to finally kiss you?"

I took his face in my hands. "I don't care what gave you the courage," I said. "Just kiss me again, okay?"

He did.

Ten minutes later I was sitting alone in the backseat of a cab, biting back a shout of happiness.

Chapter Twenty-two

July, Boston

July in New England is nice if you're spending your days at a lake or at the beach. But July in Boston just picks up and runs with late June's haziness, heat and humidity. And let's face it—haziness, heat, and humidity, annoying enough in and of themselves, also call attention to a city's grime and its unfortunate homeless population. Crime goes up in the hot weather. The average, generally peace-loving person begins to understand the impulse to commit random acts of violence.

At least, I do.

The only good thing about July is the opportunity to celebrate Independence Day. I went to a rooftop barbecue and watched the spectacular fireworks display over the Charles. I'm not a flag waver by nature, but I do admit to feeling pretty darned patriotic on the Fourth.

Anyway, one night, just after the Fourth, I met JoAnne, Maggie, and Abby at Jae's, on Columbus Avenue for dinner.

Falling off the edge of caution and into a relationship with Doug had started me thinking more closely than ever about being alone. About being single. About living single. About a married woman like my mother, choosing after over thirty years of marriage to be single, again.

"Do we even think about what it means to be living single?" I said when the wine had been poured. "Not just being single but living it, day after day, month after month, year after year?"

"I do." Maggie. "All the time."

"I don't think I know what you mean, Erin," Abby admitted.

"You know," JoAnne burst out, "I see a couple on a bus or in a theater—that's the worst! What the hell did you buy tickets for if you're not going to watch the show!—and the woman puts her head on the guy's shoulder. Okay, well, news flash, I'm tired, too, okay? But I'm alone and I don't have the option of leaning against someone. So, I've learned how to sit up on my own and how to stay sitting up on my own."

I knew I should keep my mouth shut but the temptation was too great. "So . . . are you saying the woman is weak for leaning against her husband? Is leaning on your husband's shoulder a weakness. Is it wrong?"

"In public, yeah, it's a weakness and yeah, it's wrong because it's insulting and it's showing off in front of women like me who don't have a husband to lean on!"

What?

"That's a little harsh and judgmental, JoAnne," Maggie said. "And self-centered. I hardly think either member of a happy couple is thinking of anyone but themselves."

"I think JoAnne's just jealous," Abby said. "You'll think differently when you've met the right guy."

JoAnne glared. "Don't tell me what I'll think, okay?"

"Look, what if the woman's not tired?" I said. "Maybe leaning on her husband's shoulder is a sign of affection. Are you saying that if you were engaged or married you'd never put your head on your guy's shoulder in public? Ever?"

"What am I, crippled?"

"Can she say that word?" Maggie said, musingly. "Because I don't think she can say that word."

"I've got something wrong with my spine, I need a brace, I can't sit up by myself? What am I, an infant?"

Why was I opening my mouth again?

"We're not talking about the woman going down on her husband in public," I said, "or playing tonsil hockey, or her asking him to carry her over a puddle. We're talking about a small sign of affection. Is all PDA off-limits with you? No holding hands, no linking arms? Just because you can't have it no one else can? That's not a very generous way of thinking."

"Maybe I'm not a very generous person."

"That's crap," I said. "You're a pediatrician. By nature and by profession you help people. You do services for free when the parents are strapped. You're there for your friends when they need you. You . . ."

"Yeah, I'm a regular Florence Nightingale."

"Can we please change the subject?" Abby pleaded. "Living single is too—messy."

I looked sideways at JoAnne and wondered what the hell was wrong with her. She was in a big bad mood, being more than characteristically bitter. Was it all because Martin had dumped her? Had the recent cancer scare opened up some old wounds? I felt I had to ask her to talk to me—but not right then. I was too afraid of being attacked.

However, JoAnne did have something to say and she was about to say it to us all.

"Look, I'm sorry everyone, really. Shit. It's just that I'm pissed at Martin. And . . ." JoAnne took a gulp of water before going on. "And there's something that's been weighing on my mind since that stupid cancer scare. God, I wish I didn't have to . . ."

"You don't have to do anything you don't want to, JoAnne," Abby said helpfully.

JoAnne grimaced.

"What is it?" Maggie asked.

JoAnne began. "I told Erin, right before I got the biopsy results. I had cancer as a kid, okay, and it was bad but I got over it. But it basically destroyed my family and I don't know . . . Lately I've got all these—feelings—running around inside and I don't know what the hell to do with them."

Abby and Maggie each murmured the appropriate murmurs of sympathy.

I risked it. "You said you wanted to make some changes. Maybe a therapist is a good idea."

"Ha. Only as a last resort."

"I could give you a name," Maggie offered.

"No, thanks. I shouldn't have even said anything now, but . . ." JoAnne laughed and shook her head. "I'm so confused lately, I don't know what I'm saying half the time. I should just go home and get on my treadmill, work off some energy."

"JoAnne," Abby said, "are you sure you should be alone?" Lord.

"Why?" JoAnne looked utterly annoyed. "I'm not suicidal. God. Forget I said anything."

JoAnne gathered her things and handed a few bills to me. "For the wine," she said. "See you guys around."

And she was gone.

As had become my habit, that night I spent time curled up in my reading chair, Fuzzer on my lap, an abandoned book at my feet, thinking about Doug Spears.

I couldn't deny I found the very uncertainty of becoming involved with a married man thrilling. It bothered me for about a split second, this fact, and then I pushed aside the concern. For the first time in a very long time I felt alive. Hopeful. Excited.

Who was I to analyze happiness?

A line came to me that night, something from Shelley's play *The Cenci*, something that had been floating around in my head for years. Shelley, the ultimate Romantic man— along with Byron and Keats and even DeQuincy—a precursor to twentieth century rock stars.

Anyway, the line ran:

> *O thou who tremblest on the giddy verge*
> *of life and death*

Aside from the line's context in the play, it seemed to describe the way those Romantics had lived their lives, choosing to be always on the giddy verge of being ostracized from "good" society; on the giddy verge of normal consciousness and altered states of consciousness; on the giddy verge of illicit love.

If uncertainty was a valid way of life for Shelley and his cohorts, I told myself, then it was certainly a valid way of life for me.

The Romantics were nothing but trouble, Reason said dismissively. Rabble-rousers. Rule breakers.

Yes, and they truly lived their lives to the fullest, Romance said, with reverence. Don't you want to do the same?

Yes. I did.

Chapter Twenty-three

There's a green market on Tuesdays and Fridays from about mid-June through mid-November, along the south side of Copley Square, across from the Fairmont Copley Plaza Hotel and a stone's throw from Trinity Church.

It's a nice place to go during lunch hour even though everyone else in the area has the same idea, from other thirty-something corporate types; to Cambridge-style leftover hippies in their sixties; to tiny, ancient Asian women pushing metal shopping carts full of plastic bottles and aluminum cans; to tourists in well-pressed shorts and matching wary expressions. There's a fair amount of elbow technique required to get to the produce itself and a good set of lungs is necessary to get your bags of goodies weighed and paid for. Having somewhat bony elbows and extraordinarily good lungs, I'm in and out of the market in minutes.

Fresh-baked breads, focaccia, and sticky buns from Iggy's; amazing goat and feta cheese from Crystal Brook Farm, a local, husband-and-wife-run enterprise; in late July, butter and sugar corn makes its long-awaited appearance along with bunches of pungent basil which I make into pesto to freeze and enjoy all winter long, ripe red tomatoes, and bright green beans. It's enough to make anyone want to kiss good-bye to city life and run off to Green Acres. Sort of.

For me, a noontime visit to the market is usually followed by a quick stop at Marshall's. First, a rapid eye-run through the shoes; then, up the escalator to check out clothes, lingerie, and household items, like funky picture frames and seriously discounted sheets and towels. The purchase of novelty shoes and sandals, especially when purple and under $24.99, is a marvelous Friday pick-me-up.

Of course, these midday excursions only happen once every two weeks at most. Lunchtime for me usually means a scarfed sandwich at my desk, one hand typing madly, the other shoving tuna salad into my mouth. Marshall's stock is still fine after six o'clock, though the green market's pickings are by then pretty slim. A worm-chewed ear of corn. A partly squished tomato. And only one sad loaf of whole wheat bread. I'd rather starve than eat whole wheat bread. It's the potato-leek focaccia, the olive rolls, even the simple boules that make my day.

But not my father. Whole wheat is one of his all-time favorites. He's been known to eat half a loaf for breakfast, toasted with lots of butter. A fact I'd bet he never mentions to his doctor.

I bought a loaf of whole wheat bread at the Iggy's stand and headed for Davis, Weston and Dean, the law firm of which my father was a founding partner, located on the twenty-fifth floor of the Hancock Tower on Clarendon Street.

The firm's receptionist greeted me with a slightly puzzled smile.

"Hi, Ms. Leonard," I said, choosing to ignore her puzzled smile. "Is my father available? I'll only be a moment."

"Oh, I'm sorry Ms. Weston," she said. Was that a look of guilty conspiracy on her usually bland face? "Mr. Weston is not in the office today."

Panic took hold. "Is he okay? Did he call in sick?"

Now Ms. Leonard looked slightly awkward. "No, no, he's just—taking the day off."

This was suspicious. My father never just took the day off. Maybe he was at the hospital having an emergency procedure he didn't want to worry me about. Maybe . . .

"I'm sure you can reach him on his cell phone, if you really need to speak with him," Ms. Leonard said helpfully.

"He's not home?" I blurted.

Now Ms. Leonard looked extremely uncomfortable. What was she hiding? Why was I making her so nervous?

"Um, no," she said slowly. "Um, Mr. Weston is spending the day in Newport with a friend."

About a second later it hit me.

Duh! I was such an idiot. Of course, Dad was in Newport with Abby. And neither had told me . . .

Well, Reason said, they are grown-ups. They don't have to report their every move to you.

But . . .

But what? Reason interrupted. Do you tell Abby and John every time you and Doug snatch a few hot and heavy moments together? Do you?

That's different, Romance protested. She . . .

"Ms. Weston? Are you all right?"

"Huh? Oh, yeah. Sure. Sorry."

Oh, please stop the blushing, I begged my cheeks.

"It's very warm out today isn't it?" Ms. Leonard said suddenly. She was obviously embarrassed for me. It was so humiliating.

I know I should have been happy that Dad had someone who cared about him, someone genuinely nice. But—I wasn't. Not completely. The disturbing thought came to me that maybe I'd wanted to be the one to care about him. Not in any romantic way, of course, but . . . My mother had been number one; maybe it was my turn to be number one . . . Oh, my thoughts were too tumbled and downright disturbing to deal with right then.

Maybe JoAnne had been right, back at the Barking Crab, when she'd said I'd be jealous of my father's girlfriend.

I'd think about that later. Now, I had to say and do something or Ms. Leonard would be calling the men in the white coats. You know, the ones with the straightjackets.

Think, Erin. I couldn't leave the bread at the office; it would go stale or be eaten by mice over the weekend. I could have given it to Ms. Leonard but . . . No. I couldn't admit I'd brought my father a loaf of bread; it would make me seem so pitiful. Or was it pitiable? Anyway, I considered dropping off the loaf at his place but that notion was immediately shoved aside by the fear of what I might find when I got there.

I don't remember the next few minutes clearly. But somehow I took my leave of Ms. Leonard and found myself back on the sidewalk. It was almost one-thirty, high time to get back to work. I headed toward the office.

You could give the bread to one of your coworkers, Reason suggested. You could drop it off at the Women's Lunch Place. You don't want to waste money—or food.

I could, yeah. Or, I thought, a surge of anger momentarily blurring my vision, I could just throw it the fuck away.

Which I did.

The day wasn't a total disaster. Just as I got home, the phone rang.

It was Doug. He was in his car, on his cell phone, heading home to Newton for the weekend.

"Hey. It's me."

Through the inevitable static and fuzz, I knew his voice. Who else in my life was "me" ? Well, certainly no other man. Certainly not my father. Anymore.

"Hey," I said happily. It seemed enough.

"I just wanted to wish you a good weekend."

"You did that an hour ago," I said. "When you left a message at the office. Sorry I missed your call, by the way."

Doug laughed. "That's okay. I just had to hear your voice once more before Monday."

"I'm glad. I hope your weekend is good," I said, aware that that hope was partly false. Would a good weekend include loving sex with Carol, Doug's wife and the mother of their children? A horrible thought.

But I loved Doug, even if I wasn't ready to admit that to him. I did want him to be happy.

I just felt so alone.

I just wished he could be happy with me.

"It'll be the usual," he said neutrally. "But I'll be thinking of you so I'll survive. Barely."

"Survive," I ordered. "I'm seeing you on Monday."

"Okay. I should go."

"Okay. Bye. Thanks for calling."

"My pleasure," said Doug and signed off.

Doug Spears had to love me, I concluded. To put his marriage on the line, to risk losing the domestic life he'd built, to risk losing his children, God, he had to love me so thoroughly, need me so deeply . . . The strength of his desire was an aphrodisiac. It made me feel like the most powerful woman in the world. His relentless pursuit—both romantically and professionally—went to my head and I was his.

I thought about possession.

To be possessed—with a thought, by a thought. To allow possession of oneself. To be a possession.

I thought of me and Doug Spears.

Was I betraying basic, hard-won feminist principles by wanting to be completely possessed by a man?

No, Romance argued. No you're not, Erin. You're freely choosing the state of possession.

No one freely chooses anything when they're in a state of compulsion, a state of obsession, Reason countered.

She loves him, Romance said. She wants to be his. He completes her. He is her soul's other half. He gives her life. He . . .

He's a power junkie, Reason spat, and he's got Erin so turned around she doesn't know what she really wants. She says one thing and does another. Where's the sanity in that? There's no room for responsible decision making in this scenario. She's a puppet and he's the puppetmaster. She only

makes a move when he says so and even then the move is totally orchestrated. That's ownership. That's wrong.

Hey, I protested, wait a minute. That's not how it is!

Isn't it? Reason demanded.

Romance cried, No! You just don't understand!

Reason said, Obviously not, and was not heard from again
for a long, long time.

Chapter Twenty-four

E—the 10th would have been my 34th wedding anniversary—or 35th? Just remembered! Hope all's well. Marie

For the record: I did not mention to anyone that I knew about Abby's day trip to Newport.

Brunch that Sunday was quite interesting.

"You know," Abby said when we were settled and had ordered, "I was thinking about what Erin said. About living single. I think living single means . . . learning to eat meals alone."

Maggie looked at Abby with real curiosity. "You actually eat meals when you're alone? Not just chips out of the bag and ice cream out of the container?"

"Well, sure, I try . . ."

"See, I can't do that," Maggie said. "It doesn't feel legitimate to be making a meal for myself. I mean, who am I that I should go to the trouble?"

"As for me," I said, "I've got things to do. I've got no time to waste and no one to impress. I'm hungry? Give me a block of jalapeno cheddar, I'll nuke it, tear open a bag of Tostitos and I'm set."

"You're just lazy."

I grinned. "There is that. But seriously: Does getting married mean learning how to eat meals together every single night? What if you just don't feel like eating dinner? Do you lose your independence so thoroughly that you can't even eat a half gallon of mint chocolate chip for dinner if you want to?"

"You know what this is all about, don't you?" JoAnne said. "Vegetables. You hate vegetables. And a meal implies vegetables. Protein, starch, and vegetables. Chicken you're okay with, potatoes, fine, but spinach? Broccoli? Turnips? Uh uh."

"I like turnips," I protested. "And parsnips. Especially if they're mashed with lots of butter."

"Being married is like being home again with your parents," Maggie said darkly and mostly to herself. "There's always someone watching you, judging you . . ."

"I'd love a man to cook for me," Abby said. "I think it's sexy."

"But when you want to pig out you definitely don't want a man to see you," I said. "How can you pig out when you're married unless he's away on a business trip or something? You need privacy and time to hide the empty cartons."

JoAnne laughed. "Oh, yeah, living single has its high points. It raises the art of eating disorders to a whole new level."

"I like to watch the chefs on the food network," Abby said. "I think Emeril Lagasse has the cutest smile! Bobby Flay is a bit too freckly for me, but . . . Oh, Tyler Florence, he's very handsome, and Jamie Oliver, well, I wouldn't totally mind seeing him naked . . ."

"Are you going to be okay over there?" I said, grinning.

"Abby's a Food Network groupie!" JoAnne laughed.

"Well, it's better than being a groupie of some scuzzy rock band. Like—Aerosmith."

"Okay, I'll give you that," Maggie said. "That anorexic look never did anything for me. Back when I cared."

"Living single means . . ." I said, back to the original subject.

Maggie: "No fight over the clicker."

"You could just buy a second TV," JoAnne pointed out.

"True."

"Living single means: No spontaneous sex," I said. "With someone other than yourself, that is."

"How many married couples do you know who are getting it more than once every two weeks?" JoAnne raised her eyebrows. "Not many, I can assure you."

"How do you know?"

"The parents of my patients talk. Sometimes the patients do, too. It's amazing what kids overhear . . ."

"No shaving cream all over the mirror." That was Abby.

I laughed. "Oh, my God, like you don't get toothpaste all over the sink? I've seen you brush your teeth. It's like spin art when you're finished."

Abby pouted. "Okay, well, how about: Living single means no one to hold your hand in the middle of the night when you wake up screaming from a nightmare."

JoAnne and I shared a look; I let her take the answer. "Have you ever tried to wake a guy up in the middle of the night when you're not promising sex? It doesn't work. It's something about the physiology of the male ear . . ."

"No one to hear you fart in your sleep." Maggie, of course.

"I have no rebuttal to that one," JoAnne said. "Pardon the unfortunate pun."

My turn. "Living single means: No steady vacation partner. That's a bummer."

"True." JoAnne regarded us all. "Let's face it, a woman will almost always dump her girlfriends for a guy. Girlfriends are backups when there's a man around."

"That's wrong," Abby said forcefully.

"But it's true. We should be more selective but we're not. We should honor our friendships but we don't."

"It's hard, living single," I said. "I mean, it's hard being single, but the actual living of it . . . I get so tired sometimes.

I just don't want to have to do everything myself. I just don't want to have to try so hard all the time."

"It could be worse, Erin," Maggie said. "You could wind up marrying a guy who makes you feel even more alone than you ever did when you were single."

Was that what my mother had felt with my father, I wondered, more alone than when she'd been single? Was that why she'd gone?

"True."

"Don't you think you can tell that sort of thing about a guy before you marry him?" Abby said.

JoAnne rolled her eyes. "Have you taken a look at the latest divorce stats?"

Maggie nodded. "You don't know what it's like being married to someone until you're married to that someone. You can make a few educated guesses before the wedding but there's a whole lot of unknown to come."

"Since when did you become an expert on marriage?" JoAnne asked.

I pretended to be highly interested in my leek and goat cheese salad, determined not to betray Maggie by word or look.

"I suppose there's no point in keeping it a secret any longer."

I looked up, startled.

"You're married!" Abby cried.

"No! God. I was married, a very long time ago. In grad school."

"What happened?"

"It didn't work out."

"Well, we gathered that," JoAnne drawled. "Why didn't it work out? Details, please."

Maggie blushed furiously. "I . . . We weren't compatible. And he really wasn't the marrying kind after all."

"He cheated on you?"

Maggie laughed dryly. "Many, many times. When I finally

caught him with one of my so-called friends, I got up the nerve to leave."

"Wow," Abby said. "This is unbelievable. I feel like . . . like you're an entirely different person from the Maggie I knew five minutes ago."

"Don't say that, it's not true! I'm the same as I always was. For better or worse."

"But you have all this experience we knew nothing about," Abby persisted. "All we talk about is getting married and you've already been married! That's amazing!"

Maggie eyed me. "This is why I didn't want to tell anyone."

"Wait, Erin knew?" Abby squealed.

I nodded.

"And you kept it a secret? Impressive." JoAnne.

"Look, Abby, I don't know much more about marriage than you do," Maggie went on. "We weren't married for long and it was a disaster from the start. I did learn a lesson or two but they're not the kind of lessons I want any of my friends to have to learn. Okay? So, now that you know, let's not talk about it anymore. Please?"

"No white dress, huh?"

"Nope. Not even a cheap bouquet from a Korean market. He was supposed to bring it to the courthouse and forgot."

"That's sad." Abby sighed. "Okay, I won't ever bring it up."

"Me, neither, honey," JoAnne said, patting Maggie's hand.

Maggie gave an odd sort of laugh. "Whew. Glad that's over."

So was I. My life was full enough of secrets and deceptions.

Doug and I met Monday after work at Brasserie Jo for drinks before he had to drive back to Newton.

I had something specific on my mind.

It seemed odd to me that so far, Doug had never really

talked about his wife. Odd because I'd always assumed a married man making advances toward a woman not his wife was supposed to talk about said wife—as in, "My wife doesn't understand me," or "My wife is a shrew."

But Doug hadn't said a word about his wife, except once or twice to mention her name in passing. It was as if he were single himself. Or maybe it was that his wife was so small a part of his life she didn't deserve mention. Or maybe it was that she really didn't understand him and they'd grown so far apart he virtually forgot about her once he got into his Lexus every morning for the commute to work.

It wasn't that I was hoping to hear nastiness about Doug's wife. At least, I admired Doug's not bad-mouthing her. But I was puzzled. Who was this woman at home in Newton? And why didn't she seem to matter to her own husband?

No longer being the shy, retiring type with Doug, I asked him the big question that evening. We were alone in the bar area, seated at a tiny table, sipping glasses of Merlot.

"Why don't you ever mention your wife?"

If I'd thought he'd be taken aback, I was wrong.

"Because she doesn't have anything to do with you."

"But I'm . . . we're . . . what are we doing, anyway?"

"Flirting. We're drawn to each other. We want each other."

"You're sure of yourself."

"In this case, yes, I am."

"Okay, but . . . I guess I want to know what's wrong with your wife. What's wrong with your marriage that you're here with me like this?"

Doug said nothing for a moment. Then: "Erin, you've never been married, right?"

"No, but I've been through a divorce."

Doug's smile was weak.

"Sorry," I said, and took a sip of wine.

"I made a mistake, Erin. I married the wrong woman. There's nothing wrong with Carol. But I'm not in love with her. I love her, of course, and I take care of her and the kids, but she's not my soul mate. Not by a mile."

"Then, why?" I persisted. "Why did you marry her?"

"Honestly? She was nice. I was lonely. It seemed maybe a solution to—something. I was young. My friends from college were all getting married. It's a typical story, Erin. I'm just like the majority of married men. Marriage is no big romance. It's just—settling down."

"That's wrong," I said fervently. "That's what I've tried so hard to avoid doing."

"And you've been successful. What can I say, Erin? You're smarter than I am. And now you're still free to make a choice."

I thought about that.

"And you're not free to? It seems to me that's what you're doing with me, making a choice."

"Fair enough."

"So," I said, for lack of anything smarter to say. Where did this conversation—where did we—go from here?

"So, Carol doesn't love me in the way I need to be loved. She can't. It's not who she is. I don't blame her for it."

But he's punishing her for it, Reason hissed. He's punishing her for his mistake in marrying her. Can't you see that?

Oh, that's not it at all, Romance whispered back. Now that he's finally found his soul mate, he can't just let her go. Now that he's met Erin, life has new meaning for him. He can't just stick his head back in the sand.

And neither could I.

Chapter Twenty-five

That Wednesday, at about three in the afternoon, I got an interesting call at the office.

"Hello?"

"Hi, it's Maggie."

"Hi, what's up?"

Maggie was not a big fan of the phone. A call from her meant that something was definitely "up."

"Well, I know it's kind of last minute, but I'm going to Paris on Sunday."

This was news.

"You're kidding! Why? Well, okay, stupid question, it's Paris. What made you decide to go now? Are you going alone? Is it a trip through MIT?"

Maggie laughed but it sounded forced.

"One question at a time. Yes, it's sort of a trip through—work. And I'm going now because the airfares are dirt cheap. The airlines are desperate to get people to fly. And one of my—colleagues—is coming along."

"That's nice. Who?"

"Who?"

Hmm. Curiouser and curiouser.

"Yeah, who?"

"Oh, you don't know—Dr. Bruce," Maggie said dismissively. "Just a—colleague."

"Well, gosh, I hope you have a fabulous time . . ."

"It'll be mostly work stuff," Maggie interrupted. "Look, Erin, I've got to go. I'm running off to WLP. I just wanted to let you know I wouldn't be around till next weekend. Tell the others?"

"Maggie, it's only Wednesday, I'm sure I'll—"

"Thanks. I'll call you when I get back, okay?"

"Okay," I said, very puzzled by my friend's obvious discomfort. What was she hiding? "Bon voyage."

And Maggie was gone.

> *Erin—sorry haven't written. have been sick, malaria, ok now. don't worry. don't tell yr. father. spare any $? med bills pile up. hope you're ok. m.*

It was time.

Doug and I had already kissed, more than once and with increasing intensity. It was clear the passion was there. I wanted to have sex with Doug Spears. I felt as if I would go crazy if we waited a moment longer.

I was ready.

I made the decision. Or the very fact of Doug Spears made it for me. Maybe I had no part in choosing. He was my fate. He came into my life and our tale was already told. It had only been a matter of time.

It was hardly the setting I'd imagined.

Trident's offices were located in the Prudential Center, on the forty-ninth floor of the tower. As a bigwig, Doug had a massive office, complete with couch and minibar.

We made love for the first time in Doug's office. On the big brown leather couch. Handily, Doug also kept a blanket in his office for midafternoon catnaps. No point in staining nice leather.

Everyone had long gone home or to dinner or wherever everyone went at the end of the workday. Doug and I had grabbed a bite at Radius—the site of our first sort-of date—and strolled through the Commons for a bit, arm in arm, dangerously tempting fate and risking discovery. At seven-thirty, we headed for Trident.

We had to sign in at the building's after-hours reception desk. Mac, the security guy, knew me from my increasingly frequent daytime visits to Trident's offices.

"Burning the midnight oil?" he quipped as Doug wrote our names and the time of our entry in Mac's ledger.

"Ha!" I was mortified. Mac had to know what we had come back to the office to do.

"Big presentation next month," Doug said calmly, looking Mac square in the eye. "You'll probably be seeing a lot of us."

Maybe Doug had given Mac some sort of guy signal—one that said, Ask no questions and we'll tell you no lies—because Mac looked away and mumbled, "Sure, sure."

Doug and I walked to the elevator bank.

"You okay?" Doug asked.

I nodded. But no, I was not okay. I was about to pass out. Would Doug grab me in the elevator? Would my clothes be half off by the time we reached the forty-ninth floor?

"What if someone else is up there?" I whispered.

"Mac would have told us."

"How do you know?"

"He would have told us."

Okay.

The elevator opened and we stepped into the car. Doug didn't grab for me. I didn't grab for him. We stood silently, looking into each other's eyes. It was not something I'd ever really done, looked calmly and deeply at a lover, as he did the same to me. It was exhilarating, intimate in a way that drove me to a pitch of desire I thought would knock me over.

The forty-ninth floor. Silently, we stepped off the elevator. Doug took my hand and we walked—we didn't run—down the long carpeted hallway to his private office. Through the blood beating in my ears I listened for voices and other telltale signs of occupation and heard none.

At the door of Doug's office he turned to me. "Okay?" he said.

I nodded.

And we closed the door behind us.

I lay in bed that night and remembered. I remembered every moment of our time together, every inch of his skin, every word breathed into my ear.

In spite of the less-than-romantic setting, I had never had sex that good. Not just sex, though, the whole thing, the entire experience, the need and desire and how we looked at each other and how I was completely unaware of anything but the two of us. It was spectacular.

What a cliché, I'd always thought. It just doesn't happen, the world shrinking to encompass only the two lovers, time seeming to stand still, the moment seeming eternal, comprising past, present, and future. Please. Spare me. What did John Donne and Emily Dickinson and John Keats and all those other dead poets I'd studied in college think they were trying to pull? Okay, their use of language was beautiful but what fantasies were they creating, what lies were they perpetuating? How could real life ever touch the splendor of poetry?

Well, it had for me that night. And it had changed everything.

Chapter Twenty-six

Still, in spite of the earth-shattering experience of sex with Doug, life went on much as usual. My life apart from Doug.

I sent what money I could spare to my mother, after frightening myself silly by going on-line to learn just how dangerous malaria could be.

I spoke to my father once a week, less than before he'd started to date Abby.

I went to work and generally stayed later than anyone else. I watched TV and read books. And I saw my friends, though I didn't say a word about what was going on between Doug Spears and me.

We four women had had tickets to the Red Sox vs. the Seattle Mariners game at Fenway Park for months now. And there was no reason for me not to go as the game was on a Saturday, not a time during which I could be with Doug. Because Maggie was in Paris, I offered her ticket to Damion. He accepted.

"This is the life," I said. "Who's better than us, huh? Sun, sausages with onions, beer." It was maybe the best day of my life. Of the summer, anyway. Of the days not spent with Doug.

"Weak beer," Damion said, sneering at his cup.

"I'll buy you a real beer later. As I was saying, a nice breeze, girlfriends, big men in tight pants. Big men running and crouching. Big men with great butts. I mean, this is great."

Just because I was madly in love with Doug, didn't mean I was dead to the presence of attractive male bodies. In fact, in a way, Doug had sexualized the world for me. He was the core and base of my sexuality and through him, the world had suddenly come alive with sexual energy.

"How can you eat those things?" JoAnne nodded at my sausage.

"Easy. Open mouth, insert sausage, bite, chew, swallow. I've been doing it since I had teeth."

"Just don't come running to me when there's a hole in your stomach the size of a hubcap."

"I think my nose is burning." Abby touched the tip of her nose with one thin finger. "Is my nose burning? I put on lots of sun block before I left the house so I don't know why my nose would be burning. But it feels like it is. Does my nose look red?"

"No, but it's going to if you don't shut up." JoAnne flipped a small tube into Abby's lap. "Here. Use some of my block."

Abby peered at the tube. "Oh. It's only SPF 15."

"Put on two layers."

"I don't think it works that way," Abby said worriedly. "I don't want to be all red when I see John tonight."

"Here." Damion took off his baseball cap and handed it to Abby. "Wear this, too."

Abby held the cap by the very tip of the brim, like it was a dangerous or very icky wild animal. "Uh, thanks, Damion. But, well, it's really not my style. It looks good on you, though!"

Damion rolled his eyes and snatched back his cap.

I laughed. Life was good.

* * *

Doug was full of small but lovely surprises in those first weeks. When I got to work one morning there was a white paper bag sitting on the receptionist's desk. It had been delivered from—and prepaid for—Au Bon Pain. Heather gave me an odd look as she handed it to me.

"Oh, yeah," I said idiotically, "I almost forgot. I . . . I had my breakfast, uh, sent ahead."

What? I dashed off to my office and opened the bag. Inside was a cup of black coffee, an Asiago cheese bagel, toasted with butter—my favorites—and a note.

> *E.—Thinking of you this morning. Think of me?*
> *D.*

There were more flowers. There were messages on my answering machine when I arrived home after saying goodbye to Doug under cover of darkness.

> *Erin, I miss you already and you just walked away.*

Simple, sweet gestures. Like Doug's first tangible gift to me. We met for lunch on the terrace overlooking the bay behind the Boston Harbor Hotel. It was like being on vacation for an hour—white sailboats and yachts, bright blue sky, sun glinting off the water, everybody in sunglasses, men shedding jackets, women in sleeveless dresses. It was a place where you could easily feel alone amidst the crowd of other diners.

When we had ordered, Doug took a small but chunky box from his pocket. It was wrapped inexpertly in shiny blue paper.

"Here," he said, placing the box on the table before me. "It's your birthday present."

I grinned, inordinately thrilled.

"But my birthday is in January. It's months away."

"But I missed your last birthday."

"But you didn't even know me then."

"Allow me my pleasures. Go on, open it."

I did. Usually, I tear open packages, destroying the wrapping in the process. This time, I carefully broke open the tape in an effort not to ruin the paper. It would be saved, like every other tidbit associated with Doug. Souvenirs of our first heady days.

A box. Inside was a large lucite ring, the kind that never really loses popularity, the kind that used to be sold in the candy stores of my youth for loose change and that are now sold in museum shops and fancy gift shops for considerably more money.

It was largely translucent with shafts of pink and purple and violet shot through. The top of the ring was shaped like a heart. It was a heart plateau.

There was no way the ring would ever fit under a glove. It was a whimsical ring for whimsical occasions. It was gorgeous.

"I love it!" I said, laughing.

Doug ran his finger along my cheek.

"I wanted to give you something special. Right now I can't give you the kind of ring I want to give you, so . . ."

Oh, God, he'd really wanted to give me an engagement ring. . . .

"Oh, Doug, it's beautiful. You make me so happy I can't stand it."

"Try to."

And I did.

For about ten days I kept the official start of my relationship with Doug—which I considered our first full sexual encounter—a secret from my friends. But I couldn't keep quiet any longer. I was dying to tell—not details but the fact that I was in love. The fact that Doug was in love with me. I just knew he was.

I met JoAnne, Maggie, and Abby for dinner at Dish, a small, cozy place in the South End. It was a lovely evening and there's not much traffic on Shawmut at that end of the street, so we took a table on the sidewalk.

I decided to dive right in.

"Well, I know you won't approve, but . . ."

"But you're sleeping with that married guy," JoAnne blurted. "What's his name? Dirk Spiral?"

"Doug Spears. And how did you know!"

"Oh, come on, Erin," JoAnne said. "You're so transparent!"

"I am?" This was news.

"And none of us has seen you since the Red Sox game," Abby pointed out. "You've been 'busy' every time we've gotten together."

"I'm sorry guys, really. But Doug and I have to grab what time we can. It's not like . . . like . . ."

"Like a normal relationship?" Abby said unhelpfully.

"See, I knew you wouldn't approve."

"It doesn't matter what we think, honey," JoAnne said. "It's your life and nobody has a right to tell you what to do."

"That's right. You're an adult," Abby said helpfully.

"Yeah, sound of body if not of mind." Maggie cringed. "I'm sorry, Erin. I think you're making a big mistake but I'm here for you if you need me."

"You mean, when she needs you," JoAnne amended. "Because you will need us, honey. There's no way having an affair with a married man is going to be a smooth ride. Unless you're looking for a little excitement and drama. Tell me, do emotional pain and trauma turn you on?"

"God, no!" I protested. "I just . . . I wish my friends wouldn't judge me."

"We're not judging you," Abby insisted. "Really. We're just worried."

"And expressing our concern," Maggie added.

"Right. Erin, none of us is perfect. We've all made mistakes and . . ."

"It's not a mistake, JoAnne," I insisted. "It's not. I know

Doug. I know what I'm doing. If you can't be happy for me, then . . ."

"Then we'll keep our mouths shut," Maggie said firmly, with a stern look at JoAnne and Abby. "Now, let's order. I'm starved."

"Thanks, Maggie. I'll be just fine. I will."

JoAnne patted my hand. "Of course you will. Now, let's see. A bottle of wine?"

At least.

"So," Abby said brightly, "when do we get to meet this person?"

Okay. Here was something I hadn't considered yet.

JoAnne laughed. "Abby, you don't meet your friend's married lover. It's a secret fling, remember?"

"Doug might want to meet my friends," I said, knowing as I spoke that he would not. Why would he? To get to know me better by meeting others I loved. Yes, that was a good reason, but . . .

"Why would he want to meet us?" Maggie said. "He's got to suspect your friends don't approve of him. No woman can approve of a cheater."

"Please don't be so judgmental," I begged. "He's not a bad person. Would I be involved with a bad person?"

Silence. Then: "Honey, again, we've all made mistakes."

"Oh, God," I cried, "I should have just kept my mouth shut about the whole thing."

The rest of the evening was tainted with—sadness. My being with Doug had somehow driven a wedge between me and each of my friends. It had set me apart from them in a more definite way than any "legitimate" relationship would have.

In the midst of chatting friends, diners, and passersby, I felt terribly, terribly alone.

Chapter Twenty-seven

August, Boston

August in Boston is brutal. End of the discussion. Okay, it's not as bad as, say, Charleston, South Carolina, where the temperature doesn't fall below one hundred degrees until well after dark.

But I don't live in Charleston, I live here, in Boston. And to me, August in Boston is horrid.

Maggie had invited us all over to see her pictures from Paris. As Maggie does not have a reputation for being a good photographer—and the fact that she has no air conditioner, only a loud, cheap-o fan—I, for one, was not really looking forward to the event.

The things we do for our friends.

At the last minute, Abby had called to cancel; she claimed a sore throat but I wondered. So the three of us sat around Maggie's comfortable but shabby living room. I chose the floor. I thought I'd seen something move in the corner of the couch.

"Lights, please," Maggie cried.

JoAnne turned off the lamp next to her chair.

With very few exceptions, slide shows are notoriously boring, whether in a classroom or in a living room. Maggie's was not one of the exceptions. After thirty unprofessional, unfocused, and slightly blurry shots of landmarks and pigeons, I was ready to explode.

"Maggie?" I said. "How come there are no pictures of people?"

"There's one of me," Maggie protested.

"Yeah, of your left elbow. I mean, why aren't there any pictures of your face? And of—what's the name of the friend who went with you?"

"Colleague. I told you, she's a colleague, not really a friend. Dr.—Bruce. That's her name. Don't wear it out!" Maggie chuckled lamely.

JoAnne gave me a look. It said: Maggie is one odd chick.

"Well, did you two get along?" she asked Maggie

"Fine. Yeah. I mean, we got along okay. You know."

Well, I for one did not know. But . . .

"Nice shot of the Eiffel Tower," I lied.

"Thanks. I'm really proud of that one."

The evening went on in much the same manner through four hundred bad slides, very bad wine, a slightly moldy tub of onion dip, a box of stale crackers, and the ineffectual whir of a fan.

The things we do for our friends.

When sex was not an option—for example, when someone else was staying late at Trident or when Doug had a commitment at home in Newton—we kissed. Doug and I spent a lot of time kissing, often in the backseat of cabs, sometimes in movie theaters, between the stacks in the big public library, once even behind a grimy old stone pillar in a ratty little church.

When Doug and I kissed it was—well, like nothing I'd ever experienced. Physically, a kiss is pretty much a kiss, and the act of kissing has a limited range of possibilities. It wasn't as if Doug had invented a hitherto impossible way in which to curl his tongue or anything. What was so different and overwhelming about our kissing was the emotional force in it, the psychological force behind it, in short, the sense that I was annihilating Doug and that he was annihilating me, destroying each other because we had to, each giving permission to the other for obliteration.

Well, that falls short of accurately describing what went on when our lips and tongues met. And at the time I kept this kind of intimate information to myself. Partly, because I was afraid of JoAnne's mockery—"Annihilation? Obliteration? Oh, yeah. Sounds real appealing, honey. Ever think of trying your hand at writing romance novels? The S&M kind?"—and of Abby's concern—"Erin, um, maybe you should talk to a therapist about this—kissing. It doesn't sound very, well, healthy."—and of Maggie's keen questioning—"How do you know what Doug's thinking while he's kissing you? Have you discussed this obliteration thing with him?"

And mostly because I *wanted* to keep such information to myself, treasure it, gloat over it in secret, like Gollum gloated over his Precious.

"I've got the kevorka."

"What?" Maggie said.

JoAnne threw her bag onto the table and plopped into the empty chair.

The four of us had met for dinner at M. J. O'Connor's, an Irish pub.

"The lure of the animal," I explained.

"Again: What?"

"Oh, never mind," JoAnne said, waving her hand.

"Who's been following you today?" I asked.

"Every man over the age of fifty-five has been pawing at me with his eyes since I left my house this morning. I'm not safe on the streets, I swear. Is that bartender looking at me?"

"Thank goodness your patients are children," Abby said.

"Some of them have older fathers," JoAnne said darkly. 'Don't get me started on Mr. Price."

"Again, for the second time: Explain kevorka."

"It's a thing from Seinfeld," I said.

Maggie rolled her eyes. "Of course. Why wouldn't it be?"

While JoAnne regaled Abby and Maggie with details of her kevorkian day, I thought about my own little theory of initial attraction. Not the kind that involves individual personality and character, not the kind that occurs during a first conversation, but the kind that takes place instantly, upon first sight, while passing on the street.

I believe that there are two basic elements that catch a man's fancy, that rivet his attention. These two elements are Mystery and Movement. Sometimes they exist together. Personally, I've always found they work best on their own. No point in muddying the powerful effect of either by mixing up their signals.

Alternately, Mystery might be called Sensuality and Movement might be called Sexuality. More accurately, the promise of each.

Generally speaking—always a dangerous thing, I know, and not necessarily true in my own case—a young woman's strength is Movement, aka sexuality. A mature woman's strength is Mystery, aka sensuality.

Here's an example from my own wardrobe. I own a dark brown faux fur hat; it frames my face in a Romantic way. My own father calls it my Anna Karenina hat. Every time I wear this hat, men of a particular sort stare, stumble, smile, blurt gentlemanly greetings. It's a magic hat. It evokes Mystery. In that hat, I become a Mysterious Woman. Perhaps I have suffered the loss of a great love. I am alluringly tragic. I offer the promise of Sensuality.

Also from my wardrobe: A beige suede jacket with lots and lots of fringe. Fringe swings. It dances. It moves with my every move. When I wear that jacket, an entirely different sort of man stares, stumbles, smiles, blurts greetings—and whistles. The jacket is magic. It displays Movement. In that jacket I become a Wild Woman. Maybe I've had rock star lovers. I am teasingly dangerous. I offer the promise of Sexuality.

As I mentioned, at the age of thirty-two I am right on the cusp, still able to pull off the fringe suede jacket with heartening results, also able to compel with the hat that suggests I have endured a tragic love affair and yet am still able to love selflessly. How long I'll be able to pull off the jacket is yet to be seen.

I tuned back into JoAnne's lengthy tale. Abby's mouth hung open. Maggie was wiping tears of laughter from her eyes.

"I was daydreaming," I said. "What did I miss?"

"Just the guy who fell off his bike because he didn't see a hole in the road because he was gaping at me."

"Oh."

I looked carefully at JoAnne, at her clothes and at the details of her hair and . . .

"It's the lipstick," I said. Sensuality. The promise of sex with a real-life tragic heroine. "Definitely the lipstick. Is it new?"

"Yeah, I just picked it up. It's some new brand, part of a retro line, you know, you put together a makeup look from the forties."

"What's it called?"

JoAnne shrugged and dug into her bag. A moment later she pulled out a black tube.

"It's called 'Rita Hayworth Red.' Are you sure it's the lipstick?" JoAnne asked. "Not my all-over irresistible feminine allure?"

"That helps. But trust me, I know these things. It's the lipstick."

"That lipstick is dangerous to society," Abby said.

"The society of men, anyway. Tell Erin about the guy who stopped in the middle of the street and then the light turned and all the cars were honking and he was still staring after you."

"You just did." JoAnne eyed the black tube warily. "That guy had to be at least seventy. Maybe I'd better save this for a special occasion."

"Maybe you'd better throw it away," I suggested. "If you have any heart."

"Forget it. I don't. I'll save it for those days when my feminine ego needs a little boost. Now, let's eat. I'm starved."

Chapter Twenty-eight

E—still regaining strength but Jorges is helping my recovery. txs for money. you didn't tell yr father did you? Mother

Where does one have sex with one's lover if A, one's lover is married; B, one's lover won't come to one's perfectly lovely home; and C, one is opposed to checking into sleazy one-hour, no-tell motels?

Answer: One has sex wherever one can.

We fooled around in Doug's office, after hours, of course. We fooled around—to what extent we could—in the dark of a movie theater's back row, at the last showing, of course. We made out—what an embarrassing teenage term—in a nightclub called Mercury, where we were by far the oldest couple in the place. After our second visit, I declared Mercury off-limits. I'd heard a snicker on our way out. A snicker from a twenty-something with the flattest stomach I'd ever seen. I thought very bad thoughts about her.

And because it was August and the weather hot and humid but not altogether unpleasant, we found ourselves—involved—in the great outdoors.

Yes, even once in an alley in the Leather District some-where near South Station. There was definitely something thrilling about doing it against an old brick wall in the dark of night. It had the prostitute fantasy-thing about it—but ulti-mately, that fantasy could not survive the monstrously huge rat I saw scoot over Doug's shoe. That was the end of the alleys.

Sex with Doug Spears was great. But the occasional excur-sion was fun, too. And romantic. It made me feel, for a brief time, as if we were a real couple. An everyday-world couple.

One day Doug and I skipped out of work and treated our-selves to a day in the North End.

"You know," I said, as we walked along Hanover Street, "I never even considered playing hooky when I was a kid. Never. Besides, if I had played hooky the guilt later would have made me confess and beg for punishment."

"What about college? Don't tell me you made every sin-gle class in college. No hangovers? No blowing chemistry—"

"Chemistry? Who do you think I am?"

"Okay, no blowing French to hang out with Pierre and get your own hands-on language lesson?"

I laughed. "Well, okay, in college I did skip a few classes. On rare occasions. But never for a guy."

"You're an example to all women."

"I'm an example of someone who didn't have nearly enough sex in college."

"I hope we can correct that sad situation now," Doug said, nuzzling my ear.

"After we eat."

"I love a girl with a healthy appetite."

"Good," I said, "because you're paying."

"Then I'd better get some more cash," Doug said and there was something in his tone I didn't get.

Until the next moment I realized that, of course, he couldn't put a midweek North End meal on his personal credit card in case Carol might see the bill and question the occasion. And he couldn't put the meal on his corporate card because he'd told his staff he had a doctor's appointment that afternoon.

We were hedged in and our happiness proscribed no matter where we went or what we did. My spirits plummeted.

"So, what's on the agenda?" Doug said when he'd gotten the cash.

If he could make an effort at enjoyment, so could I.

"Well, first stop is the Daily Catch, also known as Mangia Calamari. We order the fried calamari, which I eat with a dash or two of hot pepper oil."

"Sounds good so far. Except don't expect me to kiss you afterward."

"Ha. The best is yet to come, believe me. Then we order black pasta with aolio oilio. It's served in the pan right on the table. Maybe we'll order the monkfish marsala. Do you like monkfish?"

"I have no idea."

"Well, you will. There's something very sexy about marsala sauce."

"You open whole new worlds to me, Ms. Weston."

"Don't mock. Then, we'll go across the street to Café Vittorio for dessert, maybe some hazelnut gelato or a Napolean. And to use the bathroom."

"Why can't you use the bathroom in Daily Catch?"

"Because there is none."

"Isn't that illegal?"

"I have no idea."

We proceeded as I'd planned.

During lunch, Doug surprised me with exciting news. It seems that he and Jack Nugent had been talking about luring me to Trident.

"But I've never even considered doing branding and positioning for big corporations," I said, stunned.

"Maybe it's time you did. We're not ready to make a specific offer yet," Doug explained. "We're working on tailoring a position for you and your strengths. But Jack does want you to know what we're thinking. If coming on board with Trident is out of the question for you, we'd like to know now, before we spend any more time on the idea."

"Of course I'm interested," I said, and I meant it. I'd be lying if I didn't admit that the rest of lunch and coffee after—Doug's hand playing on my thigh under the tiny table at Café Vittorio—was more fun than it might have been if Doug hadn't dangled the lure of a lucrative career move.

I decided to do some shopping while in the North End. I dragged Doug to Monica's for cheeses and olives and prosciutto, all of which I would eat alone or with my friends, certainly not with Doug, who'd never been to my apartment and who said it was where he drew the line. Something about crossing my threshold, he said, would make him feel too guilty about our relationship to continue seeing me.

I didn't understand but I accepted his feelings, though his refusing to visit my home did hurt on some deep level. Home is where people in love should feel most in love. Doug and I had no home.

Three hours later we made our way back to the Back Bay through the circuitous path resulting from the construction nightmare known as The Big Dig. Back to our separate lives. Doug home to wife and kids. Me, home to Fuzzer.

As I walked back to the South End, clutching my bag of Italian treats, I thought about the afternoon alone with Doug and began to feel sad again.

Sometimes, escape doesn't seem worth it. It makes reality seem too horribly grim.

I had a troubling conversation with my father not long after that. I'd just gotten home from work when the phone rang. I hoped it would be Doug; we'd had plans to meet but at the last minute Doug had canceled. He'd been called home early by Carol. She had been throwing up all day and just couldn't handle the kids, now that they were home from school and activities.

Of course, I took Carol's stomach virus to be a sign of pregnancy. I was not in the happiest of moods.

It was not Doug calling. It was my father.

"Oh. Hi, Dad," I said.

He laughed. "Not a very enthusiastic greeting. Expecting someone else?"

"No, no," I said quickly. "I'm sorry. I just got in."

"Well, I won't keep you. You probably have plans. I just wanted to check in and say hi."

"Okay," I said. "Hi. What's going on?"

I walked with the phone into the kitchen to feed Fuzzer. The Great Beige Beast was yowling as if he hadn't eaten in weeks.

"Erin," Dad said, not answering my last question, "I haven't heard you talk about anyone in a long time. Have you been out with anyone lately?"

I popped open a can of food. Fuzzer threw himself on the floor at my feet and screamed.

Why did Dad have to ask me this?

"Erin?"

"Sorry, Dad. I'm just giving Fuzzer his dinner."

"Is he being his usual dramatic self?"

"Of course."

"So, what's the answer? Have you been out lately?"

"You mean, on a date? No, not really. Nothing worth mentioning."

Liar. My stomach began to squirm. I spooned chicken in gravy into a bowl and set it before Fuzzer, who immediately tucked in.

"Oh. I wish you would meet someone worthy. I don't like to think of you being alone. You're not lonely, are you, Erin?"

Oh, if only he knew. If only I had trust enough in his love to tell him the truth.

"I'm fine, Dad," I said. "I can take care of myself."

Could I?

"I know you can. But I'm your father. I reserve the right to worry about you. I want you to be happy. And, well, I know you're not entirely comfortable with my seeing Abby. I can't tell you how much I appreciate your maturity about it all."

If Dad only knew how torn up I was about—everything.

"Thanks, Dad. And I know you care. I appreciate your concern, really. And if I need any advice, I promise I'll come to you."

Would I? I hadn't thus far.

"Okay," he said. "By the way, have you heard from your mother lately?"

"Yeah," I said lightly. "She's fine, you know."

"She's not hitting you up for money is she?"

How had he known?

"No," I lied. "Of course not."

Dad didn't respond right away. Then: "Okay. Well, I guess I should be off."

"Plans?"

"Nothing much. Abby wants to see some movie." Dad's voice lowered. "I think it's one of those chick flicks."

I laughed. "Your secret's safe with me," I said. "And, Dad? Thanks. Really."

After we'd hung up I took off my shoes and lay down on the couch. I felt like a Victorian lady about to have a spell. A headache was coming on. I shivered and drew a chenille throw over my legs. A sadness settled heavily on my heart. A sadness not relieved even when Fuzzer curled up on my stomach and went to sleep.

Chapter Twenty-nine

Doug and I met for a quick lunch, sandwiches in the Common. We found a bench not occupied by a homeless man or covered by pigeon poop and sat.

"Can I ask you a question?" I said, unwrapping my mozzarella, basil, and tomato sandwich.

"Could I stop you?"

"No. Why didn't you acknowledge my thank you message for the Valentine's Day roses?"

Doug didn't have a snappy comeback. He took a bite of his proscuitto, marinated red pepper, and provolone, chewed, swallowed. Finally, he said: "It struck me when I heard your message that I'd made a huge move and though I didn't regret it, I swear, I . . . I got scared."

"For weeks. Until you called and asked me to lunch at Radius."

"Exactly. Silly, huh?"

Not at all. In fact, Doug's very human reaction endeared him further to me.

It never occurred to me that he could be lying. Covering the fact, for example, that he'd found a hotter prospect and had had fun with her for a while, knowing I'd probably be around, hooked by the big romantic gesture, intrigued by his ensuing silence.

That kind of thing just never occurred to me at all.

As it was a bright day with little humidity, when we'd finished our sandwiches we took a long and circuitous route back to our offices.

Along the way we passed an old and slightly crumbling Catholic church, St. Luke's. A midday service, mass or some prayer thing, was just letting out. The attendees seemed mostly to be very old Irish-American ladies. I spotted a few homeless people, as well.

"Well, the Church is good for something," I said dryly. "It gives the homeless an opportunity to get out of the hot sun or the bitter cold."

"So, you don't go to church anymore?" Doug asked.

"No. I'm what's known as a recovering Catholic. It sounds less complicated than it is. It's not a joke, believe me."

"I can't begin to imagine what it involves. I won't laugh. Just get better soon, okay?"

"I'm trying. My friends are a big help."

I wondered . . . Since the unhappy conversation with my girlfriends at Dish the month before, I'd been wanting to ask Doug how he'd feel about meeting my friends. In the abstract, of course. Until he and Carol separated, when he'd be free to come to my apartment and all.

"Doug," I said, "let me ask you something else. Would you want to meet my friends? You know, Abby, JoAnne, Maggie. Damion. I'm not setting something up or anything," I added hurriedly, lest he think this seemingly innocent question was a feminine-type trap. "I'm just . . . wondering."

Doug's answer was swift in coming and final in tone. "That's not a good idea, Erin."

"But . . ."

"Look, it's very important that we be careful about who sees us together. We have to be vigilant."

"But they're my friends," I said, slightly confused. "They already know about us."

Doug shook his head. "Doesn't matter. Besides, it's not like I want to become friends with them."

That was a bit of a shocker. "Oh," I said eloquently.

"And they sure as hell can't want to be friends with me," Doug said with a laugh.

"I just thought, you know, because they're important to me you'd at least maybe want to meet them, even if you can't really meet them. I thought . . ."

"Hey." Doug's voice became low and intimate. "Aren't you and I enough? Why do you want to bring other people into this?"

Because, I thought, that's what real couples do. They share friends and family. They share their full lives.

I said, "I don't. I'm sorry. Let's just forget it."

And we went back to our separate offices.

Abby had decided we all needed a little culture so she suggested we journey to a museum. She voted for the Museum of Fine Arts. Maggie suggested the Science Museum. I went with the Isabella Stewart Gardner. JoAnne won with her vote for the John F. Kennedy Library and Museum. Saturday we made the excursion. Abby drove, something she rarely did in the city of Boston itself. I kept a tight grip on the door handle and buckled my seat belt tightly.

We made it to Dorchester without accident.

"Wow," I said. "Just, wow. I always forget how beautiful it is out here and then I'm shocked all over again."

The building itself is stunning, another of I. M. Pei's contributions to Boston, and the brightness of the blue sky, the glittering water, the white sailboats and yachts bobbing gently, made the place seem magical. Like, well, Camelot.

I kept this tired old observation to myself.

We split up and wandered alone, occasionally joining for a comment or observation.

I was standing in front of a display case that contained a marked-up draft of a speech when Abby joined me.

"I forgot that once upon a time politicians had brains," she said.

"Not every politician did. And not every politician today is dopey."

"George Bush is. But Bill Clinton isn't." That was Jo-Anne. "Wasn't. Just horny."

"Granted. Something else he had in common with JFK," I noted. "An addiction to his dick."

Maggie completed the group. "Who, JFK?"

"Yes. And Bill Clinton."

"Oh, who cares?" she said. "As long as his penis doesn't affect public policy he can play with it all he likes."

"The American public is pretty unsophisticated about sex, isn't it?" I said.

JoAnne laughed. "Fixated, you mean. We're a nation of guilty eleven-year-olds. With a few exceptions."

"JFK was a good president, wasn't he?"

"He tried, Abby. I'll give him that."

"I think Bobby was cuter," she said.

Maggie grinned. "You would."

"What's that supposed to mean?"

"Nothing," I said, watching Maggie stroll off to another display. "You know, rumor has it that Jackie and Bobby were having an affair after Jack's death."

JoAnne rolled her eyes. "If you had to go home to Ethel and a passle of screaming kids, you'd make nice to Jackie, too."

"Meow. Anyway," Abby said, "it's only a rumor. Maybe they were just good friends. You know, consoling each other in their grief."

I sighed. "Anything's possible."

"If it makes you happy to think so . . ."

"You two." Abby strolled off again, obviously exasperated by JoAnne's and my cynicism. Again.

"Could we not talk about illicit romantic relationships, please?" I said when she'd gone. "For five minutes?"

"Too close to home, honey?"

"Uh, yeah. Though how we're going to avoid talk of affairs surrounded by photos of the Kennedy men, I have no idea."

"We can always blow this popsicle stand and go somewhere for drinks," JoAnne suggested. "I, for one, am beginning to get museum legs."

"You're lazy. But I'm there. I'll find Abby, you get Maggie, and we'll meet in the lobby."

"Deal."

The excursion to the JFK Library and Museum had—not surprisingly—raised the topic of marriage and two hours later, at Jacob Wirth, the topic would still not lie down and shut up no matter how often I tried to introduce a new, neutral topic, like—toothpaste preferences. So, reluctantly at first but gradually with more enthusiasm, I joined in.

The current subtopic was intimacy.

"I want the kind of intimacy that . . . that comes when you share a checking account. That comes when you buy furniture together. I mean—I want to be part of a team," I said.

"I should point out," JoAnne drawled, "that lots of teammates are miserably unhappy over the lack of romance in their lives."

"Okay. But maybe they function smoothly on a daily basis and are friends and companions and eat dinner together every night and take care of each other when they have colds. Isn't there something to be said for all that? Maybe all that starts to mean more than passion."

"You'd rather be Archie and Edith Bunker than Heathcliff and Cathy?" JoAnne said.

I rolled my eyes. "Well, they're both a little extreme, don't you think? Come on, how can you choose between ignorance and insanity?"

"Can't you have all that with a friend?" Maggie said. "I mean, a roommate or a best friend? If you take the sex out of the equation, isn't that what's left? Friendship?"

"I guess. But, no," I said. "I think there's something more than just friendship to a marriage. Look. Even if a husband and wife aren't superpassionate, they sleep in the same bed, they hug . . ."

"They clean the sleep out of each other's eyes."

"Oh, gag!"

"They know each other's bodies," I went on, ignoring the goofing around, "they have this bond that's—deeper, more tender than what exits between two people who are just friends."

"Or the bond that exists between two people who are just lovers," JoAnne pointed out. "Between two people who fool around—in his office, after hours?—but who don't go grocery shopping together and plan their yearly budgets and buy each other's mothers birthday cards."

"I know," I said miserably. "I know."

I said I wanted a marriage. And yet I chose to have an affair.

Do what I say, not what I do, Reason crowed. What kind of an example are you setting for yourself? What are you trying to prove? What are you running away from?

And how did JoAnne know Doug and I mostly had sex in his office, after hours? Were we that much of a cliché?

Maggie asked me: "Do you seriously want to be the kind of wife who makes sandwiches for her husband's poker parties? Do you really want to be the kind of mother who has her kids' Christmas portraits taken at Sears?"

I laughed. "Lord, no! I'm too jaded for that. But I do intend to use my kids' pictures on our holiday cards. I'll take the pictures. No goofy backdrops. Something tasteful, like my beautiful kids and a noble dog and a sleek cat in front of an elegantly decorated tree in my elegantly decorated living room."

"What if your kids are ugly? It happens, you know."

"Impossible," I said. "My kids will be Caroline and John Jr. cute."

"Let's hope their fates will be happier," Maggie added.

JoAnne raised her glass. "To the memory of John."

We joined her in a toast.

"To his sister's bravery in the face of adversity and loss." Abby.

"To Caroline."

"To Carolyn Bessett Kennedy."

Our toasts were followed by a spontaneous moment of silence.

"You know," I finally said, "we might not have everything we want in life, but we have each other. And that's pretty damn good."

JoAnne laughed but it sounded forced. "Uh oh. Erin's getting maudlin. Time to cut her off."

I made a face.

"Really, I've got to go," she said. "It is a school night."

JoAnne's departure ended the party. We took our leave of each other. I begged off driving home with Abby and walked.

It was a long time before I got to sleep that night.

Chapter Thirty

Trident was making a move.

I got a call asking me to come into their offices for a meeting.

I carefully chose my most high-powered, media-babe skirt suit and took with me the sleek, black Levenger briefcase I reserved for truly important meetings.

Jack Nugent was there. Doug was there, of course, carefully avoiding eye contact. A woman named Rita Berrios, VP of sales was there, too, looking less than enthusiastic about the meeting. I'd met her briefly before, a forty-year-old who'd had her first child just the year before and who seemed to radiate resentment at having to be in a corporate setting rather than at home with her child.

Or so I imagined.

Jack began the meeting. "I'm sure you know why we asked you here today, Erin."

A trick question if there ever was one! If I said yes, I'd sound like a cocky bastard. If I said no, I'd come across as disingenuous.

I smiled a quick smile and kept my mouth shut.

Jack went on.

Trident was making me an offer. They were making me an offer in Doug's office, in the very room in which he and I had sex. They were making me a spectacular offer.

It was very exciting. I felt powerful and in possession of a powerful secret and powerfully full of myself.

The offer was incredible. It exceeded anything I'd imagined. It seemed excessive and for a moment I wondered if Doug hadn't used his influence to get me more than I was worth. But a brief investigation of the salaries and overall financial packages of Trident's top people confirmed that my offer was right in line with the company's policies.

When the meeting was over, Doug left the room quickly. Jack walked me to the elevators.

"I can't tell you how excited I am about this offer," I told him. "It's given me a lot to think about."

"The job will be there, Erin. Don't rush your decision."

"Don't you think I can do the job?" I asked, only half jokingly.

"I know you can do it," Jack said promptly. "There's no question in my mind as to your skills and competency."

"Then . . . ?"

"I'd like you to think about whether you really want to do the job."

Now there was an interesting question. What had made Jack ask it?

Not for the first time I wondered if Jack knew about my relationship with Doug and if so, how much he knew. Was he worried about our behavior while working in the same office? He had to know I was a consummate professional and that I would never allow my private life to . . .

I fought down a blush of shame. I liked and respected Jack Nugent. And he was well known as an honest businessman and a sincere family man. If he did know about me and Doug, his opinion of me must have fallen hugely.

Jack and the ring of the elevator interrupted my thoughts.

"Will you promise me you'll think hard about accepting

the position at Trident? Make sure in your heart it's the right thing for you. Erin, your reputation with nonprofits is spectacular. So if joining with Trident isn't the right thing—well, I won't deny I'll be disappointed. Our team could benefit from your experience and energy. But I'll also respect your decision."

I nodded and stepped into the empty elevator car.

"Okay, Jack," I said, "it's a deal. I'll think about it."

That evening I met JoAnne to discuss Trident's offer. Among other things.

"Other things" took precedence.

"You know," I blurted, "I feel like being with Doug is, I don't know, somehow it's preparing me for marriage. I mean, I'm getting a sense of something . . ."

The look on JoAnne's face told me that I should have kept my mouth shut.

"How is dating—and I use the word loosely—a married man preparation for marriage?"

"Not preparation, exactly," I said. Too late to stop. "But . . . I can't really explain it, but somehow it's given me a—a glimpse, I guess—I can't say this right. I guess it's shown me how good marriage can be and reinforced my desire for a marriage of my own."

To Doug, I added silently.

JoAnne sipped her martini. "Well, that makes no sense at all, but whatever. It's your head, not mine."

"Yeah, it is. And I'm stuck with it."

"Oh, honey, we're all stuck with ourselves."

"I suppose a therapist would say we can all change, become someone new."

JoAnne cleared her throat. Suddenly, she looked sheepish.

"What?" I said. "Oh, I get it. You're seeing a therapist. Finally!"

"Jesus Christ, Erin, it's not like I'm insane!"

"I know. I'm sorry. I just meant that I'm glad you're dealing with the pain and all."

JoAnne shrugged. "It's okay so far. We'll see. I'm not making any promises. If it doesn't work out . . ."

"I get it, I get it," I said.

"Anyway," JoAnne said loftily, "I still say that telling people they can totally change is a lie perpetuated to keep the therapy profession flush. Change is possible but only within limits. The limits of character and personality and every little tiny thing that makes an individual who she is. For example, I will never decide to give up urban life and become a Sherpa. Maggie, on the other hand . . ."

I laughed. "I think she'd look cute in that mountaineering gear."

"Exactly. So, back to the important subject: What are you going to do about the Trident offer?"

"I don't know," I said. "I just—don't know."

"I didn't know you were feeling antsy at EastWind."

"I'm not," I said. "I love my work."

"So, what's the lure? And if you say Dirk Spiral, I'll smack you."

I shrugged. "Money, I guess. Change. The opportunity to learn something new."

"Blah, blah. That's all fine if you're bored where you are. But you're not."

"No. I'm not. I like my clients, even the pain-in-the butt ones. I mean, individual people can be annoying, don't get me started on Roy Blount from the Coalition for Informed Media, but how can I say I don't respect the work of the Conservation Law Foundation or the Symphony or, I don't know, any of my clients?"

"You can't. And you shouldn't. So, have you talked to Dirk Spiral about your dilemma?"

"A bit. I suppose we'll talk more, now that Trident actually made the offer."

JoAnne patted my arm. "Well, honey just don't lose your

own opinion in the process, okay? I know how you are with this guy."

"How am I?" I said, surprised. "What do you mean?"

"Honey, if Dirk Spiral asked you to jump off a bridge, you'd do it. I see it in your eyes."

"His name," I said, hurt, "is Doug Spears."

Chapter Thirty-one

Erin—celebrated my birthday with a two-day party! didn't get your card and present—did I give you my new address? will be here for another week. Love, Mother

Another girls' night out, though I really wasn't in the mood to talk, having forgotten—consciously?—to send a birthday card or gift to my mother and now suffering big pangs of guilt.

But judging by JoAnne's conversational opener, I was going to have to get into the mood.

"So," she asked me, "have you and Doug taken pictures of yourselves in the nude?"

Abby's mouth fell. "You mean, naked pictures?"

"The pictures aren't naked, Abby," JoAnne said calmly, "the subjects are naked. Don't look so shocked. Everybody does it."

"No, they don't," I said, kind of shocked. "I don't. Haven't. Yet. Doug hasn't suggested it."

"Of course he hasn't," Maggie snapped. "Why would he want to have a hand in producing blackmail material?"

"I would never blackmail him! That's a horrible thing to say."

"Well, I know you wouldn't, but does he? How much trust can there really be in an illicit relationship? The possibility always exists for you to rat him out to his wife. The possibility always exists for him to dump you cold and 'go back' to his wife. Like he ever had the balls to be honest with her and actually leave in the first place."

A moment of brutal silence followed Maggie's outburst.

I had to say something, didn't I?

"God, I need a drink."

Maggie's smile was wobbly. "You have one. But I'll buy you another."

Peace was offered and received.

"How are things going with Doug, really?" JoAnne said after some rambling talk about job stress and health insurance.

"Well," I said, "I do have a little problem. Doug's birthday is next Sunday."

"And the problem is . . . ?"

"The problem is I can't be with him on his birthday because it's on the weekend. Weekend is family time. It's sacrosanct. That means, no Erin. I can't even call him. And I won't be able to talk to him unless he can sneak a call to me. Which is unlikely, given the fact that his wife is throwing a big family party for him Saturday night, even though he's told her time and again that he hates big family parties. Any parties, really."

"How selfish of her," Maggie murmured.

Abby shrugged. "Why can't you and Doug celebrate on Friday? Like, at lunch or after work. Go have drinks somewhere."

"We're going to do that, but it's not the same as being with someone on his actual birthday. I feel—deprived."

"When you date a married man, you take what you can get," JoAnne said. "You've no right to complain, Erin. You knew what you were getting into."

"Did I? Sometimes, I'm not so sure."

"What are you getting Doug for his birthday, anyway?" Abby asked.

"That's another problem," I said. "I can't give him a normal gift—like a tie or a book or tickets to some event—because then he'd have to explain to his wife where it came from."

"Can't he just say he bought it for himself?"

"Maybe some men could but Doug never buys anything for himself. His wife would know something was up. And if he says the book or whatever was a gift from, say, Jack, at the office, then he runs the risk of his wife mentioning it to Jack . . ."

"Oh, what a tangled web we weave . . ." Maggie.

"You could, you know, give him something—personal."

"Abby," JoAnne asked, "by 'personal' do you mean to say, 'a sexual favor' ?"

"Well, yes. I do think about sex, you know."

I knew. I wished I didn't.

JoAnne snorted. "Huh. What's so special about a sexual favor? Their entire relationship is all about sex."

"That's not true!" I protested. But there was something to what JoAnne had said. What did Doug and I do with our time together? Kiss. Grope. Have sex. There wasn't much else we could do together so sex had taken on a whole lot of meanings it wouldn't necessarily have if we could be in an open—real—relationship.

"It's just not fair," I blurted. "How did I get into a position of constant secondary—tertiary, whatever—importance? When someone loves you you're supposed to be number one. I've plopped myself right down in the number three spot, after wife and kids."

"Doug put you there and keeps you there as much as you did and do," Maggie said. "Keep that in mind."

"No," I protested. "No, he's never promised anything and he's never lied to me . . ."

"Whoa!" JoAnne put her hand over her heart. "How can

you possibly know he's never lied to you when he's lying to his wife! The woman he's supposed to cherish in sickness and in health, till death do they part."

"It's . . . it's not like that with Doug. He doesn't like cheating—having to cheat. He'd love to leave Carol . . ."

"Oh, please," JoAnne cried. "Let me guess: She doesn't understand him."

"Why is it that we don't hold men to the same moral and ethical and behavioral standards as we hold other women?" Maggie said. "Does a penis give a man the right to be a shithead?"

Abby nodded wisely. "Lots of men think so."

"But women shouldn't."

"You could always leave him, Erin," Abby said gently.

Abby was right. I could. Boots were made for walking. I could wash that man right out of my hair. I will survive and he's not welcome anymore, and all that.

But the odd truth was that I didn't want to leave Doug. Ever. So what if things weren't perfect? Were they ever perfect, with any relationship? As my grandfather used to say, I'd made my bed and now I was lying in it.

At least it's a hell of your own choosing, Reason added.

"Anyone want another drink?" I asked.

In the end I bought Doug a CD for his birthday, after scoping his office more closely and discovering he had an old but working CD player behind his desk. Once Doug had mentioned that he enjoyed madrigals so I bought a collection of seventeenth century Italian madrigals, attached a goopy note—which I knew he would tear to pieces and throw away before we left the restaurant, secrecy and vigilance being all—and apologized for not being able to treat him to something finer.

Doug was distracted and checked his watch three times in the one hour we had to spend together Friday evening.

It annoyed me.

"Hot date later?" I quipped and then wanted to kill my-self.

"Sorry," he said but it didn't sound sincere. "I've got a parent-teacher meeting tonight."

"Why can't Carol go?" I said. The annoyance was rapidly becoming anger.

"She's sick," Doug said shortly.

"Again?" I said.

Doug swallowed the last of his drink and stood. "I've got to run."

I felt like crap.

"I'm sorry," I said. "I—I just hoped we could spend more time together for your birthday."

Doug smiled. Suddenly, he looked very, very tired.

"That's okay. I know it's hard for you," he said. "It's hard for me, too."

Doug gave my hand a quick squeeze, gathered his brief-case, and left.

"Happy Birthday," I called out feebly.

He didn't turn back. Maybe he hadn't heard.

Gloomily, I ordered another drink and proceeded to tor-ture myself. What had he meant by saying "it" was hard for him, too, I wondered. Did that bode ill for me, for us? Was I a terrible drain on Doug, was our relationship too much for him? Or was it Carol and the trappings of married life that were dragging him down? Panic took hold and I drank the next drink too quickly.

It was a long and lonely night.

Chapter Thirty-two

Saturday. A hot, horrible, sticky August Saturday. The day before Doug's birthday. Ordinarily, I would have opted to stay at home in my air-conditioned apartment—especially since I was slightly hung over—but I hadn't seen Damion for some time—what with my being busy with Doug—and when he'd asked if I wanted to drag along on a shopping expedition, I said yes. And wore the lightest clothes I own.

We drove to the South Bay Shopping Center, not far from my apartment.

"Do you want to stop at Marshall's while we're here?" Damion asked when we'd parked.

"Ugh. I hate this Marshall's. I'll only go to the one on Boylston Street. It's fabulous."

"What about Old Navy?"

"Hmmm. Okay," I agreed. "They've got good soundtracks. And there's always a bargain on tops and sweaters."

"You know those groovy soundtracks are a marketing ploy to make you spend more money."

I gave Damion a look.

"Really! Gee, I didn't know that. I'll work really hard to

resist—unless, of course, it's the eighties soundtrack. There are some excellent old songs on that."

"Fine," Damion said. "First, we'll spend all your money on cheap clothing. Then we need to go to Super 88 for ostrich steaks and Super Stop 'n Shop for—well, a bunch of things. I have a list."

"You're really going all out," I said as we walked across the parking lot toward Old Navy. "So—it's serious with, what's his name, Frank?"

"Frederick. It could be. I want it to be."

"And the way to a man's heart is through his stomach."

"That's one route, yes. Maybe not the most direct . . ."

By the time we got to Super Slop 'n Shop—my pet name for the massive supermarket—I was, indeed, slopping. Or was it schlepping? Anyway, I was tired of fighting my way through aisles of sweatshirts at Old Navy and frighteningly foreign produce at Super 88.

"How much do you need here, Damion?" I asked, helping him wrench a mondo shopping cart from a lineup of mondo shopping carts.

He took a neatly folded piece of paper from his jacket pocket, unfolded it, and considered. "Not much."

"Give me half of the list and we'll meet up later. It'll save time."

Damion eyed me. "Well . . ."

"I know the difference between sour cream and cottage cheese," I drawled. "The cartons are labeled."

"Okay. But if you're in doubt . . ."

"Right. I'll let you handle it."

Damion carefully tore the list into two vastly uneven pieces and gave me the smaller section. It was labeled: "Misc."

"Thanks for the vote of confidence. See you."

I wandered off to find the canned soup aisle—only Progresso, if you please—but got distracted by the aisle of discount books. After a quick perusal I discovered that discount

meant best-selling but shoddily written crap so I took a left
out of the aisle and . . .

It was her. It was Carol. It was Doug's wife.

For a moment I panicked, darted back to the books, then
my senses returned and reminded me that Carol and I had
never met. Unless she'd seen a photo of me, which was
highly unlikely, she wouldn't know who I was.

The woman sleeping with her husband.

I, of course, had seen a photo of Carol. Doug kept one on
his desk, along with a photo of the kids. Something about
keeping up appearances, I guess.

I took a steadying breath and once again walked out of
the discount book aisle and into the wide back aisle along
which were arranged refrigerated cases of meats, dairy prod-
ucts, and fish.

Carol was still there, now looking down into a section of
roasting chickens.

What was she doing at the South Bay Shopping Center?
Why wasn't she shopping in Newton, where she lived—where
she belonged? I felt a surge of anger. I had so little and she
had so much. She had Doug. I had to keep to my corner of
the universe to protect her. Why couldn't she keep to her corner to protect me?

Because, you idiot, Reason said, she doesn't know about
you. She belongs wherever she wants to belong. She's the one
with the ring and the title. She's not the one skulking in the
aisle, pretending to be interested in frozen tripe and Jimmy
Dean sausages.

Carefully, I glanced toward Carol, who still stood examining the roasters. We were no more than ten feet away from
each other. I noticed a small dark mole on her right cheek.

Objectively—as if I could truly be objective—Carol was
not a striking woman. She was of average height and average
build, a bit wide in the hips, but maybe that was from the two
pregnancies. Her hair was medium brown and in need of a
touch-up; grayish roots were visible even from a distance.
She wore no makeup—at least none that translated beyond a

few feet. I looked for a wedding band and caught a tiny sparkle—I guessed a thin band set with diamonds. I could see no other jewelry.

Carol looked like any other overworked, fortyish woman doing the grocery shopping on a Saturday morning, stocking up for her husband's birthday party, hyperactive kids somewhere in tow, probably raiding the candy displays. But Carol wasn't just any woman. I felt a surge of disgust. This woman was my rival. And this woman was a mess. How could Doug ever have found her attractive? No wonder he didn't find her attractive now. No wonder he'd turned to another woman. How in God's name did Carol expect to keep the interest of a man as charismatic and handsome as Doug while appearing in public in baggy jeans and a gray sweat jacket?

As quickly and as violently as the surge of disgust had overtaken me, it receded and was replaced by deep shame.

I'm so sorry, I thought toward Carol. I . . .

Reason was angry. Are you so screamingly insecure you have to trash a hardworking mother of two small children, a woman who's never deliberately done anything to hurt you, a woman whose husband is cheating on her, for wearing ill-fitting jeans and a sweat jacket while grocery shopping? Erin, you have sunk to a new low. I suggest therapy is in order.

And maybe a prescription for anxiety.

Oh, God, what if Doug is here, too? I thought wildly. What . . . If I saw him without Carol—what would I do? Greet him, of course, but with restraint. We'd be in public. His wife could come around the corner at any moment.

What if Doug suddenly strolled up to Carol—and then saw me? What then? Would he greet me, introduce me as a colleague? Would he ignore me? The possibility made me nauseous.

As much as it pains me to admit this, I followed Carol when she moved away from the meat and dairy cases and into the chip and snack aisle. Damion's shopping list was forgotten. In fact, it was no longer in my hand. I didn't know where it had gone.

A woman joined Carol then. A baby sat in the seat of her cart. Two children, about four and six, were helping her steer. Taylor and Courtney. Had to be.

"Have they been behaving?" Carol said to the woman. Her friend, I guessed. Or sister.

"Oh, sure."

"Mommy! Look what I got!" Courtney cried. She was jumping with excitement, clutching what looked like a bag of chips.

"Let me see." Carol peered at the bag as if she might need glasses for close reading.

"Daddy's favorite!" Courtney's pride in her choice was palpable.

"That's very nice of you, honey. Put it in the cart, okay?" Courtney did.

Daddy's favorite. B-B-Cue flavored potato chips.

I didn't know Doug the father at all. Or Doug the husband. Or Doug the birthday boy. Did I really even know Doug the man?

I turned away. I felt like I needed to sit down but short of collapsing on top of slabs of pork, sitting wasn't an option. I set off, a bit wobbly, to find Damion.

As I wobbled, I wondered. Would I tell Doug I'd seen Carol and the children? The urge to make a scene came over me and I envisioned myself the scorned woman, gloriously nasty and yet, somehow, heartbreakingly sad.

Thankfully, the urge was quickly replaced by a feeling of defeat. Defeat is better than anger? Sometimes. So, I'd say nothing. What would it change for the better if I told him? I'd keep the uneasiness within myself. I'd save him the split second of panic the news might cause—a split second within which he'd wonder if I'd confronted Carol, done something horrible.

"Erin!"

I looked in the direction of the voice. Damion.

"Didn't you find anything on the list yet?" he said as he hurried toward me, pushing his laden cart.

I shook my head.

"God." Damion stopped and put his hand to his heart. "You look like you've seen a ghost. What happened?"

I tried to smile. "It was a goblin. Can we go now?"

Damion eyed me more closely.

"You have something to tell me," he said. "Let's go. You can start talking in the car."

Chapter Thirty-three

E—still haven't rcvd bday gift—have you forgotten your mother? Mother

It seemed a long, long week.

Damion was not happy about my relationship with Doug. Of course, I hadn't expected him to be—I'd only told him about Doug after the unsettling experience of seeing Carol in the supermarket. Damion's clear disapproval weighed heavily on my mind. He'd assured me he wasn't about to abandon our friendship; he'd also said that he would do nothing to foster the affair.

Then he'd revealed something about his past I'd not known. When Damion was ten and his sister, Sarah, was seven, their up-and-coming father had had an affair with his secretary, the whole classic deal, complete with a humiliating divorce which resulted in Damion, his mother, and sister moving into cramped quarters; his unskilled mother facing a merciless job market; and Damion and Sarah becoming latch-key kids.

The whole thing had left a bitter taste in Damion's mouth, and if he was to be believed, and Damion never lied, to that day his mother hadn't gotten over the hurt. That made Damion mad. That and the fact that his sister, now exactly my age, was still cruising the bar scene, playing Russian roulette with her life.

"Maybe her behavior has nothing to do with your parents' divorce," I said, reasonably.

"It has everything to do with their divorce." Damion's tone left no room for argument. "Did you know that neither of us has seen our so-called father for almost ten years? Why? No reason, other than the fact that he doesn't give a shit about us, now that he's got family number two. And did you know that my mother works two jobs? And that she doesn't have the energy at the end of a long, hard day on her feet at the cash register to get out there and meet someone decent? Her life was over when her husband left. She had no current job skills, no personal savings. My father didn't hit it big until after the divorce. So my mother had no serious alimony, no real money from him other than child support. Which, of course, is long over."

I felt bad for Damion's mother. I felt bad for Damion and his sister. But maybe, I thought, maybe I should also feel bad for Damion's father. Maybe he'd been terribly unhappy at home. Maybe Damion's mother was a horrible shrew. Maybe . . .

Don't be an ass, Reason said. You want to feel sorry for a man who hasn't seen his children in ten years?

We don't know the whole story, Romance said soothingly. We shouldn't judge.

But Damion had judged and he'd found his father at fault. And he'd judged me at fault, too. Maybe I wasn't as culpable as Doug, but I was definitely a willing—and guilty—player.

It all got me thinking, and thinking got me depressed. What had Carol done, I wondered, before marrying Doug? Before having kids and staying home with them? Suddenly, I was dying to know. I hoped she had been a lawyer or financial analayst, hoped she had the sort of career to which she could successfully return. If she had to. For some reason.

Curiosity has killed more than the inquisitive cat. It's also killed countless good moods and otherwise pleasant rendezvous.

I met Doug Wednesday after work. It was the only time he was able to see me that week. Work was madness and his in-laws were visiting from Florida. Home duty called. I don't know what lie Doug had told Carol to be able to meet me for an hour or two.

"First, a big family party," he said, taking a long drink of his Scotch, "which I didn't want. Now the in-laws' visit, which I didn't want. I told Carol now was not a good time for them to come but . . ."

"But what?" I asked, trying not to sound too eager for the answer.

Doug set his glass down with a clank. "But it's part of our deal, our division of labor and duties. Carol does home and family. I bring in the money to be spent on home and family."

"That doesn't seem fair," I blurted, and wondered if I actually meant that.

"Who said anything about fair? It's marriage. It doesn't have to be fair. It just has to work."

"Until one person can't take it any longer."

Doug eyed me warily. "I'm not saying I can't take it any longer."

Shit, Erin. Stupid thing to say.

"What did Carol do before she had the kids?" I asked.

We were seated at the bar. The bartender brought us our meals and Doug gestured for another Scotch.

"What did she do?" Doug repeated.

"Yeah, like, you know, career-wise."

Doug picked at his food as he spoke.

"Not much. We got married when we were in our early twenties."

So, Doug and Carol had been married for almost twenty years. The thought was staggering.

"Did she go to college?" I pressed.

"Of course. Everybody went to college. She just never had any real interest in a career. She worked part-time, she temped. She hung out with her sister and her nieces and nephews. She always wanted kids."

I did a quick calculation. Doug's children were four and six years old. That meant Doug and Carol had been married for about fourteen years before she gave birth. Another staggering thought. What did they do alone together all those years? If Carol wasn't Doug's soul mate, what had they talked about for fourteen years?

"Why didn't she have kids sooner?" I said. Nothing mattered now but that I bludgeon myself with the intimate details.

Doug put down his fork and finally looked at me. "Because I didn't want them," he said. "I knew it would be the end for us. Not that there was much there in the first place. For me, anyway. Carol seemed happy enough."

"What changed your mind?" I said, transfixed by this sad story.

Doug laughed harshly. "What changed my mind was Carol getting pregnant."

"You mean . . ."

"I mean she got pregnant. She said it was an accident. I don't know. But she was ecstatic. She quit pretending to work. It was what she'd wanted all along. To be the wife and mother, that's it. The particular husband doesn't really matter much to her. She's that type. She's not very bright," Doug said, his tone suddenly mean.

"I'm bright," I said inanely.

Doug looked at me consideringly.

"I think you are," he said at last, placing his hand on my knee. "Don't let me down."

Chapter Thirty-four

I sat slumped on the couch. I'd made no social plans for the weekend. Instead, I'd brought home some work and rented a movie and made a long list of housekeeping chores that were long overdue.

By Saturday afternoon, I'd accomplished absolutely nothing. Unless you count eating three bagels with cream cheese for breakfast "something."

What was Doug doing at this very moment, out in Newton with his not very bright, sweatshirt-wearing wife Carol?

What was my mother doing with Julio or Jorges or Roberto?

What were Abby and my father doing at this very moment, five-fifteen on a Saturday afteroon, in Newport, Rhode Island? It wasn't quite cocktail hour. Maybe they were still on the beach.

Was Abby wearing a bikini? Was my father wearing a Speedo? I leapt from the couch and shook my body like a wet dog. Ugh. Ick. The image was repulsive. The beach was not a good way to go. What was? Certainly not the bedroom . . .

I put my hands over my ears and like a child sang out, "Lalalalala," to block the sound of my own thoughts. Of course, the tactic didn't work.

I sat back down on the couch and rested my head in my hands. Why was I torturing myself this way? Why was I dwelling on something so painful?

Because I was alone and the two people I was most likely to have spent part of the weekend with were spending it together. Without me. And that just sucked.

I made a Note to Self: "Being in a relationship with a married man is a very lonely proposition."

A few days after Abby and my father got back from Newport, we all had dinner at Davio's on Newbury Street. I'd tried to back out gracefully but Abby had insisted I wouldn't be in the way. Well, how could I not go after that lovely reassurance? Besides, I had been wanting to get my father's— and Abby's—opinion on the Trident offer.

"I can't tell you what your support means to us," Abby said, when she and I were seated.

Us? What had happened to Abby as an individual?

"I really think the weekend in Newport made us closer. I feel it solidified our relationship."

Not mine and yours, I thought.

"Good. That's, really, that's great."

"So, Erin, what did you do this weekend?"

Wallowed in self-pity. Go on, Reason urged, tell her the truth.

"Oh, the usual," I said. "Some reading. I rented a movie. You know, some stuff around the house."

"That's nice," Abby said distractedly. She smiled past my head. I turned. Yeah, it was Dad.

"John!" she called.

No, I thought, it's Dad first, John second. He's mine first, yours later.

"Ladies. Sorry I'm late. I couldn't get off a phone call."

"Oh, don't be silly, it's fine," Abby said, pecking him on the cheek.

Yeah, I've got buckets of time to waste, I thought. Then: Should I kiss him, too?

I didn't.

The waiter appeared. He was Uriah Heap. He was unctuous and obsequious and oozing.

He was not getting a big tip from me.

Dad ordered a Scotch on the rocks.

"And what will your lovely daughters have?" asked Uriah.

Abby's eyes widened to ridiculous proportions.

Dad cleared his throat.

I said, "I'll have arsenic, please. In a clean glass, hold the ice."

I wonder where Mom is now, I thought, as the silence thundered on. I wonder if she'd mind a traveling companion. Nothing in the hills and jungles of an Unnamed South American Country could be any weirder than what my life in Boston had become.

Doug called late that night. I didn't bother to ask where he was or how he was managing to make the call.

I told him what had happened at Davio's.

He laughed. "That's great. I would have loved to have been there."

"Yeah, ha, ha. You know, Doug, my life is a pain in the ass sometimes."

"Am I part of that pain?" he said.

Yes, I thought.

"No," I said. "You're the soothing balm that takes away the pain."

"Good. I've got to run, Erin."

"Okay," I said. "Bye."

After I'd hung up I realized that I hadn't thanked Doug for calling. I wondered what had made me break tradition.

Chapter Thirty-five

*E—finally got bday gift—thanks! blouse too big
tho—I've lost weight—so gave it to local woman
with six kids and one dress. Now, just have to
find her a skirt. M.*

Sunday brunch at Joe's American on Newbury Street.
Always a mob scene, especially in the summer, but it was
Maggie's turn to choose and the policy was not to argue anyone's choice. Anyway, the food was always good. Basic but
good.

We were about halfway through our brunch when . . .

JoAnne put down her coffee cup. "So, Abby, have you told
your mother about John?"

My God, I thought. Why hadn't I ever asked that?

Abby took a long sip of her Bloody Mary before answering.

"Well, no. Not yet."

"Why not?" I said.

"I . . . I want to wait until I know we're really serious. You
know how mothers can be, all full of questions."

"You've always told your mother about your boyfriends after the first date," Maggie pointed out.

"Right," Abby said quickly. "And, well, I've learned my lesson."

JoAnne eyed Abby suspiciously. "I think you're lying," she said. "I think you haven't told your mother about John because he's so much older than you are."

Bingo.

"Oh, Mrs. Walker wouldn't care," I said, not believing a word of it. "After all, she's married to a guy fifteen years her junior."

"And now her daughter is dating a guy twenty-six years her senior. Interesting."

"I don't know what you mean!" Abby said huffily. "And my mother's name is Mrs. Gilliam now."

JoAnne laughed. "Come on, honey. You think your mother will disapprove of John. You know she wants to be a grandmother and you know she knows her chances of becoming a grandmother when her only daughter's seeing an old man are slim."

"My father's not an old man!"

"He'll be sixty in less than two years," Maggie said. "That's not young."

"Whose side are you on, anyway?" I demanded.

Maggie shrugged and got back to her eggs.

"And it's reasonable to think your mother might be concerned for you," JoAnne went on. "She might worry her daughter will be a widow before her first anniversary. She might worry her daughter is going to wind up a caretaker of an Alzheimer's patient before her second anniversary."

"It's not true, any of it," Abby said, but her protestation sounded lame.

"Are you embarrassed of my father?" I asked. "Have you introduced him to anyone at the BSO?"

"No, and no, I'm not embarrassed! Just, everybody, stop, okay? I'm just not—ready to bring John home."

"Or to introduce him to your friends at work," I added grimly.

"You're being horrible, Erin. All of you."

"We're just looking out for your own good, honey, since you don't seem to be capable of it."

A moment of stunned silence. Then Abby grabbed her bag and bolted from the table.

"Nice going, JoAnne." I bolted after Abby.

Behind me, I heard Maggie say, "Pass me her plate, will you?"

I found Abby on the sidewalk, standing as if she were waiting for someone.

"Hey," I said. An all-purpose opener.

"Can we walk for a bit?"

"Sure."

Abby turned toward the Gardens and I followed. She said nothing and neither did I. When we reached the benches along the pond, Abby said, "Let's sit," and we did.

"You okay?"

"She's right, Erin. All of you are right."

"About what?" I asked, but I knew.

"About why I haven't brought John home to meet my mother. And why I haven't introduced him to anyone at work."

"Okay."

"Oh, Erin, I hate myself for it, I really do! It's just—I don't know if I'm strong enough to deal with the looks and the questions."

I smiled. "You're not dating Quasimodo, Abby. It's not so unusual for a younger woman to date an older man."

"I know, but . . . What if John has more in common with my mother than he does with me? What if he's totally uncomfortable going out with my BSO friends and their boyfriends? I mean, most of the women there are in their twenties and thirties. The married people only seem to hang out with other married people. No one will want to go out with me and John."

"Don't you think you're jumping to conclusions? One step at a time, Abby. And don't presuppose people's reactions."

Though what a twenty-eight-year-old guy-about-town would have in common with a fifty-eight-year-old divorced father, I couldn't imagine. What would they talk about at dinner? Testicular cancer or prostate problems? Horrible.

"Has Dad introduced you to any of his friends?" I asked, thinking, who? Like most long-married couples, my parents had long-married couple friends. When Mom left Dad, most of those couples had disappeared from view—after an initial show of support for Dad, the dumpee. Not unusual, I'm told. Maybe a divorced couple seemed too much of a threat to the still-married ones.

Anyway, aside from an old law school bachelor buddy— a real bachelor, not an in-the-closet gay guy—my father didn't have much of a social life these days. Aside from Abby.

"I've met his receptionist, Ms. Leonard," Abby said. "And, well, we were thinking of going to an industry dinner at the Marriott but . . ."

"But what?"

Abby shrugged uncomfortably. "John changed his mind a few days before the event. He said he hoped I wasn't disappointed . . ."

"Were you?"

"Kind of," Abby admitted. "I wanted to dress up and meet his colleagues. I . . . I wondered if he was ashamed of me. But then he took me out to Blue Ginger—he remembered I'd always wanted to go there—and we had a lovely time, just the two of us, so, I just never said anything."

"Well, that was nice," I said, but there wasn't a lot of conviction in my voice. Since when did my father pass on an industry dinner? He was an active member of the American Bar Association and a past president of the Boston Bar

Association Committee or some such organization. John Weston was a man who knew people and liked it that way.

A pigeon flapped its way across the Gardens, narrowly
missing my head. I cringed.

"Oh, Erin," Abby said with a sigh, "do you think this will
work, me and John?"

I debated giving Abby the hope she was asking for. But it
would have been false hope.

"I don't know, Abby. I'm sorry, I just don't know."

Chapter Thirty-six

E—Ricardo and I are doing wonderfully. He's helping me with my budget—you know how bad I am with figures! Hope all's well. Maria—that's what R. calls me.

Maureen, my only married-currently-pregnant-twenty-something-friend, my colleague at EastWind, told me one day that week that she was eagerly waiting for her mucus plug to pass. Having determinedly avoided reading *Our Bodies Ourselves,* I knew nothing about said mucus plug. It occured to me, as I listened to Maureen describe in detail the event she was anticipating, that until I was ready to pass a mucus plug of my own, I did not want to know about it. Now, I thought, as I listened in horror, now I am going to lie awake at night imagining the mucus plug. Supposedly, Maureen said, it resembles a clearish slug. Or thick, clear snot.

When I got home that night, desperately hoping not to think of the mucus plug during dinner, I started to obsess. Would I ever be able to eat a raw oyster again? Could you sue someone for ruining your appetite?

Though it was highly unfashionable and not politically

correct and all that, the truth was that I liked to know as little as possible about my body without being utterly, stupidly ignorant. I mean, I knew where pee came out. Beyond that, I liked to keep things a mystery. I figured that if something went wrong, the doctor would fix it. Of course, I hardly ever went to the doctor, either.

My chosen ignorance I chalked up to my being of largely Irish-Catholic descent. Add to that a classic American prudishness—a more far-reaching and influential gift from our forefathers and mothers than the turkey and Manifest Destiny—and you had a recipe for supreme denial.

What's Irish foreplay? Bernie on top, muttering, "Brace yourself, Bridget." Bridget on bottom, eyes closed, suffering with an overwhelming sense of guilt, beating herself for having entertained even the merest notion of lust, lacerating herself for having succumbed to temptation.

Not for the first time I looked at Fuzzer that night with envy. How nice it would be to act on instinct and need, with no thought to the soul.

Isn't that what you're doing by having an affair with Doug? Reason inquired.

Her soul is supremely involved in her relationship with Doug, Romance replied haughtily.

Soul or not, in the eyes of the church I was committing adultery. No matter that I considered myself no longer a Catholic. The church considered me caught until the day I died. Then, I would be handed over to God for judgment and appropriate punishment.

Catholics are admonished to avoid not only sin but the "near temptation of sin." They're not even allowed in the same room with sin. If sin is somewhere in the building, Catholics are warned to leave the building immediately. Lest sin tempt them into, say, looking at a coworker with envy. Or stealing staples from the supply room. Or, the good Lord forbid, fantasizing about sex during business hours.

Which thought led me to lascivious thoughts about Doug. Who at that moment was home with his wife.

In some bizarre leap, that depressing thought led to memories of my own depressing presex days. Occasionally, it still amazed me that I'd ever lost my virginity. Of course, alcohol had been involved. And for days afterward I'd felt as if I were walking around with a giant red S plastered to my forehead.

A giant red S for Slut. All anyone had to do was look at me and they'd know that I had done intimate things with a man—well, a college guy—and that I was going to Hell.

It was horrible. Not the actual experience, which was painful and awkward but probably worse by far for the college guy. What a responsibility! But the buildup and aftermath . . . Twelve years later it still made me shudder.

However, once the deed had been done and I realized that sex did not cause devil's horns to pop out of one's forehead, I worked rapidly to get over all those feelings of shame and guilt and I succeeded. It was easier than I ever could have guessed, actually.

Maybe that meant I really was slated for a place in Hell. That was okay. Most people I knew were going to be there, too.

I peered into the freezer the night of Maureen's revelation, hoping to find a Lean Cuisine that included nothing even remotely resembling a mucus plug. In the end, I settled for a box of Hanover pretzels. I couldn't even handle dipping them in mustard, brown or yellow. Spooning Fuzzer's ocean whitefish stew almost did me in.

I ate the pretzels dry, sitting in front of the TV, blindly watching sitcom reruns. While my mother tangoed with some leftover Casanova type in the hills of Borneo; and my lover rubbed his wife's feet and played hide-and-seek with his kids; and my twenty-something colleague and her husband planned their baby's future; and my father wined and dined a woman young enough to be his daughter.

How did I get here, I wondered suddenly.

And how do I get out?

* * *

Doug and I had an assignation—what a great word, so many connotations—the next night. I had to stay late at the office so we weren't able to have dinner together. I arrived at Doug's office at almost eight o'clock. He locked his door, opened a bottle of wine, and kissed me hello.

I so needed to spill, especially after my lapse into self-pity and depression the night before when I sat alone munching pretzels for dinner.

"I'm in the mood to talk. Is that okay?" I said. "I feel all wound up."

"Fine by me," he said. "As long as we can, you know, later."

I laughed at the broad comical expression on his face. "Of course."

Doug was generous as a listener. An hour had passed before I paused to breathe.

Nine o'clock. The lights were off, the room illuminated by the lights from surrounding buildings, other offices, and apartments. We sat on the couch, my legs curled up under me, Doug's legs stretched out, crossed at the ankles.

For one solid hour I'd been yammering on about my childhood; about the double-standards imposed by the church and my old-world Grandfather Morelli; about my best friend in high school who'd gone to college on the West Coast and never answered my letters; about my best friend in freshman year of college who'd committed suicide when she got a C+ in Advanced Calculus and who in a note had left her collection of Beatles albums to me. A collection I never got because her parents refused to acknowledge the various notes she'd left for various friends. Poor Susanne.

I'm sure the bottle of wine I'd consumed on an empty stomach fueled much of my rambling storytelling.

"You're sure I'm not boring you?" I said, knowing that I probably was and knowing that Doug would lie about it.

"I'm sure," he lied. "Go on. Your life is fascinating."

I laughed. "Well, I don't know about that. But where was I?"

"Something about priests and nuns."

"Oh, yeah. The poor nuns. Every nun I had in school, no matter how young she was, wore a cheap dark blue suit and ugly, serviceable shoes. Big black ugly shoes. Why did they have to do that? Every one of them, the nasty ones and the nice ones, just looked so—so poor. So neglected."

"What about the priests?" Doug asked.

I grimaced. "Most of the priests my family knew seemed to spend an awful lot of time eating at parishioners' homes and drinking at private clubs. And they dressed far better than nuns. Sleek black suits, shiny black shoes . . . They just seemed to be about a much more attractive lifestyle. Some of them even belonged to the country club and played golf every Saturday! Can you imagine a nun on the golf course, wearing her habit? And what about the shoes? What would she do for shoes?"

"And I used to regret my parents were atheists," Doug said, kissing my hand. "Go on."

I did.

"It's odd, you know. My mother didn't want me to be a nun, but she told me time and again that I wasn't 'cut out' for marriage. Those were her words—cut out for—like everyone was born according to a predetermined pattern and that was that; you couldn't change, there was no point in even trying. I think she meant it as a compliment—she always said it with a sort of proud smile—though for the longest time I had no idea why she thought not being cut out for marriage was a good thing. And I had no idea how she could tell such a thing about me, anyway. I mean, I was about nine when she started telling me what I was and was not cut out to be. I hadn't even begun to think about thinking about my future! I remember being worried by the fact that she could see so clearly who and what I was. I wondered if I had some sort of physical trait that gave me away or something. It was all very confusing."

"Did anyone ever ask you to marry him?" Doug asked.

The question took me by surprise.

"Yes, in fact, one—no, two guys did. Huh. I'd almost forgotten. Both right after college."

"You said no."

"I said no. I wasn't interested. Besides, they weren't at all right for the job."

"But they thought you might be. Seems Mother Weston was wrong. Maybe she should stay far away in the jungle."

"Yeah, I guess," I said, laughing. "Hey, why didn't I talk to you about all this years ago?"

"We only met months ago."

"Oh. Right. Here's another funny thing," I said. "If not being cut out for marriage was a good thing, then why weren't the unmarried women we knew happier? Or more glamorous? Or invited over more often? Why did my mother and her sister, my Aunt Margaret, whisper things like, 'Poor Alice, she doesn't have a man,' behind their backs? Where were the single women who weren't nuns, the single women who were happy and proud and glamorous?"

"In the city, having fun?"

I laughed. "Maybe. That possibility wouldn't have occurred to me then. See, because from when I was little I'd gotten the loud and clear message that for a woman to be single was for her to be somehow defective and pitiable."

"That's not an uncommon notion, Erin."

Doug opened another bottle of wine, refilled my plastic cup, and settled back.

"I know, I know. But—how did that reconcile with my mother's being proud I wasn't cut out for marriage!"

"Mothers. Can't live with them. Can't . . ."

"Don't tempt me," I said, briefly assailed by an image of Marie Weston whooping it up on a beach with a greasy Lothario. "Anyway, the point was that for a man to be single meant that he was a jolly and enviable bachelor. Which meant that, even if he was a priest, he was assumed to be a wonderful conversationalist and a serious gourmand and a connoiseur of fine wine. Which meant he was always invited to dinner. Unlike his skinny, dried-up and bitter female counterpart."

"Defective and pitiable?"

"Exactly." I smiled. My head felt a little funny. "You're such a good listener, Mr. Spears."

Doug leaned over and kissed me. "Go on. I'm interested."

"I don't remember my mother ever inviting a single woman to a meal. But charming Mr. Mahoney and raucous Father Bill, they were at our table all the time. Huh."

"What?"

"Another lightbulb," I said slowly. "It occurs to me now that Cousin Katie and Miss Adams were actually quite attractive—and a few years younger than my mother and Aunt Margaret—and that maybe the reason they weren't invited to dinner had nothing to do with their being defective and pitiable."

"You think?" Doug's smile was infectious. And his lips begged to be kissed. I kissed them.

"Oh, I think all right," I said. "Maybe it had something to do with their being independent and threatening. Wild single women out to steal the bored husbands of boring married women."

There's something familiar in those words, my brain said fuzzily. But what?

Doug seemed amused about something.

"Yes, I do believe you're on to something there, Ms. Weston," he said. "More wine?"

"Okay." I held out my empty plastic cup and Doug poured. "Hey, want to hear the real twist to the whole story? Then I'll shut up, I swear."

"You'll have to because I'm going to ravish you."

"Good. Then, I'll make it quick. Years later, I think I was in college, I found out that at least two of those jolly and enviable bachelors that were always mooching at our home were gay. Turns out they were just desperately trying to keep up appearances. Deeply in the closet. It's sad, really."

Doug took the plastic cup of wine from my hand and began to unbutton my blouse. "What would your Grandpa Morelli have said to that bit of information?"

I considered as I lay back on the couch and the room began to spin.

"I think he would have laughed," I said with a giggle.

Chapter Thirty-seven

Saturday night. Date night. Abby was with my father. Doug was with his wife. JoAnne, Maggie, and I were with each other. We met for dinner at No. 9 Park.

"Look over by the bar," JoAnne instructed. "The far end. Casually, casually, don't look like you're looking."

"What am I looking at?" I said.

"Mr. December with Miss May."

"Oh." How had I missed them even for a second?

The man was probably in his late sixties or early seventies. It was hard to tell, exactly, because he'd taken pains to preserve what looks he'd had as a younger man. He was slim, bordering on skinny. His hair was silver and artfuly swept back with about two handfuls of gel. He wore a big gold watch and a big gold ring and a big gold bracelet. His navy blazer with big gold buttons was impeccable, probably from Brooks Brothers. His trousers were gray, knife-creased. His shoes, shiny and black.

Aside from the preponderance of gold, he looked respectable enough, a seventy-year-old single man out on the town. Respectable, but also—old.

Especially standing next to his companion. She was maybe

my age, at least half his seventy. She wore a wrap-around
dress that showed off an impressive cleavage and a lot of leg.
High heels. Hair, blond—a very expensive color job. Something sparkly at her throat. A gift from Mr. December?

Neither was a caricature. Still . . . Mr. December put his
hand on Miss May's shoulder. Even from a distance I could
see the wrinkles and liver spots. Miss May tilted her head
and smiled up at him, a practiced gesture.

I looked away.

"Typical older man/younger woman scenario," JoAnne
pronounced. "If he has money, it'll last. If not, he'll have his
fling until he can't keep up with her anymore. Until going to
clubs every Saturday night until three A.M. puts him on
blood pressure medication."

"If he isn't on it already," I mumbled. Was my father on
blood pressure medication? What else about my father didn't
I know?

"Or she'll have her fun—or whatever it is she's having—
until she gets totally bored with his playing Perry Como
records while napping in his favorite chair with his reading
glasses halfway down his nose," Maggie said. "Or his wearing cardigans or something."

"Perry Como?" I repeated. "How old do you think that
man at the bar is? Seventy, tops." And, I thought, my father is
fifty-eight years old, not ninety. "Besides, no real old men
wear cardigans. Only fussy grandpas on TV commercials for
hard candies. Butterscotch hard candies."

"Point is," JoAnne said loudly, "without a lot of money to
keep a young woman around, she won't stay with an old guy."

"That is such an old-fashioned, sexist thing to say!" I
cried. "On so many levels."

Though Reason told me that JoAnne had a point. Look
at Anna-Nicole Smith, Reason said. Like she married that
skinny old man for his personality? Look at Miss May over
there. You think she's turned on by Mr. December's age spots?

"Well, what else can an older guy give a younger woman?"
JoAnne persisted. "If he's not rich, I mean. Forget about kids.

He's got his family, he's done. Forget about hanging with her friends, he'll feel too awkward. And sex just gets more and more iffy."

"Not to mention ear hair and wrinkles and empty cans of Ensure lying about the kitchen," Maggie added knowingly.

"And the nasty glares of women his own age. A total assumption on their part he's with you for sex and showing off in front of his buddies. A total assumption that you're with him for money and are nothing better than a tramp."

"And the fact that he can't eat anything spicy and can't eat dinner after nine o'clock or he'll be up all night with cramps."

"Or in the bathroom. With your *Martha Stewart Living* magazine."

"How about love?" I argued, a little bit desperate now. Suddenly, I didn't want Miss May to leave nice old Mr. December. I didn't want Abby to leave my father. I didn't want some young woman, especially a friend of mine, to break his heart. What did my father ever do to deserve two broken hearts in one lifetime!

"Companionship? Compatability?" I went on. "What if the man and woman really get along? What if they share passions, like art or . . . or hiking or whatever. I don't know. What if they fall in love?"

"Nah. Probably just a sick father fixation on her part and a pitiful desire to recapture his youth on the man's."

"That's so unfair, JoAnne," I snapped. "Okay, maybe it's true about some older men and younger women, but it can't be true about all of them. It can't be. It's not true about Abby and my father. I know it."

Was it?

JoAnne shrugged.

I snuck another look at May-December. He was sipping bourbon or Scotch or whiskey, straight. She was sipping a bright purple martini. Okay, there was something slightly macabre about their being together—but maybe that was JoAnne's opinion infecting my own observations.

I wondered if Mr. December had a daughter older than Miss May. I wondered what the daughter thought of her father going around with someone half his age.

"Ten years, tops," JoAnne was saying now. "That's my limit. Only exception, the guy's super, filthy rich. Then, I'll go to fifteen. Okay, maybe twenty. But only if he works out regularly. And has all his hair."

"That's so nasty, about the hair," I said. So much for my determination to stay out of the conversation. "A guy can't help it if his hair falls out. It's not his fault."

"Uh, Hair Club for Men? Plugs?"

"Do you know how much those things cost?" I argued. As if I cared. "Over twenty thousand dollars, something outrageous. Hank, from the office, checked into it."

"If he's really rich, he'll be able to afford it," Maggie pointed out.

"But what if he doesn't want to get plugs?" I said. "What if he's happy with the way he looks? What if he thinks any woman who loves him should accept him for who he is? Bald and all. That's what we want, right? Someone to love us for who we are, not for what we look like."

Strangely, no one had an answer to this question for a full minute. A full minute is a long thing.

Then JoAnne changed the subject.

"What do you do if a man asks you to change something about yourself?"

"What's to change?" Maggie quipped. "I'm perfection!"

"Ha ha. Every man asks a women to change something about her appearance. Without fail. If it's not hair color it's hair length. Or clothes, that's a big one. They want you to dress more sexy."

"They want you to dress like a slut," Maggie amended.

"A guy once asked me to cut my nails," I told them. "Can you imagine! I've had long nails since I was twelve! It's part of who I am. Oh, yeah, Erin. She's the one with the perfectly manicured long nails. I mean, nobody would have recognized me with short nails! I wouldn't have recognized me. I shudder to think."

"Weight." Maggie.

Communal groan.

"Why is it that men you hardly know at all feel perfectly free asking you to lose ten pounds?" she went on. "Or gain ten pounds. Even if you're healthy and happy and think you look just fine. I mean, the nerve!"

"The balls!"

"What gives them the right!"

"And then ask them to lose ten pounds or beef up or change their hairstyle, whatever," JoAnne said, with what sounded very much like a harrumph. "Forget it. He's gone."

"Women have to wait until they're married before they can ask the guy to change his appearance. It's a proven fact," I told them. "My friend at work, Maureen, totally dresses her husband, head to toe. She won't allow Mark to pick out a pair of shorts on his own anymore. She said before the wedding he was a slob. The week they got back from their honeymoon, she surprised him with a new wardrobe. It went on from there."

"And he goes along with it?" JoAnne sneered. "That sounds kind of wimpy."

Maggie answered for me. "That's how it works. He's got a wife. She's agreed to have regular sex for 'free' till death do them part. He's grateful. He'll put up with almost anything for the sex."

I shrugged. "I don't know. Maureen said Mark never liked shopping anyway, so she's doing him a favor all around."

"Hey, I just thought of something funny," JoAnne said. "What if this guy looks so good now that his wife's dressing him, other women start coming on to him and it goes to his head and he has an affair! He could argue it's all his wife's fault for dressing him too nicely."

"Mmm," I said. "That would be one way of looking at it."

While JoAnne and Maggie chatted on, I wondered.

Did Carol choose Doug's wardrobe? Did she buy him socks at BJ's Discount Warehouse? Was it her choice that he wear boxers and not briefs?

Underwear, the great leveler. I'd been touched the first time I'd seen Doug put on his boxers. It's a humbling thing, dressing in the presence of your loved one, watching your loved one dress.

Suddenly, the intimacy of marriage seemed so terribly unattainable.

Suddenly, I didn't feel much like eating.

Chapter Thirty-eight

E—when am I going to be a grandma? girls here have babies by 16. how's that job going? M.

Maureen and I went shopping at lunch one day for baby clothes.

"Infants need a certain type of T-shirt," she explained. "Their belly buttons are all sensitive at first, so the shirts have to tie at the side, not snap anywhere. Ties are less irritating than snaps."

"There are so many things to think about," I said. "How do you keep all the information straight?"

"I don't," Maureen admitted. "That's why I have so many baby books at home. And why I spend so much time highlighting. Whenever I can't remember something, like how often you're supposed to bathe an infant, or when I realize I have no idea how to suction a baby's nose when he has a cold, I just look it up."

"It's like being back in school," I said, "except the stakes are so much higher."

"I know. If you fail at being a good mommy, you just can't take the class over. The kid's a mess, end of story."

"Are you scared?" I asked then, as we rode the elevator in Macy's at Downtown Crossing.

Maureen laughed. "What do you think? I'm petrified. But I'm also so excited I can hardly stand it."

"How's Mark handling everything?" I asked.

"He's been great. I mean, what's his option? He loves me, he's totally psyched to be a father, he's already talking about another kid after this one." Maureen patted her belly. "I told him, fine, we can have another baby, as long as you go through the morning sickness for me."

"Wouldn't that be wonderful," I said.

Yes, I thought, as I flipped through a stack of baby undies, wouldn't it be wonderful to have a man so happy about building a family with me. If Doug and I ever married . . .

No, I couldn't allow myself to think about that. We'd never discussed having children together because we'd never discussed our being married. And if Doug hadn't wanted to have children with Carol, would he ever want to have them with me?

Point is, Reason said, he's married. And if you continue to stay with a married man, it's highly unlikely you'll ever be buying T-shirts for your own baby.

I waited, but Romance seemed to have been taking a nap.

Maureen and I spent fifteen minutes combing the baby department and came up empty, though I did buy the baby a mint green onesie with an adorable little frog on the chest. I couldn't help it.

"You still have some time," I said as we rode the elevator back to the first floor. "I'll keep an eye out for the T-shirts."

"Would you? Thanks, Erin. I'm so tired some days, and others, I feel totally energized. It's odd."

It's a miracle, I thought, tears suddenly pricking my eyes. New life is a miracle.

After work the following day I went to Lord & Taylor's baby department to look for the T-shirts with a tie, found two packages, and bought them.

On the way home, I decided to stop at the bookstore in the mall. My bedside reading pile was getting dangerously low and if I didn't have a good book to read at night, I was unhappy.

Once there, I began to browse through the tables piled with recent trade editions and the shelves stacked with hardcover bestsellers. I must have been engrossed in the selection because suddenly I realized I didn't have the bag from Lord & Taylor.

I glanced around, hoping I'd put it down somewhere close by, but I could find no bag.

I was angry and also sad. Those two packages of T-shirts had been the last in stock. Sure, I could go back to the store in a few weeks but . . .

"Excuse me."

A tall, nicely built man, maybe about thirty-five, dressed in a blue suit with the tie loosened, was standing there in front of me. And he was holding my Lord & Taylor bag.

He had a very nice smile.

"I'm sorry to bother you," he said, "but I found this over in the next aisle and I think I saw you with it earlier."

He'd seen me with it earlier? So, he'd been looking at me, noticing.

I smiled back and said, "Whew, thanks! Yes, it's mine. I'd just realized I'd lost it."

"Something special?" he asked and I noticed his eyes were a lovely shade of green.

"Yes," I said. "T-shirts for my friend. Well, actually, for her baby. Which isn't born yet. But infants need a special kind of T-shirt and we couldn't find them and . . ."

Mr. Helpful did not look bored.

"I didn't know infants needed special T-shirts," he said.

"There's a lot to learn, I guess, when you're having a baby."

"I bet." Mr. Helpful handed me the bag and said, "By the way, my name is Brian."

"Erin."

"Hi, Erin. Um, I wonder . . . Well, I was noticing you before and I kind of wanted to come up and talk to you but I hate just bothering someone, but then your shopping bag gave me an excuse to say hello."

He was adorable. I smiled again.

"So," he went on, "would you maybe like to get a cup of coffee or something? If you're busy now, I understand, maybe some other time . . ."

I felt rooted to the spot. Here was an attractive guy, a nice guy, asking me for a cup of coffee. But I couldn't accept his invitation.

Of course, you can't! Romance cried. You're committed to Doug. You're in love.

Maybe, Reason said. But that relationship is going nowhere, fast. This guy is single, as far as she knows, and seems nice. Why should she pass up an opportunity to talk?

Because Erin is faithful to her soul mate!

Is her so-called soul mate faithful to her? Correct me if I'm wrong, but he gets into bed every night with another woman.

Stop it, the both of you! I cried. I . . .

The truth was I wanted to have coffee with Brian. And the truth was also that I couldn't.

"I'm sorry," I said. "I'm seeing someone."

"Oh." Brian shrugged good-naturedly. "Okay. I guess I probably should have known someone as pretty as you would be taken."

"Thanks," I said, and I meant it, even if 'taken' wouldn't have been my word of choice. "If I weren't involved . . ."

"That's okay. Look, have a good night."

Brian turned to go.

"Thank you," I said. "For returning my package."

He turned back and said, "Tell your friend good luck."

I was in a bad mood. I seemed often to be in a bad mood in those days, testy, on edge, often ready to explode. It was unlike me. I wondered if something in my diet was contributing to high blood pressure or some other scary medical condition. But beyond that brief thought, I chose not to explore possible reasons for the change in my behavior.

I also chose not to explore why it was that I was able to keep my explosive anger in check at work and with my friends, but not with Doug. I wasn't always attacking him. But it was beginning to happen with some frequency.

We were sitting on a bench in the Gardens. Doug was throwing the crumbs of his sandwich to the ducks and geese.

"I wish you wouldn't do that," I said.

"Why? Birds have to eat, too."

"I don't care. I don't like birds."

Doug looked at me and grinned.

"How can you not like birds?"

"I just don't," I snapped. "They frighten me. I've told you that. Don't you ever listen?"

Doug threw the last crumb to the birds and turned to me.

"Hey, that's not fair," he said, not angrily. "I listen all the time. Even when you've had too much to drink."

Hello?

"What is that supposed to mean?"

"You talk a lot when you've had too much to drink. No big deal."

What?

"Since when have you seen me drunk?"

Doug sighed. "Oh, come on, Erin, just forget it."

"No, I want to know. When have you ever seen me drunk?"

"Just once, that night in my office. When you went on and on about your childhood and family and the nuns. It was cute."

Cute? The condescending bastard . . .

"I was not drunk!" I protested, though I knew I had been. A little.

Doug gave me one of those extremely annoying indulgent looks one gives a child who is lying outrageously.

"If you say so."

"I was not drunk. Did you even really listen that night?
Do you remember anything I said?"

"I listened. But frankly, Erin, I was mostly thinking about
the sex we were going to have when you stopped talking."

I felt sick to my stomach, betrayed. I felt like a fool.

"I don't believe it."

Doug laughed.

"Come on, Erin, I'm a guy. If you want to blab on . . ."

"Blab on?"

"Sorry. If you want to ramble on about the past and have
someone really listen, you should do it with a girlfriend."

"But you talked to me. You gave me advice."

"I know. Erin, what's the big deal? I was there, I did what
I could."

Doug reached for my hand. I snatched it away.

"Assuming I was drunk. You were humoring me."

"Why are you picking a fight? I don't need this, Erin."

And as quickly as the fury had come upon me, it receded,
leaving in its wake shame and misery.

Doug was right. I'd been trying to pick a fight. Truth be
told, I'd been fully aware of how boring I must have been that
night on Doug's office couch. He'd listened, responded, made
love to me, and then drove me home, safe and sound. I'd had
nothing to complain about then and didn't have anything to
complain about now.

"Oh, Doug," I whispered, "I'm so sorry. I'm so, so sorry.
I don't know what came over me. Please." I touched his arm.
"Please forgive me."

Doug took my hand.

"You're tired," he said. "Go home and get some rest. I'll
call you tomorrow."

I nodded, unable to speak, and God, hadn't I already said
enough?

Doug didn't kiss me good-bye. He released my hand. His
face looked drawn. He stood up and walked away.

You're an ass, Erin, I told myself.

You're rightfully angry, Reason said. You're not getting what you need.

I waited. Romance said nothing.

Chapter Thirty-nine

September, Boston

September in New England is surprisingly summerlike, though some of the oppression of August has lifted. In Boston, the streets suddenly teem with college students back from summer break and even those of us who are long past studenthood feel the energy of a fresh start. A new beginning.

Of course, September is also a time of endings.

The four of us met for drinks and appetizers at Mistral.

JoAnne had just gone to the funeral of a neighbor. She hadn't wanted to go but it seems the block association strongarmed every home owner along Bunker Hill Street to attend. JoAnne had hardly known Mrs. Murphy but she'd had the privilege of seeing her decked out in her Sunday best. Dead.

It had put her in a very bad mood.

"Funerals and weddings! I don't know which are worse."

"Uh, I'm going with funerals," I said, hoping to divert a tirade.

I failed. I went with the flow.

JoAnne tore on. "They both cost the guests a fortune.

There's the new dress and the gifts and God, then there's the people you'd never spend time with unless someone had croaked or was getting married. Which in some cases is worse than croaking."

Abby, Maggie, and I mumbled our agreement.

JoAnne turned to me.

"Erin, what do you say when some numbnuts at some horrible family function asks you why you aren't married yet? Like creepy Uncle Floyd at fat Aunt Marge's funeral."

"I say: Because no one's asked me yet. That usually shuts them up. Except," I added, "when Uncle Floyd chuckles, leans in with his cigarette breath, and says, 'Well, girlie, if I weren't already taken, I'd fix that.' "

"Well, I say: I'm not married because I'm a nymphomaniac and require lots of sex with many partners—sometimes many partners at the same time—and no one man could ever satisfy me."

"What's the reaction to that?" Maggie said, laughing.

JoAnne grinned. "Stunned silence. On occasion, a look of longing."

"I just tell the truth," Abby said. "I say, I'm waiting for Mr. Right. I'm waiting for my soul mate."

I resisted the sudden temptation to ask Abby if she thought she'd found her soul mate in my father.

"And the answer to that," JoAnne said, "is a look of pity and, 'There, there, dear, I'm sure everything will be just fine.' "

"I wish I could tell the truth," I admitted. "I wish I could say: 'I'm not married because the man I love is married to another woman and I love him so deeply I accept the situation.' "

"Yeah, that would go over big," JoAnne said. "You'd be labeled a hussy. You'd be known as 'the delusional one.' You'd be another object of pity."

"See?" I said. "The truth is just too . . . uncomfortable. There's a decided value to social lies."

Maggie's turn. "No one's ever asked me why I'm not married, but if they did I'd say: I don't believe in marriage. Marriage is not for me. I like my independence. I . . ."

JoAnne lowered her voice and frowned, probably like the mythical fat old Aunt Marge. "Independence doesn't keep you warm at night, missy."

"It does if it buys you flannel sheets and a down comforter."

"Touché!"

"All I have to say is that if I'm not married by the time I'm forty I'm never going to another wedding or funeral ever again." And I meant it. "They can say anything they want about me. I'm rude, I've cracked up, I'm on drugs, I'm gay . . ."

"Not that there's anything wrong with that," Maggie added, per our post-*Seinfeld* culture conversational rules.

"Of course," I agreed.

"Well," JoAnne said, "if I'm still single by the time I'm forty, I'm celebrating my good sense and buying myself a mondo diamond ring. Not that I couldn't afford it now, but I think I'll hold off and treat myself later. And then we'll all have a fabulous party and jet off to an exclusive spa for the weekend."

"Are you paying for that, too?" Maggie asked. "I'll be happy to go if you foot the bill for me."

Abby shuddered. "If I'm not married by the time I'm forty I think I'll die."

"Oh, come on."

"No, I'm serious. I think I'll just—die."

"No one dies from lack of marriage," JoAnne drawled. "Oxygen, yes. Marriage, no."

"What about dying of a broken heart?" Abby pressed. "Don't you believe people have died of broken hearts?"

"Dying of a broken heart is synonymous with suicide through self-starvation, i.e., anorexia. It's a Victorian conceit for 'Mary is morbidly depressed and won't snap out of it.' It's a joke. I'm a doctor and I can tell you, it's not possible to die of a broken heart."

"Sometimes I don't think you have a heart to break," Abby snapped.

"Where did that come from?" Maggie murmured.

"Didn't you ever pine for someone?" Abby pressed. "Didn't you ever long for even a glimpse of someone?"

JoAnne squinted at Abby as if pondering this question. Then: "Uh, no. Don't believe in pining. Sounds consumptive. I believe in active pursuit or cutting the cord. Neat and clean."

"You're such a doctor!" Abby huffed. "I can't imagine your bedside manner."

"My bedside manner is perfect," JoAnne replied, a hint of real anger in her voice. "Kids don't like to be lied to. They handle the truth a lot better than most adults I've known."

See? Funerals are far worse than weddings. They put everyone in a very bad mood.

"Hey," I said, stupidly trying to lighten the topic of conversation, "has anyone been to that new restaurant at Fanueil Hall, uh, Kingfish Hall? Hank, from work, says it's good. Well, okay."

JoAnne gave me a look of disdain. She's very good at giving looks of disdain. "No real Bostonian hangs out at Fanueil Hall," she said. "Please."

"Oh, it's not so bad," I replied, still attempting to make things—nicer. "It's a good place to take out-of-town visitors. And there are some cute shops. Like April Cornell and that Irish goods store."

Abby nodded. "I love that Christmas shop! Two stories of tinsel and treasures. It's so beautiful. I could just live there."

"Gives me a headache," JoAnne said. "Too many flashing lights and pwetty wittle kitties."

"Has anyone ever been to Durgin Park?" Maggie asked.

"I prefer Morton's," I said.

Maggie smiled. "You have an expense account."

"I like Union Oyster House," JoAnne admitted. Ah, her mood was finally softening. "Though it is pricey and I've never met a man there. A man I'd want to date, I mean." JoAnne considered. "I did once meet a few guys from Connecticut in town for some big golf tournament. But they weren't my type. Too much kelly green."

"But you can sit in the booth JFK used to sit in!" Abby said. "Upstairs. It's very exciting."

"I've sat in that booth," I said. "All I ever felt was hard wood under my butt."

"Oh, no one pick up on that, please!" Maggie moaned.

"Sorry. Didn't mean anything by it."

"Try their Oysters Rockefeller," I suggested to all. "Unbelievable."

"Speaking of Rockefeller," Maggie said, "I want to go to New York for that new show at MOMA. Frank Lloyd Wright drawings and notebooks, and photos of the projects and Wright's family. Anyone interested in making an excursion?"

"I'll think about it," I said.

JoAnne shook her head. "Count me out. Not a big fan of Mr. Wright's work. But maybe I'd go along for some shopping."

"Abby?" Maggie asked.

Abby hesitated. "Well, I'd have to check with John first."

"What!" That was JoAnne.

"I mean," Abby rushed on, "that maybe he'd prefer if I— uh, maybe he won't want me to go to New York alone. Without him, I mean."

"I'm out of this one," I said, putting my hands in the air in the universal sign of surrender.

"I'm not saying I wouldn't go anyway," Abby said lamely, turning away from JoAnne's glare. "Even if he didn't want me to go."

"Since when do you need permission from your boyfriend to go on a road trip with your girlfriends!" JoAnne demanded.

Abby opened her mouth but no words came out.

"Wait. You know what?" JoAnne said to no one and everyone. "It's been a freakin' long day. I'm tired and grumpy and I'm just going to let this slide. If Abby wants to be a . . ."

"JoAnne," Maggie said sternly. "You said you were going to let it slide. Okay?"

JoAnne went back to glaring.

I decided to change the subject. Again.

"Hey, speaking of New York, I just heard that old joke again: A nuclear explosion hits New York and devastates everything and everyone for miles. The next day the headline of *The Boston Globe* reads: HUB MAN KILLED IN BLAST."

"Ah, the provincialism of the Bostonians," Maggie said.

"Yeah," JoAnne said, "how can the Yankees suck when they're destroying the Red Sox? How exactly does that work?"

"It's the curse of being a second city and knowing it," Abby said wisely. "You feel you have to ignore the truth and flail away at the big guy. What we should do is accept reality gracefully."

"Right. New York is still the ruling city, even after September 11, 2001," I said.

"It's still the ruling city because of September 11th."

"It's because New York is the ruling city, that September 11th happened in the first place."

"So, what are we doing living in Boston?" I said.

"Oh, Boston's lovely," Abby said. "It's got its own charms. I like living here. But I love visiting New York. Forget about what I said before about John; I'll go with you, Maggie. I love going to New York for the museums and the galleries and the music, I really do, but it's a bit too—frantic—for me. I could never live there."

"Too dirty for me," JoAnne said. "But the men are fine."

"Not all of them," Maggie pointed out. "New York holds too many bad memories for me. You know, like of my disastrous marriage. I can visit but I'd never move back."

"What about you, Erin?" Abby asked. "Would you ever want to relocate to New York?"

I thought about that. Certainly, the idea had crossed my mind before. . . . But now there was Doug. Maybe he wouldn't want me to go to New York alone. Without him.

"No, I like my life here," I said. "I'm not into change for the sake of change. Maybe someday, I don't know, if I get some amazing job offer . . ." If Doug and I get married and decide to leave Boston together. . . . "I'm not going anywhere, though, for a while."

"Good." JoAnne raised her glass in a toast. "Here's to us, four fabulous Bostonians."

The evening got better from there.

Chapter Forty

Erin—sorry. I forgot Mrs. Cirillo died last year.
More later. M

The conversation—one part of it, anyway—we'd had at Mistral stuck with me. I thought later about the notion of leaving Boston, of moving away not only from Doug but from my father, my one true remaining tie to family.

This train of thought, of course, got me thinking about family in general. About families.

Is any one family better than the other? It seems everyone considers her own family to be the worst and sometimes, also the best. So how can you really evaluate craziness? Leaving aside the obviously criminal families, the parents who lock their kids in basements and feed them canned slop; the Munchhausen-by-Proxy mommies; the daddies who mistake their kiddies for sex slaves.

Take JoAnne's family, for example. Or, rather, what we've heard of her family, because JoAnne's the only Chiofalo we'd met. There was the brother in LA and JoAnne thought there might be a cousin or two somewhere in a trailer park in Schenectady, otherwise JoAnne was it. Parents first divorced, then dead. No aunts or uncles living. Just JoAnne and her older, estranged brother, Robert.

Then, there was Maggie's personal hell. I believed all of what I'd heard her say, which wasn't much, Maggie being both scrupulously to-the-point and generally unwilling to say anything bad about anyone unless it's totally unavoidable. What I knew was that there were too many kids, too little money, and too much alcohol by far. And where there's too much alcohol there's almost always violence. Maggie had the scars to prove it. But she got out alive and now has nothing at all to do with her siblings—both parents having succumbed to liver and heart disease—except for the annual Christmas card. I suspected even that token attachment would fall away before long.

And, of course, there was Abby's unusual circumstances, her mother married to a guy fifteen years her junior, a guy with no visible income other than his new wife's monthly allowance; one cousin in jail for trafficking in child porn; another in and out of a "drying out" facility; an eccentric grandfather who spoke only in rhyming couplets. The funny thing about Abby was that she claimed not to see anything unusual in the Walkers and the Howards, as if eccentricity and a certain constitutional delicacy—i.e., weak mind, no will power, amoral standards—was just part of what being a Walker and a Howard meant. Abby didn't seem to resent being the offspring of trouble. That was probably a healthy way to get through life.

Sometimes, when I look at my own family in comparison to others, they seem pretty normal. The Westons and the Morellis. It's a fairly small bunch now and if I don't get moving and have some children, it's going to be seriously smaller come the next generation and the one after that. It's me, all alone, in my thirties, no cousins I can—or want—to track down, no siblings. My father had an older sister who went into what I like to call the Nunnery—the convent—when she was only a teenager. Though nuns are generally reported to have unusually long life spans—something about lack of stress due to lack of demanding husbands and children—my aunt Mary, also known as Sister Dominic, died when I was a small child. She was about twenty-five. It was a ruptured appendix, a horrible accident. Her fellow sisters didn't get her to the hospital on time. Her parents—my grandparents, Dad's parents—had both died in their early fifties, victims of one spectacular car accident. To this day my father keeps a white rabbit's foot in his desk drawer. So far, he's been remarkably healthy—and lucky.

My mother's family is mostly gone now, too. There were a few cousins, living somewhere in New Hampshire, but it had been years since there'd been any communication. For all I knew they were dead or living in Wyoming.

My maternal grandparents had died within months of each other, five or six years earlier. First she died, then Grandpa. Everyone said he'd died because he couldn't live without her, the woman to whom he'd been married for almost sixty years. Maybe that's true; I'll never know for sure. Grandpa did have a bad heart; maybe Grandma's passing finally broke it.

My mother's sister, my Aunt Margaret, was, in my memory, an unpleasant woman. She was nasty and mean-spirited and judgmental. The last I'd heard, she was living somewhere in the Midwest, seemingly determined to keep her distance from her sister Marie, as she'd sworn to do after their last horrible fight. It was no great loss to me or my father. But I thought it must be to my mother, on some level. She never mentioned Margaret, though, hadn't since Margaret had gone away. When a mutual friend informed me of my aunt's general whereabouts, I'd told my mother that I'd heard Aunt Margaret was alive.

"Not to me," she'd said.

After that, I kept my mouth shut.

My mother, clearly the most rebellious and status-quo-breaking of the bunch, isn't a horrible person. She's just—unique. I mean, she was never physically abusive to me and while she was married to my father, she never cheated on him. Okay, so she did disappear once for three days when I was four and returned home with no explanation and looking none the worse for the wear—I was later told by my sneering Aunt Margaret—which should have given my father at least a clue that there would be trouble ahead. Which there was when at the age of fifty-five she filed for divorce without a word of warning and trotted off to An Unnamed South American Country to pursue a life dedicated to "social work."

Her latest postcard:

> *Erin—Met the most adorable young man in jail. (There was some unpleasantness, but that's over now.) He's a Ricky Martin look-alike! He's wonderful to me and doesn't at all mind that he's thirty years my junior. I'm supremely, gloriously fulfilled as a woman at last!—Ciao! (I know that's not Spanish, but it sounds so right!)*

It was amazing to me how anyone could actually get and stay married, what with each person bringing, inevitably, his or her own enormous Family Story, good, bad, or both.

From the minor but annoyingly important daily habits like the toilet paper flap being outside or in, over or under, ("We always did it *this* way at home!"), to the larger, lifestyle issues like vacationing without the kids ("But my parents *never* went anywhere without us!") . . . It seemed a constant struggle, a continual negotiation of ideas and actions.

Family. I was exhausted just thinking about the notion.

Especially when my thoughts wandered, as they inevitably did, to Doug's own birth family, then to his wife's, finally to the family they'd created in their ten-room, three-bath, two-fireplace house in Newton.

Family.

It was a part of Doug from which I was excluded then and from which I knew I would always be excluded, even if the amazing happened and we wound up married someday.

And when my thoughts projected themselves into the future, which they invariably did, I'd try to see Taylor and Courtney as teens, then young adults. I'd wonder what they'd be like. How they would think of their parents. And if I were still in the picture . . . Well, would they even know I was there? Would I be their official stepmother or still a dark, lurking presence in their father's life, someone kept apart from the Spears clan like rat poison is kept in a locked cabinet under the sink? And if I was the Stepmother, would Taylor and Courtney hate and despise me for breaking up their own best-and-worst family unit? Would I have to stay home when Doug went to big family functions like weddings and funerals because Carol, the Mother, now sainted by her husband's perfidy, would be there and my presence would be just another humiliation to her?

What about the humiliation to yourself? Reason routinely asked sharply at this point in my ruminations.

Yes, I'd respond. What about the humiliation to me?

I had no answer to that.

Chapter Forty-one

I still felt bad about blowing up at Doug by the pond in the Gardens. The man had a right to feed the ducks and geese without being attacked for imagined bad behavior to his lover.

I wanted to make it up to him in some meaningful way, but of course was hampered by the terms and conditions of the Situation. And I was scared. Scared of my own irrational behavior that seemed to rise up out of nowhere, a geyser of bitterness. A meaningful gesture, one that showed how much I cared, could not be accompanied by a screaming fit.

Maybe instead of focusing on the feelings of your married lover, Reason advised, you should spend some time analyzing the source of your anger and bitterness.

Maybe. But it was far easier to act than to think.

Lying to oneself produces frustration, which leads to anger, Reason intoned. Until you face the Situation squarely . . .

I shut out Reason and prepared a silly but hopefully meaningful surprise for Doug. Two days later when we met for lunch at Radius I presented him with a gallon-sized zipper-locked plastic bag filled with breadcrumbs.

"I made them myself," I said.

Doug took the bag and a grin spread across his handsome, slightly weathered face.

"What do you say we have lunch in the Gardens today," he said.

We got up from the table, apologized to the waiter, and headed out.

I might have been afraid of birds. But I was far more afraid of life without Doug.

JoAnne had asked me over. When she opened the door and I saw the scowl on her face, I took a step back.

"What did I do?" I said.

"Nothing. It's not about you. Come in already."

I followed JoAnne into the living room.

"You're pissed off or something."

"Brilliant observation."

I raised my eyebrows.

JoAnne moaned dramatically and flopped onto the couch. "Sorry. Sit down."

I did.

"What's up? And yes, I'd love some juice, thanks."

JoAnne pounded off into the kitchen and returned a few minutes later with a glass of cranberry juice, no ice.

I took a sip. "Okay," I said. "Spill."

She did.

"Look, remember back in June when I found out I didn't have cancer and I decided it was time to take care of me for a change? I mean, really take care of me, the whole me, not just my physical self."

"Of course I remember. Sounded great. Still does."

"Erin—there's a little problem."

"What?" I said.

"What the hell was I thinking? I mean, I've tried everything from aromatherapy to Wicca. Wicca! What more do I have to do to—change? What does 'being good to myself' mean, anyway? Where the hell did I get that phrase? Some dopey Lifetime Channel talk show? I don't know what I'm doing!"

I was torn between the desire to roar with laughter and the desire to pat JoAnne on the head and say, "There, there."

"Well," I ventured, "the therapy is okay, right? I mean, you feel it's helping?"

JoAnne made a face. "I guess. I don't know. Jesus, doesn't anybody make a quick fix kit or something! Need a change? Apply liberally, rinse, repeat, presto, everything's shiny and new."

I was beginning to understand something, the root of JoAnne's frustration. As far as I knew, JoAnne hadn't gone on one date since Martin.

Oh, yeah. It was time to strategize. Forget the herbs and spacey music and goddess workshops. It was time for her to get back out there and meet a man. It was time for sex.

"JoAnne," I said, "you need to get laid."

"Well, duh," she snapped. "But I'm supposed to be choosing wisely. I'm not supposed to be getting involved with just a fuck. My therapist says I need to meet someone who wants a relationship. Shit. What has my life come to?"

"Your therapist is right," I said. "Now, have you considered trying one of those seven-minute dating services?"

"Shoot me. Just go ahead, kill me now."

I grinned. "Okay, okay. Just asking. So, it looks like we're left with ye olde classic dating service. Or the personals."

"No personals," JoAnne said fiercely.

"All right then," I said, picking up a copy of the *Globe* that was sitting on a side table. "It's a dating service."

"I can't believe I'm even considering this," JoAnne muttered. "It's humiliating."

"Oh, please. More humilating than sitting alone at a bar trying not to look like a desperate sex-starved woman?"

"You do that?" JoAnne asked sweetly.

"Yes. And so do you. Do you really need another reminder? You're considering using a dating service because you're mature enough to realize you can't trust your old patterns any longer. You're considering this because you've had a second brush with cancer and you realize that your life is passing you by and that maybe a real relationship would be a good thing for a change. So be quiet."

"Yes, Mother."

"Now, let's see. We have—okay, Options. And Choices . . ."

"Sound like abortion clinics. Next."

I scanned the page. "Your Call?"

JoAnne rolled her eyes. "Sure that's not Last Call?"

I sighed. This was not going at all well. "Just try to be open, okay? Now: New Crop."

"No," JoAnne said shortly. "I'm getting produce out of that."

She had a point. "Here's one. Perfect Partners, Inc."

JoAnne considered. "Okay, not bad. A bit law-firm-like but . . ."

Now we were getting somewhere. All it took was the first little step . . . "Right-On Romance!"

"Oh, no. No way. I'm channeling *Different Strokes. All in the Family. The Jeffersons.*"

One step forward, two steps back. "Okay. Here's one. Reality Romance. That sounds, I don't know, intelligent."

"A.K.A, Time to Settle."

I looked at JoAnne consideringly. "You know you're impossible, don't you?"

"Yes."

"Okay. As long as you know. Moving onward . . . We've got: On Point Romance."

"For ballerinas only."

And weren't most male ballet dancers gay, anyway? And the ones who weren't probably weren't big on hanging out at expensive bars. I'd heard that dancers were very poorly paid. Their salaries made a tuba player's look hefty. Ballet dancers were not the way to go.

"Here's one," I said. "Couples Co-ordinate."

"Specializing in geeky mathematicians."

I laughed. "Is there any other kind? Okay, I get your point.

So, what about Perfect Partners, Inc. It's the only one you didn't entirely shoot down."

"I don't know. Read the rest of their ad."

I did.

"Where are the offices?"

"What does that matter?"

"I'm considering giving these people my hard-earned money, I want to know where their offices are located."

"Uh, Somerville."

"What! No way. Forget it. Slumerville? Uh uh."

It was a long, long afternoon.

If JoAnne was experiencing a dry spell, Damion had hit the jackpot.

I called him one evening and got the latest.

Damion's official new boyfriend was the real deal. Frederick was ten years Damion's senior and had been in a long-term relationship until his partner had died. Not of AIDS or some other illness. The poor guy, only thirty-seven, had been hit by a car while on a morning bike ride. Frederick had been awarded a good deal of money by a sympathetic court; seems the driver was seriously drunk at the time of the accident and wanted on assault charges.

After Tom's death, Frederick had sold the home they'd shared in Lincoln for almost ten years and bought a condo in the South End. He'd told Damion that with Tom gone, he just couldn't stand living alone in a big suburban house, surrounded by all the memories. Frederick had sold most of the furniture, bought new pieces, and put some other, more personal items of Tom's in permanent storage. A formal portrait of Tom stood atop the baby grand piano in Frederick's condo, the only physical reminder of him.

"Is he morbid?" I asked.

"Not at all," Damion said. "He's totally moved on with his life."

Tom had been allergic to animals, Damion explained. Frederick had always wanted a cat so after moving to the South End he'd walked on down to the Animal Rescue League of Boston and adopted two kittens, which he named Coco and Chanel.

"What happens if you guys get serious?" I asked Damion. "Two cats living with two dogs? Sounds like trouble."

But Damion wasn't worried. He was falling in love with a man who was falling in love with him.

"It'll work out," Damion said, "you'll see. True love makes all possible, chicka."

I wondered.

"How did you meet him again?" I asked.

"Erin, don't you ever listen anymore? I swear, since you've been seeing that creep your brain has turned to mush. We met through a friend of his who I did a job for last month. It's a great way to meet, through someone who knows you both."

"Isn't that what blind dates are all about?" I said glumly. "Blind dates have a lousy reputation. Everyone says . . ."

"I don't listen to what everyone says, my dear. I do what seems best for me."

"Okay. Well, good luck. When do I get to meet this guy?"

"Soon, I promise. Let me enjoy him all to myself a bit more, though, okay?"

"Sure," I quipped. "Who am I to thwart the progress of true love?"

Who was I even to recognize it?

Chapter Forty-two

> *E—is it nice in boston? v. hot here, all the time.
> miss fall and opp to wear my mink. ricardo of-
> fered to buy me one but what wld i do with it
> here? M.*

We decided that if JoAnne was going to do the dating service thing, she was going to do it right. Which meant we
were going to have to help her. We gathered at Abby's apartment and got down to work. Maggie begged off, saying she
was taking a class for a colleague who was ill.

"Perfect Partners asks that you fill out this simple questionnaire," Abby explained, "to help them get to know you. It
says in the brochure that they've successfully matched up over
two hundred couples in the past two years! Isn't that wonderful?"

JoAnne grunted.

"Curb your enthusiasm, dear," I said.

JoAnne sneered.

It was going to be a long night.

Abby wiggled in her chair and cleared her throat. "Okay,

let's get started. Now. First question. Remember, answer honestly," she admonished.

"Okay, okay. Just start."

"First question: Store you can't live without?"

"Express."

Abby looked surprised.

"JoAnne's a hoochie mama at heart," I commented helpfully. "You might want to put that down somewhere."

"Favorite ice cream flavor?"

"Oh, come on," JoAnne cried. "This is ridiculous. How do the answers to these questions reveal anything essential about me?"

"You want to register with this dating service, you fill out the Personality Profile," I said, struggling unsuccessfully to hide a grin.

"Christ. Okay. Go on."

"Favorite ice cream flavor?"

"Coffee."

"Hmmm. Interesting."

"What? What's interesting about my liking coffee ice cream? Is it too masculine or something?"

"No, no," Abby said. "Just wondering. Okay, next question. What movie star do you find most sexy: Brad Pitt, George Clooney, or Denzel Washington?"

"Why do those same three names always come up in these stupid polls? None of the above. I'm into Charles Laughton."

"The fat dead guy." I just wanted to be sure. "With the puffy lips."

"He's not fat anymore. Put it down."

Abby sighed and tossed the questionnaire on the coffee table. "You're not being honest, JoAnne. You're giving a false picture of yourself."

"Next."

Abby sighed again. I was enjoying this immensely. JoAnne's prickly discomfort was far more entertaining than a sitcom.

Three hours later, we had a profile that vaguely resembled

the JoAnne Chiofalo we knew and loved. It was going to have to do.

Doug and I went for a walk one evening after work and found ourselves at the Holocaust Memorial at Dock Square by Congress Street and the Union Oyster House.

I think it's one of the most haunting and powerful monuments ever built. It's particularly powerful when experienced at night.

We stood quietly just outside the walls of glass, etched with six million numbers representing the victims of the Holocaust.

"My grandfather was Jewish," Doug said finally, softly.

"Really?" That was interesting, as was any new information about Doug. But there was something odd about the way the words had sounded.

"On whose side?" I asked.

"My father's father."

"So, your father is Jewish, too, right?" And that would make Doug, also, Jewish, at least partly.

"No," he said. "My grandfather converted to Christianity. My father was raised in the first church of suburbia. When he and my mother had kids, they gave up the whole religion thing entirely."

"But, when you're Jewish you can't just stop being Jewish, right? I mean, it's more than a religion, it's a people, a huge and varied culture, a . . ."

"Not for me," Doug said harshly, and I knew the subject was dismissed.

I knew but I couldn't let it go. Not for the first time I wondered about Doug's wedding, about Carol's religious beliefs, about . . .

"Did you and Carol get married in a church?" I asked, attempting to sound nonchalant.

Doug answered promptly.

"Carol was raised Lutheran. We got married in the church she went to every week as a kid."

"Does she still go to church?"

"Why do you want to know these things?" Doug's voice betrayed a slight annoyance. As if—as if he thought I was intruding on his privacy?

Why did I want to know these things about Doug and Carol? Morbid curiosity? Or would knowing these domestic details somehow lead me to further knowledge of Doug as an individual? Truth was, I didn't really understand my motives in prying.

I shrugged. "It's interesting, that's all. I like to know about people."

Doug began to walk through the Memorial.

"So," I said, walking quickly to catch up. The words were going to come out of my mouth. I couldn't stop them. "If you got married again, would you do it in a church? You know, if the woman . . ."

Doug stopped short and I bumped into him.

"Sorry," I mumbled.

"Erin," he said, his voice serious and low, "I'm not getting married again."

"Oh. I just meant . . ."

"Erin, listen to me. Have I ever lied to you? Have I ever told you that I was leaving Carol?"

"No," I said, my heart shattering.

"I'm sorry. This will have to be enough, what you and I have. Okay? Do you understand that?"

I nodded, too sad to speak.

Doug took my hand and we walked on.

No, it's not okay, I thought. And I don't understand. What Doug and I have is not enough and it never will be.

Now you're talking sense, Reason said. I hadn't even known it was listening.

And no, I thought, bravely, stubbornly, I don't believe that Doug will never get married again. I believe in us. I believe in our love. I believe we can be together the way we should be.

There's my girl, Romance soothed. Don't give up hope. Love can conquer all obstacles.

Except reality, Reason said. It can't conquer reality.

Chapter Forty-three

We met at Joe's American, clearly one of Maggie's favorites, as almost every time it was her turn to choose the restaurant, that's where we ended up. I reminded myself to buy her a T-shirt with the Joe's logo for Christmas.

Maggie was late by ten minutes. Her color was high. She looked—pretty. She flopped into the empty chair, said, "Sorry I'm late," and grinned.

"What in God's name is going on with you?" JoAnne said, grinning back.

"I met someone," Maggie blurted.

"I knew it!" JoAnne crowed. "That's why you've been so secretive lately. And late. We've hardly seen you. Who is it? Do we know him?"

Suddenly, it came to me. How could I have been so blind? There was no him to know.

"Uh, not exactly," Maggie said, blushing.

"Do we know her?" I said, amazed at my own boldness.

Maggie blushed more furiously. "Uh, you might. But probably not. She . . ."

"Whoa. Whoa. Just—whoa. Her?" JoAnne looked at me, like I was the one with the Big Story. "She's a—she?"

"Yes," Maggie said. "She's a—she."

Abby smiled kindly. "Maggie, I'm so happy for you. So, what's her name, what's she like, what does she do?"

"So, you're saying—what? That you're gay?"

"Why can't you get with this, JoAnne?" I said. "We're all a bit—surprised—but it's really no big deal." I looked at Maggie. "I don't mean anything insulting by that. I just mean, you know . . . But if it is a big deal I don't want to diminish what's going on and I guess it is a big deal after all . . ."

"You can stop babbling, Erin," Maggie said. Kindly. "And yes, JoAnne, I guess this does mean that I'm gay, or maybe what it means is simply that I'm in love with a woman, I don't know. Yet. I don't really care. Look, I'm happy. For the first time in way too long, I'm happy. Jan makes me happy."

"And I think it's so wonderful!" Abby squealed. "What's Jan's last name? Is she pretty? Oh, should I ask that?"

"I don't know," Maggie admitted with a laugh. "I think she's beautiful. And her last name is Ward and she's very smart and very kind. And she loves, me, too."

"How did you meet this paragon of womanhood?" JoAnne sounded like she was choking.

"We met through the Women's Lunch Place. You know, where I volunteer. So does she."

"When did you meet?" Abby asked.

Maggie considered. "Exactly two months and eleven days ago."

Bingo.

"Wait a minute!" I cried. "She's Dr. Bruce, isn't she? You went to Paris with Jan, didn't you?"

Maggie blushed furiously.

JoAnne clapped. "You dog, you."

Abby's mouth opened wide. "You mean, there is no Dr. Bruce?"

"Jan owns a bookstore in Harvard Square," Maggie said hurriedly. "She's very successful. I mean, she'll never get rich being an independent but she provides a great service to the community with special orders and readings and events. She can pay the mortgage and still have enough left over to . . ."

"Take you to dinner?"

"Actually," Maggie said coyly, "Jan's a fabulous cook. We usually eat at home."

"Hmm. I have noticed you've, er, filled out a bit lately."

"And I look better, don't I?" Maggie challenged.

Actually, she did, I realized.

"I'll be right back." Maggie got up and walked toward the ladies' room.

When she was out of sight, JoAnne leaned close to me.

"I'm sorry," she hissed. "I just don't understand how you can go to bed one night straight and wake up the next morning gay. Something weird's going on here."

Abby said nothing but looked at JoAnne with concern.

"That's not how it happens, JoAnne," I said. "Come on, you know better."

"Do I? Look how hard it's been for me to change my life, even a little bit and Maggie just . . . just . . ."

"Just what, JoAnne?" Maggie had returned from the ladies' room.

JoAnne looked stumped for about half a second then recovered her usual aplomb.

"Look, Maggie. I could use some advice. Nothing I'm doing seems to be helping all that much. Individual therapy, group therapy—"

"People still do group therapy?" Abby said. "I thought that went out with fondue pots."

"Fondue pots are back," I said. "Check the Crate and Barrel catalog."

"Anyway," JoAnne said loudly, "and art therapy and Ti freakin' Chi and touchy-feely goddess-within workshops. Why am I not happier than I was when I started all this self-help crap? All I've accomplished is a piece of cardboard with macaroni pasted on it. And I haven't heard one word from that bogus dating service."

"So, what you're really saying is that you're jealous of me?"

JoAnne looked hard at Maggie. "Yes, I think that's what I'm really saying. You got happy. You fell in love with someone who fell in love back. I didn't. Haven't. Yeah, I'm jealous. And—well, I guess I'm proud of you, too."

Maggie grinned. "Plenty of people have been proud of me, but I don't think anyone's ever been jealous of me before. Thanks."

JoAnne grinned back. "No problem."

A weekend in Newport, just me and JoAnne. Abby was with John. Maggie was with Jan. Damion was with Frederick. Doug was with Carol.

And JoAnne was not pleased. I suppose she had reason to be pissed.

We were sitting at the bar at Christie's, looking out over the sparkling water of the Narragansett Bay. JoAnne was having some trouble keeping her voice down to a civilized level.

"You come to Newport for the weekend—what's probably the last gorgeous weekend of September—so you can mope? So you can pine for your married lover who's probably at this very moment firing up the grill for the kids and the neighbors, playing Mr. Suburbia?"

"Thinking of me while he's doing it," I said. The woman he said he would never marry.

"Oh, yeah, I'm sure. Come on, Erin, you're no fun."

"Sorry. If you want to talk to some guy you can. Nothing's stopping you."

"This is supposed to be a singles weekend. You know, as in, we're both single, it's late summer, we're looking for love."

"I've got love."

JoAnne sighed dramatically. "Whatever. I'm not saying you have to sleep with anyone, but maybe smiling every once in a while would be nice. For my sake. God, Erin, Doug's made you into a dishrag. He's got you all locked up and waiting for him, all untouchable, while he goes on and lives his life as he pleases. What right does he have?"

"The right I give him to ask me to be faithful."

"Oh, honey, I give up. Look, let's just have a drink and stare at the water if that's what you want to do."

"We could talk," I suggested, smiling. "See, I'm smiling."

JoAnne grunted. "As long as we don't talk about Dirk Spiral, fine. But if Mr. Gorgeous approaches me, I'm flirting. Perfect Partners hasn't come through with one guy for me yet."

"Fair warning. Nice yacht."

"Hmm. Wonder what its owner looks like?"

Wonder if he likes cats, I thought. Because in spite of my protestations to JoAnne about being content to be faithful to Doug, even on a beautiful, late summer weekend in Newport, Rhode Island, I was, in fact, experiencing a glimmer of discontent.

Just a glimmer, but it had caught my eye and wouldn't go away.

Maybe since shopping with Maureen for baby clothes. Maybe since the night at the Holocaust Memorial. Maybe only since earlier in that past week when Doug and I had met for a quick lunch. The lunch itself was unremarkable, as was our conversation. Doug seemed tired and overworked; I know I was both. When it came time to part, Doug said, in a far too casual voice for a truly spontaneous thought: "By the way, Erin. I found several cat hairs on my suit jacket the other night when I got home. They must have rubbed off you. Luckily, Carol was asleep, but you've got to be more careful. You've got to think of me more in this. You've got to consider my position."

The words and Doug's fake-casual tone hit me like a slap.

"You don't like cats?" I'd quipped feebly.

Did he really think I didn't consider his feelings? How could he claim to know me and think that I was being careless with his reputation as husband and father?

"I hate them," Doug said sharply, "but that's not the point."

"I know," I said, feebly still. "I'll be careful."

Doug smiled but it seemed obligatory, not a freely given gift.

"Thanks. I'll talk to you later."

He turned away and I said, "I'm going to Newport this weekend with JoAnne."

Doug turned back. His face was expressionless. "Good," he said. "Have fun."

And that was that. No, "Think of me," or, "Don't let any guy pick you up," or, "Be careful." At that moment it occurred to me that Doug had never actually asked me to be faithful to him, even though I'd managed to convince myself that he had.

And he'd never told me he loved me.

The thoughts were too disturbing so I shoved them away.

By the time I'd gotten back to the office that afternoon, I'd partly convinced myself that Doug's ill temper—or lack of concern?—was due to his being exhausted by the demands of his job. By the time I got home that night, the glimmer of discontent had made its appearance.

Fuzzer met me at the door, as was his wont, and yowled. I scratched his head and followed his fleeing paws into the kitchen. As I watched him eat his dinner noisily, I was overcome with a growing anger.

"Screw you, Doug Spears," I said to the kitchen. And to Fuzzer, eyeing me for seconds, I said, "You can shed on me all you want, guy. It's my life."

Now, Saturday afternoon in Newport, here I was effectively lying to one of my dearest friends, implying that Doug had asked me not to sleep with other men, stating flat out that I was content with my relationship and its demands.

"JoAnne?" I said suddenly. "Want to go dancing tonight?"

I got home late Sunday night to find a call from Doug on my answering machine. It was hurried but it lifted my heart.

Doug said he hoped I'd had a fun weekend—but not too fun—and apologized for being "distracted" at lunch the other day. Distracted was not exactly the word I would have chosen, but hey, at least Doug had acknowledged he'd been a less than perfect date. He suggested we meet at Pignoli after work the following day.

It felt good to be home.

Chapter Forty-four

*E—will be out of touch for a while, don't worry.
M.*

For some reason, Pignoli was mobbed, an unusual thing for a Monday evening. There was only one empty seat at the bar. I took it with reservations. The woman to the left seemed innocuous. The guy to the right—the one in black pants and shirt with a pale, slightly shiny, printed sports jacket—was going to be trouble. The moment I sat . . .

"So, is that an Irish nose?"

I don't know. I threw away the box it came in. What kind of dumb-ass question was that?

"I'm part Irish, yes," I said. And you? What kind of honker is that?

"Me, I'm Italian-American, all the way. Ba-da-boom, heh?"

Tony Soprano this guy wasn't. He wasn't even James Gandolfini, whom I would have dated in a moment if he—and I—suddenly became single. This idiot next to me at the bar was as far away from Soprano/Gandolfini as Spam is from fine duck liver pâté imported directly from France.

The thought made me hungry. I looked over my shoulder

at the door. Where was Doug? I checked my watch. Ten minutes late. As usual. I had probably another twenty-minute wait ahead of me. And the excuse would be the same—he'd called Carol to say he was going to be home late and got caught listening to every detail of her boring day.

"Hey, what's a nice Irish girl like you . . ."

"American. I'm an American. And I have the passport to prove it."

"A babe like you must get a lot of invitations to travel, right? Bermuda, Bahamas . . ."

Oh, my God. I blocked out the offense of Joey Bag-a-Donuts's voice and quickly cased the bar area. Still no empty seats I could slip away to. Shit. I wished someone would call me at that moment and get me out of this moron's way. Can you will a phone to ring, I wondered. Maybe a psychic could do it. . . .

Ring . . .

"Excuse me," I said brightly.

Bag-a-Donuts shifted noisily on his chair and scoped for another "babe" to bother.

"Hi," I said.

"It's me. Have you been there long?"

"Only since the time we were suposed to meet." I turned my back to Mr. Ba-da-bing. "Is everything okay?"

"No, it isn't."

I felt that all-too-familiar burst of fear and dread and panic in my stomach. For an irrational moment I knew Doug was going to dump me via cell phone. For that same irrational moment I thought he was going to tell me he was dying of cancer.

"Erin?"

"What is it? What's going on?"

"Carol called. Courtney had an accident. They're in the hospital. I've got to get home."

"Oh, Lord, is she okay?"

"Yeah. Has a broken leg but otherwise she's okay. She was at a friend's house for a play date and—God knows how it happened—but she fell down the kid's basement steps. The mother isn't being too clear on what role her bully of a kid might have played."

"Doug, do you really think another kid pushed her!"

"I don't know what to think yet. Look, Erin, I'm really sorry, but I've got to run. Have a good weekend, okay? I'll try to call but with all the stuff going on at home—"

"I know," I interrupted. "It's okay," I lied, "really. If you can call, great, but don't worry about me. Just take care of Courtney."

Doug signed off. I flipped closed my phone and took what I hoped would be a steadying breath. The bartender gestured toward the almost empty glass of Vernaccia in front of me. I shook my head and reached for my wallet.

Every family joy or crisis threatened my relationship with Doug. Taylor's getting chicken pox might make Doug realize just how much he cared about his family and how wrong it would be to leave them. Carol's getting her real estate license could result in Doug's experiencing a burst of pride in his wife and a rededication to her happiness. A school play could stir up long-dormant memories of the vows he'd made to Carol to be faithful to her till death did them part, no matter his own distress.

Romance was not bothered by this fact. But consider the frisson of The Affair, Romance said. Oh, Erin, you are so lucky! The secrecy of your love demands a bravery and a truer devotion than a love that announces itself to the world.

Reason snorted. And you like this nonsense? I never saw you as a drama queen, Erin. What's happened? Reality not good enough for you? The mature security of marriage too mundane? You need to spice things up by . . .

All right, already! I shouted in my head, but the woman to my left flinched, so loud were my troubled thoughts. My body was radiating emotion, it had to be. Flesh is only so solid.

I drained the last of a glass of water I'd asked for when I came in.

It was horrible of me to resent Courtney's broken leg,

horrible and selfish. But it was the reality of my situation. I was living the life of the Other Woman. My position in Doug's life was nothing if not precarious.

But that didn't mean I had to lose my native kindness and generosity of spirit, did it? I'd be there for Courtney in what way I could.

I felt calmer already.

Doug did the right thing by going home, I told myself. He's a good father.

Right, Romance agreed. And that's one of the qualities you most admire in him, his love for his children.

How is fucking you showing his love for his kids? Reason often had a foul mouth. Nevertheless, Reason usually had a point. If I were willing to listen to it.

"Hey, beautiful."

"What? Oh, sorry."

Bag-a-Donuts grinned in an oily way. "Get stood up?"

"No," I lied. Lying was second nature to me now. "That was my boyfriend telling me to meet him at the Four Seasons instead. He wanted to surprise me."

Bag-a-Donuts shrugged and made a face. "Hey, if you get bored, I'll be right here. I ain't going nowhere."

That's the truth, I thought and smiled nicely. Bag-a-Donuts slurped his Scotch.

Rats. I had been looking forward to Pignoli's homemade gnocchi. I couldn't hang around for dinner now that I'd lied about being wanted elsewhere. I'd just trudge home and nuke something, maybe rent a movie along the way.

I gestured for the bartender, paid my bill, and added a generous tip—to show myself that even though I'd been hurt I was big enough not to take it out on the world—and left.

The night air felt wonderfully cool on my heated face. I breathed deeply.

"The hell with him," I said to the world. "I'm going to the Four Seasons if I have to go by myself." I adjusted my bag on my shoulder and started walking.

Chapter Forty-five

Of course, Doug apologized again for not being able to meet me Monday evening. I didn't doubt his sincerity. We made plans to meet at his office at six on Thursday for— for whatever we pleased.

At five minutes to six I walked through the lobby of the Prudential tower and toward the reception desk.

"Hi, Mac," I said, in my artificially bright, don't-come-too-close greeting voice.

"Miss Weston," Mac answered, properly cowed. "Who you here to see?"

I busied myself signing in. "Mr. Spears and I have a meeting."

"No, you don't."

My head shot up.

"What?"

Mac reddened. "I shouldn't've said it that way. It's just that Mr. Spears didn't come to work today. Didn't his secretary tell you?"

No, she had not. Neither had Doug. Obviously, he'd forgotten about our date and so had given Janey no instructions for canceling it.

"Well," I said, forcing a laugh, "I'll certainly have to speak to him when he returns. To think I could have been home by now, eating dinner."

Mac smiled conspiratorially. "I like an early dinner myself, Miss Weston."

"Well." I looked down at the registry. "Guess I should cross out my name, huh?"

Mac did it for me. "Have a nice evening, now," he said.

I forced a smile this time but I don't think it convinced even Mac. "You, too, Mac," I said. "Bye."

When I got home a half hour later, Fuzzer was there to greet me. And there was no message from Doug.

I dialed his office number and left a carefully worded message I hoped he'd find first thing in the morning.

He did. At nine-fifteen, the phone rang.

"Meet me for lunch?" he said.

"Where?"

"At the Boston Harbor Hotel."

The last time we'd been there Doug had given me the pink-and-purple Lucite heart-shaped ring.

I said okay and hung up.

I arrived at the hotel at one o'clock. Doug was already there, waiting for me on the terrace.

I didn't want to start a big fight. All I wanted was an apology. At least, I told myself that was all I wanted.

He suggested we get a table. I told him I wasn't hungry. We walked down to the water's edge.

"Why didn't you let me know you hadn't come into the office?" I demanded.

Doug sighed. "I'm sorry, Erin. Honestly, I forgot. Both kids were sick and Carol needed some sleep and between cleaning up vomit and taking temperatures, it was all I could do to remember to call in at all."

Let alone remember to tell your girl on the side that the

date was off. On Doug's list of priorities, I came after wife, kids, and work.

I'd always known that, hadn't I? Well, hadn't I?

Suddenly, I was furious. The fury had come upon me again like a cramp. I didn't know what to do with it. I thought it would kill me.

"I looked like an ass!" I screamed. Doug jumped, startled. "I've never been more humiliated in my entire life."

"Erin, don't yell."

"I'll fucking yell if I want to yell," I yelled.

Doug turned away from me and stared out at the water.

"Nice. Just turn away like I'll disappear or something. Is that what you do with Carol?"

God, I was treading on such dangerous turf but I couldn't stop myself. What was going on with me? Why was I always so angry? Why was the anger so vitriolic?

Still, Doug said nothing.

"This—this whole thing," I sputtered, "it's bullshit, it's just a lot of crap."

Doug turned and looked dead at me.

"Do you want to end it?" he asked calmly.

I felt the blood throbbing in my temples. Did I? Did I want to end it?

"No," I blurted.

"Are you sure?"

"Yes."

"Then will you let me apologize?"

"I can't stop you."

"Yes, you can. If you don't stop talking I'll never be able to say I'm sorry."

"Are you?" I spat.

"Yes. I've already said it. And if I weren't sorry, I wouldn't be standing here taking this abuse."

"Abuse?"

"When you scream at me it's abusive."

You always hurt the ones you love, I thought inanely. What sort of monster was I becoming?

"I'm sorry," I mumbled. "And I accept your apology. I'm sorry."

The tears started to roll down my face. Because we were in public and because it was the middle of the day, Doug couldn't comfort me.

Even if he had wanted to.

Chapter Forty-six

After the latest wrong episode with Doug, I was determined to have fun with the girls. I certainly didn't seem to be having much fun with Doug those days.

"What's the craziest thing you've ever done to meet a man?" I asked.

"A particular man? Or just a man?" Abby.

"Does it matter?"

"I'm out of this," Maggie said. "But go on. I'm curious."

"A woman in my office," I said, "was crazy about one of the guys in the building but she never had the nerve to talk to him in the elevators. So, one day she overheard him talking to someone from his office about sailing and how he had his own sailboat and all, so she signed up for sailing lessons at Boston Community Boating, down on the basin. I guess she figured she'd run into him there."

"And?"

"And during the first lesson she slipped and somehow managed to break her leg. Needless to say, she didn't feel so crazy about Elevator Guy after that."

"Once, in high school," Abby said, "I waited outside the

boys' locker room after a big game for a guy I had a crush on to come out."

"Wild. You crazy woman. What happened?"

Abby blushed. "Well, it didn't go very well. When he came out and saw me there, well, he and his friends kind of— laughed. It turns out he was dating some gorgeous cheerleader for our rival's team."

"He was a traitor. You deserve better."

Abby blushed. "Besides," she said, her voice low, "I heard later that he wasn't circumcised. Ew!"

"Has anyone ever seen an uncircumcised penis?" I asked. "I haven't. Up close and personal, I mean."

JoAnne shuddered. "Like Elaine Bennis said, no personality."

"I can't believe you're quoting a TV character," Maggie said. "Again. Do you ever read? You know, like, books?"

"I've heard sex is better for the uncircumcised man," Abby said.

"Nice. It's always about the man!"

"It's like Viagra being covered by insurance," JoAnne said, "but, at least in most cases, not birth control."

"Someone please tell me the logic in that!"

"There is no logic but that of the All Mighty Dick," Maggie pronounced. "It's a classic Dick Issue."

"Again, to quote Elaine: How do they walk around with those things? And yes, I do read," JoAnne said haughtily. "You know, like, books. Medical journals. Patients' charts. It's just that I find sitcoms a good form of relaxation. And they're funny. Sue me, I like to laugh."

"Speaking of laughter . . ." I murmured and nodded to the left. A Britney Spears wanna-be and her Christina Aguilera buddy had just taken seats at the bar.

"I think it's sad," Abby said with conviction. "Those girls have no self-esteem. They don't even know who they are!"

"And they're at least twenty-five," Maggie added. "Old enough to know better."

JoAnne made a face. "Leave them alone. Who cares? You want to date the kind of guys who'll ask them out? Not me."

Abby frowned and I snuck another look at the bimbos.

Suddenly: "Has anyone read any of the *Left Behind* series?" JoAnne's question hung in the air like a bad smell. All thoughts of Britney and Christina were expelled.

Finally, I said, "Oh, no. Please don't tell me you've read that trash."

JoAnne shrugged. "I admit to an occasional bout of sheer morbid curiosity."

"But when you buy one of the books you're helping to support those Rapture nutbags," Maggie said, her tone uncharacteristically fierce.

"Didn't Debbie Harry do a rap song called 'Rapture' ?" That, of course, was Abby.

JoAnne made a face. "Who said I spent any money? I read the first installment in the bookstore. It's not exactly serious literature. Basically, the writing is juvenile. And the authors have no idea how to write a female character. None. But there is something bizarrely fascinating about people believing so literally in the fantasies of the Bible."

"Don't get me started on the born-again Christians," I said, my tone not so uncharacteristically fierce. "I barely survived the regular ones."

"Catholics are not the same as Christians, Erin. You know that."

She had me there.

Abby's expression became dreamy. "I bet Satan is cute. You know, all manly and dark and brooding."

Here was an interesting twist to the conversation. I knew I would regret it but . . .

"Okay, Abby. I'm going to ask. Why do you think Satan is a hottie? Aside from his living in eternal flames."

Abby didn't seem to get the unintended pun. She rarely did. "Well, Satan is supposed to be the Anti-Christ, right? Anyway the opposite of Jesus. And paintings of Jesus always make him look so—girly. Effeminate. Like he's a whiner."

Maggie hid a smile behind her bottle of Tremont Ale.

"Er, you know paintings have nothing much to do with any historical Jesus, right?" I said. "They're about the artist and his time."

Abby shrugged. "I know. Still, every time I think of Jesus I think of those pictures where he's sad and morbid and skinny. Who'd want to go out with him? I need a man with a little more—oomph."

"Oomph?" Maggie repeated, no longer bothering to hide her smile. "You think the devil has oomph."

JoAnne gave me the eye. "Ah, yes. The appeal of the bad boy. Something we're all supposed to outgrow."

"Does anyone, ever?" I challenged.

JoAnne took me up on the challenge. "Honest opinion? No. Does everyone continue to act on those urges? Also no."

"I think good boys are sexy," Abby said. "Some of them. The ones with oomph, like your father, Erin."

"I don't think any boys are sexy," Maggie said, happily. "Not anymore."

I was having fun with the girls.

That night, in spite of the good time I'd had with my friends, I couldn't sleep.

Three o'clock saw me settled on the living room couch, staring blankly at a rerun of E!'s *Mysteries and Scandals*. Somebody was having an affair. There were drugs. And an angry, gun-toting wife.

It got me to thinking. A person wouldn't cheat on his soul mate, would he? That would be a horrible violation of trust, the absolute worst.

How can you grade violations of trust? Reason wondered.

What was Reason doing awake at three A.M.?

Doug's cheating on you would be worse than his cheating on Carol? Reason went on. You both love him. How are Doug's actions any less immoral?

Okay, I see, I shouted. It does sound stupid, but . . .

But Doug would never cheat on me, I knew that as clearly as I knew my own name. How could he? When there was an all-encompassing intimacy, one that brought joy and passionate satisfaction, there was no room or reason for anyone else.

Reason snorted. If you say so.

Sounding a little cynical these days, aren't you, I retorted.

Comes from working with you. Let me ask you this: Isn't Doug's sleeping with his wife while he's having an affair with you cheating on his soul mate?

I cringed. It wasn't the first time I'd wondered if Doug was still having sex with Carol now that we were together.

Oh, he'd never do that, Romance cried, suddenly awake. I'm sure the thought of sex with anyone but you, Erin, is abhorrent to him. No, I'm sure he refrains from sex with Carol. After all, she doesn't love him in the way he needs to be loved. He told you that himself.

Of course he has sex with Carol, Reason shot back. For several reasons. One: To keep up his cover as a loving, devoted husband. Two: He's a man. Men want sex in a different way from women. They want it more often. They'll say and do practically anything for it.

That's sexist thinking, I protested feebly.

Why don't you just ask him, Reason suggested reasonably. You're an adult. You said you knew what you were getting into. You said you could handle the truth.

I got up to go back to bed.

I was wrong, I thought. I can't handle the truth.

Chapter Forty-seven

E—miss me? went on a little excursion, will tell you later. has yr father met anyone yet? he shldn't be alone. M. P.S.—what abt yr love life?

It was a typical late September day—cold and rainy—so we'd gathered for a comfort food dinner at Silvertone, one of those superpopular restaurants that declares it hip to eat meatloaf and mashies.

Abby looked all flushed and dropped her fork three times before the entrées arrived.

"Okay, spill it," JoAnne said. "You're driving me nuts."

Abby grinned.

"I think—oh, I can't believe I'm saying this out loud! But I think John's going to ask me to marry him on my birthday!"

"Ask or marry?" JoAnne drawled.

"What?"

"Leave her alone," Maggie said. "Wow, that's big news, Abby."

I took a deep breath. It didn't help. "Abby, what makes you think, uh . . ."

"I just have a feeling," Abby gushed. "The way he looks at me sometimes over dinner . . . Like he's wondering what style of ring I might like . . ."

In my experience, guys didn't ponder women's jewelry styles. Unless they were architects or artists and Dad was definitely neither. Nor was he a cross-dresser. But I said nothing.

JoAnne nodded. "Uh huh. Has he, you know, said anything specific? Has he even hinted, given you any verbal clue at all?"

Abby frowned prettily. "Well, no, but you know how men are! I just know he wants to surprise me."

Another thing my father disliked—surprises. Getting them or giving them. Again, I said nothing.

Abby babbled on for a bit and I tuned out. I thought about my meatloaf. It was good. I thought about the meeting I still had to prepare for that night. I . . .

"Erin? Aren't you excited?"

"Huh?" I refocused. Abby was beaming but the longer I stared at her the dimmer the beam became.

"Are you . . . okay with this?" she said, hesitantly.

I patted her hand. "Of course, I am, Abby. I'm sorry, I just . . . I was just daydreaming. You know, about the wedding. I . . . it's so great. I'm happy for you. I . . ."

I shut up and grinned. It hurt.

But Abby didn't seem to notice my discomfort. She babbled on again and I left JoAnne and Maggie to their own devices while I let my own mind wander into the abyss.

Nice, I thought. My father gets two weddings before I even get one. And men don't even care about the wedding part. . . .

Back up, Erin, Reason said. Think carefully here. I did. And I realized that my father hadn't mentioned anything about marrying Abby to me. Not that he had to. Could Abby be imagining the relationship was progressing so well so quickly?

Could I be in deep denial?

Possibly.

Oh, Erin, Romance fluttered. It's right out of a fairy tale!

No fairy tale I'd ever heard of. But Romance wasn't always concerned with the truth and/or with accuracy.

I got through the rest of the dinner admirably, if I do say so myself. At least, I didn't throw any punches.

I had to talk to Abby again about this marriage thing. We met after work the next day for a quick drink at Hamersley's.

Abby was relaxed and happy and somewhat festive in a red sweater set from—of course—Talbots. A little doggie pin sat near her left shoulder. I wore a somber black pantsuit. Armani Exchange, but the point was my mood, not the brand.

We ordered, a glass of Proseco for me, a Cosmopolitan for Abby. As soon as our drinks arrived, I launched.

"Have you really thought about what marrying my—about marrying John—means?"

Abby looked puzzled. "What it means? It means I love him. If he asks me to marry him I'll say yes because I love him."

Okay. She had me there.

"What about kids? You've always wanted to have kids. I don't know for a fact but I'm pretty sure—John—doesn't want to start another family."

God, I hoped he didn't.

"Well, Erin, I've thought a lot about that since John and I have been together. And . . . Well, I'm willing to give up being a mother as long as I can be his wife."

Stepford wife, you mean.

"That's an awfully big sacrifice to make for a man you met only a few months ago," I pointed out. "Why are you the one giving up your dream? Did he ask you to?"

Abby blushed. "We haven't actually talked about it. I mean John mentioned once that he didn't want to start another family, so I came to my decision myself."

I wondered. I didn't think my father was the sort of man who'd ever deny his wife a child. In fact, I was pretty sure he was the sort of man who wouldn't be in a committed, long-term relationship in the first place with a woman who definitely wanted a child when he definitely did not. He was too honest. I hoped.

What did my father and Abby actually talk about when they talked? If they talked . . .

"Abby, have you considered what it would be like marrying a man over twenty years—God, almost thirty years!—your senior? That's huge."

Abby smiled with what I'm sure she thought of as a wise smile.

"Love makes all possible, Erin."

After the previous few months, I had no idea if there was any truth to that adage. I let it go.

"Abby, if you marry my father, you would be my stepmother. Have you thought about that?"

I had. And I was stubbornly opposed to it happening. It could not happen. My best friend would not and could not become—Mom.

How would I introduce her? "This is Abby. She sleeps with my father." Or: "Meet Abby. She looks thirty-two but she's really fifty-five. Really."

"Well, that could be . . . nice," Abby said, hesitantly.

I knew it. This was even too much for the Romantic Princess to bear. I ordered another round of drinks.

"I mean, at least you know me, Erin. I'm not mean or anything."

"Abby, we're a cliché," I said, leaning over and grabbing her hand. "You realize that, don't you? We're like, I don't know, an episode of *Love American Style 2002*. We're a sitcom. I'm embarrassed even to be alone with myself. Single thirty-two-year-old daughter of newly radical mother and fifty-eight-year-old attorney father who's dating daughter's gorgeous brunette friend, also thirty-two."

And where did that scenario leave me? I'll tell you where. It left me alone. And embarrassed. And suddenly, very, very tired.

Why couldn't things stay the way they were, even if the way they were sucked? That was the Big Question I now struggled with on an almost hourly basis.

Abby was silent. I couldn't keep my mouth shut.

"Why do you have to do it? I mean, why? There's no other man out there in the entire city of Boston and its surrounding suburbs good enough for you marry so you have to marry my father? Why my father? Why not someone else's father?"

I didn't really expect an answer to these questions. But I had to ask them. Self-pity compelled me.

Abby looked stricken and very sad. I felt awful.

"Oh, come on, I'm not mad," I said. "And you know I'll support you whatever happens." I did mean that. "Just, you have to admit it's a little—odd—our situation. I just need some time to get used to the idea of having a stepmother only a few months older than I am. Be patient with me?"

Abby smiled weakly. "Okay. And, Erin? Can I ask your opinion on something?"

By now I was feeling quite generous.

"Of course you can, Abby. What is it?"

"Do you think a marquise cut is too tacky?"

Chapter Forty-eight

Many of Boston's sidewalks—particularly in the South End and Beacon Hill and by the waterfront and Faneuil Hall and the North End, etc.—are buckled brick and old cobblestone. Boston is not a high-heel friendly city. No woman with a shoe addiction should ever move here. Ankles are turned and sprained, heels are ruined, a confident stride is reduced to an on-the-toe mincing step . . . All I can say is, thank God for Marshall's, Filene's Basement, and Discount Shoe Warehouse.

By the time I reached Les Zygomates my left heel had a nasty nick. That, and the luncheon mob scene inside, did not improve my mood.

Neither did Doug's insistence that we talk about my career.

"Where do you want to be in five years?"

I raised an eyebrow. "Is this an interview?"

"Maybe. I mean it, what are your career goals? What's your plan all about?"

I thought about that.

"I don't know. I just . . . I just work. I see what happens, what comes along. I don't really have a plan. But I've done all right so far. I mean, I make pretty good money . . ."

"Erin, be serious! You could make double your salary at Trident."

"How do you know my salary?"

"Let's just say, I know it."

This bothered me somehow. But before I had time to think it through or to respond, Doug shot another question at me.

"What do you value as a professional?"

That was a relatively easy question to answer.

"I value hard work. I value people who have the work ethic. I also value work itself, especially if it brings some sense of fulfillment to the worker and I really value it if it helps other people in some meaningful way."

Doug quirked an eyebrow.

"You sound like some cheesy personal happiness guru, Erin. Nice sentiments, but if you really want to get ahead . . ."

"Of whom? Why do I want to get ahead of anybody?"

"Okay then, if you really want to succeed in the business world, you have to start valuing smart work over hard work. You have to learn to play with the big boys, like Trident, and not waste time with the little girls, like EastWind, and their symphonies and dance companies."

"First of all," I said hotly, "you sound like a cretin. And second, why does the business world have to be apart from the rest of the world? What if I want to succeed in life as a whole, meaning I want to be happy and healthy and loved and I want to love back and work and . . ."

"And what?" Doug prodded.

And have a family of my own. Have babies.

"Nothing. That's it," I said uncomfortably. "Can we please just eat lunch now?"

Doug sighed like a man long put upon, said "Fine," and tucked in.

My appetite was gone.

It was just the three of us that night. Maggie was with Jan. Of course, these days she was spending more of her time with her partner and less of her time with her girlfriends. It was natural. But it was—weird. I missed her.

"I've been wondering," Abby said.

Abby was with us because my father was burning the midnight oil on a big case.

Always the second choice, Erin, a nasty voice inside me said. Always the fallback.

"Do you think Maggie's really, you know, gay?"

"Does it matter?" I asked. "She's happy with Jan."

"Besides, who would decide, 'Oh, I think I'll live in a homosexual relationship' just for the hell of it?" JoAnne added. "Who would choose to be reviled? Living gay isn't easy."

"Easier than it used to be, thank God. In some places, anyway."

"True."

"I still wonder . . . Maybe Maggie got so turned off by lousy men she, you know, turned gay. Meaning she's not really gay-gay but just fell in love with a woman because—because the woman isn't a man and Maggie hasn't been in love in a long time and she wanted to be."

JoAnne and I sat in stunned silence. But not for long.

"Okay," I said, "why I'm even responding to that is beyond me, but, if I understand what you're saying—and I am not so sure I do—Maggie's being with Jan is just another version of girlfriends being substitutes for men. You're saying that if Maggie got a better offer from a man, she wouldn't need Jan."

Abby considered. "Well . . . yeah."

"Please," I begged, "please don't let her hear you say that, okay?"

"So, Abby," JoAnne said, "have you ever been attracted to a woman?"

"Me!" she squealed. "No, of course not!"

"Even when you couldn't find a guy to go out with?" I said. "Or when some guy treated you really badly?"

"Yes. I mean, no. I'm all confused. No women."

"Well, that destroys your theory that women fall in love with women because they're sick of men, doesn't it?"

Abby shook her head. "I don't want to talk about this anymore."

JoAnne grinned.

"Fine. This conversation never happened. Agreed?"

Abby nodded.

I said, "What conversation?"

Chapter Forty-nine

October, Boston

October in Boston—in all of New England, really—is magical. There's a good reason we northeasterners brag about our brilliant foliage, bright blue skies, and chill, crisp air. There's a good reason early autumn, especially, is the most popular time of the year for L.L. Bean-clad tourists to invade Boston. October is the season of high Romance.

> *Erin—glad John is with someone; why no details? hope she doesn't hurt him; he's a good man. does she have money? have you considered a dating srvc? yr. not getting any younger. Marie*

Perfect Partners, Inc. had done its job. Finally. At least, they'd introduced JoAnne to one Peter Leonard. I was curious to hear more.

JoAnne and I went shopping at Filene's.

"So, what's going on with this Leonard fellow?" I asked.

"I really like him," JoAnne said simply.

"That's great." Unless he's a shit, I added silently. Was the new JoAnne as perceptive as the old?

Doubtful, Reason said. Once you let your heart have a say, perception and discrimination get all screwed up.

Romance cried, That's not fair!

Reason chuckled slyly.

"He's just, I don't know."

Point proven, Reason crowed.

"What does he do for a living?" I asked, as we stepped down into the Basement.

"Oh, he's something or other at Fidelity. Something with money. He says he loves his job.'

"That's—good. And? What else?"

"Well, he's very good-looking, in a kind of Robert Redford way. A young Robert Redford."

"I thought you didn't go for blondes," I teased.

"That was back when I was superficial. When I was dating just to get laid. It's different when you date for a relationship. The specifics like hair color don't matter anymore. As much."

The guru had spoken. I wonder if they'd sold her that line at Perfect Partners, Inc.

"So, how many times have you seen him?" I asked.

"We had dinner twice and we went to the movies last Sunday afternoon." JoAnne smiled like she had a juicy secret. Then: "We shared a popcorn."

I hesitated. The precancer scare JoAnne probably would have been implying something sexual by "shared a popcorn." But the postcancer scare JoAnne—I just didn't know.

"A jumbo size."

Okay.

"Er, do you mean you—uh, had sex?"

JoAnne looked up from the blouse she was regarding and frowned.

"No. I mean we shared a jumbo size popcorn. Really, Erin, sometimes your mind is in the sewer."

Better than it being in the clouds, I replied silently.

"Perfect Partners suggests you date at least four times before doing anything sexual. Holding off a bit has been proven to be good for a budding relationship."

Uh huh. This was JoAnne Chiofalo talking?

"Well, I hope it works out for you," I said.

JoAnne smiled. "Me, too. Hey, look at this cute sweater! And it's only $11.99."

Since when do you use the word "cute," I wanted to ask, but I kept my mouth shut.

One late afternoon in mid-October, I called my father for brief instructions on how to fix a constantly flushing toilet.

He rattled off something about jiggling this and poking that. Something was up. Dad's instructions were usually quite clear and precise.

"Are you okay?" I said. "You sound distracted."

"Yeah, yeah, I'm fine. Just busy. So, anything else new?"

"Uh, no," I said, a whir of tension beginning in my gut.

"Okay. I really have to go, Erin. I'm sorry. Enjoy the weekend."

"Okay. Thanks, Dad. You, too."

I hung up and felt the room spin.

Dad knew. The truth hit me hard. My father knew that I was having an affair with a married man.

How I leapt to this conclusion from our brief, nonspecific— nay, innocent—conversation is indicative of my emotional state at that time. My emotional state was not good.

Within minutes I was sunk in a pit of paranoia.

I felt exposed. I felt naked and shivery in a completely negative way.

How could I ever face my father again? Now he'd have to live with the ugly fact of both his wife—former wife—and his daughter being in some ways adulterers, home wreckers, heartbreakers.

I jumped up from the couch and began to pace. Fuzzer turned his back to me.

And how could my best friend have betrayed my confidence, I raged silently. But I knew exactly how. The vault didn't lock properly when it came to women, their men, and secrets about the women's friends. I myself had told an asshole or two something I shouldn't have about a female friend's woes. Why? Had I thought that revealing JoAnne's yeast infection or Maggie's financial troubles would bring intimacy to the relationship? Stupid. Especially when my friends had asked me not to repeat their secrets to anyone, particularly the Sideshow Bobs and Fat Bastards we'd all dated, however briefly.

Still, I wanted to know. I wanted to hear from Abby herself what had happened. I dialed Abby's number.

"Hi. It's Erin. Are you alone?"

She said she was.

"Abby?" My voice shook, I could hear it. "Will you answer me honestly?"

"Of course, Erin."

"Did you tell my father about me and Doug?"

"No! You told me not to. You told me you didn't want him to worry about you. Remember, Erin?"

"So—he doesn't know?"

"Well, he never said anything to me about knowing. And if he does know, he didn't hear it from me. Erin, why are you asking me this? It's insulting. You know I don't break my promises."

My relief was enormous. At least Abby was a good person, even if I wasn't.

"I'm sorry, Abby, I'm sorry. It's just . . . Oh God, I can't even explain. I thought . . . I'm sorry. I'm being paranoid. Sometimes this whole thing is just so hard."

"Erin? Will you answer me honestly?"

I laughed. Bitterly. "I'll try. I haven't been on great terms with honesty lately."

"Are you happy?"

"What's happy?" Maybe I could joke my way out of this disastrous conversation.

"Happy is happy, don't be a jerk," Abby snapped. "Just answer the question."

In all my years of friendship with Abby, I'd never heard her really angry. I felt chastened. Even my friends were becoming disappointed in me. If I were no longer someone my friends respected, who was I? What was I?

But if I answered honestly it would mean I had to do something I didn't think I had the strength—or the desire—to do. Yet. And if I lied . . .

"No," I said. "I'm not happy."

But I was about to be.

Chapter Fifty

It had been a busy morning. Clients needed hand-holding, Heather, the receptionist, was out sick, and Hank needed help on a brochure he was writing. By noon, I was whacked. When the phone rang I cursed. Sure to be another problem, I thought.

"Erin Weston."

"What are you doing this weekend?"

I relaxed. Doug.

"I don't know. The usual. Why?"

"How would you like to run away to Vermont with me?"

"Don't tease me, Doug."

"I'm not teasing. We'd leave Friday after work and drive home late Sunday afternoon. I found a quiet, very private little B & B on the net and—well, I made a reservation so you have to say yes."

I was too stunned to speak.

"Erin?"

"Oh, God, of course I'll go! How . . ."

"Good. Look, I have a meeting. I'll call you later, okay?"

"Okay," I said. "Bye."

I hung up the phone and sat there grinning like the Cheshire cat. A very happy Cheshire cat. A Cheshire cat with a big fat belly full of cream.

It was unbelievable. Honestly, I don't remember ever having been so excited. The prospect of spending a weekend with Doug—Friday evening through late Sunday afternoon— was stunning. I never learned how he'd managed to arrange it at home. I assumed he'd told Carol he was going somewhere on business, but when I asked him later, he smiled and said nothing.

It didn't matter. What mattered was that it was happening. Or would happen if disaster didn't strike, if Tyler or Courtney didn't get sick, if I didn't have to run off to a funeral in an Unnamed South American Country, if . . . if Doug didn't change his mind and decide the risk was too great.

That way lies madness, Romance said, voice a-flutter. Just think happy thoughts!

I did, or tried to. That evening I packed and it only took three hours to choose the perfect Vermont autumn weekend ensembles, including, of course, a pair of suede pants for day and a slim-fitting wool crepe dress, just in case. I still hadn't told anyone about the trip—something about jinxing it all. But by the next morning I had to tell someone or burst. I called Abby from the office. She was suitably excited and promised to feed Fuzzer and get my mail. I left a purposefully nonchalant voice mail at JoAnne's office and a more honestly emotional message on Maggie's home machine.

It occurred to me then that in the course of casual conversation my father might ask Abby if I had plans for the weekend. What would she say? For the obvious reasons I'd asked all my friends not to tell my father I was involved with a married man. And then I'd panicked and accused Abby of breaking her promise of secrecy. But she hadn't broken her promise, and so far, the secret had held. When Dad had asked me if I was dating anyone new or special, I'd lied and said no.

But with my going away for the weekend with Doug . . . I quickly called Abby again at the BSO. I didn't want to bother her so much at work but if I left a message on her home machine I ran the risk of Dad's overhearing the message. Ditto, home e-mail. Who knew how much John and Abby shared?

Covering your butt has become second nature to you, Erin, Reason drawled. How nice.

Reason could be awfully judgmental at times.

Abby picked up on the second ring.

"Abby? It's me again. I . . . I, uh, have a situation."

Long story short: While Abby claimed she didn't have a big problem keeping my relationship with Doug a secret from my father, she did have a smallish problem keeping my weekend whereabouts a secret. Something about an active lie versus a lie of omission.

And, of course, it probably didn't help that I'd recently accused her of breaking her word.

"What if there's an emergency?" she asked. "What if John needs to get in touch with you? I'll have to tell him I knew all along where you were and then I'll look like a horrible person. Lying destroys a relationship, Erin."

She had a point. In the end I apologized for having asked her to lie for me. It was agreed that if Dad asked if Abby knew what I was doing for the weekend she would be as honest as she felt comfortable being at the moment. It was all I could rightly ask of her. Now I just had to pray that Dad was so smitten with Abby that all thoughts of me fled from his head the moment he saw her.

Strange what we wind up wishing for, isn't it?

Friday morning dawned cold, bright, and clear—classic mid-October weather, with a promise of a very chilly night.

I got through the workday with only half my usual focus. That bothered me for about a minute, then guilt went out the window. I was going away for the weekend with the man I adored.

Adoration was not too strong a word to describe my feelings for Doug Spears.

In spite of our troubles and my increasingly angry response to the Situation, I wanted to be with Doug and no other man.

Inexplicable, Reason muttered.

Yes, true love is an enigma, Romance replied.

I saw the weekend in Vermont as a turn for the better, as a gesture from Doug toward a happier future—and a more secure one. I didn't even consider the possibility that it might be a last hurrah. For the moment, unbelievably, Negativity was dormant.

We'd met at the parking garage under the Prudential Center and as far as either of us could tell, no friend or colleague had seen us. Doug was driving the 2000 Lexus I'd seen before, his usual commuting car. It was on the tip of my tongue to ask why he hadn't arranged to borrow a company car since he'd probably told Carol he was going away on business, when the absurdity of that question stopped me cold. Lies upon deceit upon secrecy.

I tried to pull my thoughts back to the moment. Thus far, everything had gone smoothly. Too smoothly? Maybe Doug and I were just tempting fate by escaping this way. . . .

Stop it, Erin, I commanded my unruly brain. Just enjoy this time alone while you can.

Yes, Erin, Romance advised, savor every single moment.

"Happy?" Doug asked, lowering the volume on the blues station.

"Yes," I said.

This was only the second time Doug and I had been in a car together—other than a cab, of course—something so mundane, exactly the kind of activity we were largely denied by our status as illicit lovers. It struck me that there was romance in everything, if you chose to see it.

Doug's hand on the wheel and stick shift, his foot depressing the gas pedal and brake, his slight squint of concentration—every normal action and gesture had enormous allure. Doug was the sexiest man on Earth.

While we drove I indulged in fantasies of domestic bliss.

I was Doug's wife, sitting in my proper place at my husband's side. I was Mrs. Erin Spears, choosing a china pattern, selecting fabric for the living room's custom-made draperies, being a gracious hostess to Doug's colleagues. I was a loving companion, caring for Doug when he had the flu, checking in on his parents weekly, supporting his decision to leave his job and open his own firm again. I was . . .

Enough with the fantasizing, Erin, Romance counseled. Come back to the present and experience each and every moment.

Romance was right. The life that had been playing through my head wasn't real, it wasn't truth. Reality was Doug and me, alone together, driving toward a lovely weekend in Vermont. Truth was that we were in love.

I told myself that it was all I knew and all I needed to know.

As we got closer to our destination, my thoughts focused on the idea of actually sleeping with Doug—eyes closed, breathing slow and even . . . It was something I'd never hoped for and now, facing the actuality, I was thrumming with anticipation.

Was he a spooner? Did he sleep like a mummy, all tight and straight? Did he—God forbid—snore? It didn't matter. There was so much to learn and that prospect was exciting.

True intimacy was what I was seeking, after all.

Sleeping with someone new—spending the night, I should say—had always been uncomfortable for me. It usually took several weeks before I could manage some serious shut-eye, especially if we were at his apartment. Those were lonely nights, staring at the ceiling, counting cracks, cringing at night noises no woman certainly would want a guy to hear. At least in my apartment I had Fuzzer to keep me company. At least in my apartment I didn't feel—creepy.

Somehow, I knew things would be different with Doug. I knew that I would sleep comfortably and soundly. I knew that I would be safe.

Doug parked in the leaf-strewn yard before the B & B. It was a classic Vermont-style house, a bed and breakfast right out of an issue of *Martha Stewart Living,* two stories tall, white with black shutters, two chimneys promising fireplaces. On the front door hung a large wreath made of some sort of bramble, decorated with pine boughs and little red apples. In each of the windows stood a small electric candle, burning brightly in the chill dark night.

A small desk was set in the foyer. Behind it sat a robust woman of about sixty.

"Oh, yes, you must be Mr. and Mrs. Spears," she said, then introduced herself as half of the owning partners. Mrs. Nelson's wedding ring sat tight on her finger, clearly unremoved for ages, solid and permanent.

My own ring finger felt horribly naked.

"Yes, that's us," Doug said smoothly and signed his name to the register.

"Erin?" He handed me the pen.

I managed to scrawl something illegible.

Later, Doug told me he'd thought it would simply be easier to mask ourselves as husband and wife. Fewer questions and wondering glances that way. Still, he said, he thought we should split the bill and pay in cash. Not as much of a paper trail that way.

"Of course," I said coolly, but inside I was a heady wreck.

Chapter Fifty-one

I couldn't sleep.

You jinxed it, Erin, I told myself, all that stuff about how it was going to be different sleeping with Doug. You just shouldn't have thought about it at all.

What had I told myself, exactly? That I'd be able to sleep right off because I'd be safe with Doug. What did that mean, anyway?

Well, it certainly didn't mean how I felt after Doug grilled me on my thoughts about joining Trident all during dinner at a small local restaurant. No matter how hard I tried to get him off the topic, I failed.

Finally, I'd just given up and concentrated on my butternut squash soup.

Safe also doesn't mean how you felt when Doug called home, I reminded myself as I stared up at the dark ceiling. Doug had explained it was his routine while on a business trip to call home twice a day, once at night, once in the morning.

"I'm sorry, Erin," he'd said. "Would you like me to go into the hall?"

I'd forced myself to smile and said, "That's okay. I want to take a shower."

So, while I took an unnecessary shower, Doug spoke to Carol from the bedroom. From our bedroom. I strained to hear over the running water but could hear nothing. It was probably better that way, though a sick curiosity was killing me. By the time I turned off the water and stepped out of the shower, Doug had ended his call and was leaning in the bathroom's doorway.

"Everything okay?" I'd said, feeling strangely ill.

"Fine," he'd answered. "Now, come here."

Of course, we fooled around.

Doug had gone straight to sleep after we'd had sex. Okay, that was pretty standard behavior for a guy. It didn't piss me off. What pissed me off was his habit of turning over every five minutes and my freakin' inability to go to sleep.

I groaned and turned onto my side, wishing Fuzzer were there with me.

Or that I was home with Fuzzer.

The next morning we had breakfast in the breakfast room, alone but for one other couple who nodded a greeting and left us to ourselves.

We went back to the room to grab coats. I took my automatic camera from my travel bag.

"No pictures, Erin," Doug said.

"What?"

"I don't want you to take pictures of us."

"But they're only for me," I protested. "I mean, I'll show them to you but . . ."

But what? But I'd never send them to Carol? I'd never blackmail you? That awful conversation I'd had back in August with my friends had come back to haunt me.

"I'd really prefer if you didn't," Doug said. "Please."

"Okay." I tossed the camera back into my bag. "Sure."

Doug pulled me to him.

"Thank you," he whispered. Then he kissed my ear and my cheek and my neck and my lips.

Everything was okay.

Note to Self: "Wear helmet when apple picking." I was a walking disaster with the apple-picker. Somehow I managed to unloosen a barrel or two from one particular tree—on my head. Somehow I also managed to whack Doug in the shoulder with the picker end. It caused a tear in his sweater I knew I could never mend.

On the other hand, Doug wielding an apple-picker was like Doug wielding a sword or lance. Romance was absurdly pleased. At the same time Doug and the apple-picker gave me a glimpse of the domestic, at-home Doug, the guy who got the cat out of the tree and strung the Christmas lights on the eaves, the guy who mowed the lawn. The power tool Doug. The toilet-fixer, lightbulb-replacer, clogged drain-clearer that every single woman dreams of. Competent Doug.

When we'd loaded the trunk of Doug's Lexus with the apples I would take home—it was unspoken that Doug would not, could not, appear home with apples freshed picked during a "business trip"—I dragged Doug into the country store.

"Everything in there is going to be a rip-off," he warned. "They're just waiting for us city folk suckers."

"I know," I admitted. "But I want to look anyway."

While Doug wandered among the various homemade ciders, I poked through shelves of kitchen towels, jugs of maple syrup, and organic soaps.

And then I found her.

She was wonderful. Her name could be Hannah or Martha. She wore a calico dress and a white apron. Her boots were black. Her hair was made of yarn; it, too, was black. Her eyes were calm and deep.

"What's that?"

I turned. "Oh, it's an apple doll. See, the face is made of an apple that's been carved then dried. She looks very wizened, don't you think?"

"Do you like her?"

I nodded. "Yeah, I do. I was never one for sugary sweet dolls. I'm more the Strega Nona type."

"Then she's yours."

Doug plucked the apple doll from my hands and while I stood stunned, mouth open to protest the gift but no words coming out, he took the doll to the cashier.

A moment later, I followed.

"Her name is Martha," I told him, as the cashier wrapped the doll in tissue paper.

"How do you know?"

"She told me. You just have to know how to listen and most dolls will tell you their names."

"You're wonderful, do you know that?"

Yes, I thought. Now I do.

Needless to say, Sunday afternoon came far too soon for me. We drove back to Boston largely in silence. I felt sadness creeping along my bones and after a while asked Doug if he'd like to listen to some music. We found a blue grass program and had some fun singing along—making up the words, of course—until we reached the B.U. Bridge. Then, Doug turned off the radio. More silence.

We pulled up in front of my building at around six-thirty.

I didn't ask him to come up. I knew he'd say no—he had his rule about not crossing my threshhold and I assumed Carol was expecting him home at a certain time.

Doug cut the engine and turned to me in the blue dark.

"Well."

"Yeah." I attempted to laugh. "Well."

"It was great, Erin. Wasn't it?"

He took my hand and held it tightly.

"Yes, it really was."

Doug leaned forward and so did I and we kissed and it was very tender.

"We should do this again," he whispered and my happiness was complete.

Romance swooned.

Reason snorted in derision.

Doug went back to his wife and kids in Newton.

And I went home alone.

Chapter Fifty-two

E—imagine! lovely old gentleman made me a mar-
riage proposal! sapphire ring v. elegant. said no
but let him down gently. gotta run! M

October twenty-fifth. The day after Abby's thirty-third birthday. We met at Sel de la Terre. At my suggestion. They have
amazing french fries, sprinkled with rosemary. After a drink
at the bar, we took our table and waited for Abby. She was
not so uncharacteristically late.

I kept my eye on the door. After fifteen minutes—

"Here she comes," I said, without moving my lips. Sort
of.

"Can you see anything?" JoAnne whispered.

I tried not to be too obvious but . . .

"No. Not from this distance. Maggie?"

Maggie bent down and pretended to reach into her bag.
After thirty seconds, she straightened. "No ring."

The woman should have been a spy.

"Are you sure?" JoAnne hissed.

"Yup."

"Act natural," I said, and smiled up at Abby, now only two tables away.

"What the hell does that mean?"

"It means, don't jump on her."

"Hi, Abby."

She stood there for a moment, holding her bag before her in two hands, looking like she'd much rather flee than join us.

JoAnne, Maggie, and I shared a look. None of us wanted to blurt out the question uppermost in our minds.

"Hi, honey, have a seat." JoAnne pulled the free chair away from the table.

Abby smiled but the smile didn't reach her eyes. Actually, it hardly reached the ends of her lips. "Hi, everybody."

"Happy birthday again, Abby," Maggie said and raised her glass of wine.

"Thanks." Abby sat and immediately began to unfold and refold her napkin. "I really love the book, Maggie. I've started reading it already."

"A biography of Mozart," Maggie explained.

Thoughtful gift. I'd given Abby a Diana Krall CD—we all loved Diana Krall. And JoAnne had given her a gift certificate to Talbots, Abby's favorite store. We'd done good.

But now one of us was going to have to ask . . .

"So, Abby." It was JoAnne, her voice completely neutral. "Did you and John have a good time last night?"

"Oh, yes, it was very nice," Abby said quickly.

Maggie shot me a glance. "Um, where did you go for dinner?"

"He took me to Upstairs at the Pudding. I guess he knew it was one of my favorite restaurants."

JoAnne nodded. "Very romantic. Very pink."

"Was the food as good as ever?" I asked. I did actually want to know.

"Uh huh. It was—very nice."

Well, that confirmed our suspicions. Abby had definitely

not gotten an engagement ring for her birthday. But should one of us acknowledge that—or should we all just leave it alone?

There was more than a moment of uncomfortable silence.

"He also gave me a book," Abby said suddenly. "A novel I'd mentioned I'd wanted to read."

"Well, that's thoughtful, too." JoAnne looked across at me with a look that said, "How do we stop this game?"

Abby did it for us. "No ring, though," she said. By now her napkin had been smoothed to super flatness.

"Oh."

"I'm sorry, Abby," I said, and I meant it. She looked so sad. No one wants to see their dear friend looking so sad.

"That doesn't mean it's not going to come at Christmas, honey."

I glared at JoAnne. Since when did she spout sentimental crap? My gut was telling me the engagement ring wasn't going to come at all. But it wasn't my place to share my gut.

"It's okay," Abby said. She shook her head, fluffed her napkin, and put it on her lap. "Could we—could we not talk about it tonight? You guys are wonderful and all but . . . Let's just have fun. Okay?"

"Okay," Maggie said heartily.

And we tried.

I shared a cab with Abby. When we got to her place she asked if I'd come up for a few minutes. To talk. I agreed. How could I not?

Abby opened the door to her apartment. As always, it was spotless and neat as a pin. Not surprising that after years of my mother's less than competent housekeeping, Dad should have been attracted to such a fabulous housekeeper.

I kept that observation to myself.

"I'm going to get into my robe," Abby said and went off to her bedroom.

I sat on her chintz-covered couch, wishing I could get into my own bathrobe right then.

So, there had been no ring. I'd never seen Abby looking so disappointed. So—vulnerable. More than ever, tonight Abby had reminded me of a lost little girl.

A moment later Abby emerged in her pink flannel bathrobe and pink fuzzy slippers. She'd been crying.

"Can I get you anything?" she asked, with an attempt at a chin-up hostess voice.

"No, I'm fine. Why don't I get you something. Tea?"

Abby curled up in a corner of the couch and nodded. I went to the kitchen and nuked a cup of her favorite—plum-and-cinnamon-flavored tea. I took it back to the living room and as I handed her the cup, she burst out.

"How could I have been so stupid, Erin! I just . . . I just thought that everything was going so well and I thought, well, of course he'll surprise me on my birthday. Engaged at thirty-three, married at thirty-four . . . Oh, Erin, I can't bear being thirty-five and not married!"

Abby dabbed at her eyes with a tissue. I felt a headache coming on.

"Honey, you're jumping to conclusions. Just relax. And remember, Abby, Dad—John's—from a different generation." Oh, Lord, was I saying this? "He does things differently. Maybe he thinks it's too soon. Maybe he wants to take things slowly, be a gentleman."

Okay, my father went to college during the Vietnam War, not World War II. He hadn't worn beads or smoked pot for thirty-some-odd years but he was hardly a fussy old man. But I had to say something.

It seemed to do the trick. At least, temporarily.

"That's true," Abby said musingly. "About his being different. But . . . Erin, I feel so embarrassed! I could barely get through dinner last night without bursting out crying. How can I face him again when I feel so disappointed and he doesn't even know what he did!"

Or didn't do, I amended silently. Because he doesn't want to make a commitment yet. To anyone? To Abby.

"Abby, things will be fine," I offered lamely.

"He didn't say anything to you?" Abby asked, hopefully and fearfully.

"No, not at all, and I didn't say anything to him about . . . about what we thought might happen, either. So, don't worry. He has no idea about—the ring."

Or did he, I wondered. My father wasn't exactly dense. And Abby wasn't exactly subtle. I couldn't imagine that John Weston hadn't picked up on Abigail Walker's probably less than gentle hints about marriage. Or that he'd failed to notice her general despair the night before.

"That's good," Abby said but she sounded doubtful.

"Look, I think you should go to bed." I got up and took her empty teacup. "It's been a trying twenty-four hours and sleep sounds like a good thing."

Abby nodded. "Okay. Be careful getting home. And, Erin?"

"Yeah?"

"Thanks. I mean it."

We hugged. "I know you do, Abby. I know."

Chapter Fifty-three

Ex-boyfriends are a problem no matter what way you look at them. They're a problem when you run into them on Saturday morning, on your way to the dry cleaners, not looking your post-breakup best. They're a problem when they won't stop calling, either to beg you to take them back now that the women they left you for dumped them, or to harrass you for having left such a stellar guy. They're a problem when they date again before you do. They're a problem when memories of intimate moments with them make you cringe.

There should be a way to excise exes from our lives. They should be removed, like suspicious tumors are removed, just cut right out. I suppose murder is one possibility, though the getting caught part isn't very appealing. A lobotomy is another possibility, though I wouldn't want to sport a nasty scar on my head for the rest of my life.

Doug and I were strolling through the Gardens at lunchtime when I saw him. Post-college, Ex-Boyfriend No.4. Or No. 5. I'd lost track.

"Huh," I said.

"Huh, what?"

"Ex-boyfriend, two o'clock."

"Which one?"

"The big dumb-looking one in the gray coat. Bert. Bert Something."

Here was a challenge. Would Bert remember me? Would he guess that Doug was my married lover? I dripped nervousness. Doug seemed to be enoying my discomfort, which, I'd begun to notice, was something he often enjoyed.

I'd also noticed that Doug had taken to telling me to calm down, lighten up, stop overreacting, lower my voice, and stop being so emotional. Was everything I said or felt or did, wrong?

Maybe, I thought, Bert won't see me. Or I could snub him. Or maybe . . .

"Hey! Erin!"

"Shit."

Bert was coming our way, a big grin on his beefy face. Doug and I stopped and waited until he joined us.

"Hey, Erin, long time no see."

He did not shake my hand. I was glad.

"Yeah. Uh, Bert, this is—this is my colleague, Doug Spears. We're—we're coming from a meeting."

Bert shook Doug's hand. Interesting.

"Erin was crazy in love with me years back," Bert said, lightly punching Doug's arm. "Had to beat her off with a stick. Not literally, of course, don't go in for hitting the ladies . . ."

"What!" I cried. "I was never in love with you!"

Bert raised an eyebrow and Doug chuckled. He actually chuckled.

This can't be happening, I thought. It just can't.

"But now I'm a married man," Bert said, and I swear he stuck out his chest as he said it. "Got hitched five years ago. Got two kids already. Wife's in banking, quit to stay home with the kids. Maybe she'll go back to work someday, not necessary. I make more than enough money, don't need her salary."

Doug looked at me with that annoying, amused smile. He said nothing. He was waiting for me to say something.

Bert defined the term "blowhard." There was no way I was going to get out of this alive, except by playing along.

"Well, that's just great, Bert," I said tightly. "We really have to go now. I—"

"What about you, Erin?" Bert pretended to peer at my left hand. "No ring? No hubby?"

"No, no husband," I said. "No kids, either."

Bert clapped me on the shoulder. "Well, don't worry. You've got some time yet. You're not half bad-looking. Not getting any younger, though. Don't wait too long!"

Like what I was doing with my life was sitting around waiting to say, Okay, I'll get married now. Just like that.

"Okay," I said, urging a tiny smile to my lips. "I won't."

Bert loped off and Doug and I continued through the Gardens.

"Can you believe that moron!" I hissed. "What a freakin' nerve! He's hallucinating!"

"Oh, come on, Erin. Aren't you exaggerating, just a bit?" Doug's cocky smile just fueled my fire.

"I was not in love with him," I said fiercely.

"Maybe you were, just a little. It was a long time ago, right? Maybe you forgot."

"Oh, I haven't forgotten. I'll tell you what really happened. One night Mr. Numbnuts said to me, 'Hey, babe, don't fall in love with me.' Believe me, falling in love with Bert was the last thing on my mind. So, I answered, quite nicely, 'Uh, love? This is just a fuck.' And he looked at me like I'd just strangled his pet puppy. He was horrified. He just couldn't imagine meaning nothing more to me than his technique. Which wasn't so fabulous, by the way. Well, that was the end of that. He acted all huffy and injured and then he broke up with me."

Doug eyed me.

"You really didn't care?"

"I really didn't care. But obviously, Bert did. It's been how many years and he still can't let it go?"

We walked on. Anger made me want to run, not walk.

"Why did you go out with him in the first place if he was so lame?" Doug said suddenly.

I felt my heart go hard.

"Why does anyone do anything?" I said. "Boredom."

Jan was at a meeting of independent booksellers. Maggie was free to have dinner with us. We gathered at my house for takeout from Jae's. It was an amusing challenge keeping Fuzzer out of the chicken dishes I'd ordered.

When the food was distributed, JoAnne said: "So, tell us. What's it like with a woman?"

"JoAnne! God . . ." Abby gulped her water.

"I'm curious. I mean, I have an idea but I've never gotten a first-hand report from an actual . . ."

"Lesbian. You can say it, it's okay. Pass the spring rolls?"

"Really, Maggie, we don't have to talk about this . . ." I said as I handed her the plate.

"I know. But we've spent hours talking about sex with men so JoAnne is right to assume she can ask me about sex with women."

"See?"

"But I'm not going to tell you anything."

"What? Why not?" JoAnne demanded.

"Because my sex life—now that I'm having one again—is private. It's no one's business but mine and Jan's." Maggie grinned sheepishly. "Besides, I'm too shy to talk about it."

"Well, you guys are still new," I said. "It's normal you'd want to keep things special."

"That, too. But I'm not going to be giving a course in lesbian sex to you chickies any time soon so . . ."

"Rats." JoAnne. "Anyone going to eat that last dumpling?"

"I'm relieved," Abby said, then clapped her hand to her

mouth. "Oh, I didn't mean . . . I just . . . Maggie, you know I'm shy, too!"

It was a good evening, the four of us just hanging around, drinking wine, eating Asian food, taking turns scratching Fuzzer's head. It was like old times.

But it wasn't. Things had happened to us. Other things were happening. And still other things were about to happen.

Chapter Fifty-four

November, Boston

November in Boston is often gray, rainy, and cold. But that's only after the trees have exploded with color and the air has freshened.

November the first. The day after Halloween. A holiday best left to children, in my opinion. Too many adults find it license to be idiots. Idiots in stupid costumes. Drunken idiots in stupid costumes.

I'd stayed home and distributed candy for the few kids who came around. All were accompanied by their parents. Maggie and Jan had gone to bed early, pooped after a day of serving and cleaning up after a holiday meal at WLP. Abby and my father had rented the old black-and-white *Dracula* with Boris Karloff and popped popcorn.

JoAnne had donned an expensive rented costume and gone with Peter Leonard to a party given by someone from his office.

JoAnne had gone as Cleopatra. Peter, it seemed, had gone as himself. An asshole.

The four of us met at Tremont 647 for dinner.

"Gather round, girls," JoAnne said when we were all together. "I have a little story to tell."

Peter Leonard had turned out not to be a perfect partner, at all.

"From the minute we got to the party," JoAnne said, "Peter acted as if I didn't exist. He didn't introduce me to anyone. He got his own drink. Then he got me one, but only after I'd asked him to. So, being the social butterfly that I am, I began to mingle. And it didn't take me long to see that every woman at the party but me was a twenty-something. A young twenty-something. I tried to strike up a conversation with one girl dressed as a genie but it's hard to have a meaningful talk with someone who doesn't know the name of the current mayor of Boston."

"Ugh," I said. "I know the type. Dumb as a bucket of hair. What about the men? Anyone eligible?"

JoAnne laughed. "If you're looking for late thirty-something assholes who make far too much money for their own good. Judging by the conversations I overheard, Peter isn't even the worst of the bunch."

"So, what happened?" Abby asked. "Did you just leave?"

"Well, that was the plan. First, being a well-mannered social butterfly, I figured I'd find Peter and tell him I was out of there. And I found him all right. With his tongue down the throat of the dumb-ass girl I'd tried to talk to earlier."

"Loser," Maggie pronounced.

"Oh, yeah. Total loser. But I wasn't leaving without his knowing I'd seen him. So, I shouted his name and when he came up for air, I picked two apples from the bobbing bowl and tossed them to him."

My jaw dropped like a cartoon character in shock. "You didn't."

"I did. And I said, 'Here. You might need these. I noticed you don't have any of your own.'"

Abby looked puzzled.

"The apples were, like, his balls," Maggie explained.

Abby gasped. "Oh, my God. Did he do anything? Did he say anything? He must have been so embarrassed!"

JoAnne shrugged. "I don't know. I don't even know if he got my meaning. I walked out of the room, grabbed my coat, and got the hell out of there."

"You . . ." What could I say? I was so proud. "You amaze me. Kudos, woman, and kudos again."

"What are you going to do?" Abby asked. "You really liked him."

JoAnne laughed. "What do you think I'm going to do? It takes more than a bimbo in a freakin' genie costume to keep me down."

"Hurrah for you!"

"See," I said. "Being open to emotional experience doesn't mean giving up all powers of discrimination. It doesn't mean you have to be anti-intellectual. And it doesn't mean issuing an open invitation to be trod upon."

JoAnne eyed me. "Just who are you preaching to?"

I didn't answer.

"My advice," Maggie said, "is to stay away from those dating services and just live your life."

"Not exactly the most original words of wisdom . . ." JoAnne grinned. "But I like them."

> *Erin—any snow yet? don't miss nov in boston*
> *one bit! thinking of writing memoirs of travels.*
> *think it wld sell big, if i do say so myself. M.*

Abby had come over to watch an Audrey Hepburn movie. She owned just about all of them on video and was slowly replacing them with DVD versions. I was the happy recipient of the slightly worn videos.

It should have been a light, fun occasion but from the moment Abby walked into the apartment, it was clear she had something on her mind.

I popped the tape into the VCR—*Breakfast at Tiffany's,*

this time—and got us settled with champagne, cracked black pepper crackers, a variety of cheeses, and olives.

"Ready?" I asked, though I knew in my heart it would be some time before we would get to the movie.

"I have to talk," Abby said, sitting upright on the edge of her chair, busily twisting the tassle on a throw pillow.

"Okay." Yes, the movie would wait.

"Erin, could you . . . Do you think you could talk to John? You know, about me and him."

It was not what I was expecting to hear.

"Oh, Abby," I said, "I can't do that. First of all, I doubt he'd say anything but 'Mind your own business.' Second . . . well, I think I should mind my own business. Why can't you, you know, just ask him if anything is wrong?"

Abby flopped back into the chair and rested her head against its back. Fuzzer immediately leapt onto her lap. "I'm afraid," she said. "I'm afraid of what I'll hear."

"What if I hear something—bad. You'd want me to tell you, right?"

"No. Well, yes, I suppose. Erin, I just can't figure out what's going on! John's been so distant lately. Since my birthday. Not mean, not really cold, just—kind of like a stranger. I feel he's uncomfortable with me suddenly and it makes me feel uncomfortable. Erin, I swear, last night both of us couldn't wait to get home. To our separate apartments."

"I really don't know what to say, Abby. Except that you should talk to him. Maybe something at work is driving him crazy, I don't know. And you won't know either, unless you just ask him if everything's all right between you."

"Maybe if I just say nothing and act like everything's fine—which will be hard but I can do it—whatever's going on will pass. They say that sometimes ignorance is bliss."

And, I added silently, they also say that having your head up your butt means you're a big sack of stupid.

"Well, it's up to you, Abby," I said. "I'm sure it'll all work out."

Another lie, but it seemed to satisfy Abby, who now busied herself with scratching Fuzzer under his chin and humming softly.

I took a sip of champagne and started the tape.

I'd done what I thought was the right thing. I'd advised Abby to speak honestly with her boyfriend. But I had developed a strong curiosity now and knew I'd butt in where I shouldn't. I'd talk to Dad. I just wouldn't tell Abby that I had.

Secrecy and lies, deceptions and falsehoods. The words were like a chant in my head. They were becoming my own personal mantra. I could see my tombstone now: HERE LIES ERIN WESTON. ADULTERER, CONSUMMATE LIAR, BETRAYER. MAY SHE ROT IN HELL.

Chapter Fifty-five

Friday. The end of the week, the beginning of another weekend without Doug. We'd spent a lot of time together Monday through Thursday and I probably should have had the strength not to pop in on him at Trident's offices Friday late afternoon but . . .

I knew that Doug usually didn't leave work before six on a Friday. At five-forty-five I knocked on his open office door. As far as I could tell, everyone else at Trident had gone home. Odd. But promising. Maybe we could slip in a few kisses, at least.

Doug looked up from his computer.

"What are you doing here?" he asked, obviously startled.

I smiled. "Just wanted to say hi before you left for the weekend. I'm sorry if I scared you."

"You didn't. But I need to finish something before I leave."

"Rush hour traffic's a bear, isn't it?" I said, moving into the office and perching on the edge of his desk.

Doug looked at me and something flickered in his eyes. I felt sick suddenly.

"I'm not going home," he said. "I'm staying in Boston this weekend."

I felt sicker now. Oh, God, I thought, Doug's seeing another woman . . . How could he, after our weekend in Vermont?

"Oh?" I said, my voice cracking slightly. "Why didn't you tell me?"

Doug leaned back in his chair, as if relaxing. "Because it's really none of your business, Erin. It's my anniversary. Carol's coming in to meet me at seven and we're staying at the Ritz for the weekend."

I've never been shot by a gun and hope never to be. But I can't help thinking that what I felt at that moment was what a gunshot victim might feel at the moment of impact. Nausea. Pain. Shock. Disbelief. The world growing fuzzy and dark at the edges.

"You're doing what?" I said finally, voice shaking with rage.

"Oh, come on!" Doug laughed. He roared. He really didn't get it. "I can't believe you're upset about this."

"You can't believe I'm upset that you're taking Carol to the Ritz for a weekend?"

"She's my wife and the mother of my kids. I respect her, I've told you that. It's our anniversary and I want her to feel special."

Okay, Reason said, he's got a point. He can give his wife whatever gift he pleases. You have no right to object.

It's good that he treats his wife well, Romance said stoutly. It bodes well for you.

But on the other hand, Reason continued, voice more sharp, what an amazing load of crap this guy is spewing.

I struggled to keep my voice at a calm pitch and my hands from picking up the giant stapler and lobbing it at Doug's head.

"Doesn't it strike you as a bit, oh, I don't know, insincere, to be celebrating your anniversary when you've told me you know you married the wrong woman—and when you're fucking another woman? When you've taken another woman away for the weekend?"

I couldn't help it. My voice had risen to a horribly hysterical screech. I could hardly stand myself.

Doug looked unperturbed. His smile was gone—but not entirely. "No," he said, "I don't think I'm being insincere. I think you're being childish."

For one thrillingly nasty moment I determined to call Carol and blow it all up, tell her that her shithead of a husband was cheating on her, tell her we were both better off without him, crack open Doug's world like my grandfather used to crack open walnuts in his bare hand. God, that would feel good. I'd be free and clear and . . .

And you'd be leaving Carol to clean up the mess, Reason pointed out. You'd be cracking open her life, too, destroying her hard-won illusions of a happy marriage. She doesn't deserve that, Erin.

But doesn't she deserve the truth? I demanded.

Yes. But not from you and not in this way. Not as an act of vengeance.

That gave me something to think about. I knew so little about Carol—the real Carol. Was she mentally tough, emotionally resilient? Would she receive my revelation with mature stoicism—or would she collapse with grief? Maybe even try to kill herself. What would become of the children if I destroyed Carol and her personal version of marriage?

Damn it, Reason was right. I'd keep my mouth shut.

But oh, did my heart—and my dignity—hurt.

"I can't be with you right now," I said. I couldn't even look at Doug's face. I reached for my bag and his hand shot out for mine. I yanked both hand and bag away and still without looking directly at him, I left.

Behind me I heard an amused chuckle.

On the way home that evening I forced myself to stop in CVS for the few items on my list. You'll be home soon enough, I told myself soothingly. And then you can let loose. Cry.

Stomp. Eat. Drink. Whatever. All by yourself. For the entire weekend.

No matter what time of the day, CVS was mobbed.

Mouthwash and ibuprofen. Last stop, the makeup aisle.

I took my purchases to the back counter, which is really the prescription pharmacy counter, but the people who work there are much smarter than the ones who work at the general checkout counter up front. So, if you don't want to be charged six times for one stick of deodorant, and then spend fifteen minutes waiting for the slack-jawed cashier to cancel out the order and start from the beginning, you take your purchase to the drug counter.

The guy behind the counter wore a name tag that read JARED. Nice name. He said hello and asked if I had a CVS card. I didn't. He rang up the mouthwash, ibuprofen, and liquid makeup.

"Oh," he said, examining the box of face powder. "There's no price on this. Did you by any chance notice what it costs?"

"No," I said. "I didn't. Sorry."

"No problem." Jared looked over his shoulder. A twenty-something girl stood several feet behind him, hair streaked false red, lab coat open to reveal a tight tank top. He held up the box of face powder.

"Suzy? Do you know the price on Revlon Age-Defying face powder stuff?"

The girl laughed. "How would I know?" she said loudly. "I'm not, like, old."

Jared whipped back to face me. One look at my face and he knew I'd heard the girl's careless remark. At least Jared had the decency to blush.

"I'll go check the price myself," he said and rushed out from behind the counter.

Which left me looking directly at the girl, and her looking at me. Suzy's expression was carefully blank. And then she turned away from me.

So, there I was, waiting for my age-defying formula. Trembling—slightly—with anger. Trembling—largely—with hurt.

Single, thirty-two, and with no more prospect of marriage than I had back in January when I'd vowed to get serious about my life. When I'd promised myself I'd start living more consciously and wisely.

Who ever knew I was such a liar?

I had another dream about Doug that night. Maybe "about" isn't really the most accurate word. It was more like the dream was Doug, like the dream was reality, like Doug was there physically, in my bedroom, in me, on me, overwhelming me. It wasn't a sex dream as much as it was—what? I was beneath Doug, he was hovering over me, then pressed against me and I couldn't breathe and it was thrilling and at the same time horrible. I looked up as best I could, not being able to move all that easily, and Doug's head was thrown back but it lowered when he sensed my watching and blood gushed from his mouth . . .

I woke then, scared and breathing fast. No blood on my face, no Doug in the bed, just Fuzzer sleeping heavily against my leg. I got up and went through my usual morning routine and put the disturbing dream from my mind. It wasn't easy but I did it.

Chapter Fifty-six

*E—think i can pay you back soon—going in on a
surefire venture with nice man i met at local bar.
always wanted to own my own business. will keep
you posted. M.*

The offer from Trident was still on the table. I called Jack
Nugent to confirm that and to let him know I was still considering. I apologized for taking so much time with my decision. He told me there was nothing for which to apologize.
He wished me a great day.

Face it, Erin, I told myself. The more you imagine working with big corporate clients, the more you pull away from
taking the job.

Am I crazy, I wondered. Crazy to reject an opportunity
for serious money and corporate power? Reason weighed in
with an opinion. No, not crazy. But examine your motives.
Are you really satisfied with what you're doing and what you
have? Or is fear holding you back from taking this step? Say,
fear of success? Fear of something new and challenging?

Romance had an opinion, too. Consider this, Erin: Maybe
it's crazy to turn your back on work you've always found ful-

filling. You make enough money now to support a comfortable lifestyle. Is it worth giving up work about which you feel passionate for a few thousand dollars?

Several thousand dollars, Reason corrected.

On the other hand, Romance said musingly, if you accept the position at Trident you'll get to see Doug every day and it just might provide an oppportunity for the relationship to grow and flourish.

A traitorous thought erupted: Did I want to see Doug five days a week? Did I want the relationship to grow and flourish?

Reason seems not to have heard. Is choosing your lover to be your boss wise, Erin, it asked.

What would happen if we broke up, I thought, suddenly panicked. Would Doug try to get me fired?

Again, Reason ignored me. It said: How realistic is it to expect to maintain a true separation between your personal and professional life—especially since everyone at Trident knows—or will know—that you're sleeping with the boss?

No one knows anything! I protested. Doug and I have been very discreet.

Oh, Erin, your love shines from every inch of you! Romance cried. You've proclaimed your love to the world!

Yeah, and rumor has it that Erin Weston is sleeping her way to the top. Reason was very smug.

It does not! I protested. It's not true.

Prove that to your colleagues, Erin. Take the job at Trident. Go ahead. I dare you.

I called Doug at the office for no reason other than the desire to hear his voice. But when I heard it, I wished I hadn't succumbed to such a nonprofessional desire. Especially after the scene I'd made about his anniversary weekend with Carol. I'd clamped down on my anger, grasped at rationality, and apologized. Still, the memory rankled.

"What is it Erin? I'm busy."

"Oh, sure, sorry. I just wanted to say a quick hi."

"Okay."

"So, hi."

"Is this about our offer?" he said, with a distinct change in tone. Suddenly, Doug sounded interested in talking to me.

"No, no. I haven't made a decision yet. I . . ."

"Trident can't wait forever for you to make up your mind, Erin. Honestly, it doesn't say much for your decision-making ability to be fooling around with us all this time."

I was shocked. "I'm not fooling around with you!" I cried, then cringed and lowered my voice. "Doug, this is a huge decision. I'm sorry, I don't mean to . . ."

"Erin, I've got to go, there's a meeting. Just focus, okay, and if you're holding out for more money than we've offered, tell me, don't play games. Trident wants you on board by the end of the year."

"Yeah, okay . . ."

The line went dead.

He could at least have been polite, I thought, and tears pricked at my eyes.

My boss called a meeting the following morning. A few months earlier I'd talked to him about the Women's Lunch Place and about Maggie's involvement. As far as I knew, Terry hadn't given the place another thought after our brief conversation.

I thought wrong. Seems Terry had spoken to the people at WLP, done some research about their past involvement with public relations and publicity, checked out their financials. Finally, Terry had come to a decision. He wanted EastWind to offer its services to WLP pro bono.

"It's my firm, I know I can do what I want," he said, with a grin. "But I don't want us to offer ourselves if we're not all in agreement. I don't want to force anyone to participate. Some of you have kids at home, some of you are already putting in too-long hours. All of you have lots of responsibilities. I don't want to force you to accept another set. But I do want you to consider EastWind's doing everything we can for this shelter."

"I'm in," I said, surprising myself. The words had come without thought and they felt right.

"Just so we're clear," Terry said. "It might mean some long hours with no compensation. No monetary compensation, anyway."

"What's their annual operating budget?" Hank asked.

Terry passed him a piece of paper.

"Ow. How they get anything done is a miracle. Okay, I'm in."

And it went like that around the table.

"Me, too," said Edmund.

"I don't see how we can say no." That was Maureen.

Each and every one of us made the commitment.

"Good," Terry said, grinning broadly now. "I'll call WLP right now. Thanks, everyone. You people are the best."

I looked around the table at my colleagues. Yeah, they were the best.

Chapter Fifty-seven

E—business venture fell thru. lost abt $1,000.
cld have been worse. how is yr job? still no man?
M

I needed to see Doug. I'd made up my mind. The formal note to Jack Nugent was already written, signed, and sealed, waiting to be mailed. I wanted Doug to know first. I thought he had the right.

I asked that we meet at Radius. That first lunch, back in March, had gone well for us. Maybe there was still some good fortune in the air.

Doug was agitated.

"I don't want to talk about work," he said, before even saying hello. "It's been a hell of a morning."

That did not bode well for the success of my planned topic.

I kept my mouth shut until our entrées were served. But then I had to get on with things.

"Doug," I said, "I know you don't want to talk about work. But I really need to talk about Trident's offer."

Doug looked up as if he were stunned I'd broken his command.

"I'm eating. And you heard what I said. Do we need to discuss this now?"

"If not now, when?"

"How about never? Is never okay with you?"

Blood rushed to my face. "Stop quoting *New Yorker* cartoons at me. Come on, we need to talk about this."

Doug sighed and made a production of putting down his fork. "Okay, so talk."

"I'm not taking the job at Trident."

The look on his face frightened me. For a moment I thought of retracting madly. But I didn't.

"What?"

"I've decided to stay at EastWind. I know what you're going to say . . ."

"Oh, you have no idea." Doug pushed his plate away and took a gulp of his water with ice.

"It was a really hard decision to make, Doug, and I'm sorry it took me so long . . ."

"You're making a big mistake." Doug's voice was cold. And angry.

Oh, yes, I've been making a big mistake for a long time now, I answered silently. But not for much longer.

"Why can't you support me on this?" I asked uselessly.

Doug didn't answer my question. "You're not going to be happy, Erin."

Oh, yes. I was. If it killed me, I was going to get happy.

I laughed nervously. In the privacy of my own head I felt brave. The hard part was translating that feeling to words and actions.

"I hope . . . I hope you're wrong," I said.

It was Maggie and Jan's housewarming, a celebration of their having moved in together and making the big commitment.

Abby and I stood alone by one of the many bookshelves stuffed with books of all sizes and knicknacks of all kinds.

"Are we . . ." Abby began and then stopped with a look of confusion. Or was it surprise?

"Oh, yeah, I'd say so."

JoAnne joined us with a small plate of goodies. "You'd say what?"

I gave a quick and hopefully unnoticed glance around the room. "The three of us are—I think—the only straight people here."

"I'm not sure we should say 'straight,' " JoAnne said nonchalantly. "It implies that homosexuals are crooked and wrong."

"Whatever, fine."

"It's kind of—weird," Abby whispered. She took a mini-quiche from JoAnne's plate and popped it into her mouth whole.

"Being the minority?" I said and Abby nodded. "I know. It gives you a teeny glimpse into what, say, Jan or Damion, must feel almost all the time."

JoAnne rolled her eyes in the direction of a particularly fierce, macho-looking woman in a black leather jacket. "Scared. Like you're about to get your butt kicked."

"Looks are deceiving." It was Maggie, joining us with a coffeepot. "Sally's a kindergarten teacher, one of the best. She's a total softy."

"Sorry, Maggie," I said.

She shrugged. "Why? Sally scared the life out of me the first time I met her. Refill, anyone?"

Abby held out her cup.

"Why don't you guys mingle?" Maggie suggested as she poured. "You kind of—um, stand out—huddled over here by yourselves."

"Like we don't belong?"

"You belong, JoAnne," Maggie said. "You're my friends."

Maggie moved off to serve others. JoAnne went right and Abby went left. I went for more food.

Just as I popped a mini-quiche in my mouth . . .

"Hi, Erin."

It was Jan. I gestured to my stuffed cheeks and put up my hand to say, Wait just one minute while I finish gulping my food.

"Sorry," I said and wiped my mouth.

Jan laughed. She had a nice laugh. "My fault. My timing has never been great."

"This is a wonderful party," I said. "Did you make all the food?"

Jan looked proud but not smug. "Yeah. I love to cook."

"So Maggie says. And she loves your cooking."

"So, she's talked about me to you guys?"

"Sure. Not a lot—Maggie's kind of quiet about her personal life. But she feels comfortable talking about you, if that's what you mean."

"I guess I do. I . . . I wondered what her friends' reactions would be when she told them about me."

I considered. "Honestly, I wasn't totally surprised. I mean, I'd kind of suspected she'd met someone and was just being extremely cautious about the whole thing. I just didn't think the someone would be a woman."

"Not that there's anything wrong with that."

I laughed. "That's my line, but yeah. Seriously, Maggie seems really happy. And she looks better than she's ever looked, since I've known her anyway."

"So, I must be doing something right?"

I liked this woman. "Yeah. I'd say you're definitely doing something right. And could you invite me to dinner sometime? The spicy shrimp is awesome."

We left the housewarming a half hour later.

"It's a little—weird—isn't it?" Abby said. "Not Maggie and Jan's being gay but their being together. It's almost like we're losing her."

"I know. I feel the same way," I admitted. "Like one of us grew up and left home. I'm happy for her and all but . . . I'm kind of sad, too."

"And angry."

That was a surprise from JoAnne.

"Uh," I said, "why?"

"I admit it. I'm angry that she's more mature than I am. The very fact that I'm angry shows just how immature I am. Maggie's settled into a loving, monogamous relationship—which takes plenty of guts—and where am I? Maggie took the lead. I've fallen behind."

"Think of Maggie's relationship with Jan as a personal challenge," I suggested, only half jokingly. JoAnne loved a good competition. "Now you've got to prove you can be just as mature as she is."

Pay attention, Erin. That was Reason. This might just be an opportunity for you, too.

I woke up that night in a cold sweat. I must have been dreaming, caught in a nightmare, but the moment I woke, my mind was blank.

I stared up at the ceiling and took deep, calming breaths. I wondered if I was getting sick. I wondered why I felt so depressed.

Because you are depressed, Reason suggested, not unkindly.

I know, I admitted. Depressed and unhappy and downright miserable.

And whose fault was it?

The truth was ugly. The fault was my own.

It occurred to me as I lay there that maybe there was truth in what Maggie had gently suggested to me once. Maybe I was afraid to find real love, the kind I talked about wanting and yet the kind I was not in the least pursuing by having an affair with a married man.

It occurred to me that I was afraid that what my mother had told me when I was a kid was right, that I wasn't cut out for marriage after all. Maybe I'd been deceiving myself by thinking otherwise. If I did manage to pull off a wedding I'd soon after ruin the marriage. Should I have continued to listen to my mother?

No. I threw off the covers, disturbing Fuzzer, and sat on the edge of the bed. No. My mother was wrong. I did want to be married and I knew somewhere deep down that I could make it work. It would be hard but—I could do it. I wanted to do it.

But first, I had to get off the going-nowhere path I had taken when I'd started the affair with Doug. And in the dead of night, alone and growing cold, that seemed a Herculean task I just wasn't up to undertaking.

Chapter Fifty-eight

I liked my father's Back Bay apartment. It was cozy in that men's club sort of way, but without the mournful heads of long-dead elks and the moldy skins of long-dead bears. And here I was about to get thrown out of it for good.

We each settled in a high-backed leather armchair with a glass of wine.

"How's work, Erin?"

"Okay. Fine. Look, Dad, I know it's none of my business—I really know that—but . . ."

"But you're going to ask me anyway," he said with an indulgent smile.

"Yes," I said, looking down at my clasped hands. "And you have to know that Abby has nothing to do with this, honestly. She'd die if she knew I was talking about this with you . . ."

"Erin, before I run away in trepidation, what is it?"

"Okay. Well, see . . ." I hesitated. It really was none of my business, what was going on in my father's head about Abby.

Oh, but, Erin, it is your business, Romance cried. These are two people quite dear to you and their happiness does concern you!

You're butting in, Erin, and you know it, Reason countered, with a voice like a slap.

Yeah, well, it wouldn't be the first time.

"Dad," I said, looking steadily at his face, "are you serious about Abby? Because she said things seemed a bit—off—between you two lately and I know she was so excited about your relationship and . . ."

"Yes, Erin, I'm serious about Abby. I care about her. Which is why I'm going to have to end our relationship."

What?

"You're breaking up with her?" I said, though I'd heard him just fine. "I don't believe it!"

Dad smiled, a bit sadly. "Why? Because I'm old and should be grateful that a younger woman is in love with me?"

Well, yeah, for starters, I thought. But I said nothing.

"Erin, Abby's a wonderful woman. She's beautiful and smart and caring. But . . . she's too young for me. We're just not at the same place in our lives. I know she wants to get married—it's written all over her—and in all good conscience I can't let her continue to hope—to believe—I'm going to marry her."

This is what you get for being a buttinski, Reason said. I thought I heard a note of gloating in its voice.

"Did you . . ." Oh, Lord. I had to ask, didn't I? "Did you ever tell her . . . Did you do anything to make her believe there was a possibility of marriage?"

"Erin, you know Abby. I'm a man. Therefore, I'm a possible husband. I promise you, I never mentioned the subject. I never talked about the future."

"She did," I said glumly.

Dad sighed. "I know. She's been dropping hints since October. At first, I ignored them and then when the hints got broader, I tried to confront her with my feelings but . . . Well, you know Abby. She doesn't always hear what she doesn't want to hear."

Yes, that much was true.

"Is there another woman?" I said, hoping there was because I was angry and needed a better excuse to be pissed off at my father than his trying to spare Abby's feelings.

"Yes."

Bingo.

"I met her just last week. We haven't dated yet, just had lunch once with some other people. But I intend to ask her out."

It just got worse and worse.

"So, you weren't cheating on Abby with her?"

"Lord, no. Erin, I was faithful in word and deed to your mother for over thirty years. And I've been faithful to Abby since we met at the party. I'm happy being faithful. It's who I am. I want to marry again. Just, not Abby."

"You think this other woman—"

"Marilyn."

At least it isn't Tiffany, I thought.

"Marilyn. You think she might be the one."

"Oh, it's far too early to tell. She might have no romantic interest in me at all. But if she does, Marilyn and I stand a better chance of making a relationship work for the long haul. She's in her late forties or early fifties, I'd say. She's been married and has a son who's now in college. Our experiences are at least similar. We're compatible, Erin, or we could be. Truly compatible. And that's what most of marriage comes down to. Compatibilty. Being comfortable just sitting in the same room together. It's something I never really felt with Abby."

"Why did you go out with her, then?" I challenged.

Dad laughed. "Well, for one, she liked me. Do you know how flattering it was to find a thirty-two-year-old woman interested in me, especially after my wife had left me so unceremoniously? And, as I said before, Abby's charming and pretty and . . . Well, she gave my ego a much-needed boost. She helped bring me alive again. And I'll forever be thankful to her for that."

"You know you're going to break her heart. You do know that."

"I know. But it won't be broken for long."

"How do you know about Abby's heart? How do you know anything about her?" I said angrily.

Dad replied calmly. "Mark my words, Erin, before long Abby will see that we weren't meant to be. Abby told me she always wanted a family of her own. Suddenly, she's willing to give up that important life goal for me? No. Abby deserves to have that family. She'll make a fine mother and I can't deprive her of that experience."

"Isn't it her choice to make, whether or not she wants to have kids?" I asked stubbornly.

"Believe me," he said almost sternly, "if Abby and I married she'd come to resent me. I've seen a similar thing happen with one of my colleagues. He grabbed at the chance to be married to a beautiful, much younger woman, without regard for his own emotional needs—or hers—and it's a disaster. He's getting a divorce and he's a mess over it. Erin, nothing's for certain, but with a decision as important as choosing a life partner, you have to read the signs. You have to try to be smart. I have to try to be smart for me and for Abby. What I want is a companion and a wife. What Abby wants right now is a father. She'll get over that, but not if I stick around."

Well, what could I say to all that?

Who was I to tell my father he was making a huge mistake, dumping Abby? First, deep down, beneath the shock, I didn't really believe his leaving her was a mistake. And I was proud of him for being a real gentleman. Second, I wasn't exactly batting a thousand in the romance department, was I? Sex, sure. Commitment, zero.

"Do you want another glass of wine?" Dad's voice was gentle. "I've also got some cheese and crackers I could put out."

I nodded. "Okay. Thanks," I said and to my own ears my voice sounded like that of a little girl who'd just been scolded for naughtiness.

Dad stood and headed for the kitchen.

Well, I thought, leaning back into the chair, it looked like

I wasn't the only one not getting a piece of important jewelry any time soon.

> *E—thinking of sending card to yr father, just to say hi. gets lonely sometimes. how's it going with him and that woman? M.*

The end came a few days later. Abby called me on her cell phone, sobbing. She said she had just left work. I told her to go home immediately. I told her I'd be right there.

I knew what had happened, though Abby hadn't made much sense through her tears.

When I arrived, Abby's apartment door was ajar. I entered cautiously.

"Abby?"

She was curled up on the couch, a box of tissues at her side. Her hair was wild, as if she'd flung herself onto the couch and rolled in grief. Her face was red and puffy.

"Your door was open," I said softly. "You have to be more careful."

"I don't care."

"What happened?" Suddenly, I felt terribly creepy, pretending to be all innocent. Why hadn't I warned her? I sat next to her on the couch.

"John broke up with me at lunch today," she said, and the words brought more tears.

"Oh, honey, I'm so sorry."

And Dad, I thought, how did you expect her to get through the afternoon at work after dumping her at lunch! Not very considerate.

"It's all your fault, Erin!" Abby blurted. "You told your father to break up with me! How could you! You know how I feel about him!"

Why had I come, if only to be attacked? I'd come because my best friend had been dumped by a guy she was in love with. Duty called.

I put my hand on her shoulder. "Abby, I swear, I had nothing to do with it!"

"You never wanted us to be together . . ."

"In the beginning, yes, but, Abby, I was fine with it after a while, you know that. I'm sorry. I'm so sorry . . . I'm so angry at him . . ."

Which was true and not true.

"Oh, what am I going to do, Erin?"

"You're going to feel awful for a while," I said. "And then you're going to be fine, Abby. I promise."

"At least you don't break your promises to me."

"Did John?" I asked, wanting very much to hear her side of the story.

Abby lowered her eyes. "No," she said in a soft, low voice. "It's just . . . just that it hurts . . . Oh, Erin I love him . . . I thought he was my soul mate."

And that was the end of the talking that night. A box of tissues and a half gallon of chocolate fudge ice cream later, Abby fell asleep on the couch and I went home, locking the door behind me.

It had been a long night.

Chapter Fifty-nine

Thanksgiving. Thursday, November 24. It was not a memorable day. And because of its very lack of memorability, I'll never forget it.

I spent the day with my father at his apartment. We watched part of the Macy's Thanksgiving Day parade—in silence. When Santa came gliding along in his magnificent sleigh, a few tears slipped down my cheeks. Dad was tactful enough not to comment.

Neither of us was much in the mood for cooking so we'd ordered a fairly traditional meal from Savenors. At three o'clock we heated up the turkey roulade, and made Bloody Marys. Food and then a buttery Chardonnay eased some of the tension and softened some of the sadness and we talked. But by five o'clock we'd run out of small chat and I packed up my share of the leftovers—including some for Fuzzer—and went home. Dad and Marilyn were getting together briefly that evening, if she got home from her parents' assisted living center at a reasonable hour. I was going to bed.

Of course, the first thing I did when I got home was check my answering machine. No messages.

You hadn't really expected Doug to call on Thanksgiving,

had you? Reason asked. Come on, Erin. It's more of a family day than Christmas.

Maybe that was the reason Abby hadn't called, either, I thought gloomily. She'd gone home to the Walkers in Lincoln— her true family, not the Westons, who'd betrayed her. Romance in its tragic mode was just dying to take hold and I didn't have the energy to put up a good fight.

Yes, you do, Reason said. Snap out of it, Erin.

Reason was right. Here I was moping around while Maggie and Jan were devoting their Thanksgiving to helping the guests at the WLP have a wonderful meal. They'd been baking at home for days and had signed on as volunteers for both the breakfast and lunch shifts. . . . Why hadn't I offered my time or other support, I wondered. True, neither had outright asked but I could have volunteered. There and then I made a decision to ask Maggie how I could get involved at Christmastime. Wasn't it always said that the best way to forget about your own problems was to do something about the problems of others? And what were my problems compared to hunger, poverty, and homelessness?

Even JoAnne had spent her time more usefully than I had that Thanksgiving. She'd flown to California to spend the holiday weekend with her brother and his fiancée. She hadn't seen Robert in almost ten years, but true to her word about making some serious life changes, she'd picked up the phone and tracked down her only living relative. I hoped she was having a good time. I hoped she wasn't storming her way back to Boston, convinced she'd made a huge mistake in caring.

> E—won't contact yr father if you think it bad idea. glad all's well with his relationship. really. oh—happy turkey day. must be off—have a rendezvous. Mom

Turns out my worry was for naught. JoAnne got back from LA the Sunday after Thanksgiving. We met briefly for a drink at Brasserie Jo. Much like an authentic French bistro, the bar offered free hard-boiled eggs and olives for nibbling. I was a particular fan of the eggs. None of my friends seemed to understand or share my passion.

"How was the trip?" I asked when we'd taken two stools at the bar and ordered. A glass of Macon-Lugny for me; a Cosmopolitan for JoAnne.

"Let me put it this way, honey. LA is not my kind of town."

"Did you think it would be?"

"Not really. It was more like my suspicions were confirmed."

"So, how was it spending time with Robert?"

JoAnne considered. "Interesting. He calls himself Bobby now, by the way. My mother refused to use nicknames for us so I guess this is his way of rebelling, of distancing himself from his past."

"Yeah, changing his name and moving to the opposite coast. Pass me an egg?"

She did, with a grimace. "And becoming engaged to a woman born and raised in Israel. On a kibbutz, no less."

"You're kidding. Pass me the salt."

She did, with raised eyebrows. "Oh, no, I'm not. Bobby's converting for her. My brother the Jew. It's a good thing my parents didn't live to see this day."

"Is she nice, his fiancée?"

"Oh, Rachel's lovely. Probably the best thing that ever happened to my brother."

"So, you'll see them again?"

JoAnne sipped thoughtfully. "Someday. Not soon and not often, I imagine."

"But you don't regret the visit?" I said, hopefully.

"Not at all. Robert—excuse me, Bobby—and I will never be superclose, but at least now the ice is broken. I'll be invited to the wedding and I'll go. You know."

I did, kind of, know.

"Sometimes I still wish I had a brother or sister," I said.

JoAnne grinned. "You have me, honey. Isn't that enough?"

Actually, yeah. It was.

"To us," I said, raising my glass.

"To us. And to the East Coast!"

"Care for an egg?" I asked.

"Who are you, Cool Hand Luke? No, thanks. But I will take another Cosmopolitan. And ask you a question. How's it going with Doug?"

"You don't have to ask," I said. "I know you don't like my seeing him."

"I asked because I want to know. I might not like the guy but I do like you."

I laughed feebly. Truth was, I'd been wanting to talk to someone about what was happening—or not happening— between Doug and me. But I hadn't wanted to burden Abby with my pain; she had enough of her own to contend with. And Maggie's current state of bliss shouldn't, I believed, be marred by my personal misery. Of course, Dad was out. And Damion wanted only to say, "Leave the asshole now."

That left JoAnne, next to Damion, the friend who felt most strongly that I was ruining my life by seeing Doug Spears.

Better than no one, Reason said. Besides, she was right there.

"Well," I said, accepting my second glass of wine from the bartender as JoAnne took her Cosmopolitan, "the truth is, things haven't been so good lately."

"Oh?"

"Yeah."

I explained that Doug's reaction to my refusing the job offer at Trident had been less than supportive.

"Are you happy with your decision?" she asked.

"Absolutely."

"So, that's what's important. He's just being a man, all pissy because he didn't get his way. Because his little sex slave won't be at his beck and call, just down the hallway."

"You're harsh, you know that?" I said, but a similar, un-comfortable thought had occurred to me.

"Sorry."

I shrugged. "It's okay. Anyway, it hasn't been getting better. In fact, the more time passes, the more—I don't know—the more distant Doug becomes. It's like I've disappointed him or something. Or like . . ."

Banish the thought. . . .

"What?" JoAnne urged. "It's like what?"

"Like . . . like he's tired of me now."

JoAnne frowned.

"The sex is suffering."

"Oh, yeah," I admitted. "I hardly see him anymore, you know, for—personal stuff. And . . . When we do get together, it's . . ."

"Not as exciting as it used to be?"

I rubbed my temples. How had it come to this? How had the intensity of our erotic relationship suddenly become so . . .

"It's not the same. It's just—sex. It's not as intense."

It almost feels—boring, I added silently.

"That's got to be tough," JoAnne said and the note of sympathy in her voice was real. "After all, I've said it before, you two are pretty much all about sex."

In the past, I'd angrily rejected JoAnne's assessment of my relationship with Doug. Now, I was beginning to think that all along she'd seen my life much more clearly than I had.

What were Doug and I without wild, clandestine, sinful sex? Were we even friends? Had we ever been more than two randy adults with a little time on their hands to indulge in our guilty pleasures?

"Erin?"

I startled.

"Oh, sorry," I said. "I was just thinking."

JoAnne looked at me closely.

"Let's change the topic, okay?"

I smiled wanly.

"Okay."

Chapter Sixty

December, Boston

December in Boston can be magical. The month dawned very cold and bright; snow held off until just days before Christmas. And as much as I fear falling on ice, I do love to see snow for Christmas.

But back to the start of that month.

Attending an industry function, especially a fancy-dress ball, was not my favorite way to pass the time. But a few times a year it was important that I attend—important for my career to be seen and to see, to talk and to compare notes. In the past, I'd certainly never dreaded a function. At the very least there was usually shrimp and champagne on ice.

Now, facing the Society for Marketing Arts and Sciences annual Christmas ball, I was a wreck. Doug would be there, he had to be. And with him, his wife. No one came alone to the ball. I had asked Damion to be my escort and he'd agreed. No one would mistake us for a romantic couple, but that hardly mattered. People had been known to drag a brother or sister along for the night.

The event was on Saturday night. On Thursday morning,

Doug called at the office, ostensibly on a matter of business, though since my refusing the job at Trident, he'd ceased to ask for my advice on client matters. What he really wanted to talk about was the SMAS ball. He wanted me not to go.

After a quick greeting, Doug got right to the point.

"The ball is this Saturday."

"I know. I'm bringing Damion. My friend."

"I'll be bringing Carol."

"So I figured."

"It will be awkward."

For whom, I wondered. For you? For me? For Carol? Who did Doug care about in this situation?

"Uh, huh," I agreed eloquently.

"It's probably not as important for you to be there as it would have been if you'd taken the position at Trident," he said.

Ah ha. So it wasn't me Doug was concerned about at all. I was insulted—and angry.

"So, you don't want me to be there?"

Doug laughed derisively. "Why in God's name would I want you to be there? I want you to stay home, far, far away. But I know you won't."

"I can't," I answered. "It's an important event. I need to be seen there. EastWind Communications needs my representation. I'm not going to hurt you or to cause a scene. You must know that."

"Erin, I don't know anything about you, anymore. Not after you strung me along with the Trident job and then rejected me."

"It," I snapped. "I rejected a job, not you." But inside I knew that to Doug, my refusal to take the job had meant my refusal to bring myself further under his control. Yes, in a way I had rejected Doug by turning down Trident's offer.

"Whatever. The point is, I can't read you anymore. Maybe I never could. I thought you were someone I could trust."

I gasped. "I don't believe this!" I cried. "I never lied to you, not once. I never said I would take the job. I only said I would consider it."

"That's how you see it," Doug said coldly.

"Are you breaking up with me?" I said finally, ears buzzing, fingers tight on the receiver. Wishing he would say yes. Wishing he would say no.

There was a moment of silence. Two moments. Then: "Of course not. You're always so overdramatic, Erin. I'll see you at the Park Plaza."

And he was gone.

For obvious reasons, my heart was not into preparing for the big event. Still, I had a reputation to sustain for looking perfectly put-together and at the same time stand out—a difficult balance to achieve. Where heart failed, instinct and training stepped into the breech.

First step: Go shopping. Any woman who cares at all about clothes will tell you that an event of any sort requires something new. The same long, silk, taupe skirt can appear twice in one season when worn first with a fitted, black suede jacket with mandarin collar, and second, with a brown satin, ruffled, to-the-waist jacket. Shoes, bag, jewelry, and hairstyle change appropriately, of course.

As depressed as I felt, the act of shopping—of being in the Copley Mall amidst early holiday shoppers—finally lifted my spirits. It's the energy of shopping I love, the sense of abandon, and the sense of hope that with a perfect new velvet jacket will come the perfect new life. New York City may be the ultimate shopper's paradise, but trust me: Retail therapy is alive and well in Boston.

I finally found the dress in Lord & Taylor, just across the street from the mall, on Boylston Street. Lord & Taylor is a gem of a store, with sales ladies who've devoted twenty, thirty, and yes, sometimes even forty years to its service. I love these ladies, love chatting with them, soliciting their advice on hats and handbags, hearing about their dead husbands and fifty-year-old kids.

What I finally chose came very close to the outfit worn by the Julia Roberts character, Tess, in the remake of *Ocean's 11,* the night of the big fight. The night her eyes were opened to the fact that her current boyfriend was scum and her thieving ex-husband the real worthy man.

The dress was gold and glittery, slim-fitting, with a slim halter neck and open back. It came to the knees. Over the dress I would wear a slightly longer evening coat, of a gentler gold, and with a slight swing. The outfit struck me as dignified yet ultrafeminine.

I figured I'd need the dignity in a big way.

I called Doug at the office the next day. He wasn't at his desk. He did not return my call.

That night I went straight home after work and crawled into bed with Fuzzer. Doug and I hadn't had sex in almost two weeks. Something deep inside me knew we'd never have sex again.

I curled up on my side, pulled the covers over my head, and mourned.

Chapter Sixty-one

Damion met me at seven and we took a cab to the Park Plaza hotel.

"Thanks again for doing this," I said when we were settled in the cab's backseat.

"You should thank Frederick for lending me out on a Saturday night," Damion teased

"I will thank him," I promised.

Damion wore a tux of his own, a Filene's Basement, single-breasted Hugo Boss special. He looked very handsome. Frederick was a lucky man in many, many ways.

At the hotel we checked our coats and headed for the ballroom in which the ball was to be held.

"Are you going to be okay?" Damion said softly as we approached the fancy double doors.

"Yeah," I said shakily. "Maybe."

Once inside we got glasses of champagne and I introduced Damion to a few people I knew from the industry. I restrained myself from glancing around for Doug, not an easy thing as glancing around is a natural response to a room full of gowns, tuxedos, and glittering jewelry.

But the inevitable finally happened. I spotted Doug across

the room, with a woman in black I recognized as Carol. As casually as I could, I described him and his placement to Damion.

"I've got him in my sights," he said. And then, under his breath, "I don't believe it." He turned to me and said, "Erin, hold on, okay? The asshole is headed this way. He's dragging the poor wife with him."

The champagne glass shook in my hand. Damion took it from me and put it down on the serving table behind us.

"Let's go," I said. "I can't face them!"

"It's too late. Just—hold on. Smile pretty, honey. Make him squirm."

I turned fully to face the Spears as they approached and felt myself quail.

It was unmistakable, the gleam of—mischief? cruelty?—in Doug's eye. He didn't have to be doing this, introducing his wife to his girlfriend, but he was, and it was giving him a kick. He was enjoying humiliating me. I couldn't imagine what he thought he was doing to Carol.

Since when had Doug become cruel?

Maybe he'd always been and I just hadn't wanted to see it.

And then they were in front of us and Doug was saying hello to me, eyeing Damion almost warily, and introducing his wife.

Subtly, Damion put his hand on the small of my back. It was a comforting gesture, if any gesture at that moment could be.

In her party clothes, wearing makeup and with her hair recently "done," Carol was far more attractive than she had been in Super Stop 'n Shop back in August. She wasn't a beautiful woman but she'd put herself together with a sure hand. The dress was simple, black, and elegant, calling attention to no particular body feature but flattering overall. Her roots were no longer grayish. A diamond pendant on a yellow gold chain shone against the black dress. Her wedding set, not the simple band she'd worn grocery shopping, also diamond and yellow gold, was large yet tasteful.

Good job, Carol, I thought. I wanted to cry.

Clearly, the conversation had been going on without my being aware. Suddenly, I became aware of Carol's voice.

"Oh, Doug's such a workaholic," she was saying, with a fond laugh. "He just loves what he does and he's so good at it. Well, so I'm told! I hate how he has to work late all the time but I know it's really what makes him happy so . . ." Carol shrugged in a coquettish way that seemed entirely natural to her.

I smiled stupidly, at a loss for even one word.

"You must be very proud of your husband," Damion said brightly. His ironic intent was not lost on Doug. Doug looked suddenly furious. If I wasn't up to playing this sick game, Damion was totally willing to play in my place. With deadly intent.

"Oh, I am!"

"Carol," Doug said abruptly, "I want to introduce you to someone from the Society." Without a farewell, he took his wife's elbow and forcefully turned her from us.

"Nice to meet you both," she said over her shoulder and for a second I thought I saw a look of embarrassment flicker across her face. I wondered if Doug had her trained to think it was a social faux pas that had made him drag her across a room.

"I need to . . ." I murmured.

Damion took my arm and gracefully escorted me from the ballroom and toward the ladies' room.

"I'll wait right here," he said as I stumbled on.

Inside, I avoided the eyes of the other overdressed women and darted for an empty stall where I threw up. Thankfully, I hadn't eaten since late morning. As undignified an act as vomiting is, it does on occasion ease the intensity of pain.

I waited until the room sounded empty and emerged. I patted my face with a paper towel soaked in cold water, rinsed my mouth and reapplied my makeup. It didn't completely cover the blotchiness, or stop the slow trickle of tears that insisted on staining my cheeks.

Finally, I rejoined Damion. He steered us to a settee in the hall.

"Thanks," I said.

"For what? For not having taken all this more seriously before? I could kick myself when I think . . ."

"It's not your fault, Damion."

"In some ways, it is. Friends have responsibilities to each other. Anyway, it's not too late for me to say this: End it, Erin. Now. This is no good for you. It's no good for anyone."

Damion was right. Of course he was. I'd known the end was near since I'd refused the position at Trident. Maybe since before. And I'd been holding on to the shreds of my feelings, reluctant to end things with Doug for good, still scared of being without him, even though being with him was making me increasingly ill.

"I don't understand him," I said. "I don't understand how he can be so nice and supportive one day and so awful the next."

"You don't have to understand him. You just have to walk away."

"Okay," I whispered through tears and the congestion that always accompanies them. "I look . . . I look horrible. Maybe I should wait until Monday . . ."

"No, Erin," Damion insisted. "Let him see what he's done to you. Let him see you, Erin—for once let him see you and not his tricked up, super career woman slutty version of you. Be yourself for the first time since you met this creep."

Well, Romance whispered waterily, you do look the part of the tragic heroine.

I nodded.

"Good." Damion stood and patted my shoulder. "I'll wait for you in the bar. Don't leave without me. I want to be sure you get home safe."

"You're good to me," I whispered.

Damion smiled. "Feels nice, doesn't it? Now promise to find a straight guy to be good to you. It's not rocket science, Erin. Now, go."

* * *

I spotted him by the coat check. The hall was empty but for the two of us.

"Doug." I sounded harsh even to my own ears.

He stopped and slowly, slowly turned around. He was not pleased.

"What is it, Erin? Carol's waiting for me."

He was so handsome in his beautiful tux, so compelling, in spite of the coldness in his eyes. I wanted to be with him even then. How our bodies betray us . . .

"It's over, Doug."

He glanced around and seeing no one started toward me. "Erin, come on . . ."

I put up my hand and if I looked like a traffic cop, so be it. "Don't," I said and the old fury rose within me. Hopefully, for the last time. "Right now I want to kill you."

He stopped. He looked disgusted. "Don't make a scene, Erin."

"Go fuck youself," I spat.

And it was over.

Chapter Sixty-two

The first time he called was Sunday evening, less than twenty-four hours since our scene in the lobby of the Park Plaza. I was vastly surprised. I'd expected never to hear from Doug Spears again.

The conversation was not pleasant.

"What the hell was that about last night?" he snapped.

I was in no mood for his crap.

"Where are you calling from? A street corner? Don't want to risk Carol finding your corporate cell phone bill lying around the kitchen."

"That's enough, Erin," he replied in a voice that made me wonder how he spoke to his kids when they acted up. Poor kids. "When can I see you? We have to talk."

"No," I said. "We don't."

I disconnected the call, slammed down the receiver and burst out crying. God, why had he called! Suddenly, the room felt dirty somehow, tainted, like a filthy creature had slithered its way through my pristine home, leaving slime and ruin in its wake.

You might consider changing your phone number, Erin, if

you're so upset, Reason suggested, not unkindly. Get an un-
listed number.

Traitorous Romance leaned in close and whispered. But
what if he really does love you and really does need to talk to
you. Maybe he needed you to shock him into leaving his wife.
Maybe . . .

"No!" I said aloud. "Just let me . . . leave me alone."

I wanted to sit down and think. Because Romance had
given me something to think about. The truth was, a tiny part
of me was hoping that what it had said was true. That Doug
had been panicked into taking action, into filing for a divorce, into . . .

Unplug the phone, Erin, Reason said firmly. And, no. I
will not leave you alone. He's an ass. And it's my job to help
you keep that in mind.

Doug called again Monday morning. I was on another line;
Heather gave me the message that I was to call back on "an
urgent matter." I didn't. Briefly, I considered asking Heather
to hold my calls for the rest of the day but a nagging sense of
responsibility to my clients stopped me.

Monday afternoon, Doug called again. I had the misfor-
tune to answer the phone.

"Why won't you talk to me?" His voice was low. I'm sure
his office door was closed.

"Because there's nothing to say," I answered. That wasn't
quite true but if I opened my mouth I'd be lost—either in a
torrent of rage or in a flood of left-over feeling. Neither would
lead to appropriate office behavior.

"That's bullshit, and you know it."

Okay. He had me there.

"Erin?"

"What?"

"I want to see you."

Oh, and how a part of me wanted to see him! For one

delirous moment I wavered, thought: What could one fifteen-minute meeting hurt, thought: Your hard-won self-esteem, thought: I'm strong enough to resist his power over me, thought: Am I?

Answered myself: No. I'm not.

Finally, I said, "That's not a good idea. Look, I have to go. I have a meeting."

He'd used that excuse often enough to get me off the phone. I hung up, took a deep breath, and laughed. Disaster averted. Narrowly, but averted.

I wasn't much in the mood for socializing but my friends insisted I get out and join them for drinks at the bar at Tremont 647. Its location—very close to home—and its atmosphere of warmth and conviviality swayed me.

Still, I know I was not good company.

Abby, once again proving her native kindness and generosity, didn't mention her own recent loss once but was all sympathy, even offering to stay with me for a while if I needed the company. She made me cry.

JoAnne seemed to enjoy the chance to curse loud and long. She called Doug names I swear I'd never heard before, and some I'd heard but had never had the nerve to say myself. She made me smile.

Maggie brought Jan along and I was glad for that. They brought a bouquet of flowers from Lotus Designs, my favorite florist, and not an inexpensive one. Jimmy's work is brilliant and always inspiring. Maggie and Jan's concern was genuine and fell somewhere between Abby's gentle care and JoAnne's kick-ass name-calling.

When I got home that night, I forgot to check the answering machine and went straight to bed.

Wednesday night, around ten o'clock. The phone rang.

I knew it was Doug.

Why couldn't he just stop calling? Why didn't he just give up?

I didn't see Doug's calls as proof of his love for me or as a sincere effort at apology. I saw them for what they were—halfhearted attempts to bring me back under his control. And probably not for long. By then I wouldn't have put it past Doug to win me back only to fling me off a short time later, like a cat finally flings away the dead mouse that no longer amuses it. Doug would see it as justifiable payback, all being fair in love and war.

The phone continued to ring. I hesitated, considered letting the call go to the answering machine. Instead, I lowered the volume on the stereo and answered.

"It's me."

I didn't respond. There seemed no appropriate greeting.

"Erin?"

"Yes."

"How are you?" he asked.

Oh, why didn't I just disconnect the call?

"Fine. Okay."

When Doug spoke again I heard a thin, familiar note of impatience.

"Have you thought about us? About our getting back together?"

"Yes," I admitted.

"And?" Doug laughed "Christ, Erin, this is like playing twenty questions."

Okay, now I was impatient, too. And annoyed.

"And I still think it's a bad idea," I said.

Doug sighed and tried another tack.

"Erin," he said, voice softer, "think about all we mean to each other."

"What about it? What should I think?"

"Think about losing it all."

"I already have. If I ever had anything to lose in the first place."

"Oh, come on, stop being foolish. You . . ."

I replaced the receiver in its cradle. The phone rang again almost immediately. I turned down the sound on the answering machine, turned off the stereo, and went to bed.

Chapter Sixty-three

It was time to make Christmas commitments. Maggie and Jan were planning on hosting a dinner for Jan's extended family. Unlike Maggie, Jan was close to her parents and siblings. It was a bit uncomfortable for Maggie at first, being social with relatives, but after a meeting or two she began to relax and enjoy herself. Especially when Paul and Colette applauded their daughter's announcement that she and Maggie were tying the knot in a few weeks. Mr. and Mrs. Ward were everything the Branleys had not been. They were warm and intelligent and funny. Finally, after more than thirty years, Maggie had gotten the family she deserved.

JoAnne surprised me—only a bit—by accepting Abby's invitation to join the Walkers in Nantucket for an "old-fashioned" Christmas—which, I imagined, probably had a lot to do not only with old-fashioneds but with brandy Alexanders. "I'm thinking the country club's Christmas ball might prove interesting," she told me. Seems Abby had enticed JoAnne with tales of well-heeled eligible men in well-fitting tuxedos.

Abby asked me to join her, too, but I declined—with only minor regret. Dad was cooking Christmas dinner for Marilyn and her son, Kip. I boldly invited myself to the party. Dad was genuinely pleased and assigned me the role of pie bringer.

There was another reason I wanted to stay in Boston for the holidays, one I hadn't yet told Maggie, JoAnne, or Abby. The reason was my mother. Marie.

> *Erin—Will be in town for Xmas. Will you? I have a surprise . . . Marie P.S. Miss you.*

This latest caused me some trepidation, which in and of itself was nothing new. My first thought: Oh, crap, she's pregnant. That's what she means by the surprise. My second thought: Oh, crap, she's bringing some greasy-haired stud muffin with her. Third thought: Oh, crap, she's moving back to Boston. My fourth thought: Mom misses me?

My fifth, and most startling, thought: I miss her, too.

I called my father later that night and told him the news. He was silent for a moment.

"Dad? Are you okay?"

He laughed. It sounded confused. "I don't know, Erin. I . . . I guess I didn't expect her to just—show up again."

"I know. Neither did I. But Mom hasn't been predictable for a long time now, has she?"

"True. Well—are you going to see her?"

The question startled me. "Of course. I mean, if she even calls. She is my mother, you know."

Although truth be told, if Mom had shown up only a few months earlier, I'm not sure I would have had the maturity to see her.

"Good."

"Dad?" I hesitated but had to know. "Will you see her? If she asks to get together."

More silence.

"Dad? You okay?"

"Yes, yes, I'm fine." He sighed. "Erin, honestly, I don't know. This is all so sudden. I need to think a bit. I'm not sure I have anything to say to her, really. I'm not sure I can handle asking about her life and hearing about her young men."

He had a point. If her postcards were any indication, Mom was not into keeping her love life under wraps. At least, not with me. But I doubted she'd be discreet with Dad, either. And there was always the possibility she'd arrive at Logan with that greasy-haired stud muffin in tow.

"That's okay," I said. "Let's just wait and see what happens. Maybe she won't even show up."

"Would you be disappointed if she didn't?" Dad asked.

I didn't have to think hard about my answer. "Yeah, I would. Not devastated. But I do want to see her, now that she's made the first move."

"You're a good person, Erin Weston."

I smiled. "I had an excellent role model."

The following morning I had a dentist appointment so I didn't get to the office until around ten-thirty. The mail had already been delivered. On my desk sat a plain, white, letter-sized envelope. There was no return address. My name and office address were typed; the postage was from an office meter.

I'd never seen anything more ominous.

A scathing, attacking letter from Doug?

If it was, I'd throw it away immediately, unread. No, I'd tear it to shreds first, then throw it away, unread.

I closed my office door behind me and without taking off my coat, opened the envelope. Inside was one folded sheet of white paper. The note was also typed.

This is what it said:

> *You don't know me but I know of you through our extended business connections. I probably should have written before now. I wanted to warn*

*you but I was too jealous and angry; I wanted
you to suffer.*

*Doug Spears and I had an affair two years
ago. We met through work. Eventually, I found out
I wasn't the first. Believe it—you won't be the
last.*

*I don't know what he told you or even if you're
still with him, but I just couldn't stay quiet any
longer. Watch out for yourself. He's not a good
man. The sick thing is I still have feelings for
him. I hope you make it out in better shape than
I did.*

A friend.

I don't know quite how to explain what I felt in that moment. They say that actions speak louder than words. That
actions articulate feeling far more lucidly than words.

This is what I did.

I tore the letter into little bits and tossed them into the
trash. It wasn't something I'd ever forget; no need to keep
the evidence.

I opened the top drawer of my desk. The chunky lucite ring
Doug had given me back in the summer—a belated birthday
present, he'd said—was there, amidst the mess of paper
clips, rubber bands, a single dried-out red rose, and emergency packs of knee-highs and trouser socks.

I took the ring from the drawer and wiped it against my
coat. It was a pretty thing and somehow it, more than the
anonymous letter, made my heart ache. I knew I could never
bear to wear it again, probably because it had given me so
much pleasure. But a voice inside me I didn't immediately
recognize said, Let someone else enjoy its prettiness, Erin.
Make it a gift and by doing so you'll find pleasure again.

Well, I wasn't so sure but, still wearing my coat, I walked
down the hall to Edmund's office. He was just coming in,
cheeks red with cold, a slightly leaky brown paper bag in his
gloved hand.

"Careful," I said. "Coffee's leaking."

Edmund grunted. "Story of my morning."

"Edmund, you have a daughter, right? She's—six?"

"Just seven, actually. Why?"

I hesitated, then held out the ring.

"Well, someone gave me this and it's really, you know, not right for me. It's really more for a little girl. I wonder . . . I thought that . . ."

Edmund smiled and reached for the ring. "Hey, thanks, Erin. Becky will love this. She's wild for anything pink."

I smiled and felt—okay.

"No problem," I said and went back to my office.

Chapter Sixty-four

Christmas shopping lacked its usual thrill for me. Still it had to be done so on a Sunday in mid-month I headed through the Gardens then the Common for Filene's Basement. If you're a good girl, I told myself, and buy presents for all your little friends, you can treat yourself to a stroll through DSW.

Just past the Frog Pond there's a playground. And around the slide were gathered a family. A family who looked oddly familiar.

I came to a stop. It couldn't be. I peered more closely, hoping I wasn't looking like a child molester scoping out her next victim.

It was a bit hard to tell for sure. For one thing, the mom was hatless. The woman I'd seen on the ice had been wearing a fuzzy, brightly colored hat. They all had, and they all were now, except for Mom.

Boston's a small city, I told myself. It's entirely possible this family is the same one I saw back in January. At the Frog Pond. The night I met Doug.

Then the mom laughed and I knew. Almost a year later I recognized the joy in a stranger's voice.

Still, the symmetry of the thing was hard to believe. A sign? A message? A confirmation from—above? Or simply an accident. A coincidence.

Whatever. I chose to give meaning to this family's reappearing in my life. It was a not-so-gentle reminder of the promises I'd made to myself almost a year earlier. It was a tough reminder of how I'd failed myself.

I walked on and left the family to get back to their own lives, unwatched by a lonely single woman.

I passed out of the Common and stood waiting for the light on Tremont.

I'd been battered and buffeted. I hadn't asked for the pain but I'd grabbed for the experience, so there was no one to blame but myself. I was almost a year older and if not deeper in financial debt, then certainly more aware of my emotional deficits.

What doesn't kill you makes you stronger, Romance told me with a trembling, brave little voice. And a little more saggy, wrinkled, and battle-scarred, Reason added. Unnecessarily.

A facial was what I needed. And change.

Life was going to have to change all around. My life was going to have to change.

JoAnne had been on me for months to take a yoga class. She swore—as did the experts—that yoga helped reduce the powerful effects of stress on the body. Considering I could hardly turn my neck from left to right most mornings—worse after sleepless nights—I decided finally to sign up for an introductory class at The Yoga Studio on Joy Street in Beacon Hill. It was as close as I was ever going to get to working out, that much I knew for sure.

My life was going to change, but within the boundaries of me. The point was to explore and expand those boundaries to their real, not assumed, limits. JoAnne was exploring her boundaries. Ditto, Maggie. Even Abby had talked about making some healthy changes.

For the first time, the word "health" and all it implied

sounded mighty appealing to me. There'd be no nuts and berries diet, but there would be calm and productivity and love. Definitely love.

When I got home late that afternoon I busied myself with some straightening up. Among the pile of papers on my kitchen table I found a business card I'd almost forgotten I had.

CANDACE RECKLET, LIFE EXPRESSIONS CONSULTANT.

Suddenly, I remembered my embarrassment at Candace's suggesting I show the group at Abby's house pictures of Fuzzer. Almost everyone in that room had been married; many had also been mothers.

And suddenly, I was mad at myself for having been ashamed of being without husband or child. And I remembered now the part of Candace's message I hadn't taken to heart that night. That every life has value. That every life should be celebrated in words and pictures, as well as in song and action. Candace hadn't said it in so many words but her message had been clear: Living single did not make me unworthy of praise.

I thought of all I'd accomplished. I thought of the wise career choice I'd recently made. I thought of the dear, dear friendships I'd built over time. I thought of Fuzzer, whom I adored. And I thought of my maturing relationships with each of my parents. John and Marie. No longer just Mom and Dad.

I had a lot to celebrate and even more to be proud of.

I looked again at the card and made the call. Candace's answering machine picked up.

"Hi, Candace? This is Erin Weston. I was at a class at Abby Walker's house a few months ago? I was wondering if I could host a class here sometime. In my home. Maybe before Christmas?"

* * *

About a week before the wedding, I went over to Maggie's place to help her box up the last of her belongings. She'd finally found a renter and was completing the move into Jan's house the following morning.

Naturally, as we worked we talked, interrupted only by the scream of clear plastic packing tape coming off the roll.

"Have you told any of your brothers and sisters about Jan?" I asked.

Maggie laughed. "Are you on drugs? Of course not. I don't need the grief."

"Okay, that's what I thought. But are you going to let them know your new address?"

Maggie considered. "No," she said, "at least, not right yet. I'm not selling my place for a while so I can still have mail sent there if I want. I'll work it out somehow. I just don't want to be—tracked down at this point in my life. I'm too happy for family."

It was my turn to laugh. "I so know what you mean. Hey, I never told anyone this but . . . When I turned twenty-one and was still unmarried, my grandfather called a family conference. He wanted to discuss the very disturbing likelihood that I would wind up an Old Maid. He wanted the family to talk about how my future would be provided for."

Maggie grimaced. "At least he cared. Sort of."

"It was downright surreal. I mean, I'd just graduated from college suma cum laude and my death knell was being tolled because I hadn't yet managed to drag a man down the aisle."

"Did you tell him you were quite capable of taking care of yourself?"

I taped up another box before answering. "No. I took the high road. I laughed off the incident as quaint and harmless, but it got to me. On some level, it really got to me."

"Poor kid."

"The point is, you know, it's so hard to shake off those prejudices of your youth. It's so hard to completely reject those 'truths' you were taught for years."

"Don't I know it. So, how do you feel now?"

I stopped working and looked at Maggie. Her eyes were kind.

"I feel—I feel that even though I'm most definitely not ashamed of being single—on some level I am. Especially since I turned thirty."

"That's horrible, Erin. I wish you wouldn't feel that way."

"I know," I said, fighting back sudden tears. "Me, too."

Later in the day we took a break for sodas and a pizza from Trentino's. Maggie flipped on the TV she was leaving for the tenant's use. It was tuned to CNN. As we munched we watched a report on the latest developments in cloning.

"I just can't get my head around the whole idea," I said finally. "I'm embarrassed to admit that. I mean, I'm not anti-intellectual. I don't believe in circumscribing human endeavor. I don't even think it's really possible without disastrous results. Still, reproducing a human being, making a copy . . . "

"I know," Maggie agreed. "There's something so Frankensteinian about it."

"Yeah and look what happened to him," I said. "Dr. Frankenstein died 'blasted' in his hopes and his poor monster ended his days referring to himself as 'miserable' and 'abandoned' and an 'abortion.'"

"I always did have a soft spot for the monster. The original, the character in the book, not the dopey movie monster."

"The whole cloning thing. . . . It just doesn't sit right with me. I don't know, Maggie. Maybe I'm just paralyzed by fear of the possible negative consequences. Maybe I'm just too morally provincial to handle such a challenging circumstance. Maybe the vestiges of my Catholicism won't let me support the idea of cloning. I don't know. Stem-cell research—okay. But once you start learning, how can you possibly stop? Why would you want to?"

"You could stop because you're afraid of what you'll find, of what horrors you'll unleash. But scientists aren't by nature afraid of the unknown, right? Even the ones concerned with the ethics of their work."

"I guess. So, maybe we have no choice. As a species we're going to go forward into ever more strange places and eventually we might not be able to back our way out. Maybe we're just inherently suicidal."

Maggie considered.

"Maybe," she said. "Or maybe we're just hubristic slobs. Either way, we're going to kill ourselves."

I nodded. Yeah. Maggie was probably right.

"You know, Maggie," I said, snagging the last slice of pizza. "You're the only one in my life I can talk to about stuff like—important stuff, issues and all. I don't know why that is, but it is."

Maggie smiled. "Glad to be of service. Can I have half of that slice?"

And it occurred to me full blast that after Maggie and Jan finally moved in together one hundred percent and especially after they got married, I might hardly ever—never?—have the chance to hang out with Maggie and just talk. About important stuff. About our childhoods. About how I still somehow missed Doug, at least our early days together. About anything.

"Come on," Maggie said, getting up from the floor where we'd picnicked. "We still have lots to do."

In a way, that day of packing was a farewell, if not to a friendship then to a stage of a friendship. Maggie was moving on. I was releasing her to do so with my blessing. And with sadness. I wasn't afraid for Maggie. But I was afraid for me.

Chapter Sixty-five

Almost two weeks Doug-free. It was hard but not as hard as I'd once thought it would be.

I wasn't the only one moving on with my life, no matter how slowly. Abby had decided to go into therapy. She wanted to examine why she, too, was still single when she wanted so badly to be married. She also wanted to know why she wanted so badly to be married in the first place. At least, why she said she did.

JoAnne, on the other hand, had quit therapy, stating it wasn't really her style. But I saw a change in her, a change for the better. It was subtle—JoAnne was never going to be all warm and cuddly—but it was there all the same. She'd begun to have feelings for a doctor, an oncologist she'd known for years and with whom she occasionally consulted on particularly difficult cases. His name was Merv Frankl and he was fifty years old. He'd been married once before and had a daughter in college. Most interestingly, he was a grandfather; his son had married young. On the surface, JoAnne said, he wasn't the sort of guy she would ever have expected to fall for. He was even slightly overweight and hated Cancun. But things between them were moving along nicely and JoAnne was pleased.

I was pleased for her. I was pleased for us all.

Maggie Branley and Jan Ward tied the knot on December 18th at a little nondenominational church in Kendall Square. It was a simple ceremony. Maggie wore a red blazer; Jan, a red blouse. Each wore a sprig of holly, all in honor of the season. Afterward, the guests went to lunch at a family-style Italian restaurant, where more friends joined the party. Plans for that night included another gathering at Jillian's to play pool and eat nachos. I declined that invitation out of sheer weariness. Weddings take it out of me.

"Well, that was depressing," JoAnne said once we were back on the T after lunch.

"And lovely." Abby was still dabbing at her eyes.

I thought for a moment. "And encouraging. At least one of us has found true love."

"That doesn't necessarily increase our chances, Erin."

"I know, JoAnne. Jeez, I'm just trying to be optimistic."

"I know. I'm sorry. Let's get off at Park Street and go to the Federalist and have a celebratory drink. We'll toast Maggie and Jan . . ."

"And maybe I'll meet my soul mate!" Abby said brightly.

I laughed. It felt good and genuine.

"Oh, Abby," I said. "For our sake, I hope so."

I was awake far into the night.

I was wiped out. It was a stupid, self-defeating thing I'd done, especially right after a wedding ceremony, looking at photos Doug had given me of his life before his marriage. All the photos he'd been able to sneak out of his house without Carol noticing them gone. The photos he'd kept in shoeboxes marked "personal storage"—shoeboxes I'd heard about but would never see.

"Why do you want to see this old crap?" Doug had asked when he handed over the photos.

"It's not crap to me," I'd answered.

"You're sentimental."

Doug, it seemed, wasn't. He'd never asked me to return the photos.

I'd asked him once why he'd never put his childhood and young adult photos in an album. He had no answer. I'd wanted to ask if Carol had ever expressed a desire to see photos of her husband as a boy. I didn't have the nerve.

Now, my decision had been made. I'd send all the photos back, have them delivered to Doug's office, marked "personal and private," of course, because no matter how badly I'd been hurt, no matter how devastated I felt, getting Doug into trouble was not going to make me feel any better. I've said it before—I'm no saint but I'm not an evil soul-sucker. And, the sorry truth was that I still loved the man. Hated him, too, but still loved him. The love part, maybe, was habit. Someday, hopefully, both feelings would pass into oblivion. For the time being, as odd as it seems, I still cared about what Doug thought of me and didn't want him to know me as a vindictive bitch.

Even though you have a right to be, Reason pointed out.

Erin's a victim of Love! Romance cried. How can one rail against Love?

She's a victim of a shithead, Reason snapped.

I believe that someday Erin and Doug will be reunited. . . .

Stop it! I cried. The both of you are going to have to learn how to get along if I'm going to get to where I need to be.

But . . . Reason.

But . . . Romance.

No buts. Learn how to work together. That's an order.

You'll make a good mother someday, Erin, Reason said, albeit reluctantly.

Romance nodded.

Thanks, I said. I know.

I got back to work. One photo remained unboxed. I picked it up. Doug as a kid at someone's birthday party. His face was surprisingly round, his hair super short, a haircut he'd told me he'd hated, a haircut his grandmother had taken him to get. I marveled at the innocence the little boy in the photo seeemed to embody, the smiling face, the uncorrupted energy . . . We're all innocent as kids, and never after that. How much of the hurtful things we do to ourselves and others is our fault and how much the fault of the burden of living? Of getting through the mundane challenges of each day and facing the prospect of another, and another? Can any of us who stick around willingly in this life really be blamed for our minor transgressions?

I had no answer then and still don't. Why should I, when brilliant philosophers throughout the ages have been wrestling inconclusively with the questions of man's—if not woman's—free will, guilt, and redemption?

I peered more closely at the photo, hoping to see something else—some clue as to—what? The man the little boy had become? Doug had said he was four or five when the photo was taken. That meant it was taken in 1959 or 1960. Nine or ten years before I was born.

Who was Doug Spears before Erin Weston?

It came to me then that the man I'd fallen in love with was the boy in this picture. I loved the Doug I thought he must once have been. A shadow of a wish of a memory. My love had been poorly bestowed on something as insubstantial as a fantasy.

For one mad moment I decided to keep the photograph as . . . as a reminder of my folly? As a sort of talisman, a token for good luck? I had no answer. All I knew was that I wanted so badly to keep the picture—but I could find no good reason for keeping it. Plenty of bad ones, and they were so seductive, but not one that made clear sense.

Reason won that battle. If I was going to grow up, finally, I had to do it right out, full throttle, no backsliding—at least no conscious backsliding. I had to be fair to and honest with myself—and to the man who would one day be my husband. I put the photo of a charming little boy in the box with the others, sealed it, and went to bed.

Chapter Sixty-six

I sat at my desk trying to focus on work. In the past, I'd found that I could lose myself in work and so forget—at least temporarily—whatever pain or heartache I might be experiencing. That was the past. Things were different now.

Maybe work alone just wasn't enough for me anymore. Maybe I was indeed growing up, filling out emotionally.

Maybe it was time to take the next step.

A day or two earlier Maureen had told me she knew someone she thought I'd like to meet. I'd told her I wasn't ready yet to date again and then felt sick when I realized what I'd said. As far as Maureen knew, I hadn't been seeing anyone for the past months.

Right?

Maureen had come into my office then and closed the door behind her. She was due to give birth at any moment and I cringed as she lowered herself slowly into my guest chair. She was a trooper.

"Erin, it's okay. I know about—that you were in a relationship."

I put my head in my hands. "Oh, crap. Do you know the name of the guy?"

"Yeah. Look, don't worry about it, we all make mistakes before we meet the right one."

I raised my head. "Maureen, I'm so sorry."

"Why?"

"Because I violated another woman's marriage and my friend Maggie says that's like violating every woman's marriage."

Maureen grinned. "Your friend Maggie sounds a little grim. Forget it. Just don't come near Mark. He's my version of Prince Charming."

We both laughed. "Okay," I said, "I won't."

"So, you want to hear about this guy I know?"

"Sure. No promises though."

So, she told me. His name was Nick Alexander. He was thirty-eight years old and an architect. He was divorced. He had a son aged ten with whom he was very close. Mark had met him through a mutual buddy in construction.

According to Maureen, Nick was "manly."

"Not macho," she said, "but manly. And a very good father. And his ex-wife is reasonable. She's even getting remarried in a few months."

I said I'd think about it.

I'd thought about it.

I dialed Maureen's extension.

"Hi, it's Erin. Okay. Tell Nick he can call me."

"I will." Maureen's voice sounded—huffy. Puffy. "Right after I drop this baby. My water just broke, Erin. Get me to the hospital!"

The night before Christmas Eve.

Maggie and Jan were at a reading and book signing at We Think the World of You on Tremont and Hanson Street. The author had written a book on the latest fertility methods. Seems Maggie and Jan had been planning to start a family almost from the time they met. At least I knew something about infant T-shirts.

JoAnne, their prechosen pediatrician, was with Merv at some hospital function, probably ragging on him for not going to the gym.

Abby was on a date with a thirty-five-year-old accountant she'd met on line at Finagle a Bagel. Seems they'd both ordered the exact same breakfast. Joseph had asked her out on the spot. Seems he believed in soul mates . . .

My father was on a date with Marilyn.

Damion was cuddling with Frederick; Coco and Chanel were draped across their laps; Lucy and Ricky were asleep at their feet.

Maureen and Mark were rocking little Jules to sleep.

My mother was in the air, somewhere over the Carribean, headed for Boston.

And I had a date the following afternoon, Christmas Eve day, with Nick, the architect. We were going skating at the Frog Pond. He'd promised not to let me fall. I'd dug out my rabbit fur pom-poms.

"Looks like it's just you and me tonight, Fuzzer," I said, rubbing his forehead the way he likes it to be rubbed. He began to purr. I smiled and opened the book on my lap, a collection of Lord Byron's poems and letters.

I'd opened randomly to the play entitled Manfred, and to these words:

> *I have not been thy dupe, nor am thy prey—*
> *But was my own destroyer, and will be*
> *My own hereafter.*

And my own saviour, I thought. I'm the one responsible for my life. It's all up to me.

And I can have what I want, can't I?

Fuzzer yawned, stretched, and settled back against my thigh.

Life wasn't so bad at all.

Epilogue

So, there it is. A year in the life.

In case you're interested, Marie's big surprise was the news that she was giving up her "social work" in various Unnamed South American Countries for a spiritual quest. Seems she'd heard of a guru named Lancelot Ali Yen who guaranteed to bring his followers deep joy and fulfillment.

Two days ago, Marie left for his compound in New Mexico. I went with her to the airport and watched as the plane took off.

We'd spent a good deal of time together, Marie and I, during her brief stopover in Boston. I told her about Doug Spears. She'd taken my hands in hers and said, "My poor baby." Then she'd asked for yet another loan. I gave it to her, of course.

Marie and John did not get together. She didn't ask to see him and he didn't ask to see her. I guess it was less painful that way, for both of them.

Nick Alexander was true to his word. He did not let me fall at the Frog Pond. I like him, a lot. He even has brown eyes.

So, maybe this is The Year.

Wish me luck?

Holly Chamberlin, bestselling author of LIVING SINGLE, returns with a sexy, sassy new novel of three women on the brink of turning thirty—and on the verge of finding themselves. A house share in Martha's Vineyard sets the stage for a summer of cold margaritas, hot guys, and hilarious adventures. The kind of summer that can break hearts—and make lifelong friendships . . .

THE SUMMER OF US

Gincy Gannon isn't exactly an easy fit with the upper crust Vineyard scene. Raised poor and precocious in Nowheresville, New Hampshire, she escaped to Boston after high school. Now a career at PBS fills her days, while her freewheeling sex life keeps her otherwise stimulated. Commitment is definitely not her thing. So why, when Gincy's supposed to be reeling in lifeguards, is she getting hooked on a single dad?

Life is good for Danielle Leers. She's got a close-knit family, a killer wardrobe, and a job that keeps her in manicures and massages. As far as Danielle's concerned, pampering is a right, not a privilege. Besides, now that she's set her sights on settling down, her good grooming will attract great husband material. Which should mean a well-heeled Jewish professional. *Not* a townie who fishes for a living . . .

Blueblood Clare Wellman doesn't worry about keeping up appearances—her boyfriend, Winchester Carrington, III, is in charge of that. Actually, he's in charge of pretty much everything . . . and never lets Clare forget it. Some time on her own is just what Clare needs to get to know herself again. Then Win proposes. An engagement ring shouldn't feel like an albatross—and this summer may be Clare's last chance to see what could be—before what *is* ties her down for good . . .

Three city-smart girlfriends are about to take the plunge into love, lust, and letting it all hang out, Vineyard-style. It will be a summer of change—but long after the tan lines have faded, they'll still have each other.

Now, get ready for an exciting sneak peek of
The Summer of Us
coming in May 2004!

Gincy
The Go-To Girl

The crisis was discovered at four forty-five in the afternoon. Fifteen minutes before ninety-nine percent of the staff hurried out of the building to enjoy their sixteen-hour vacation.

My boss, Mr. Bill Kelly, Kell for short, was frazzled. He didn't handle crisis well. What he did do well was delegate responsibility.

He came tearing into the center of our office area, what little hair he had on end, plaid shirttails untucked.

"Listen up, people. We have a problem. The idiots at the copy shop lost our proposal and we've got to recreate it. Now. It's got to be at the printer's tonight."

I watched the predictable reactions of my colleagues.

Curran, the senior designer, slipped out of the room backwards.

Norton, the copy editor, suddenly found the piece of blank paper he was holding extremely interesting.

Vera, the administrative assistant for our division, feigned a sudden hacking cough.

"Kell," she gasped, "I wish I could help, but I think I'm really sick. If I don't get home and into bed soon . . ."

Kell turned to me. "Gincy, you'll stay, right?"

"It's gotta get done," I said, shooting my coworkers a look of disgust. "I'm here."

That's me. The go-to girl. Virginia Marie Gannon.

I guess I got my work ethic from my father, though our choices of work couldn't be more different.

Dad manages a hardware store, the small, privately owned kind that monsters like Home Depot have mostly put out of business.

I'm the senior editor of the monthly publication sent to subscribers of a public television station here in Boston.

Come to think of it, I'm not sure how much of a choice my father had when it came to a career. He didn't go to college. When I was about twelve I heard a rumor from a cousin that he'd never even finished high school.

To this day I don't know the truth about that. I'd never ask Dad straight out. It would embarrass him, and though my parents aren't my favorite people in the world, I treat them with respect.

It's what you do. Work hard and respect your parents. In that way, I'm a typical Gannon. In other ways? Not so much.

Anyway, the job got done and at six thirty-five I left our office on Bowdoin Street.

By the time I raced through the door of George, An American Cafe, it was almost seven o'clock. The place was a cemetery.

"Where is everybody?" I barked to the dimly lit room. "There's nobody here!"

A dark-haired girl about my age stepped away from the bar. I noticed she had breasts the size of Pamela Anderson's. Almost.

How can you not notice something like that?

"Uh, hello?" she said. "We're here. Me and—Clare, right?"

Another girl, a blond one, all clean and healthy-looking, like she could star in a soap ad shot at a mountain spring or something, slipped off a barstool and joined the first girl. She nodded and looked at me warily.

Okay, maybe she had a reason to. I'd caught a glimpse of my hair in the window before charging through the door. It was pretty wild. I think I'd forgotten to comb it that morning.

I had, however, remembered to wash it. Which was more than I'd done the day before when I'd been up since four A.M. working on a report for Kell the Inefficient. Next thing I knew it was eight-thirty and if I'd stopped to shower I would have been late for a nine o'clock meeting.

You know how it is.

"So," I said. "I thought there was supposed to be a meeting here tonight. You know, to hook up with roommates. For a summer place. In Oak Bluffs."

"There was a meeting," the dark-haired one drawled, "but it seems it was over at, like, six-oh-five. By the time I got here at six-thirty, everyone had already hooked up."

She nodded toward the girl next to her. "Except for Clare. And me. I'm Danielle, by the way."

"Hey. Gincy."

"That's an unusual name," Danielle said flatly.

"Yeah," I answered flatly. "It is."

The one named Clare stuck out her hand and I stared at it. She let it drop.

"One girl told me all the good houses are taken," she said. She sounded apologetic. "I think you're supposed to rent them by February or March and then look for housemates. Not the other way around. I didn't know."

I propped my fists on my hips. What there was of them.

I tend toward the skinny.

"Crap," I said. "Well I didn't know, either!"

Danielle heaved this big dramatic sigh. "None of us did," she said. "I guess."

I was seriously disappointed. I really wanted this summer to be something special.

And then, inspiration struck.

"Wait," I said. "All of the good houses might be taken but that doesn't mean there aren't still bad houses to rent. Right?"

"I suppose," Clare said doubtfully.

"A bad house?" Danielle rolled her eyes. I noted she was wearing a lot of eye make-up. Personally, I'd owned the same tube of mascara for three years. "See, I don't like the sound of that," she went on. "That means, like, a bathtub but no shower, right? Ceiling fans but no central air?"

I guffawed.

Ms. Fresh Mountain Air tried to hide a smile. "It might be worth taking a look," she said. "I . . . I kind of had my heart set on this."

There was a beat of silence and then I said, "Well, what's it gonna be? Are we going to do this or what?"

"Well, I'm not spending the entire summer in the city," Danielle declared fiercely. "The grime is murder on my skin. And speaking of murder, I just read in the Globe that street crime has like, tripled from last year. And you know how they get in the hot weather."

I narrowed my eyes. "How who gets?"

Danielle looked at me incredulously. "Duh. Criminals?"

Okay, I thought. But I'm watching closely for any signs of bigotry.

"I'm allergic to cigarette smoke," Clare said suddenly.

I eyed her keenly.

"Well," she admitted, "not allergic, exactly. It's just that I don't like it. It gives me headaches."

Danielle nodded. "And cigarette smoke stinks up my hair, not to mention my clothes. No smoking in the house. Agreed?"

I considered this.

Truth was, I wasn't a big smoker. I was kind of a social smoker. A wimpy smoker. It was the only thing about me that was wimpy. I could live with a no-smoking rule.

Still, I kind of hated to let things go.

I kind of liked to win. It was one of my more obnoxious traits.

"What about on the porch?" I countered. "If there is one. Or in the yard?"

Danielle and Clare discussed this with eye language and then Danielle nodded.

"All right. But if the smell starts getting in the house . . ."

"Yeah, yeah, fine. Anyway, we're jumping ahead making house rules before we even have a house."

Clare didn't answer but checked her watch for about the tenth time.

"Hot date?" I asked.

She blushed and hefted off a barstool what I realized was a suit in a plastic dry-cleaners' bag. "Oh, no! I have a boyfriend. He's working late tonight. We live together. I just want to get home before he does. You know."

I didn't at all know, but shrugged. "Fine. We'll hammer out the rules later."

"Good, because I want to watch something on Lifetime at eight," Danielle said.

She suggested a time, date, and place for us to meet for an excursion to the Vineyard; we each promised to bring any rental listings we found and Clare said she'd make an appointment with an Oak Bluffs real estate broker.

After we'd exchanged phone numbers and e-mail, the odd couple left and I gratefully settled at the bar and ordered a beer and a plate of nachos. I hadn't eaten all day. The six cups of coffee I'd drunk were eating away at the lining of my stomach. I could hear them munching.

So could the bartender, who after a particularly loud growl gave me a funny look.

I smiled sweetly. "If you could hurry with those nachos?"

I'd always hated snobs.

Maybe because I grew up among people whose idea of culture was a monster-truck rally followed by super-sized sugar drinks at the local DQ.

I was pretty sure half of the residents of my hometown—which I not so fondly called DeadlySpore, New Hampshire—were related. I guessed for some people, inbreeding was a goal; incest, something to kill the slow passing of rural time.

The evidence was clear, at least to me. Every single class in our local grammar school and high school had at least one member of the extensive Brown family.

Maggie Sullivan was a Brown.

Bobby Manigan was a Brown.

Petey Ming, who looked as Asian as his last name, was a Brown; I don't know how, exactly, but he was.

Basically, you threw a rock, you hit a Brown.

Note to the uninformed: Rock-throwing was a sport of choice in Pondscum, New Hampshire, as was name-calling, merciless teasing of anyone who ate whole wheat bread instead of Wonder white, and expert wedgie-giving.

Not that I, of course, ever participated in any of these sports except as a horrified spectator.

I swear.

See, for as far back as I can remember, say from about the age of four, I felt different from the infuriatingly dim-witted morons—okay, do morons come in any other kind?—who populated the neighborhood where I lived from the time of my birth to the day I left MooseDroppings, New Hampshire for school in Boston, Massachusetts.

Addison University. Ah, the haven for wanna-be artistes. (Yeah, use the French pronunciation here.)

Also known as losers.

That's not fair. Not everyone who went to Addison was a loser.

Sure, some started out that way and just perfected the role over time. Everybody knew these kids. Every high school had them. Kids who blustered and swaggered about their Hollywood-style future and somehow, in the end, came running home, proverbial tail between proverbial legs, to take a job tending bar at the local dive. For the rest of their lives.

Other kids started their freshman year at Addison bright-eyed and truly, touchingly optimistic about preparing for a life in The Arts. Then they became losers, usually by the middle of their sophomore year, when they realized they had absolutely no artistic talent whatsoever.

Losers or posers, or a fascinating combination of both.

Me? I started at Addison an eighteen-year-old combination

of loser and poser. Pretty impressive, I'd say. Not everyone can pull off such a loathsome personality at so young an age.

Even more impressive—and rare—is that by the end of my four years of higher learning (you know, higher as in "wanna toke, man?"), I was neither a loser nor a poser.

(See? I know how to use neither/nor, either/or. Losers don't know anything about good grammar. They spell grammar "grammer." Posers don't give a crap about good grammar. They have sycophants write their stories for them.)

So, if neither poser nor loser after four years of dopey seminars on the latest fad in acting methods (taught by people whose one and only claim to fame was a television commercial for deodorant) and ridiculously unhelpful internships at the tiny offices of sadly illiterate neighborhood newspapers (whose staff always included a totally bored party boy at the switchboard) and far too many theme parties (such as, Come as Your Favorite Living South American Philosopher!), what, then, was I?

One: Highly unemployable and not proud of it. That made me not a poser.

Two: Possessed of a substandard college education and embarrassed by it. That made me not a loser. And explained my desire to teach myself the rules of grammar.

Still, I knew that if I had to do it all over again—what a joke!—I'd probably be the same jerk I was the first time around. I doubted I'd be enrolled in Harvard or Brown or Northeastern, even knowing at eighteen what I now knew at the ripe old age of twenty-nine.

And counting. Thirty loomed.

Not that calendar year, but on the first day of the next. I missed being the first baby born in WormSlime by three minutes. Nancy Harrison, married to a Brown, delivered a bouncing baby boy at 12:02 A.M., to the eternal frustration of my mother.

I wasn't sure she'd ever forgiven me for being late, let alone for being born.

Anyway, turning twenty-nine had made me think. About age and accomplishment and roads not taken. Yet. The reality was that I'd been working since I was nine, baby-sitting, mowing lawns, running errands for the elderly neighbors.

And then I'd put myself through college.

And then I'd gone on to develop a not-so-terrible career in public television.

Don't get me wrong. I loved to work, even if I didn't have any major assets, liquid or otherwise, to show for my dedication. Student loans ate most of my salary; rent ate another large portion.

The fact was that I was tired. Really tired.

And so I determined that in those last months of relative, if not starry-eyed, youth, I was going to have some fun. Meet a bunch of cute guys. Stay out all night. Sleep all day, at least on the weekends.

Before getting back down to work.

Sitting there all alone at the bar, sipping a beer, I determined to rent a house on Oak Bluffs even if it was the rattiest dump imaginable.

And even if I had to share it with the odd couple.

The blond one, Clare. She looked as if she'd stepped out of the pages of an Eddie Bauer catalog, all scrubbed and healthy. I doubted we had anything at all in common.

And worse, the Pampered Princess, Danielle. With her red nails and her gold necklaces. Seriously not the kind of person who could be my friend.

But then again, who was? I could count my female friends on a fingerless hand.

The nachos finally arrived. I dug right in, slopping guacamole on my shirt. My tummy quieted immediately.

Gincy, I told myself, this is going to be one hell of a summer.

Clare
She Can't Say No

I never said no to Win. I wasn't sure I knew how.

"So, get the low-fat milk," he went on, his voice slightly distorted by his speakerphone. "And Clare, sweetie? If you could also pick up my black suit, that'd be great. It won't be ready until five-thirty, but that shouldn't be a problem for you, right?"

Plus, I hadn't told him about the summer house. I didn't want to pick a fight over something as silly as dry cleaning when I knew a truly big fight was to come.

"Sure," I said, folding clean laundry while I held the portable phone between my shoulder and chin. "No problem."

"Thanks, sweetie. You know, with your afternoons free—"

"They're not free, Win," I replied, automatically. We'd been through this so many times. "I have to grade papers and review lesson plans and then there's housework and—"

Win chuckled his indulgent chuckle. "Okay, okay, I get it. Sorry, sweetie. Look, I've got to run. See you later. Oh," he added, as if just remembering. "I probably won't be home until at least nine so grab some dinner for yourself, okay?"

Win lowered his voice; now it held a note of long-suffering.

"I have to take this client out for drinks after work. You know how it is."

No. I didn't know how anything was.

But I was beginning to figure things out.

"Sure," I said. "Bye."

We hung up and I finished folding and putting away the laundry. The simple task always gave me a feeling of accomplishment. At least something in this world was clean, neatly folded, and put away just where it had always belonged.

Like my so-called life?

I never could say no to Win, not even at the beginning of our relationship.

To be honest, Win had never asked me to do anything dreadful or dishonest or criminal.

He wasn't abusive. Not in any common sense of the term.

It was just—it was just that he was powerful and I was . . .

Not powerful.

But not stupid, either.

See, I'd finally come to understand that Win had power over me because I allowed him to have power over me.

I'd given it to him from the moment we'd met just over ten years earlier. I hadn't known what I was doing, not really.

And if I had?

At eighteen years of age I welcomed Win—a strong-willed, decisive, career-focused man—into my life with a sigh of relief. Not a literal sigh, you understand.

But having Win around made things easier for me. For example, in spite of my parents and professors pressuring me to think seriously about my future, I had no idea what I wanted to do or be until Win helped me decide on a career in teaching.

I liked being a teacher, very much. What was more, I was a good teacher. I was dedicated and sometimes even inspired. At least, my fifth graders at York, Braddock and Roget seemed to like me.

Win, it seemed, knew me when I didn't even know myself.

There were other reasons for my falling in love with Win Carrington.

I knew he wanted someday to be married and have a family, and I wanted those things, too.

My mother, who'd never worked outside the home, having married just out of college, urged on our budding relationship. Maybe she recognized in Win something of my father, a man who was a stellar family man if you looked at it in terms of financial support.

My father.

Daddy had always loved me, in a formal, distant sort of way. But he never paid much attention to me for the simple reason that I wasn't a boy. James, five years my senior, and Philip, two years older, were his major concerns.

His heirs.

Daddy was so old-fashioned he almost seemed like a character straight out of a Victorian novel. But he was all too real. And quite early on he assigned me to my mother.

His two girls.

Mother chose my clothes and took me to Girl Scout meetings while Daddy brought my two brothers to his beautiful office at the University of Michigan Medical Center where he was chief of urology.

Mother attended my ballet recitals while Daddy took my brothers on fishing trips up north.

Mother taught me how to sew and knit while Daddy encouraged the boys to excel in school and sports.

Nothing changed this dynamic until I started to date Win. Suddenly, I became visible to my father. Suddenly, I was worth his personal attention.

And the more Win achieved, the higher in Daddy's esteem I rose. At least it seemed that way to me.

When Win was accepted at Harvard Law, Daddy took us all to Chicago for the weekend.

When Win made Law Review, Daddy gave me a big fat check, as if I'd been the winner of the prize.

And when Win was offered a partner-track position at the

law firm of Datz, Parrish and Kelleher, Daddy treated us both to a weekend at Canyon Ranch in the Berkshires.

Everything was just fine.

Still, not long before that May evening when I committed myself to spending a good part of the summer with two strangers, and in spite of my father's gifts and approbation, something inside me began to change.

I felt as if I was waking up. I felt as if I was falling asleep.

And for someone who was known for her even keel, this was frightening.

I'd feel terribly restless, then lethargic; full of nervous energy, then barely able to get out of bed.

My favorite pastimes, like knitting and power-walking along the river, suddenly held no interest.

I started to screen all calls so that I wouldn't have to fake a good humor.

I lost what little sex drive I'd had.

Clare Jean Wellman. I'd always been the girl who was so pleasant and easy to please.

But suddenly, I felt all discontented.

And angry. But I wasn't sure why.

Sad, too, but I couldn't identify the source of the sadness.

Win didn't seem to notice my altered mood and behavior. At least, he didn't say anything to me about it. I guess I was grateful for that. Strange, but true.

I was grateful for his oblivion, or what passed for it.

I started searching out articles in popular women's magazines on mood swings and hormonal shifts, on something astrologers call the Saturn Return, and finally, on depression.

But members of the Wellman family didn't go to therapy.

Besides, I asked myself time and again, why did I need therapy? I had a steady job, a good family, a nice home.

I had Win.

Maybe, I came to think, there's nothing wrong with me. Maybe . . .

And then, one day while flipping through a magazine called New England Homes, I saw a promotional article about

Martha's Vineyard and it occurred to me, just like that, that I could go away for a while.

By myself. At least, without Win.

Classes ended in mid-June and the fall semester didn't start until after Labor Day.

Why did I have to stay in Boston when I could be somewhere closer to nature?

I missed spending time in the country and being by the water. It wasn't my choice to live in a big city. But Win had made his decision, New York or Boston, and I'd chosen Boston as the lesser of two urban evils.

A summer in the heat of the city? Or a summer by the sea-shore?

Besides, Win worked such dreadfully long hours and I knew he'd be starting a major case sometime in August, which meant we wouldn't be able to take a vacation together anytime soon.

The idea was tantalizing. Going away without Win.

I felt as if I had a dirty, thrilling secret.

For two days I did nothing more but fantasize about spending part of the summer without Win.

And then I saw a sign taped to a streetlight, a sign advertising the housemate event at George.

And there it was. Just like that I made a verbal commitment to share a summer house in Oak Bluffs with two strangers.

What had I done?

I asked myself this question over and over again on the way home to our spacious loft on Harrison Avenue in the South End. It became a chant in my head, matching my footfalls; What have I done, oh, what have I done.

I passed a tiny, bustling restaurant called the Dish on the corner of Shawmut. It was a balmy evening and several diners were seated at the small tables on the sidewalk.

At one table sat a woman alone, her pug resting at her feet. She was about forty-five and simply dressed; she looked content and relaxed.

I could never do that, I thought. *Eat alone at a restaurant.*

Or could I?

I spent an awful lot of time alone for someone with a live-in boyfriend.

It would be nice, I thought, *to work up the nerve to actually do more on my own, like enjoy a warm spring evening at a friendly local restaurant.*

The woman caught my eye as I passed, and smiled. I returned her smile, awkwardly, and walked on.

Courage, Clare, I told myself. *Taking this house for the summer is a step in the right direction. It's a step toward independence.*

That's what you want, right?

Independence?

But what does Win want for you? a teeny voice questioned.

He wouldn't be pleased with my plan, that much I knew for sure. The real question was: Would I have the nerve to stand up to his desires?

In other words, would I have the nerve to say no to him and yes to me?

I stopped at Foodie's, a midsized market across from the big cathedral, for Win's milk and for something prepared for my dinner.

And as I waited for the plastic container of macaroni and cheese, I thought about the two women who'd likely be my housemates.

Danielle seemed okay. She was a bit flashier than most of the people I knew but she seemed like a nice person.

I liked nice people.

Niceness, I'd always thought, was an underrated quality.

Gincy?

Well, I was a bit worried about her. About how we'd get along. Already I could sense that she was a bit pugilistic. Kind of a troublemaker. Kind of wild.

Maybe, I thought, *I should reserve any further judgment until we all meet again.*

I paid for the groceries and, juggling a white plastic bag and Win's dry-cleaned suit, headed over to Harrison Avenue.

All anxiety aside, I was excited. On some level I really didn't care what Win thought about my plan. And that brought a sense of freedom, something I don't think I'd ever felt before.

I took a deep breath and for a moment imagined I was on the beach, alone with the stars and moon and pounding black surf.

My life suddenly seemed very scary.

And quite possibly, very wonderful.

Danielle
She Likes Herself

It wasn't my fault that I was late for the meeting.

I mean, in the business world, what meeting ever starts exactly on time?

I'll tell you. None. Not many.

I'd been the senior administrative assistant at the Boston offices of a large construction firm for seven years and I'd seen my share of meetings.

Not even engineers, known for being all precise and focused, are on time for meetings. Not always.

So who would expect a meeting of random twenty- and thirtysomethings with some money to spend on a nice summer vacation—a meeting held at a totally casual bar like George—to begin exactly at six o'clock?

Please.

Most people in my office, located near Northeastern's attentuated urban campus, didn't even leave the building until at least six-thirty. So they told me because I made sure to be out of there no later than five. I didn't make enough money to work until seven.

That was my husband's job.

At least, it would be when I found him.

Anyway, I left the office that day at five on the dot, per usual, giving myself plenty of time to take a leisurely stroll through the mall on my way from Huntington Avenue over to Boylston Street, almost up by the Gardens. It was a very nice day in late May and for a moment I considered avoiding a short cut through the mall in favor of a bit of fresh air.

And then a disgusting bus roared by, belching thick black smoke, while I waited for a traffic light, and I thought: *What? I should destroy my lungs more than they're already destroyed by this foul city air?*

No thank you.

I suppose I didn't have to walk through the entire mall. It did take me out of my way.

And I suppose I didn't actually have to detour upstairs. But I did and that's when it happened. I saw the cutest pair of slides in the window of Nine West and they just called out to me.

"Danielle Leers!" they cried. "Look at us! Just imagine yourself wearing us to dinner at Davio's."

Well, as any self-respecting woman would tell you, when a pair of fabulous shoes cries out to you, you march right inside the shop and you try them on.

Of course, the slides looked spectacular on my feet, especially with the Raspberry Royale I was wearing on my toenails.

Sure, once summer came I'd be wearing Sassy Strawberry, but I was expert enough to know my color matches—without the help of *InStyle* magazine.

I bought the slides. And when I left the store, feeling that special after-purchase glow, I suddenly remembered that I'd forgotten all about the summer-house rental meeting.

I checked my watch to see it was already six and, with a shrug, headed off toward the closest exit. I figured it was better for me to stick to the streets if I were to make the meeting at all.

Which I didn't. Because by the time I got to George the meeting was over and everyone was hooked up with housemates but for me and two other girls who'd come in late.

Well, long story short the three of us decided to just go to the Vineyard and hope to find something decent to rent.

So there I was, committed to sharing a house—well, at least to trying to find a house—with two total strangers.

Neither of whom seemed anything like me at all.

Maybe, I thought, that was a good thing.

Maybe it would be fun to hang out with the one named Clare. She was okay. Her clothes were a bit bland but at least her hair was nicely, though simply, done. And she had a boyfriend, so she'd be no competition.

Though I did wonder why she was renting a house without said boyfriend.

The other one, Gincy? I wasn't so sure about her. The girl's hair was a disaster. And she hadn't been wearing any jewelry. Unless you counted ratty little silver studs in her ears as jewelry. Which I did not.

Still, she'd be no competition, either. No man I'd want to date would ever in his right mind want to date that mess of a girl.

In the end, it didn't really matter how well I got along with my two housemates. I wasn't renting a summer house to make new girlfriends.

Actually, I'd never been much for girlfriends.

True, I kept in touch with a few girls I grew up with in Oyster Bay. That's on Long Island, part of New York. We e-mailed on occasion and I saw them whenever I went home to visit my family.

But I didn't have a lot in common with Amy and Michelle and Rachel. Not only because they were all married and I wasn't.

I'd kind of been different from the start.

Like, I was the only one of the group to leave home for college.

While Amy and Rachel attended a local community college and Michelle made the commute to and from New York University every day (her parents didn't want her to live in the dorms), I went off to Boston University and majored in communications with a minor in art history.

For four years I flew home to Long Island for holidays and for summers and, though I always had a nice time, I was always happy to get back to Boston and my own life.

Then, as graduation drew closer, it became clear that my parents assumed I'd be returning home to find a job in New York.

I rebelled against the notion.

I loved my family. But I didn't want to start my so-called adult life under their gaze. They'd given me enough grief about going to Boston for college, but I'd stuck to my guns. I'd needed to be alone, to grow.

And there was just no way I could go home after those four years.

My privacy had become too important.

Amy, Michelle, and Rachel were each married by the age of twenty-three.

My father hinted that maybe I might want to marry, too.

My mother wondered what was wrong with those stiff New Englanders that they couldn't tell a lovely young woman when they saw one.

Honestly, I was in no hurry to marry. At first.

Which brings me back to the summer house. I had chosen to rent a place in Oak Bluffs because I couldn't afford to take a house on Nantucket or one of the super-expensive areas of the Vineyard, like Edgartown.

I knew I could ask my parents for money. They'd give it to me, but first they'd try to get me to drop the idea of a house and come home for a few weeks that summer.

And I didn't want to do that. Their love could be so overwhelming. I'd never stopped being afraid that I would get lost in their emphatic embrace.

And it was someone else's embrace that interested me.

I was taking a summer house in the first place because it was time to find a husband.

A husband worthy of Danielle Sarah Leers.

Who was Danielle Sarah Leers that fateful summer? Let me tell you a bit about her.

Height: five feet, four inches tall. Just right.

Coloring: medium olive complexion, brown eyes, and perfectly arched eyebrows, thanks to Studio Salon.

Hair: thick and dark brown; I liked to wear it to my shoulders and it was always perfectly groomed.

Figure: some had called me voluptuous. Others said that I resembled a young Sophia Loren.

Or a Catherine Zeta-Jones.

Or, on one of my best days, a Jennifer Lopez.

Really. People told me this. You can ask my mother.

Once, a very long time ago, a guy had the nerve to tell me I was a smidgen too fat. I told him to take a leap. What I looked like was my business and my business only. He tried to back-pedal and claim he meant the fat remark as a compliment, but it was too late. He was history in my book.

See, I'd always believed that self-esteem was a very good quality to have. I owed mine to my parents. They taught me early on that I was beautiful and intelligent and entirely worthy of happiness and love and social success.

They taught, and I listened. I might not have listened so well all the time at school, especially during geography and social studies—like I've ever had my day ruined by not being able to find, I don't know, Uruguay, on a map! But at home I listened very carefully.

It wasn't that I was full of myself. I'd known girls who were full of themselves and they were just insufferable. Insufferable was, is, and always will be unacceptable. But I did advocate feeling good about myself. Feeling worthy of good things.

Why not?

As my grandmother was fond of saying, "You're dead a long time."

Think about it.

Anyway, I didn't worry obsessively about an extra pound or two. I knew I was beautiful with or without the pound.

And I didn't tolerate anything less than total gentlemanly behavior from men.

I went for regular massages and facials and had a manicure and pedicure every two weeks. Once, someone at the office asked me why I bothered to have my toenails done during the winter.

"It's not sandal weather," she pointed out. "No one sees your toes."

"Correction," I replied. "I see my toes. And I'm the one that matters."

Since high school I'd worn only yellow gold, never silver. Not that I hated silver; it's just that I'd decided to have a trademark, a signature style. And I'd learned early on that every woman should have a personal jeweler, someone she trusted.

Every woman, I believed, should have a lot of things all for herself. It all came back to self-esteem.

It all came back to self-respect.

It made me want to scream when I saw women allowing themselves to be trampled by men who wanted them to pay for their own dinner, men who didn't call when they said they were going to call, men who wore sweat pants in public.

I thought: *What is the world coming to when this bad behavior is allowed?*

Here was the thing: You gave men an inch, they took a mile. You had to set boundaries. You had to make them play by the rules. And if they didn't want to play by the rules, they were out of the game. Period.

I considered myself a good person.

I donated the previous season's clothes to a homeless shelter. You know, the mistakes, the pieces you just shouldn't have bought.

Not that I made many mistakes.

At the end of each year I wrote a check to the Women's Lunch Place.

"When you have as much as we do," my father often said, "you should give a little back."

Someday, I'd think, *when I have children, I'll teach them what my parents taught me. I'll make sure they're proud and strong and generous, and then happiness and success will follow.*

At least, that's what I was told should happen. Sometimes I had my doubts about the happiness part. Not that I talked about those doubts or anything.

Though I had doubts, I did have faith, of a sort. My family didn't keep kosher or go to synagogue, but on the high holy days we did gather for the special meals. The women cooked and the men sang and read some prayers.

Most of which I didn't understand because I'd never taken Hebrew in school.

Please. There was enough in life to keep track of, what with a job and a social life.

Still, I'd always felt that tradition was important and vowed that when I married, my husband and I would instill the importance of tradition in our children.

Back again to the topic of a husband.

I had a plan once, a long time ago, to meet Mr. Right by the age of twenty-five or so.

Maybe it wasn't so much of a plan as a felt certainty. I just never thought I wouldn't meet Mr. Right by my midtwenties.

But there I was, twenty-nine and single. And turning thirty that summer, August tenth.

Thirty.

I could hardly believe it.

Suddenly, I was very, very aware that many of the other women on the streets of Boston were younger than me. I took to scrutinizing them, the clarity of their skin, the thickness of their hair, the brightness of their teeth, the firmness of their flesh.

Rivals. Dangerous rivals.

Not that I'd lost confidence in myself, but . . .

Face it. Thirty is old for a woman.

Danielle, I told myself, *it's high time you got down to business. It's high time you tied the knot.*

Marriage was a sign of maturity, right? It said to the world, "Look, I'm an adult. I can talk about mortgages and gutters and snowblowers and property taxes and in-laws and school systems and life insurance with the best of them. With my parents."

Marriage was an end to childhood or a prolonged adolescence or something.

It was an end to something.

Well, I was ready to put an end to something.

I was ready to be an adult.

I was ready to join the club.

Now, all I had to do was find Mr. Right.

No big deal, I told myself. He was out there somewhere.

And he was going to love me in my new slides.

BOOK YOUR PLACE ON OUR WEBSITE AND MAKE THE READING CONNECTION!

We've created a customized website just for our very special readers, where you can get the inside scoop on everything that's going on with Zebra, Pinnacle and Kensington books.

When you come online, you'll have the exciting opportunity to:

- View covers of upcoming books
- Read sample chapters
- Learn about our future publishing schedule (listed by publication month *and author*)
- Find out when your favorite authors will be visiting a city near you
- Search for and order backlist books from our online catalog
- Check out author bios and background information
- Send e-mail to your favorite authors
- Meet the Kensington staff online
- Join us in weekly chats with authors, readers and other guests
- Get writing guidelines
- AND MUCH MORE!

**Visit our website at
http://www.kensingtonbooks.com**

Discover the Thrill of
Romance With

Kat Martin

__Hot Rain
0-8217-6935-9   **$6.99**US/**$8.99**CAN

Allie Parker is in the wrong place—at the worst possible time . . . Her
only ally is mysterious Jake Dawson, who warns her that she must play
the role of his reluctant bedmate . . . if she wants to stay alive. Now, as
Alice places her trust—and herself—in the hands of a total stranger, she
wonders if this desperate gamble will be her last . . .

__The Secret
0-8217-6798-4   **$6.99**US/**$8.99**CAN

Kat Rollins moved to Montana looking to change her life, not find
another man like Chance McLain, with a sexy smile of empty heart.
Chance can't ignore the desire he feels for her—or the suspicion that
somebody wants her to leave Lost Peak . . .

__The Dream
0-8217-6568-X   **$6.99**US/**$8.50**CAN

Genny Austin is convinced that her nightmares are visions of another
life she lived long ago. Jack Brennan is having nightmares, too, but his
are real. In the shadows of dreams lurks a terrible truth, and only by
unlocking the past will Genny be free to love at last. . .

__Silent Rose
0-8217-6281-8   **$6.99**US/**$8.50**CAN

When best-selling author Devon James checks into a bed-and-breakfast
in Connecticut, she only hopes to put the spark back into her
relationship with her fiancé. But what she experiences at the Stafford
Inn changes her life forever . . .

Available Wherever Books Are Sold!

Visit our website at **www.kensingtonbooks.com**.